Time Undone

Benjamin McGill

Sullivan and Walsh

This book and all subsequent books will be dedicated to the most beautiful, sexy and hardest working girl I know. My amazing partner in crime, Becky.

And to my two incredible children.

Lilly McGill.

Without you, this book would have been riddled with (way more) spelling errors. Watching you grown up and rule this world has made you my hero.

And to Dean (Sam)

Your constant joy and ability to force me to relax and enjoy life more has been the best.

My Wife and children will always be the thing I take the most pride in. You are all my inspiration.

Contents

1
Feldmarschall

The air hung heavy, smothering each breath as my mother's cries shredded the silence. "Please, I beg you! Not my children! Not my babies!"

Her voice, a desperate, cracked whisper, clawed at the frigid darkness, but the soldiers stood rigid and unblinking, stone-faced beneath their peaked caps. The once-familiar room around us lay in ruin; wooden beams were splintered, the walls were crumbling, and every corner was cloaked in the ghosts of our past. The windows were jagged holes now, gaping like empty eyes, letting in gusts of wind that slashed through us, cold as the grave.

My brother and I clung to the edge, half-hidden in a sliver of shadow, our thin bodies pressed against the rough stone wall. A candle flickered weakly around us, casting fleeting shapes that danced and twisted across cobweb-strewn surfaces. All that mattered was the sound of her agony; it was the sound of something precious unraveling, of any hope we had that this may soon be over being crushed to dust.

She was on her knees now, hands scraping across the broken floorboards and leaving crimson trails smeared in the dirt. "Please, we're not harming anyone... Please, just..."

Her voice broke, splintered, as a tall silhouette filled the doorway. He stood there, a figure of shadow and menace, framed by the ruins of what used to be a home, and the weight of his gaze swept over us.

"ENOUGH!"

The word cracked like a whip, slicing through the air. Every soldier straightened at once, their postures snapping to rigid attention as if pulled by invisible strings. He strode forward, boots striking the floor in sharp, measured steps that crushed the breath out of the room. His presence swelled, choking and bending everything around him to his will. The uniform he wore clung with a cruel precision. Every seam, every polished button was a testament to a brutality cloaked in discipline. The red band on his arm flared in the dim light, its twisted symbol barely visible in the dim light.

"Now," he murmured, his voice a dangerous purr, smooth as velvet yet barbed with malice. "What, pray tell, is this disturbance?"

He moved slowly, almost leisurely, eyes flitting from the shattered remnants of the room to the crumpled figure of my mother on the floor. Her trembling seemed to mock the stillness he demanded, each shuddering breath betraying her terror. Blood mixed with grime stained her cheeks, smudged like the smears of a broken artist's hand, painting her despair across her gaunt face.

One of the soldiers shuffled uneasily, his gaze darting to the man in the doorway. He stepped forward hesitantly, shoulders hunched, as if flinching from a blow yet to fall. "The Jew whore won't stay silent, Feldmarschall."

A gloved hand jerked onto the back of my neck, fingers clamping down like a vice. I bit back a cry, my body curling inward instinctively as his grip tightened, pain searing through me like a live wire. I tried to shrink away, but his hand only dug deeper, the pressure spreading hot fear through my veins. His face, pale and drawn, turned towards the Feldmarschall as if pleading for approval. The man in the ironed uniform merely smiled, a cold, thin curve of his lips like a predator savoring the helpless twitch of its prey.

"Amram! Be still," my mother begged, her voice frayed, unraveling under the weight of fear.

Feldmarschall's eyes flicked to me; his smile held no warmth. He stepped closer, and the air seemed to thicken, every breath tinged with the icy chill that rolled off him.

"Amram, is it?" His voice was a low murmur, soft and almost coaxing.

I nodded quickly, tears spilling down my cheeks as I kept my gaze averted. "Do you know what happens to little boys who don't obey their mothers?"

The question lingered in the room, gentle as a lullaby, yet edged with something dark that made my heart thud wildly in my chest.

I tried to shake my head, but the soldier's grip on my neck tightened like a noose, the leather of his gloves biting into my skin. The Feldmarschall didn't wait for an answer. He moved with slow, unhurried purpose, his gaze never leaving mine as he raised his foot and pressed the hard heel of his boot onto my mother's outstretched hand.

The scream that tore from her throat was a sound I'd never heard before-- raw, primal-- filled with such agony that it seemed to split the world in two. It echoed through me, piercing every fiber of my being, leaving me paralyzed in the suffocating silence that followed.

"STOP IT, YOU MEAN MONSTER!" a small voice rang out, fierce and trembling all at once.

My brother—Isaiah, brave, stubborn Isaiah—threw himself forward, his tiny fists flailing as he kicked out at the soldier's leg. "Leave Mama alone!"

Time itself seemed to freeze. The soldiers exchanged quick, bewildered glances, caught off-guard by the audacity of a mere child. Even the Feld-marschall stilled, a flicker of surprise flashing across his face. Then he straightened slowly, turning his gaze on the trembling boy standing before him.

"And what is your name?" he asked, his tone soft, almost gentle. But there was a stillness beneath it, a calm so cold it sent ice down my spine.

"Isaiah... sir," my brother whispered, his voice wavering as his courage began to crumble.

He stood there, his small chest rising and falling rapidly, shoulders quaking under the weight of his fear. The Feldmarschall's smile widened, the expression stretching grotesquely as he leaned in, his face just inches from my brother's.

"Such a brave boy," he murmured, the words dripping with mockery.

Then, like a viper striking, his arm lashed out. The sound of the backhanded slap was sharp, reverberating through the shattered room. Isaiah crumpled to the ground, a choked cry escaping his lips as he curled into himself.

"But bravery," the Feldmarschall sneered, looming over my brother's trembling form. "Is nothing more than stupidity wrapped in pride."

He straightened, the smile vanishing from his face, replaced by something colder, something infinitely more dangerous. My mother's sobs filled the room again, ragged and shattered, clawing desperately at the silence. "Please… mercy… please, just—"

"Mercy?" he barked, voice twisting into a snarl. "Like the mercy your kind showed when they crucified our Lord? When they polluted our blood with their filth and disease?"

He stood straighter, a look of cold disgust contorting his face. "There is no mercy for you, Jew."

With slow, deliberate movements, he unfastened the small pistol from his holster, metal gleaming dully in the murky light. Everything seemed to warp and slow as he raised the gun. For a moment, the barrel hovered in the air inches from Isaiah's head. The room shrank, collapsing around that singular, horrifying image: the muzzle of the gun, the trembling form of my brother, the monster behind the trigger.

"NO!" I screamed, but the word splintered uselessly, swallowed by the roar of the gunshot.

BANG! The sound ripped through the room, deafening, final. Isaiah's tiny body jerked violently, crumpling to the floor in a heap. A dark pool of crimson spread like a bloom beneath his head, staining the broken boards.

"No!" my mother wailed, a raw, keening cry that shattered through the cold air, tearing something fundamental inside me.

She lunged forward, her mangled hand outstretched, fingers grasping desperately. But a soldier stepped in, shoving her back with brutal efficiency.

"Just like a Jew to take what isn't his. Hope is not for you." The Feldmarschall's voice was almost contemplative, as if speaking to himself.

His eyes slid toward me, the corners of his mouth curling into a sickening parody of a smile. And then the gun swung my way.

My heart stuttered, a wild, frantic beat that echoed in my ears, drowning out everything else. I couldn't move. My limbs felt encased in ice; paralyzing terror locked every muscle in place. "Mama, help me, please!"

The words tore from my throat in a strangled sob, but they barely left my lips before white-hot agony detonated in my stomach. The pain twisted my insides. I screamed, the sound ripping free of my chest as I clutched at the wound to no avail.

BANG! Another shot, and another explosion of pain, this time higher, tearing through my ribs. My body convulsed, every nerve alight with fire, every breath a desperate, shallow gasp.

I crumpled to the floor, the room tilting, the world blurring as the agony consumed everything. Blood filled my mouth, choking me, and the darkness closed in, blotting out the horror.

"Mama. Please Mama, hold me..." I whispered, each word a struggle, wet and gurgling as blood pooled in my mouth.

It tasted of iron and finality, thick and suffocating. The room swam around me, the edges blurring, dissolving into a murky haze. Everything felt distant, slipping through my grasp like smoke. The cold crept in, numbing my limbs and stealing the warmth from my skin.

Through the narrowing tunnel of my vision, I caught one last, fleeting glimpse of my mother's frail silhouette, arms flailing as she was dragged away. Her cries, ragged and broken, echoed in the darkness. But her voice, too, was fading, swallowed by the void.

Above it all, the Feldmarschall's laughter rang out, sharp and hollow, reverberating through the shattered remnants of our world. It was a sound that seemed to vibrate with malice, devoid of humanity. It was the laughter of the father himself.

"What happened next, Orin?" Ferkin asked, leaning forward with interest.

"Nothing happened. I woke up," Orin's words slipped out, dull and lifeless, falling flat into the night air.

He stared at the ground, fingers tracing aimless patterns in the dirt, his chest still coiled tight with the lingering grip of fear. Ferkin's eyes glittered with barely concealed amusement. "No beautiful girls to rescue, then?" he teased, his mouth twitching with suppressed laughter.

He tried to smother it, but a few stifled snorts broke free, sharp and grating, each one gnawing at Orin's nerves like sandpaper against raw skin.

"Or maybe one of those giant metal bird with the wings that don't bend?" Ferkin pressed on, lowering his voice dramatically. "You're always talking about those beasts with the clouds that shoot out the sides of them, aren't you? Was there no mighty cloud maker to slay for the honor of the village, oh brave Orin? And what is this gun thing anyways?"

"Shut up, Ferkin," Orin muttered, though there was no bite to his words.

Ferkin was doing what he did best, picking at him until he cracked. But not tonight. The fear still hung around Orin like a cloak, heavy and damp, seeping into his bones.

"Aw, come on, just having a bit of fun!" Ferkin's grin widened as he gave Orin's shoulder a light shove. "Don't be so serious all the time. Maybe you dreamed yourself into the middle of a grand feast, eh? Piles of food, mountains of roasted tusked pig, and sweet dandle wine with you at the head of the table! Or were you back in that little shack of yours, sitting beside your old man while he prattled on about the Great Mother and her blessings?"

Orin flinched, the words hitting a little too close. "So, what do you think it means?" he snapped, trying to yank the conversation away from Ferkin's jabs.

Orin's fingers dug into the earth, seeking something solid, something real. "Is this something I should be worried about?" he asked.

Ferkin's expression shifted, his brows knitting together as he took his time, leaning lazily against the rough bark of the tree. He didn't answer right away—he never did. Most people would say it was thoughtfulness, a habit of careful reflection. But Orin knew better. This silence was just the slow, deliberate pull of the bowstring before Ferkin let the arrow fly.

"Worried?" Ferkin let the word dangle between them, savoring it like a ripe fruit. "Maybe you should be. I mean, strange dreams, mysterious prophecies, the usual hero's curse... Or," he shrugged, his eyes narrowing playfully. "Maybe you're just eating too much of Mrs. Salem's cheese before bed."

Orin scowled, but Ferkin just grinned wider.

"Well?" Orin growled, fists tightening in the dirt. "You think it's just a dream?"

Ferkin tilted his head, considering. "Mmm, maybe. Or maybe it's more than that. Maybe it's fate knocking at your door. Or maybe it's just the wind in your head. Who's to say?" His grin turned wolfish. "But if you ask me, I think you're making it all up just to get out of chopping firewood in the morning."

"Can't you ever be serious?" Orin hissed.

Ferkin's face softened then, just for a heartbeat, his gaze flicking over Orin, assessing. "Serious? Sure. You want serious?" He leaned in closer, his voice dropping to a low murmur, the humor melting away. "I think you're scared, Orin. Scared that these dreams mean something. Something you don't want to face."

Orin swallowed, his throat tight. "I'm not scared," he insisted.

"Liar," Ferkin whispered, but his tone wasn't mocking now; it was almost... gentle.

With a sigh, Ferkin flopped back against the tree and shrugged. "Fine, don't tell me. Keep your nightmares to yourself if that's what you want. But just remember that dreams don't hurt you, Orin. It's what you do with them that matters."

"Do with them?" Orin repeated, confusion lacing his voice.

Ferkin waved a hand dismissively. "Yeah, like... I don't know, ignore them. Or chase after them. Or, you know, maybe go rescue a beautiful girl next time instead of waking up like a scared little Gophen rabbit."

Orin stared at him, torn between frustration and a grudging sort of gratitude. Only Ferkin could twist a conversation from serious to ridiculous in the span of a few breaths.

"Forget it," Orin muttered. "You're impossible."

Ferkin laughed, the sound deep and rich, shaking the silence loose from the forest. "Orin! Can't you just think about fucking like the rest of us?"

The laughter echoed off the trees, his voice bouncing through the shadows until it seemed like the woods were joining in. For a fleeting second, Orin almost smiled. That was Ferkin's gift—pushing someone right to the edge of their patience and then pulling them back with a laugh so genuine it seemed to light up the night. But not tonight. Tonight, the cold knot of fear buried deep in Orin's gut stayed knotted, refusing to unravel.

"Why do you even care?" he grumbled, folding his arms over his chest. "You never take anything seriously."

"Because you do," Ferkin replied simply, the humor in his eyes dimming. "You always have. Someone's got to remind you to breathe once in a while. And hey, if that means making a fool of myself to get you to loosen up, then so be it."

Orin blinked, caught off guard by the honesty in Ferkin's tone.

"So, what then?" he muttered, glancing away. "You think I'm... I'm fine?"

"Fine?" Ferkin scoffed. "You? Not a chance. But you'll survive. You always do."

And with that, Ferkin clapped Orin on the back, the familiar grin sliding back into place.

Years before the Eye of Mother started sharing light with the red sun, Orin and his papa would be out here. His father would always lean back against a cozy spot, a twinkle of a story in his eye. Even now, Orin could almost smell it—those leaves, pungent and sharp—mingling with the thick aroma of dandle beer. His father would lean forward, voice softening, reverence creeping into his tone. "You're a low-lander, Orin. You are bound to the land spirit. It is through her that you must draw your strength."

Orin's lips twisted into a grimace at the memory. That's how it always ended, with his papa's voice slipping lower, slurring as he drowned deeper into his own words. Stories of desperate men fighting tooth and nail through endless winters, their feet swallowed by the frozen earth and their breath hanging like ghosts in the air. Tales of powerful realms, once mighty and unbreakable, crumbling under the weight of their own greed and ambition, leaving behind only hollow ruins and whispers of their glory. His father's gaze would grow vacant, as if he were staring through the thin veil of reality into something far darker, his mind spiraling into the same twisted fantasies that had scared Orin as a boy.

He spoke of soldiers lost in dense jungles, soaked in mud and rain, never knowing if the ground beneath them was hiding an enemy or a trap. He described ships torn apart by fire in sudden, blinding flashes, and of men clawing their way through clouds of smoke and metal to survive. There were trenches filled with bodies, faces hidden behind grotesque masks that filtered the choking air, surrounded by the chemical burn of invisible death. Orin's father recounted the horrors that blurred one into the other—people slaughtered, generations erased—of fires that burned the air itself, turning night into a blinding flash of white and leaving shadows where men once stood.

His voice would drop to a whisper then, talking of lands that had been torn apart, divided and stitched back together by rulers who saw land as nothing more than something to be divided by lines on a map. Nations split apart, families divided, only to be fused back in uneasy unions and shattered again when the earth was stained with blood. And always, at the edge of his words, were the haunting tales of men who created a terrible fire, one so powerful that it bloomed like a giant mushroom, swallowing the sky and turning the ground to ash and the very air to poison. These were tales of blood and sacrifice, of ancient spirits trapped in endless night, bound to the places where they perished, lingering still in the scars that marked the earth.

By morning, he was gone every time, lost in his head. His eyes glazed and far away, he spoke to a world Orin couldn't see—a world that seemed to creep closer with every dream.

Everyone in the village whispered about it when they thought Orin wasn't listening. "Jupin and dandle root beer will rot your mind," the elders muttered as Orin's father staggered through the narrow streets, eyes glazed, rambling about the Great Mother and the land of Terra.

"It's a shame," old Marla would sigh to the blacksmith's wife, shaking her head. "A man who was once so strong, reduced to this."

"And his poor boy—what will become of him?" the slaughterer's daughter would murmur, glancing at Orin with pity as she wrapped a slab of meat in thick leaves.

"I heard he speaks to the shadows," one of the farmers whispered one evening when they thought Orin was out of earshot. "Said he sees faces in the mist."

"Nonsense," scoffed another. "It's the drink that's poisoned his mind. A once-proud man, ruined by his own vice."

And they weren't wrong. By the end, he couldn't tell his nightmares from real life, spinning stories of spirits and forgotten lands until the line between truth and delusion blurred beyond recognition.

"The Great Mother watches," he'd rasp, wild-eyed, to anyone who would listen. "She watches, and when she wakes, the land will remember. All will become one."

"Enough, you mad old fool!" one of the bolder villagers would shout, waving him off with a sneer. "No one wants to hear your cursed tales."

But he would only smile, a sad, faraway smile, as if he saw something they couldn't—something just beyond the veil of this world. The whispers would continue, hushed but insistent. "He was a good man once, before all this," they'd say. "But now? Best steer clear of him and the boy, too. Whatever darkness has taken hold of the father might yet take the son."

And that's what got him killed in the end. Lost in his own mind during a Flesher skirmish, he hesitated—a single heartbeat of confusion as he shouted out non-sensical gibberish "United flight 93..." Then looked up in the sky. That was all it took. A blade flashed, and he fell, soul snuffed out before anyone could even shout a warning. Orin still remembered the look on his mother's face when they brought his father's body back. Something in her broke that day, something that never healed.

The village's gaze turned to Orin and Ferkin then, full of pitying eyes and murmured condolences. But behind it, there was something sharper. There was a sense that they were tainted by the same madness that had taken Orin's father. His mother carried on, shoulders squared against the whispers, refusing to bow to their pity, but Orin saw the way her hands clenched tighter and the nights she stayed up long after he'd gone to bed, staring into the empty dark.

For all his madness, though, Orin's father hadn't been wrong about everything. He always said, "Find yourself a woman who doesn't put up with your shit, and you'll do just fine."

That was the one piece of advice that stuck. It had served him well—until it didn't—and it sure as hell served Orin. His mother, fierce as iron, proved him right. She was the first woman to make it into the Guard and the only one who clawed her way up the ranks until even the men followed her orders without question.

She was the only person crazy enough to take in Ferkin and his sister. He had been a wild, feral kid back then—more stray animal than boy—stealing and scrapping to survive. The whole village said she was out of her mind, that he'd be gone in a week, maybe two. But she made people fall in line. She never gave up on him, not once, even when he pushed her to her limits. If anyone asked Orin, taking Ferkin in was the bravest thing she ever did, but probably also the most reckless.

And then she was gone.

It happened quietly, like the sun slipping behind a cloud. One moment, she was fierce and unstoppable, barking orders and holding the whole village in the palm of her hand. The next, something inside her just... flickered out. No amount of love or loyalty could reach her anymore. Grief wrapped its fingers around her, digging deeper each day, draining the fight from her step by step. It hollowed her out, eating away at her laughter, at the fire in her eyes, until there was nothing left but a shadow of the woman who'd once seemed larger than life.

By the time she finally stopped breathing, it felt like she'd been gone for a long, long time.

After she was gone, it was just Ferkin and Orin. The silence between them was heavy, like an unspoken promise. Orin guessed he could call Ferkin his brother, if brothers were made of brawling and bad jokes. He was the kind of man whose laughter cut through the worst of days, even if it sounded more like a roar than anything human. But when everything crumbled, he was the one Orin wanted next to him, standing like a rock in the storm.

Orin sighed, rubbing his hands together as he stared into the campfire's dying embers. The flames had dwindled down to a soft orange glow, casting flickering shadows across the clearing. The night pressed in around them, cold and vast.

"Get some shuteye, Orin," Ferkin muttered, shifting against a pile of ferns until he found a comfortable spot. His massive frame seemed almost to merge with the darkness, a slumbering beast at the edge of the firelight.

"Night, Ferkin."

"Night, my dashing, wonderful, loveable—"

"Ferkin! Shut up!"

He just laughed, low and rumbling, the sound carrying warmth that seeped into the cold corners of the night. Even when the world felt empty, even when everything else fell away, Ferkin's laughter was solid, a reminder that the two weren't alone. He couldn't help but smile a little, letting the sound wrap around him like a blanket as he leaned back and closed his eyes.

2

The Prophet

"**Y**ou missed it!" Orin called up, stepping back from the base of the towering Sefmore tree.

Its massive trunk, lined with craggy bark and thick vines, shot up into the sky, where its branches tangled into a thick canopy that swallowed the light. Ferkin shifted in the branches high above, peering down through the layers of leaves. He squinted as if he could burn a hole through the overgrowth by sheer willpower. "Missed one?" he scoffed, his voice tight but playful. "You miss plenty, and you don't hear me complain, do you?"

Orin snorted, keeping his gaze on Ferkin as he moved cautiously. "Wouldn't know," he shot back. "You talk to much. You never shut up long enough to let anyone hear it."

"Talk too much, huh?" Ferkin retorted, shaking a nearby branch. Dried leaves and dust rained down like a fine mist, forcing Orin to back up. "Everything I say is poetry."

"More like endless drivel," Orin countered, grinning wide as Ferkin snapped off a dry, crumbling branch and flung it down. Ferkin scowled as it bounced uselessly off the trunk and landed at Orin's feet.

"This tree's no good, Orin," he finally grumbled, rubbing his hands together to shake off the debris. "Too far gone."

"Then come down already!" Orin called, folding his arms in anticipation.

What happened next was pure Ferkin. He threw his leg over one branch and lost his grip, scrambling for another, half-dangling there with his limbs flailing like some enormous, panicked bird. He dropped, caught himself, and slipped again. The whole descent was less climbing and more controlled plummeting. By the time he hit the lower branches, Orin was doubled over, tears of laughter blurring his vision.

With one final, graceless stumble, Ferkin dropped the last few feet, landing in a cloud of dust and broken twigs. "You alright?" Orin managed to choke out between gasps.

Ferkin brushed himself off, looking utterly unbothered. "Flawless," he said, straightening up with as much dignity as he could muster. "Not a single misstep."

Orin grinned, shaking his head. "Yeah, flawless. Like a falling boulder."

"You're getting too old to be climbing down like that."

"Old?" Ferkin landed in a crouch, shaking broken twigs out of his locked hair. His brow furrowed as if Orin had just insulted his entire lineage. "What do you mean? That was perfection itself."

"Right, right," Orin teased, laying it on thick. "Just like you mastered that baby Snore you swore you could handle solo. Or that time with the—"

"Enough!" Ferkin barked, though the grin twitching at his lips betrayed him. "How your wife puts up with your mouth, I'll never know."

"She's got the patience of a mystic," Orin said with a shrug. "And the stubbornness of a dwindle beetle."

Ferkin chuckled, the sound rumbling through the stillness of the woods. "Well, can't say I didn't go easy on you. Didn't want to make you look old by comparison," he said with a wink, his eyes dancing with mischief.

"Yeah, thanks for sparing my pride," Orin shot back, rolling his eyes but unable to suppress a smile. "Now, let's get this last tree and get out of here."

They wove their way through the thick underbrush, their boots sinking softly into the mossy carpet underfoot. The forest was a living, breathing thing. The scent of pine and damp earth hung heavy in the air, and the trees, ancient and towering, whispered with every brush of wind. Hidden birds called from high up in the canopy, and the rustle of unseen creatures stirred in the undergrowth. The place buzzed with life, yet there was a stillness to it too, as if the forest was holding its breath, guarding secrets only it knew.

"There!"

Orin stopped, staring up at another enormous Sefmore tree. Its roots coiled out like the limbs of a sleeping giant, burrowing deep into the soil. He reached out, fingers brushing over the rough bark as he leaned closer. "What the...?"

His hand recoiled. A thick, viscous sap oozed from the tree, glistening darkly in the dappled light. The substance clung stubbornly to his fingers, stretching in shimmering threads like spider silk when he tried to pull away.

"Something's wrong here, Ferkin," he murmured, his eyes narrowing as he examined the sticky residue. "This shouldn't be happening."

Ferkin's roar of laughter exploded through the stillness, nearly making Orin leap out of his skin. He doubled over, clutching his sides as he wheezed, "Watch your hand there, Orin!"

Tears streamed down Ferkin's face as he slapped his knees in a fit of glee. Orin gritted his teeth, his face burning as he tried to smear the sticky sap off onto a patch of moss.

"Say, isn't it your turn to check this one out?" he shot back, narrowing his eyes at Ferkin.

Ferkin finally straightened, wiping the last of his tears away. "Oh no, my friend," he said with a broad grin. "I wouldn't dream of taking this moment from you. Besides—" he gestured to the strands of sap stubbornly clinging to Orin's fingers, his grin turning devilish—"it looks like you and this tree are already getting along splendidly."

Orin scowled, glancing up at the towering trunk. The tree stretched on and on, its bark winding in thick ridges like the scales of some ancient beast.

"What're you waiting for?" Ferkin called lazily, making himself comfortable against a patch of soft moss. His smug grin was impossible to miss. "That tree's not going to heal itself."

Orin bit back a retort and drew in a deep breath, craning his neck to take in the sheer height of the Sefmore. "I don't think I've ever gone this high before," he admitted.

Ferkin tilted his head, squinting up into the leafy abyss above. "That has to be one of the tallest in all of Terra."

"Almost the size of the Emerald Lady herself," Orin murmured, swallowing hard as he sized up the climb ahead. The top seemed to vanish into the clouds.

"Well… here goes nothing."

He lunged for the nearest groove in the bark, fingers digging into the scaly ridges. The rough texture bit into his skin, and he gritted his teeth against the sting. With a heave, he hauled himself up, inch by inch, his boots scraping against the gnarled surface as he climbed. The branches above shifted with his weight, swaying and creaking like old bones.

Muscles straining, he forced himself upward, ignoring the fire spreading through his limbs. His breath came in ragged gasps as he reached for the next branch, gripping it tightly as it bent beneath him. Don't look down. Just keep going.

"Good luck up there!" Ferkin's voice floated up, muffled but unmistakable. "And if you happen to fall—or, I don't know, jump—I'll take real good care of that wife of yours!"

His laughter rang out, rising through the layers of leaves like some triumphant battle cry. "Shut up, Ferkin," Orin growled under his breath, muscles straining as he hauled himself up another few feet.

The ground was a blur of green and brown far below—a dizzying smear of colors that made his head spin if he glanced down too long. Focus. One branch, then the next.

The air thinned as he climbed higher, the wind whipping through the branches. And then, all at once, he broke through. He clung to the topmost branches, chest heaving, and blinked out at the world beyond. The sun hung low, a blazing orb dipping toward the horizon, its fiery light spilling across a rolling sea of treetops. The scent of wildflowers and distant streams drifted up, crisp and sharp, cutting through the burn in his lungs. Far below, like a toy village, rooftops peeked out from the forest's embrace, the tiny steeple of the town hall jutting up through the foliage. Home.

"JUMP, JUMP, JUMP!" Ferkin's chant echoed up, faint but relentless, cutting through Orin's brief reverie.

"Shut up, Ferkin!" he roared, gripping the rough bark to steady himself.

With a deep breath, he fumbled for the hand saw strapped to his boot. "Watch yourself down there!" he called out, though his voice sounded small and far away in the open air.

He positioned himself carefully, bracing against the swaying branches, and set the saw teeth against the brittle wood. Snick, snick, snick. The vibration hummed up his arm as he worked, muscles straining against the stubborn, rotting fibers. The branch beneath him shivered, creaking like a wounded animal, and then—

CRACK.

The world dropped out from under Orin. His stomach twisted violently as gravity yanked him down, the branches blurring into a chaotic swirl of green and brown. A breeze whipped past, roaring in his ears, and every muscle locked, frozen in place. For a split second, time stretched, and he felt weightless—a leaf caught in a gale. Then panic seized his chest, squeezing his ribs like a vice. He was falling, plummeting.

His mind went white, every thought wiped away by a single, blinding fear: he was going to die.

Below, Ferkin sprang to his feet, eyes narrowing in fierce concentration. He thrust his hand skyward, veins bulging as they turned an unnatural black. His voice cut through the wind, low and guttural, each word like a command rippling through the air. "Aeris, aeris autem invisibilia vi funsesto da mihi tu virtutum."

The wind roared in response, swirling through the trees in a wild frenzy. Leaves tore loose, whirling around Orin in a vortex of green and gold, pressing against him, resisting his fall. His stomach lurched as his descent slowed, the atmosphere cradling him like invisible hands. Above, the shattered branch snapped back into place with a sharp crack, and the world righted itself in a blur of motion. He clung to the trunk, gasping for breath, his heart pounding like a war drum.

"Ferkin!" he shouted, craning his neck to see him.

Ferkin stood rigid, hand outstretched, a thin trickle of black blood winding down his cheeks like dark tears. Orin slid down the rough bark as fast as he dared, scraping his palms and barely feeling it. When he hit the ground, Ferkin was slumped against a jagged rock, his shoulders heaving.

"What did you do?" Orin grabbed his arm, yanking him upright.

The black stain smeared across Ferkin's beard, his face pale and drawn, eyes half-closed in exhaustion.

"I saved your ass," he murmured, swiping weakly at the blood streaking his face.

"Using father's energy!" Orin hissed, the words catching in his throat. Father's energy. Forbidden, lethal. "If the elders find out—"

The sentence hung between them, unfinished. The penalty for invoking the forbidden prayers of the old gods was death. For both of them.

"Fuck, Orin," Ferkin muttered, lifting his gaze to meet Orin's. His eyes were bloodshot, the whites tinged with crimson. "I saved your life. You could at least say thank you."

"Thank you," Orin whispered, his hands trembling as he pulled away. "Just... don't do it again, alright?"

Ferkin's lips twitched into a tired smile, the expression hollow and weak. "No promises."

Orin watched him warily, noting the lines etched deep around his eyes, the way his frame sagged like an old, weary man. He looked drained, his vitality sapped away—the steep price of the forbidden prayers. And he'd paid it. For Orin.

"Come on," Ferkin murmured, a low whistle slipping from his lips as he signaled for the Snores. "Let's go home."

With a bit of a clumsy stumble, Aya trudged up and lowered herself next to Orin. She wasn't the biggest snore, but he still had to leap to get up.

"Race you back!" he shouted, his voice breaking through the stillness as he leaned forward, gripping Aya's reins.

Aya shifted beneath him, muscles bunching, her powerful frame coiling like a spring ready to release. Orin froze, fingers tightening on the leather straps at the sight of Ferkin's expression. The usual easygoing grin had vanished, replaced by a tight-lipped frown. His gaze was sharp, fixed on something deep in the shadows beyond.

"What is it?" Orin whispered, a shiver crawling down his spine. Ferkin wasn't one to scare easily. If he looked tense, something was very wrong.

"I'm not sure," Ferkin murmured, leaning forward in his saddle. "I think I see something over yonder."

Orin's heart skipped as he turned to follow Ferkin's line of sight. The forest loomed around them, thick and dark, the towering Sefmore trees standing like silent giants. Tangled branches and heavy foliage blurred together in a maze of shapes and shadows. For a moment, it seemed like nothing more than the ordinary chaos of the woods. And then—

There. A shape, almost indistinguishable against the dark backdrop, slithered between the trunks. Orin's breath caught. It moved with a strange, fluid grace, like smoke caught in a breeze, its form shifting and contorting in ways that made his skin crawl.

"There's nothing there but a bunch of—" he started, but the words withered away as his brain registered what he was seeing. A figure—no, a shadow, darker than the night itself—crept out from behind a distant tree, sliding along the forest floor like living ink. The aura around it shimmered, thickening, and Aya, usually fearless and steady, let out a deep, guttural grunt.

Her tail lashed, snapping through the underbrush, claws scraping against the ground as she shifted uneasily. Orin's brave, battle-hardened Snore, who had faced down fleshers without so much as a blink, was... afraid. "Steady, girl," he murmured, his voice trembling as he patted her neck.

She flinched under his touch, nostrils flaring, eyes rolling wildly. The sharp edges of fear clawed at his chest, twisting tighter with every skittish movement of the creature beneath him. "Who goes there?" Ferkin's voice rang out, sharp and commanding, cutting through the heavy quiet.

He sat up straighter in his saddle, shoulders squared, every muscle tensed like a drawn bowstring. The words hung in the air, unanswered. The shadow didn't pause, didn't flinch. Instead, the leaves above exploded into frantic rustling, thrashing as if caught in a storm. But no wind touched Orin's skin.

A chill crept through his veins, spreading like ice. The sky, still streaked with the fading light of day, darkened in an instant. Thick, heavy clouds gathered overhead, swallowing the sun's last glow until the world was cast in a murky twilight. Silence fell—absolute, suffocating. The chittering of birds, the hum of insects—gone, as if the forest was holding its breath.

Then it came. It was a sound, thin and wavering, drifting through the stillness. Not quite wind. Not quite animal. It was a moan, a low, mournful wail that seemed to echo from everywhere and nowhere at once.

"What is that?" Ferkin whispered, his voice tense, eyes wide as he scanned the shadows.

"I don't know," Orin breathed, his gaze locked on the shifting darkness that pulsed and twisted as it edged closer.

The aura around it rippled, recoiling in invisible waves. "I said, who goes there?!" Ferkin shouted again, but the words were nearly drowned out by the wind that had suddenly sprung up, howling through the treetops with a ferocity that made the branches creak and groan. The edges of his voice, usually steady as bedrock, wavered—almost desperate.

The shadow didn't stop. The wind shrieked louder, ripping leaves and branches from their moorings, tearing them loose and hurling them through the air. The trees shuddered, swaying violently, their roots straining against the ground. It was as if the forest was trying to repel the intruder, to force it back. But the figure pressed forward, moving with a relentless, terrible purpose.

Then, faint at first, Orin heard it. A murmur. Words carried on the wind, broken and scattered, like someone whispering through clenched teeth. He leaned forward, heart pounding in his ears, straining to make it out.

Nothing.

The sound came again, a soft, breathy susurration winding through the roar of the storm. Orin's chest tightened. This time, he caught it. The fragmented syllables twisted through the air, thin and venomous.

The whisper was coming from the shadow.

"He's saying something," Orin croaked, his voice barely audible above the wind.

Fear tightened around his throat like a vise. He glanced sideways at Ferkin, but Ferkin didn't look back. His gaze stayed fixed on the figure, his face drained of color beneath his beard, as still as stone.

"Are you okay, sir?!" Orin shouted, raising his voice, but it felt hollow and useless against the howling storm.

"What in the spirits is he saying, Orin?" Ferkin demanded, his words clipped and taut.

They fell silent, straining against the roar of the wind, ears aching as they tried to catch the whisper of syllables that seemed to dance just out of reach. Then, like a blade slicing through the chaos, the voice broke free: "Time is gone… death is coming."

The words reverberated, low and hollow, sending a shudder through the earth itself. They thrummed through the air, burrowing into Orin's bones. The figure, no longer just a vague blur of shadow, emerged from the trees, stepping forward with a ghastly, deliberate gait.

Orin stared, his mind stumbling over what stood before them. A man—or what remained of one—shuffled into the open, draped in a shredded, blood-drenched cloak. The fabric hung in tatters, clinging to a body that looked more like ruin than flesh. Bones jutted through decaying muscle, black and slick beneath the pale, fraying skin. One arm dangled at an unnatural angle, the exposed bone cracked.

"Time is gone… death is coming," the creature crooned, his voice swelling into a haunting, singsong lilt.

His eyes—dark red, bulging grotesquely from sunken sockets—rolled wildly as if they were trying to look in every direction at once. Thick blood oozed from the hollowed-out spaces in his cheeks, dripping in sluggish, crimson rivulets that pooled at his feet.

"Spirits, what are you?" Orin whispered, the words trembling on his tongue.

The sight of the figure burned itself into his mind. A nightmare made flesh. The skin, if it could be called that, peeled away in patches, sagging and sloughing off in wet, yellow clumps that evaporated into curling, inky tendrils as they hit the ground. The mist twisted and swirled, forming symbols that flickered and writhed, alive with dark, frantic energy.

"Time is lost... death is coming... time is lost..."

The words tumbled out in a fevered rush, rising into a shrill crescendo. The figure's body convulsed, spasming violently as chunks of rotting flesh tore free, revealing the shriveled sinew and splintered bones beneath. One leg, stripped almost entirely to the bone, jerked as it took another unsteady step. The brittle tibia cracked, splintering under its weight.

"Sir, what happened?" Orin forced the question out, though his voice wavered, barely a whisper. He didn't want to know. He didn't want to hear it. But the words slipped free, helpless against the terror that clawed at his chest.

The creature's gaze snapped to his, red eyes wide and wild. It grinned, lips peeling back to reveal jagged, yellowed teeth. The grin stretched, splitting and tearing at the corners of its mouth.

"Time is gone," it whispered softly. Then, louder, a scream that shattered the silence: "Time is lost!"

Ferkin shot Orin a look, eyes wide and frantic. "Orin, you don't think… you don't think this has something to do with—"

"No!" Orin barked, cutting him off before he could finish. The word tore out of him, sharp and fierce—more to silence the fear coiling in his chest than to reassure Ferkin. "This has nothing to do with what you did."

"What do you want?" Orin shouted, his voice cracking. He didn't expect an answer. Part of him hoped there wouldn't be one.

The man—no, the thing—threw its head back, mouth gaping wide, and screamed. The sound shattered through the air, a raw, piercing shriek that burrowed deep into Orin's skull, reverberating like nails scraping against bone. Aya reared up, muscles bunching as she fought against the reins, and Orin clung on desperately, the world tilting wildly beneath him. Ferkin's snore, Beastly, let out a high-pitched bellow, twisting and bucking under him.

"DEATH IS COMING!" the creature howled, its voice splintering into a keening wail. "DEATH IS COMING, DEATH IS COMING, DEATH IS—"

"What's coming?!" Ferkin roared, struggling to control Beastly's thrashing. "What the hell is it?!"

"DEATH IS COMING!" the creature screamed again, frenzy escalating in its voice, eyes bulging grotesquely from their sockets.

Blood vessels burst, dark veins spider-webbing across the whites. And then—with a wet, sickening pop—its eyes fell free, rolling loose across the mossy ground. Orin's stomach churned as he watched them bounce once, twice, before coming to rest at his feet.

His grip tightened on the reins as the last shreds of skin peeled away, hanging like torn paper before dissolving into nothingness. The creature's tattered cloak and shredded clothes crumpled to the ground. It wavered, legs buckling. Then, with a brittle snap, one decaying limb shattered like dry kindling. The thing collapsed, crumpling in on itself.

"De… de… de…" The sound was a horrible, rattling gasp, each syllable scraping up from what remained of its throat. "De… de… DEATH."

With a final, jerking spasm, its jaw dropped open, bones splitting and cracking, and black mist poured out of its ruined form, spiraling upward in oily tendrils.

Silence crashed down. For a heartbeat, the world held still.

"Great Mother, what the fuck was that?" Ferkin's voice broke the stillness, high and strained.

He cursed again, a litany of panicked, disjointed words tumbling out as he stumbled forward, grabbing for one of the crumbling bones. It disintegrated on contact, the dark mist slipping through his fingers like smoke.

Orin stared at the dissipating remains, his breath coming fast and shallow. His mind churned, piecing through fragments of half-remembered stories—hushed whispers exchanged in the dead of night around campfires. Tales of dead men who wandered the earth, their twisted bodies heralds of doom, sent forth by dark forces to warn of something terrible on the move.

"A prophet," he whispered, staring at the dissipating tendrils of black mist. They twisted lazily before vanishing completely, leaving the forest unnervingly still. "He looks like a prophet from Davaro."

"Looks like a prophet?" Ferkin choked out, voice tight with disbelief. "He looked like death itself!"

Orin's gaze dropped back to the ground where the creature had crumbled. The moss, once lush and green, was scorched black, the earth charred and brittle. And there, etched into the smoldering remains of the forest floor, a symbol glowed faintly—a jagged, cruel mark that pulsed with a sickly, greenish light.

"What... what does it say?" Ferkin breathed, the words barely more than a ghost of sound.

"I—" Orin's throat tightened as he took a step back. The symbol seemed to shift and writhe, the lines warping as he stared. "I don't know. But... we need to tell the elders."

"No!" Ferkin's response was instant, sharp enough to snap Orin's gaze up to his face. His expression was drawn tight with panic, eyes wide and wild. "If they find out—if they know what we did..."

"Then what?" Orin demanded, fear bubbling up and spilling over. "What are we supposed to do?"

"We forget," Ferkin muttered, dropping to one knee. He ground his heel into the moss, dragging his boot over the glowing symbol again and again until it was nothing more than a smudge of dirt and ash. "We forget this ever happened."

But even as they turned away, Orin knew it was a lie. The image of the twisted, glowing mark burned itself into his memory, searing deeper with every step they took. They could scrape away the symbol, bury it in the dirt—but it wouldn't matter.

3

Home

It was a while before reaching the village. On the ride back, they didn't talk much; there was nothing to say. They both agreed there was no point in frightening everyone, and there was a shared worry about what might happen if, during the questioning, it came out that the Ferkin used the Father's prayer.

On any normal trip back, they would always ride into the village together, but it felt wrong today, as if his presence would somehow do something. In unspoken agreement, they parted at the Serpent's arch, long before entering the village. "This is good, this is okay. He'll be okay," Orin murmured to himself, though Aya swung her head to side-eye, as if trying to weigh in on what was being conveyed.

The village spread out before them like a vivid tapestry, each brushstroke of life vibrant and full of warmth. The scent of freshly baked turpin bread wrapped around them, the sweet, nutty aroma mingling with the memory of sunlit kitchens and soft laughter. Steam curled from pies on every windowsill, their golden crusts bulging with spiced fruits and honeyed glaze that dripped down in sticky rivulets. Shutters creaked shut as shopkeepers exchanged final goodbyes, their voices a gentle murmur in the cool evening air.

The road beneath Aya's hooves was knotted and unruly, a ribbon of dirt twisted through a forest of gnarled roots and weathered stone. Her hooves drummed against the uneven ground, her steps jittery as she tossed her head and flicked her tail, ears pricked toward something unseen. The dying light filtered through the branches above, painting the path in long, jagged shadows that seemed to writhe and reach for them. The last slivers of sun slipped behind the treetops, and the village seemed to pause, holding its breath before surrendering to the stillness of dusk.

In that breathless quiet, the night flowers stirred. One by one, their petals stretched open, as if waking from a long slumber, unfurling to reveal blooms of indigo, red, and gold. A faint, shimmering glow radiated from each blossom, spreading like ripples of light that shimmered against the smooth stone walls and the rough bark of the trees. They swayed gently, as if caught in the rhythm of a song only they could hear, their soft illumination casting the village in a dreamlike glow.

The air vibrated with the gentle hum of Dixin fairies—a soft, melodic thrum that shimmered through the trees, slipping between branches and leaves like a shared breath of the forest. Tiny shapes flitted in and out of the twilight, wings flashing with iridescent colors that danced like sunbeams on water. They darted through the glowing blue of the narvanor bushes, peeking out with quick, birdlike movements, their playful antics adding a layer of magic to the evening.

Acorn-sized faces framed by wisps of silvery hair appeared, curious eyes wide and bright as they watched from their hidden perches. One bolder fairy edged closer, her wings beating in a blur of delicate color, hovering just at the tip of Aya's reach before flicking away in a burst of laughter and light. It was impossible not to smile. It was always like this—the fairies testing the boundaries of their courage, the air filling with their soft, tinkling whispers as they finally deemed the world safe enough to dance. Soon, they would spiral through the ferns, weaving around each other in a joyous blur of light and motion, turning the forest floor into a living constellation.

The village wasn't grand or imposing; no songs would be written of its people, and no stories of mighty deeds or great heroes would bear its name. But that didn't matter. It was a place where every creaky floorboard and worn roof beam spoke of belonging, where even the smallest sound—the snap of a twig or the low murmur of voices—felt like part of the heartbeat of home. There was no grandeur here, no crackling magic or ancient power hidden in the woods. Just a quiet village cradled in the sheltering arms of the sefmore trees, its presence soft and steady like a well-kept secret.

Guiding Aya past the familiar curve of the aging Town Hall, Orin took in its dark slate walls that were weathered but stubbornly proud against the twisting roots and flowing wooden structures surrounding it. One couldn't help but notice the iron root pillars that stood rigid and defiant, they seemed almost out of place in this land of organic curves and natural patterns—a relic of a time when people sought to bend nature to their will rather than walk beside it. It was there, under the ironwood trees that shadowed its entrance, where Shira and Orin had first crossed paths, the memory etched into the very bark of those ancient sentinels.

The scene replayed in his mind: Shira, delicate but determined, navigating the tangled web of gnarled roots with a basket of flour precariously balanced in her arms. Her brow knitted in fierce concentration, eyes fixed ahead until her foot snagged on a root. The basket went flying, and with it, a puff of flour exploded into the air, drifting in lazy, white swirls. Orin had expected her to gasp, curse, or stamp her feet in frustration. Instead, she simply paused, taking a deep breath to steady herself. Then, with the poise of a queen, she brushed the dirt from her knees and stood tall, dusty but unbroken, her eyes clear and calm. There was a grace about her, an unshakeable presence that left him stunned. Two days later, he asked her to be his wife, and they wed beneath the great Emerald Lady. Her massive figure towered above them, its light shimmering like stained glass, casting patterns of gold and amber that shifted and danced in the light of the setting sun. He remembered the moment of saying, "I do," as the blue sun sank below the horizon, bathing them in a soft, radiant glow that made the whole world feel suspended in time.

As the road unfurled ahead, the familiar silhouette of the house came into view, nestled amid a tangle of crimson and white blooms. The flowers spilled over the base of the house, their tendrils winding up the walls, brushing against the windows as if seeking a way inside. Overhead, the ancient Sefmore trees stretched their limbs protectively, their sprawling branches creating a canopy that left only a small patch of sunlight to pierce through. That slender beam of light fell on a quiet corner of the yard, where simple moss-covered headstones marked the resting place of Orin's parents and grandparents.

When the village fell silent each night, he would retreat to the back garden, pipe in hand, the sweet scent of tobacco swirling lazily in the cool evening breeze. Fireflies drifted like tiny lanterns among the bushes, their glow a soft, pulsing rhythm that matched the distant hooting of owls. Through a single opening in the treetops, he would stare up at the stars, tracing imaginary paths to places far beyond the village borders. Each exhale of smoke carried a dream—of adventure, of roads untraveled, of something beyond this small, familiar world. But now, those dreams seemed hazy, smothered under the weight of duty and the lingering shadow of the day's events, leaving only a hollow longing in their wake.

The front yard lay cradled within a low stone wall, its crumbling rocks blanketed in thick, velvety moss. Waist-high and uneven, it stood as a quiet guardian, drawing the line between the untamed sprawl of the forest and the quiet refuge of home. A sagging white gate clung to rusted hinges, swaying gently with each whisper of the wind, its forlorn creak echoing faintly. It hadn't latched properly in years, not since he was a boy chasing fireflies and Dixin fairies in the twilight, and though its slant had grown more pronounced, he had never once tried to mend it. It was a stubborn remnant of those long-gone evenings, holding fast to its place in time.

He nudged it open, the gate groaning softly in protest, and stepped onto the familiar path of smooth river stones. Each stone was a piece of the past, plucked from the streambed by his father's roughened hands as he splashed beside him, a child's joy mingling with the steady rhythm of flowing water. Now, they formed a winding trail through the yard, their surfaces gleaming faintly under the last traces of sunlight. The path curved gently toward the house—an old soul, hewn from the heart of a Sefmore tree that his great-great-grandparents had planted with hope and reverence. The bark, thick and gnarled, was streaked with dark veins that seemed to hum quietly in the fading light, its presence rooted deep in the soil and in the family's story.

Shira's touch was woven into the house, her spirit present in every brushstroke of red she had painted along the windowsills. The bold color stood out against the rich, earthy browns of the tree's bark, making the structure seem to breathe with life. She had insisted it needed to be "alive," spending long days staining the front door with tiran tree nuts until the wood shimmered with a deep, glowing red. The door handle, a coiled twist of black metal, ended in a delicate emblem—a pair of intertwined trees, the crest of their family, its roots and branches forever entwined.

Stepping inside, the warmth wrapped around Orin like a beloved old blanket. The fire crackled softly in the hearth, flames leaping and flickering behind the iron grate. Two well-worn rocking chairs, their curved arms smoothed by years of touch, sat side by side before the fire—a wedding gift from his parents, aged but enduring. Books lined the shelves, their spines faded, interspersed with small trinkets and keepsakes—a shell here, a carved whistle there. Each object held a history, a voice in the quiet symphony of home. Beneath his feet, the soft, spongy wood floor gave gently with every step, its polished surface catching the warm glow of the firelight, reflecting memories of evenings spent just like this—safe, familiar, and steady.

This was his sanctuary—a place where the warmth of family and the quiet of peace breathed through every corner. But as he stood by the hearth, staring into the flames, a chill clung stubbornly to his skin. The dark shape from the forest, the decaying figure with eyes hollowed by death, lingered at the edges of his thoughts like a shadow he couldn't quite catch. Even the crackling fire, its glow licking at the stone, seemed powerless to push back the creeping dread. He turned, glancing through the window into the black expanse of trees beyond, half-expecting to see that twisted figure lurking in the gloom, watching.

But there was only silence. Just the stillness of the village settling under the blanket of night.

He stepped further into the room, the soft glow of the fire casting a warm, golden light over the hand-carved wooden walls. Shadows flickered and danced across the grain like phantoms, pulled into a rhythm by the snapping and popping of the logs. Tiny embers spun up the chimney in a whirl of fiery spirals, momentarily lighting the room with a vivid burst before fading into the dark. The heat curled around him like a familiar embrace, but even its touch seemed unable to banish the cold knot in his chest.

He inhaled deeply, letting the scent of home wrap around him in a tight hug. The rich aroma of ale pie—thick and savory, with the sharp brightness of citrus nectar weaving through the hoppy base—mingled with the earthy warmth of freshly baked turpin root bread. His stomach tightened, hunger roaring to life at the reminder of how long it had been since he'd last eaten. The nuttiness of jupin seeds roasting over the fire added another tantalizing note, their fragrance wafting through the room, layering itself into the blend of scents that seemed to embody the essence of comfort and belonging. It was the kind of smell that tugged at old memories, making his chest tighten with a sense of homecoming he could find nowhere else.

But what truly made this place feel alive was the melody drifting softly from the kitchen. Shira's voice—light and lilting—floated through the air, weaving its way through the wooden beams and across the polished floors, filling every corner with a quiet, unassuming joy. It was a song he'd heard a thousand times, but its sweetness never faded. He closed his eyes, letting the simple, gentle tune surround him, each note settling over him like a soft blanket, warm and reassuring.

Then came the sound of quick, pounding footsteps—a small stampede tearing down the hallway, punctuated by a high-pitched, breathless shout. "Papa, papa, papa!"

Before he could react, a whirlwind of energy barreled into him, a tangle of limbs and golden hair flying as a small, freckled face buried itself in his chest. Orin laughed, the sound bursting out of him as he scooped up his boy, whose wild, shaggy hair tickled his chin as he squirmed and wriggled in his arms.

"Cal, my little rascal!" he called out, hoisting the boy up and feeling his small frame buzz with excitement.

Cal's ragged brown sleeping gown trailed behind him like a cape, the sleeves too long, and his knitted black socks flopped loosely around his ankles. Even so, his vivid blue eyes—just like his mother's—sparkled with mischief. A wide grin spread across his flushed, freckled cheeks. Only eight years old, Cal was already bursting with boundless energy that seemed to fill the entire room.

Orin glanced up and caught sight of Shira standing in the kitchen doorway, moving slowly toward him, the soft light of the fire casting a halo around her. The smile on her lips made his heart skip a beat. "Hello, beautiful," he murmured, unable to keep the warmth from his voice.

She stepped forward, her movements fluid and effortless, like water slipping over river stones. Her long golden hair spilled down her back in a cascade of shimmering waves, catching the light like spun sunlight. The ivy-green dress she wore clung softly to her form, the fabric flowing in soft, elegant lines, its pale green sides accentuating her every curve. A faded gold band encircled her left forearm, snug against the fabric just below her elbow, and the delicate lace at the ends of her sleeves covered her hands in a soft, cloud-like veil. Every detail—the way the firelight danced in her eyes, the small smile at the corners of her mouth—etched itself into the moment, lingering like the final note of a perfect song.

"Missed you," she said softly, her gaze meeting his.

"Missed you, too," he replied, his voice low and quiet as he set Cal down.

The boy darted away, a blur of motion once again, but Orin stayed still, rooted in place, taking in Shira as the weight of the world seemed to melt away. The scent of home and the sight of her filled every empty space inside him.

Her smile lit up the room, a bright, effortless glow that always caught him off guard. Even after all these years, the way she looked at him—eyes soft, lips curving with affection—made his breath hitch. She reached out, brushing a stray lock of hair away from his brow before letting her fingers drift lower, combing through the rough curls of his beard. A shiver of warmth spread through him as she twirled a bit of his hair between her fingers, her touch delicate and almost reverent.

Then she leaned in, her lips brushing his forehead in a kiss that felt more like a promise than a greeting. "Welcome home," she whispered, her voice soft, lingering in the space between them.

Her breath carried the faint scent of turpin root and sweet spices from the kitchen, mingled with the ever-present earthy fragrance of the forest outside. As she stepped back, the firelight caught in her eyes, making them appear to dance.

A sharp tug on his chin broke the spell. "Papa, come see what I made!" Cal's voice rang out, his excitement bubbling over as he bounced on the balls of his feet, his small hands clenched into tight, eager fists.

"After dinner," Shira interjected, her tone firm but gentle—the kind of voice that left no room for argument. She raised an eyebrow at the smudges of dirt streaking Cal's fingers. "And only after you wash those hands."

Cal's shoulders drooped, his face falling into a practiced look of utter despair, a pitiful plea written across his freckled features. He turned his wide, imploring eyes upward toward his father. A soft chuckle escaped as his father reached out to ruffle the boy's messy hair. "Even mighty warriors need clean hands, son. Off you go."

Grumbling under his breath, Cal spun around and bolted down the hall. Orin turned back to Shira, a grin tugging at his lips. "And what about me, Mrs. Arator? Must I go and wash my hands, too?"

Shira tilted her head, a playful glint lighting her gaze. "You, Mr. Arator," she replied, dropping her voice to a low, mock-serious tone. "Have something far more important to do first."

"Oh?" he leaned in, arching an eyebrow.

She stepped closer, the space between them vanishing as she gazed up at him with a look that made his heart stumble. "Yes," she murmured, her lips curving into a teasing smile. "You owe your wife a proper kiss."

A soft laugh escaped him as he lowered his face until their noses brushed. "Then a proper kiss you shall have."

Their lips met in the lightest of touches, a feather-soft brush that sent a thrill through him. Time seemed to slow, the world narrowing to just the feel of her—her warmth, her scent, the soft sigh of her breath mingling with his. For that moment, everything else faded. There was no forest, no shadow lurking at the edges. Just her, and the unshakable certainty that this was exactly where he belonged.

She pulled away slowly, a small smile tugging at the corner of her lips, but then her gaze shifted past him. "Where is Ferkin?" she asked, her expression growing puzzled.

He leaned back slightly. "He was in the mood to go to the tavern tonight," he said casually.

But she gave him the look that said she knew better. For years, Ferkin always returned with him after being away. He always sat down and filled Cal's imagination with stories of the adventures he'd been on. But not tonight.

"Should I be concerned about him?" she asked, turning back toward the kitchen.

"No, everything is fine," he replied. Another lie. And again, she knew it.

The kitchen stretched out around them, its cozy walls and counters curving naturally from the trunk of the Sefmore. The smooth grain of the wood swirled in patterns that seemed to shimmer faintly under the fire's glow. The warmth of the room enveloped them, the air filled with the comforting scents of home and the quiet hum of contentment. A sturdy wooden table dominated the center, its surface scarred and nicked from years of lively family meals and shared laughter. Shelves lined the walls, crammed with mismatched plates and bowls—a testament to Shira's love of collecting. Glass jars filled with preserved fruits and vegetables glistened in neat rows, their vibrant ruby reds, deep ambers, and verdant greens catching the firelight like a row of glittering jewels. It was a room that hummed with life, shaped by years of small moments woven together to create the home they'd built.

Shira placed the steaming ale pie on the counter, its golden crust shimmering under a delicate glaze of butter and herbs. The rich aroma filled the room, carrying the scent of slow-roasted meats, caramelized onions, and the sharp bite of fermented ale. It unfurled around them like a comforting embrace, wrapping them in warmth. He closed his eyes for a moment, inhaling deeply as the smell tugged at his senses, promising comfort and satisfaction.

"Sit down, love," she murmured, already reaching up to pull his favorite mug from the shelf.

The wooden plank creaked softly as she shifted the mug free, the small sound echoing through the quiet kitchen. Outside, the garden lay shrouded in darkness, the blossoms tucked tightly into themselves as if they were asleep. Shira filled the mug with a generous pour of dandle beer, the frothy head foaming just over the rim, and set it down before him.

"You look like you could use a drink," she said, her voice soft with understanding.

4
The Eight

He took the mug in hand, savoring the bitter, floral notes of the beer as it danced across his tongue. "Ahh, perfect," he sighed, feeling the day's tension begin to unravel.

"Cal!" Shira called, her voice ringing out clear and bright, slicing through the stillness. "Dinner's ready!"

Cal came charging into the room, a blur of energy and tousled hair, only to freeze as Orin caught him mid-sprint, scooping him up with a grin. "Hold on there, warrior! Did you wash your hands like your mother said?"

"Let me go!" Cal squealed, squirming as Orin tickled his sides, laughter spilling out in uncontrollable bursts.

"Well, did you?" he pressed, trying to keep a straight face as he held Cal aloft.

Cal stuck out his hands triumphantly. "See? Clean!"

Shira's eyebrow arched in that way that made both of them pause. "And the backs?" she asked, her voice stern but tinged with amusement.

Cal's grin faltered, and he quickly tucked his hands behind his back, drawing a chuckle from him.

"Hmm…" Orin pretended to examine Cal with exaggerated seriousness, peeking around at his hidden hands. "I suppose that'll have to do."

Shira shook her head, lips twitching with a smile she tried to hide. "Alright, let's eat."

They gathered around the table, the rich smells of the meal filling the space between them as they dug in, the room coming alive with the simple, happy noises of a family at dinner—spoons scraping against plates, the soft hum of satisfaction, and bursts of quiet laughter. He watched as Cal attacked his slice of pie, cheeks puffed out with every bite, his enthusiasm boundless.

"Papa?" Cal mumbled, crumbs spilling from the corner of his mouth.

"Yes, my boy?" He leaned closer, wiping a stray crumb from Cal's chin.

"Can you tell me the story of the Eight Lands?" Cal's voice was small and hesitant, his eyes wide with the kind of hopeful expectation only a child can muster.

"Not during dinner," Shira gently interjected, her gaze softening as she looked at their son. "Your father's had a long day."

But when Cal's eyes met his, full of that pure, unguarded eagerness, something inside him melted. "Maybe after dinner," he murmured, ruffling Cal's hair. "If you finish all your pie."

"Really?" Cal's face lit up, eyes sparkling like the first light of dawn.

"Really," he promised, feeling a deep contentment settle in his chest. For that moment, the outside world faded, the darkness at the edge of the forest distant and powerless. Around this table, there was only light and warmth.

He tipped the last of the dandle beer into his mug, the amber liquid glowing softly in the firelight as it pooled at the bottom. The frothy head bubbled up, cresting just above the rim before settling. He glanced over at Shira, who watched him with that familiar look of half warning, half fond exasperation. Her gaze was soft, and her lips quirked in a knowing smile. He couldn't help but grin, lifting the mug in a mock salute. "It's fine, love. Besides, who better to tell the tale than me?"

She sighed, but the laughter in her eyes said everything. "Just don't rile him up too much before bed," she teased, her voice carrying a playful lilt.

He leaned back in his chair, savoring the moment—the warmth of the fire, the scent of roasted meat and fresh bread, the sound of his family's laughter wrapping around him. For tonight, there were no shadows, no fears. Just them, bathed in the golden glow of home.

Shira sighed, her shoulders relaxing as her gaze softened. "Alright," she relented, though her expression turned playful as she raised a finger in Cal's direction. "But I expect you in bed after this, without any fussing, young man."

Cal puffed up his chest, shooting a defiant look her way. "I'm not a young man!" Cal announced, his small voice brimming with indignation.

Shira's lips twitched, the corners pulling upward despite her efforts to keep her stern facade. "Oh, you're not?" she asked, arching a brow, amusement dancing in her eyes. "And what are you, then?"

"A great warrior, like my grandfather!" Cal proclaimed, standing a little taller, his face lit with fierce pride.

Shira's gaze dropped pointedly to the nearly full bowl of ale pie sitting in front of him. "Well, great and powerful warrior," she said, her tone mockingly grave. "You need to finish your dinner. And I expect it to be gone before the story ends."

Cal's expression shifted to one of exaggerated despair as he eyed the hefty portion still in his bowl. "All gone?" he echoed, as if confirming the sheer magnitude of the challenge set before him.

"Yes, all gone," Shira replied, biting back a laugh as his shoulders sagged in defeat.

"Okay," he groaned, shoulders drooping dramatically, as if resigning himself to a battle of epic proportions.

With a deep, resigned sigh, he picked up his spoon and began shoveling mouthfuls of pie with the exaggerated movements of a soldier heading off to war. Orin stifled his own chuckle, shaking his head, and took a long, slow drink from his mug, letting the bitter tang of the beer linger on his tongue. Then, setting the mug down with deliberate care, he turned to Cal, leaning forward as he lowered his voice.

"Many years ago, before our kind walked the land, there were only the spirits," he began softly, his tone slipping into the rhythm of an old storyteller. "And the creator of all—the Great Mother. The Eight Spirits ruled over the land together for many thousands of years, each one embodying a part of the world itself. One day, the Great Mother brought another child to show her eight others. And this child," he paused, letting the silence hang heavy between them. "Was the first man."

Cal's spoon hovered mid-air, his eyes wide and bright as he leaned in closer, his dinner momentarily forgotten. His father leaned towards him, lowering his voice to a hushed murmur, as if sharing a secret meant only for them. "While seven of the eight spirits were loyal to the Great Mother, cherishing mankind just as she did, the first of them—the eldest, the strongest, the most beloved—became consumed by jealousy. He was called Him, and Him couldn't understand why his mother would create such a weak and flawed creature when she already had her perfect children."

He paused, letting the words hang heavy in the stillness, watching the flicker of emotions cross Cal's face. The boy's brows knit together, a tiny crease forming between them. "What is it?" he asked softly, his voice barely more than a whisper.

Slowly, Cal wriggled off his stool, his small form sliding into his father's lap. He looked up at him with eyes far too serious for his age, searching his face. "Am I a flawed creature, Papa?" he whispered, his voice so small, so uncertain, that it sent a pang straight through his father's chest.

"No, not at all." Orin breathed, fiercely wrapping his arms around the boy. "You are in no way flawed, my boy."

He glanced over at Shira, her expression soft yet steady as she watched them. Cal's fingers lifted to his mouth, tracing the delicate scar that marked his upper lip, the reminder of a struggle he'd fought even before he'd drawn his first breath. Shira leaned forward, her hand enveloping his as she pressed a kiss to his cheek.

"Don't ever let anyone tell you that you're anything less than perfect," she murmured, her voice gentle but firm, a strength lying beneath each word. "Do you understand?"

"But some of the other kids—" Cal's voice wavered, trailing off.

"Listen to me," Orin said, cutting in softly. "You are the most unflawed, precious thing in this world. We wouldn't change a single thing about you."

Cal blinked up at them, his small brow furrowing as if weighing their words against the taunts and whispers of others, trying to sort truth from hurt. Slowly, hesitantly, he nodded. "Okay," he whispered, though doubt still lingered at the edges of his voice.

Shira looked at her husband, her eyes saying everything she couldn't in front of their son. Her gaze flicked to Cal and back to him, conveying a silent conversation that spoke of shared worry and fierce love. "Maybe that's enough story for tonight," she suggested softly.

"No!" Cal shook his head, his eyes widening with a sudden spark of desperation. "Please, Papa, finish it! I want to hear the rest. Please?"

He turned those pleading eyes to his father, his little hands clutching the fabric of his shirt as if afraid he'd vanish if he let go. Orin glanced at Shira. She sighed, a soft breath of resignation, but her gaze remained tender. He shifted Cal slightly, adjusting so the boy could lean back against his chest, his small body fitting perfectly against him.

"Alright, my warrior," he murmured, pressing a kiss to his son's hair. "But just a little more. The rest will have to wait until tomorrow."

Cal beamed up at Orin, his face lighting up with anticipation. "When the Great Mother learned of His defiance," Orin continued, keeping his voice low and measured. "She tore Him away from her love, casting Him into the dark lands at the edge of the world."

Orin paused, watching as Cal's eyes widened, the boy's small hands clutching at his sleeve. "But Him's anger was like a flame that wouldn't die. Furious at being cast out, He tore the flesh from His body and used it to create new beings—children born of shadow and hate—shaped by a dark power stolen from the threads of time itself."

Leaning closer, Orin let his voice drop to a murmur. "They were vile, twisted things, their souls bathed in black fire. These monsters, these Voders, became his army."

Cal's breath caught, his small frame tensing as the dark images formed in his mind. Orin tightened his hold around the boy, feeling his heart race beneath his arms. "But Him wasn't satisfied. No—He wanted to strike at the Great Mother's heart, to shatter what she cherished most. So, He took some of her beloved men and twisted them, too, bending them to his will, their bodies warped into horrifying shapes. These creatures—the Fleshers—were no longer men. They were abominations, created to sow terror and pain."

Cal shuddered, his face tilting up to peer at Orin, eyes wide with a mix of fear and wonder. "Him sent his army of voders and fleshers into the lands of the other Spirits, sparking a war that scorched the very earth and darkened the skies."

Orin spread his arms wide, fingers splayed as if to mimic the chaos that had torn through the realm. "The Spirits fought back, each wielding the power of their land, pushing Him's monsters back into the darkness, but the battle was so terrible, so fierce, that it split the ocean itself." He swept his hand through the air in a dramatic motion. "The sea shattered, its waters bleeding into the land, carving the once-whole realm of Irada into eight separate lands."

Cal's mouth dropped open, a soft gasp escaping him as he tried to picture it all—a world torn apart by war, oceans breaking like glass. His wide eyes flicked back to Orin, searching for more.

"The Great Mother, enraged by Him's betrayal, cursed His land, filling it with eternal pain and fire." Orin leaned in closer, his voice dipping to a conspiratorial whisper. "And to protect her remaining children, she placed the other seven Spirits—one in each of the new lands—to watch over mankind."

Orin paused, letting the room fall still, the only sound the soft crackling of the fire. "And now," he murmured, "they sleep, hidden deep within the earth and sea, guarding us from Him and his vile creations, ensuring that His dark reach can never again touch our world."

Cal stared up at Orin, eyes impossibly wide, his small mouth forming a silent O. The flickering firelight danced in his gaze, casting shadows across his face as the story unfolded in his mind. He could almost see it—the spirits standing guard, the vast ocean splitting apart, and dark creatures slinking through the shadows, waiting for their master's call.

Orin's gaze softened as Cal seemed lost in the tale, his small brow furrowed with thought. But then, with a sudden flicker of movement, Cal turned, his wide eyes darting toward the darkened window, as if expecting to see those twisted forms lurking just beyond. Instead, all he found was the quiet garden, night flowers closed in slumber, and the gentle silhouettes of trees swaying softly in the breeze.

Orin pressed a kiss to Cal's tousled hair, his voice a reassuring whisper. "You're safe, my boy," he murmured, pulling Cal closer into his arms. "The Spirits are still there, even if we can't see them. Watching. Protecting."

Cal nodded slowly, snuggling deeper into Orin's embrace, his small body relaxing. His gaze drifted back to the flickering fire, the warm glow reflecting in his thoughtful eyes. Across from them, Shira's eyes met Orin's over the boy's head, her expression soft but filled with something unspoken. In that shared glance, they both understood—it wasn't the monsters outside that they needed to guard against, but the ones that might creep into Cal's heart.

"For tonight," Orin said softly, his voice barely above a murmur. "All is well."

Cal exhaled, the tension in his small frame easing. "And the Spirits will keep us safe?" he asked, his voice a faint whisper.

"Yes," Orin replied firmly, tightening his hold. "The Spirits and us."

Cal's lips curled into a small smile, and Orin knew the darkness of the story had receded, leaving behind a warm glow of comfort and safety. But then, in a quiet voice, Cal whispered, "What if they wake up?"

A small smile tugged at the corners of Orin's lips as he leaned in closer, as if to share a secret. "Then," he whispered, his voice low. "When the darkness threatens to swallow everything, they will rise again. And Him..." Orin's voice dropped to a murmur. "Will walk among us once more, knocking at the doors of little boys and girls."

Without warning, Orin reached under the table and rapped his knuckles hard against the wood. "Bang, bang, bang!"

Cal shot off Orin's lap with a yelp, his eyes wide and startled before he burst into a fit of giggles. "PAPA!" he shrieked, his whole body shaking with laughter.

Even Shira jumped, her hand flying to her chest, her eyes wide in shock before she too erupted into laughter. "Alright, that's enough!" she gasped, her own amusement bubbling up despite herself. "Settle down and finish your food."

Cal scrambled back onto his stool, still grinning with excitement as he shoveled the last few bites of pie into his mouth, his earlier reluctance forgotten. Between bites, he blurted, "The Emerald Lady is our Spirit, right, Papa?"

"That's right, my boy," Orin said, pride swelling in his chest. "The Emerald Lady watches over Terrae. She is steadfast and strong, guiding us through the darkness when all else fades."

Orin closed his eyes, picturing the towering tree in his mind. The Emerald Lady was formidable, her iron roots winding deep into the earth, her root covered arms stretching wide and sheltering. Her crown glowed with an inner light that held back the shadows.

"And remember," he continued. "Cavatio guards the Divine Cavern, filled with hidden mysteries and secrets. Caelum reigns over the majestic mountains, offering glimpses of the future from his high perch. Aquam cradles the vast ocean, holding the secret of health and life. Ballator, the mighty rock warriors, know nothing but battle. Caprale, the eternal swamp lily, remembers every whisper of the past. Secretum is shrouded in roaring waterfalls and deadly mists. And then," Orin's voice grew deep and guttural, barely more than a breath. "There is Devoro...the cursed land of the fleshers."

Cal shivered, his wide eyes darting nervously toward the shadowed window, as if expecting to see dark shapes lurking just beyond the glass. "But they can't come here, right?" he whispered, his voice tight with worry.

Orin drew Cal closer, feeling the boy tremble slightly against him. He pressed a gentle kiss to the top of Cal's head. "Not while the Spirits keep watch," Orin promised, his tone steady and reassuring. "As long as they are with us, we are safe."

Yet, even as the words left his lips, a flicker of unease twisted deep in his chest. It was an uninvited thought, creeping in like a cold draft beneath a door. Because somewhere out there, Him was watching. And Orin knew—deep down—that even the Spirits couldn't protect them forever.

"Alright, that's enough excitement for one night," Shira interjected, her tone light but firm.

The set of her shoulders left no room for argument. She caught Orin's eye, a silent reminder not to push the boy too far. But something in Orin's expression must have given him away, because Cal leaned forward, eyes wide and still brimming with wonder. "Papa?" Cal pleaded, gazing at Orin, then flicking it to Shira.

Cal's lower lip jutted out, the way it always did when he was trying to coax a little more time out of them, a look that tugged at Orin's heart every time. "Please, can't we hear just a little more?"

He turned his gaze back to Shira, his wide, round eyes pleading in the way that usually earned him a few more moments of play before bed. Orin felt his resolve waver.

Shira sighed softly, her eyes drifting toward Cal's bowl. Bits of bread and meat were carefully spread across the bottom, arranged just so in a clear attempt to make it seem like he'd eaten more than he had. Her expression hardened, the playful smile fading as she fixed him with a stern look.

"Bedtime," she declared, her voice firm and final, leaving no room for argument. "Kiss your papa goodnight."

Cal opened his mouth to protest but stopped at the sight of her arched brow, his shoulders slumping dramatically in exaggerated defeat. With a heavy sigh, he slid off Orin lap, his steps slow and burdened with the weight of a child denied his bedtime story.

His eyes flicked back to Orin's, still pleading silently for just a few more words. "Goodnight, my warrior," Orin whispered, ruffling Cal's hair softly as the boy turned to go.

"Don't forget," Shira added gently, her voice softening as she watched Cal trudge toward the door. "Even great warriors need their rest."

Cal sighed dramatically, glancing back over his shoulder with one last look of longing before finally disappearing down the hall.

"What? No kiss for me?" Shira called after him, feigning hurt, though a smile tugged at her lips, betraying her struggle to stay stern.

Cal spun around, eyes wide. "Oh! I forgot!"

He dashed back, standing on his toes to plant a messy kiss on her cheek. The warmth of it lingered on her skin even after he pulled away, his earlier gloom evaporating like mist under the morning sun. With a grin, he bounded off down the hall, his small feet thudding softly against the floorboards.

Shira turned back to Orin, her smile fading into a more thoughtful expression as Orin leaned back, tipping the last dregs of his dandle beer into his mouth.

"You tell him too many fanciful tales," she murmured, her voice gentle, more teasing than scolding. But beneath her words, there was a note of unease, something deeper as her gaze searched Orin's face. "You'll fill his head with nonsense."

Orin let her words hang in the air for a moment, a ghost of a smile tugging at the edges of his lips. He didn't respond right away. Instead, he met her gaze, letting the silence stretch between them. The weight of what he had seen—what he knew—sat heavy in his chest. "Maybe not all stories are childish," he murmured quietly, his voice low and edged with something raw.

The shift in Orin's tone didn't go unnoticed by Shira. The playful spark in her eyes dimmed, replaced by a shadow of worry as she slipped onto the bench beside him. Her hand hovered just above his, hesitant, before she laid it gently atop his knuckles, her fingers cool against his skin. A chill crept into the room, the warmth of the fire suddenly feeling distant and thin.

"What is it?" she whispered, leaning closer. The tremble in her voice betrayed the fear she tried to mask. "Tell me, Orin."

Orin's throat tightened, the words tangling themselves into a knot that he struggled to free. "Ferkin and I—" he began, then faltered. The memory clawed at him, dragging him back to that shadowed grove. "We saw something today. Something of Him's."

Shira's eyes widened, the flicker of alarm sharpening into focus as she leaned in, clutching the edge of the bench as if bracing for a blow. "What did you see?" she whispered, her voice thin and taut, the unspoken plea of please, don't say it hanging heavily between them.

"A man came out of the woods," Orin whispered, his words raw and jagged. "Or what was left of him."

The color drained from Shira's face, her knuckles going white where she gripped the fabric of her dress. "What do you mean?" she breathed, the tremor in her voice growing.

Her gaze darted over Orin's face, searching and pleading. "His flesh—" Orin's voice cracked, the memory flashing before his eyes: that twisted figure staggering through the trees, everything thick with the scent of rot and something far worse. He closed his eyes, fighting a wave of nausea. "His flesh was stripped from his body."

Shira's breath caught, her fingers tightening painfully around his. She stared at him, her eyes wide and glistening. "Stripped? But—"

"He walked out of the tree line," Orin continued hoarsely. "His skin just... slipping off. Like wet parchment tearing away into pieces. It fell to the ground in a black mist. And the mist, it was coming from his wounds, swirling around him like it was alive."

A shudder ran through him, the chill deepening, as if the forest's darkness had slipped into the room, coiling in the corners, whispering. Shira's eyes shone with unshed tears; her lips parted in silent horror. The room felt smaller, the fire's light dim and frail against the shadows pressing in on them.

"Alive?" she whispered, her voice barely audible, as if speaking the word aloud might make it real.

"It moved, Shira," Orin murmured, his voice rough. "Like it was trying to escape. It was crawling out of him."

She recoiled, a strangled sound escaping her lips. Her fingers dug into his arm, her grip tight enough to bruise, but he didn't flinch. He couldn't. The image of that twisted, skinless form loomed in his mind, the memory of its stumbling steps, of the mist curling and seeping from the ragged remnants of its flesh, clinging like a nightmare that refused to fade.

"What... what did you do?" she asked, her voice trembling, barely more than a breath.

"Nothing," he whispered, his voice hollow. "There was nothing to do. He was already gone, Shira. Whatever that... thing was, it wasn't a man anymore." He looked down, staring at her small hand clutching his, the contrast of her pale skin against the roughness of his own. "It's like the forest spat him out, like it was trying to purge whatever darkness had twisted him."

For a long moment, silence hung between them, the crackle of the fire a distant murmur. Then Shira drew a shaky breath, her gaze locked onto his, fear and determination warring in her eyes.

"We need to tell the council," she said, her voice steadier, though her hand trembled against his. "If... if there's more of them—"

"I know," he cut in quietly, squeezing her fingers gently. "I know. But tonight, let's just..."

He trailed off, glancing toward the hallway where Cal's shadow had disappeared, picturing his small form burrowed under blankets, his face peaceful and untroubled. "Let's just keep this between us, for now."

Shira swallowed hard, then nodded slowly, her gaze softening as she followed his glance toward their son's room. She leaned into him, the warmth of her body a fragile barrier against the cold that had seeped into his bones. He wrapped an arm around her shoulders, drawing her close, and for a moment, they sat in silence, listening to the fire and the distant, steady beat of Cal's footsteps bouncing around his room.

"Just for tonight," she murmured finally, her voice a soft breath against his neck.

"Yes," he whispered back, holding her close. "Just for tonight."

But the image of that skinless figure lingered, and in the darkness of the room, the shadows seemed to shift and watch, waiting for something—something he couldn't yet name.

"What did he say?" The words slipped out in a ragged breath, barely a whisper against the low crackle of the dying embers.

Orin swallowed hard, the memory of the prophet's voice clawing at his mind. "He said..." He faltered, his throat tightening around the words. "He said, 'Death is coming, and time is lost.'"

The phrase dropped from his lips, leaden and cold, each syllable settling between them like stones thrown into a still pond. "He just kept saying it, over and over, until…" His voice broke, and he looked away, the last image of that man—what was left of him—seared into his thoughts. "Until there was nothing left."

Shira flinched as if struck, her whole body jerking back. She stumbled a step away, eyes still locked on his, then turned sharply, her movements quick and unsteady. She made for the wooden chair by the fireplace—the one she always sought out when sadness and worry pressed too close. The chair creaked softly as she sank into it, her fingers trembling as they twisted in her lap. Her face was ashen, lips parted in a silent plea as the weight of what he'd said seemed to close around her, settling in like a crushing, inescapable truth.

"Oh, Orin," she whispered, the sound fractured and raw as it left her lips. Her hands flew up to bury her face, shoulders curling inward as if folding around a wound only she could feel. "What does it mean? What... what are we going to do?"

He crossed the room in two strides, dropping to his knees beside her, his hands reaching out to cradle her tear-streaked face. "We don't do anything," he murmured, his voice firm, though the lie tasted bitter on his tongue.

He wiped the wetness from her cheeks, brushing away the streaks with his thumb, but it did nothing to erase the fear lingering in her eyes. "Shira, it's been years—decades, even. No Flesher, no dark creature has touched Terra in generations."

"But the prophet—"

"A prophet who wandered too far into the cursed lands of Devoro," he cut in, the words tumbling out fast, desperate. He squeezed her hands, trying to steady both of them. "Whatever happened to him... it was his own doing. It means nothing. If there were any Fleshers—"

A sudden, violent crash shattered the silence, the sound splitting through the room like a lightning strike. Orin's heart jolted, freezing for a single, breathless second before pounding painfully against his ribs.

Shira gasped, her eyes darting toward the doorway, wide and wild. The blood drained from her face, leaving her pale as a ghost, her fingers digging into his arm.

Orin shot to his feet, his pulse roaring in his ears as he turned toward the source of the noise, muscles coiled tight, breath held. The quiet that followed was thick, almost suffocating, the darkness outside the windows pressing closer, as if holding its own breath, too.

"Stay here," he breathed, his voice rough and strained. He stepped forward, every instinct screaming for him to run back, to shield Shira from whatever lurked beyond the door. But he couldn't—wouldn't—let fear rule. Slowly, he moved toward the hall, the creak of the floorboards underfoot the only sound breaking the stillness.

"Orin—" Shira's voice trembled, tight with the terror she was trying so hard to keep from spilling over.

He glanced back at her, his heart aching at the sight of her clutching the arms of the chair, knuckles white. "It's alright," he said softly, though the words felt hollow, empty. "Just—just wait here."

He edged around the doorway, peering into the darkened hall beyond. The shadows seemed to thicken, shifting uneasily at the edges of the lamplight. Orin took another step, breathing shallowly as he strained to catch any sound, any hint of movement.

Then, from the far end of the hall, there was a soft creak, barely a whisper against the silence. Every muscle tightened, a chill crawling up his spine as he stared into the murk. "Who's there?" he called, his voice low and steady.

Nothing answered but the faint rustle of wind against the windows. Swallowing hard, he edged forward, his gaze fixed on the shadows, nerves stretched thin. Another creak... Closer this time. His hand instinctively dropped to the knife at his belt, fingers wrapping around the hilt as if seeking reassurance from the solid weight of it.

"Orin!" Shira's sharp cry yanked him back, his heart leaping into his throat. He spun around, sprinting back into the room just as she rose from the chair, her eyes wide with panic.

"Orin, it's Cal!" she gasped, the words tumbling out in a rush. "He—he's not in his bed."

The knife slipped from his grasp, clattering use-lessly to the floor as a new, deeper fear clawed at him. "What?" he breathed, the world narrowing to a single point, a single, terrible thought. Cal—alone in the dark.

Without another word, he was running, his feet pounding against the wooden boards as he tore down the hall, the walls a blur of shadows and fear. He burst into Cal's room, the door slamming against the wall with a force that rattled the windowpanes.

Empty.

The blankets lay twisted on the floor, the bed cold and rumpled. The small lantern by his bedside flick-ered weakly, its light casting long, thin shadows that seemed to stretch and twist, mocking his frantic gaze.

"Cal!" he shouted, the sound ripping from his throat, desperate and raw. He whirled around, scanning the corners of the room, the hall, every inch of darkness pressing in.

Nothing.

"Cal!" Shira's cry was sharp, her voice breaking on the name.

Orin spun around, heart hammering, and there stood their son, frozen in the hallway. His eyes were wide and glassy, shimmering with unshed tears. At his feet lay the shattered remains of a small clay bowl, jagged pieces scattered like fallen petals. Cal's tiny shoulders shook, trembling with the weight of fear and guilt, caught in the act of eavesdropping.

"I, I, I—" he stammered, the words stumbling over each other, barely more than a breath.

His gaze darted between them, desperate and frightened, as if searching for a way to undo what he'd heard. "What did you hear, boy?"

The question snapped out of Orin, harsher than he intended, laced with the panic surging in his chest. His voice cut through the silence, and Cal flinched, shrinking back. Orin cursed himself, forcing the anger down, but the fear coiled tighter. "Tell me at once!"

"I—" Cal's small face crumpled, and in an instant, he was running to Orin, throwing himself into his arms. Tears soaked into Orin's vest as Cal buried his face against his chest.

"I'm sorry, Papa!" he sobbed, his little fists clutching desperately at the fabric. "I just—I just wanted to see what you were doing!"

Orin exchanged a quick glance with Shira, catching the worry etched deep into her expression as she wiped at her own damp cheeks. He took a breath, willing himself to calm. "What did you hear, Cal?" he asked again, softer this time, lifting his son's chin gently to see his face. "Tell me, my boy."

Cal sniffled, his breaths hiccupping as he struggled to speak through the tears. "I—I heard you and Mama talking... about a man who died. Is it true, Papa?" His wide, frightened eyes locked onto Orin's, searching, pleading for reassurance. "Is it true?"

The truth caught in Orin's throat, tangled with a thousand lies he wanted to tell. But he could only nod slowly, feeling the weight of the admission settle between them. "Yes, son. It's true. But it's nothing for you to worry about."

"But—but what if—" Cal's voice quavered, a tremor running through his small frame.

"Listen to me," Orin said quickly, gathering him close, holding him as if he could shield him from every fear, every shadow. "There are many dangers in the world, yes. But your mother and I would never let anything happen to you. Do you understand?"

Shira stepped closer, her arms wrapping around them both, the warmth of her body a steady, calming presence. "Nothing," she whispered fiercely, leaning in, her voice low and firm despite the fear still lurking in her eyes. "Nothing in this world, not even the powerful Him, could harm you while we're here."

Cal's tear-streaked face tilted up toward her, eyes still swimming with doubt. "But what about that man?" he asked quietly, the words barely more than a breath. "The one with no skin?"

Orin clenched his teeth, fighting back the curse that threatened to spill out. "That man," he began carefully, keeping his voice steady. "Broke an old law, Cal. He stepped into a place no one should go, and the darkness there... it consumed him."

Cal's small brow furrowed, the question already forming on his lips. "Will I ever be taken by darkness, Papa?"

"Never," Orin vowed, pressing a kiss to his forehead. "You and your mother will always be safe. I promise."

Shira's gaze softened as she glanced down the hallway toward Cal's bedroom, a forced smile touching her lips. "As long as little boys stay in their beds where they belong," she teased gently, ruffling his hair with a light touch.

A small giggle escaped Cal, fragile but real, his tear-streaked cheeks dimpling with the ghost of a smile as he scrubbed at his face with his sleeve. "Wait 'til Noro hears about this!" he blurted, the excitement in his voice cutting through the remnants of fear.

"Cal." Orin said his name sharply, feeling the word slice through the room. Cal froze, looking up at him, eyes wide. "You must never tell anyone what you heard tonight. It would frighten too many people."

Orin held his gaze, willing him to understand. "Promise me, son."

"I promise, Papa," Cal whispered solemnly, his small face serious as he nodded, the weight of the vow settling into his eyes.

"Good," Shira murmured softly, brushing a stray curl back from Cal's forehead as she stood. She smoothed the wrinkles from her dress, drawing in a deep, steadying breath. "Now, I think it's bedtime—again."

Orin scooped Cal up, his small body warm and solid in his arms as he carried him down the dim hallway. The house felt quieter now, the echoes of their earlier conversation fading into the soft creak of the wooden floorboards beneath their feet. The only light came from the faint glow of the dying fire behind them and the small, steady flame of the oil lamp Shira had lit as they entered Cal's room.

The golden light spilled softly across the walls, casting a gentle glow over the small space. Orin laid Cal down, tucking the blankets carefully around his slight form, smoothing them as if he could somehow tuck every fear and shadow away with them. "Rest now, my boy," he murmured, leaning close. "And remember—no matter what shadows creep, the warrior in that painting will watch over you."

Cal's eyes drifted to the painting on the wall, a figure with his sword raised high, standing against the tide of darkness. He blinked sleepily, the tension slowly easing from his small face. "Just like you, Papa," he whispered, his voice trailing off, soft and drowsy as sleep pulled him under.

"Just like me," Orin whispered back, brushing one last kiss against Cal's brow as his breathing evened out, the shadows retreating from his dreams.

Orin stayed there a moment longer, watching his son's face relax into the peace of sleep, feeling the steady rise and fall of his chest. But as he stood and turned away, the promise he'd made echoed in his mind, hollow and fragile. Because he knew, deep down, that no warrior—no father—could guard against what was coming.

In the stillness of the room, the painting seemed to watch him, the warrior's raised sword a silent, unmoving sentinel against the darkness that gathered beyond their walls.

5
Reflection

Orin and Shira lingered in the kitchen, the fading warmth of the fire casting a gentle glow that flickered shadows across the wooden beams. He could feel her gaze on him, eyes filled with an emotion that wrapped around the tightness in his chest, making it hard to breathe. After the evening's chaos, a quiet calm settled between them, accentuated by the way her expression softened and the corners of her lips curved, as if sharing a secret known only to them.

"You, my handsome husband," Shira murmured, her voice barely more than a sigh. "Look like you need to sit out back and smoke a pipe."

The words brushed against the silence, and he felt her fingers, feather-light, tracing a path along his cheek. There was a glimmer of mischief in her eyes, a spark of playfulness that stirred something warm within him.

"How right you are, dear," he replied, stepping closer until the space between them disappeared, just a breath apart.

His hand slid down her spine, gliding over the curve of her waist, fingers mapping the familiar terrain of her body. As he reached the soft swell of her bottom, she let out a soft, startled breath, her cheeks blooming pink. In that moment, she was still reminiscent of the younger woman he had fallen for all those years ago.

"And what do you have in mind, Mr. Arator?" she teased, arching a brow and taking a half-step back, just out of reach.

Moonlight streamed through the window, turning her hair into molten gold. Her smile widened, eyes dancing as though daring him to chase her. "Well, Cal's in bed, and..." he began, letting his voice drop to a husky whisper as he leaned in, closing the distance again.

"And," she interrupted him gently, pressing a finger against his lips while brushing his hand away. "I need to finish these dishes unless you want to eat off the ground like a Snore."

Her laughter bubbled up, bright and musical, as she spun away to pull open the little drawer by the sink. She retrieved his old pipe—worn, simple, with a long stem and a scuffed bowl. Running her fingers over it, a small smile tugged at her lips, eyes softening with memories. "I'll call you when I'm done."

He took the pipe, its rough wood warm against his fingers. Leaning in, he brushed a kiss against her cheek, lingering just long enough to breathe in the scent of lavender mingling with the spices from the meal she'd prepared. "Don't get lost out there." she whispered before he slipped out the back door.

The night air wrapped around him, cool and crisp, carrying the scent of wet earth and blooming Garling flowers. He followed the winding stone path through the garden, the gravel crunching softly beneath his boots. Above, the sky stretched out, a dark green, endless sea.

Settling onto the soft, dew-kissed grass beneath the only clear patch of sky in their backyard, the overgrown branches of Sefmore and ironwood trees arched overhead, weaving together like the ribs of an ancient beast. A protective canopy cradled him in shadow, except for a small, jagged window of stars glimmering high above. Beyond the garden's edge, the Nolin stream murmured, its waters tumbling over weathered stones, the sound resembling a hushed conversation carrying secrets only the night could understand.

Everything around him seemed to pause, as if the world held its breath. Sweeden flowers dotted the garden, their leaves glowing softly with a pale luminescence that swayed gently, stirred by an unseen hand. Lofen flies flitted between the blossoms, hovering with wings beating in a blur, casting faint halos of light as they landed on shimmering petals. Their songs were whispers in the dark, fragile melodies weaving in and out of the stillness, barely more than a breath against the air.

He drew out the shredded, dried Gargen root, its sweet, earthy fragrance rising as he packed it into the bowl of his pipe, tamping it down with practiced care. The scent was rich and grounding, filling his senses like the comforting embrace of an old friend. With a quick flick of flint and steel, the root caught flame, and he drew in a deep breath. Warm smoke curled up and around him, the spicy, complex aroma mingling with the crisp night air, wrapping around him like a dear friend as he leaned back into the grass.

Above him, the sky stretched wide, a canvas painted in the deepest black, the cracked moon hanging low and heavy like a fractured pearl. Its pale light bled over the treetops, casting a ghostly sheen that turned the leaves into silver shadows. Beyond, the Eye of Mother loomed in the heavens tugging at the tail of the moon, a faint, shimmering ring etched against the darkness. Orin stared at its vast, far away body, familiar awe tinged with something sharper tonight. It was a reminder of the world's expanse, of powers churning far beyond the borders of their village, and of mysteries slipping through the cracks of understanding.

He traced the moon's tail with his eyes, watching as it arced into the ring of the Eye, a celestial path as constant and unyielding as time itself. But the sight, usually steadying, felt hollow tonight. Shadows at the edges of his mind coiled tighter, conjuring the image of what he'd seen in the woods: a figure stumbling out of the dark, its flesh hanging in tattered strips, the aura around it thick with a black mist that moved as if alive, as if it were breathing.

A shiver prickled down his spine. What had it been? An omen? A warning? Or something far more sinister, something that had no name but lurked at the fringes, waiting? He took another draw from the pipe, smoke filling his cheeks, but it did nothing to dispel the chill creeping through him. Even here, under the cracked moon and the watchful Eye of Mother, the night felt different. It was alive with unanswered questions and a silence that seemed to listen.

And then there was Ferkin. The wild, almost fever-ish gleam in his eyes had made Orin's blood freeze the moment he had invoked Him's understanding. It wasn't just desperation he had seen; it was something raw and untamed—like a flame on the verge of devouring itself. The memory hit him like a punch to the gut, dredging up a story his father used to tell around the fire: a woman who had turned to Him's understanding to save her people. She'd started with good intentions, but the understanding had warped her, twisted her until she could no longer control them. She had become the very thing she tried to protect them from, turning everything she loved to ashes.

Could that happen to Ferkin? Orin's throat tightened as if bound by iron. Had that one act, born out of panic, already begun its work on him? Had it planted the seed that would twist him into something unrecognizable?

He took a long draw from the pipe, letting the smoke dance on his tongue, but it did little to loosen the knot in his chest. Losing Ferkin to something so foul, seeing him consumed and torn apart by that understanding... Orin clenched his jaw against the thought. Ferkin was like a brother to him. He couldn't—wouldn't—let that happen.

But doubt gnawed at him, hollow and sharp. What if he couldn't stop it? What if it was too late?

The question lingered, cold and insidious, a dread that no amount of Gargen root could numb. He exhaled slowly, watching as the smoke coiled up into the night, twisting and writhing like tendrils of the same dark mist that had clung to that cursed figure. When the last wisp faded into the black, he set the pipe aside and lay back on the cool grass, staring up at the stars as if they might hold some answer.

The chill crept through his clothes, sinking into his bones. The grass prickled against the back of his neck, and he felt small—smaller than he had in years. The sky above stretched out in a vast, indifferent sea of black, and for a moment, he was weightless, adrift in that endless void. The world was too big, too full of things he couldn't grasp, too full of powers that dwarfed any hope of understanding.

"Orin." Shira's voice, soft and low, slipped through the quiet like a gentle breeze.

He blinked, turning his head. She stood in the doorway, bathed in moonlight. It wrapped around her like a silvery veil, highlighting every curve and line, making her skin shimmer like polished marble. The night breeze stirred her hair, sending a cascade of golden waves tumbling over her shoulders, brushing against her collarbone and spilling lower, grazing against the pale swell of her bare breasts. She looked almost unreal, a figure carved from moonlight and shadow.

"I'm ready for bed," she murmured, her words a warm caress against the cool night air. She turned, glancing back at him with a smile that stole the breath from his lungs, her hips swaying as she stepped inside. Every movement, every shift of her body, was pure grace, and as she disappeared into the soft glow of the lantern light, the fire's flickering warmth painted her silhouette in golden hues.

"I don't expect to be kept waiting long," she added over her shoulder, her voice teasing, a promise and a command wrapped in one.

Then she was gone, the door swinging shut with a soft click. Orin's heart started racing in his chest, all thoughts of twisted figures and dark understandings evaporating in an instant. He scrambled to his feet, the pipe forgotten in the grass.

6
Crucify

Orin stumbled through the fog-choked woods, crying out for Cal, his voice swallowed almost instantly by the oppressive silence. It felt as though the darkness itself absorbed his words, pulling them away before they could reach the twisted trunks looming in the mist. Above him, the sky roiled in a black, starless sea, heavy clouds shifting as if something massive and unseen stirred restlessly behind them.

Everything was wrong. The forest, usually alive with the hum of crickets and rustling leaves, was now smothered in a silence so profound that it made his skin crawl. There was no wind, no movement—only a stifling stillness weighing down on his chest, making each breath a struggle.

"Papa!" A shrill, frantic cry pierced the dead air—Cal's voice, small and close.

Orin's heart raced as he wheeled around, straining his eyes against the dense gray murk that blurred the world into shifting shadows. "Cal, where are you?" he called, but the sound warped around him, making it impossible to tell which direction it had come from. Panic surged through him as he shouted again, "Cal, stay there! I'm coming!"

He broke into a run, branches tearing at his sleeves like clawed fingers as he plunged deeper into the suffocating gloom. His foot caught on a root, nearly sending him sprawling, but he pushed forward, ignoring the sting of bark scraping against his skin.

The ground was treacherous, a maze of twisted roots and rocks jutting out like broken bones. He leaped over a dry streambed, its stones crumbling under his weight, kicking up clouds of gray dust that hung in the stagnant air. The trees loomed ominously on all sides, their bare, gnarled limbs reaching out like the grasping arms of the damned.

"Papa, please!" Cal's voice, trembling and raw, sliced through the suffocating stillness, twisting something sharp and painful inside Orin.

Fueled by panic, he pushed himself harder, dodging the ghostly shapes of wilted flowers and brittle bushes that snapped underfoot. Everywhere he looked, colors had bled away, leaving the forest a hollow, gray husk of itself. Flowers that once bloomed brightly were now shriveled remnants. Leaves crumbled to ash at his touch, dissolving into nothingness.

"I'm coming, Cal," he cried, the words a thin thread of hope against the crushing dread threatening to swallow him whole, but the fog closed in tighter, the world shrinking with every step.

"Cal, stay there! Don't move!" Orin's voice tore through the stillness again as he plunged forward, each stride a struggle against the fog that tightened around him, thick and unrelenting.

The forest floor blurred beneath him, and then—snap! His foot caught on a branch, the world pitching sideways as he crashed down hard, breath driven from his lungs.

Pain flared through his ribs, a bright, searing agony radiating up his side, but he didn't have time for it. Gritting his teeth, he pushed himself up, dragging his body over the cold earth until he was on his hands and knees.

And then he saw them.

The ground ahead was littered with tiny, broken forms—Dixin fairies, hundreds of them. Their shredded wings glinted faintly in the murk, a sick parody of their once-vibrant glow. Torn limbs and delicate bodies twisted beyond recognition were scattered like fallen leaves. He reached out with trembling fingers, touching one of their tiny thorn swords, now a lifeless scrap smeared with the dark stain of their own blood.

His stomach twisted. These were the guardians of this place, the symbols of life, of everything the forest had stood for. Now, they were nothing but remnants of a massacre.

"Papa!" Cal's scream ripped through Orin's horror, yanking him to his feet.

He staggered forward, forcing his legs to move as the mist coiled around him, resisting and clinging to his clothes, pulling him back. But he wouldn't stop. Couldn't stop. "I'm coming, Cal! I'm almost there!" he shouted, his voice raw with desperation.

The fog pressed in on all sides, twisting and thickening until the shapes of the forest became dark smears in the haze. As he lurched ahead, something shifted. The mist rippled, shadows deepening until the blackness bled into twisted, unnatural forms clawing at the edges of his vision. Then, the darkness itself began to move.

He skidded to a halt, breath catching in his throat. From the center of the trees, something massive unfolded, stretching and distorting until it loomed high above the twisted ferns. It was a cross made of something blacker than shadow, a substance that devoured the light around it. Thick, inky mist oozed from its base, spreading outward in tendrils that choked the ground, curling around every blade of shriveled grass and every rotting leaf, drawing them into itself.

"Cal..." The whisper escaped him, barely audible.

He stumbled back as the mist pulsed and thickened, writhing around the cross. It twisted into grotesque forms that clawed at the air like trapped spirits, shrieking silently in their torment. Above, the gnarled branches of the trees bent toward it, straining as if pulled by an unseen force.

And then it screamed.

A high-pitched, keening wail tore through the forest like a blade, so shrill and piercing that Orin clapped his hands over his ears. But the sound was inside his head, reverberating through his skull.

"Cal!" he choked out, the word lost in the wail.

The darkness surged, the mist churning and boiling around the cross, and he felt it—an immense, malevolent presence bearing down on him, hungry and ancient.

"Papa!" Cal's scream cut through the oppressive silence, his voice thin and desperate, swallowed almost instantly by the suffocating darkness beyond the cross.

Orin strained to see his son, his eyes darting frantically through the haze, searching for any sign of movement in the shifting black. Nothing but shadow and fog. "Cal, where are you? I don't see you!" His voice wavered, raw with fear, as he staggered forward, hoping Cal would step out from behind the dense shroud.

Then the mist twisted, curling back just enough to reveal a shape bound to the cross, high above the ground. Orin froze, his gaze locking onto the figure nailed there, a twisted, broken idea of a man. Limbs jutted out at jagged angles, stretched tight against the dark wood by thick, rusted nails that dug deep into decaying flesh. The sight made his blood run cold.

The figure hung limp, head bowed forward beneath a crown of thorns and iron barbs that gouged deep into his skull. Dark, viscous blood oozed from the punctures, sliding down the battered face in thick rivulets. And then, slowly, impossibly, the head lifted.

Empty, sunken eyes rolled in their sockets, milky white and blind, until they fixed on Orin. A slow, horrible smile cracked across the lips—splitting the dried, blood-caked skin—and a low, guttural laugh bubbled up, a sound that seemed to come from somewhere far beneath the earth. Orin recoiled, a wave of nausea surging up, bile rising in his throat.

The smile widened. Those eyes glinted with a sickly, unholy light, and the figure began to move, hands twitching, fingers spasming as he strained against the nails pinning him to the wood. Then, with a sickening pop, his right hand tore free, the iron stake ripping through bone and sinew like wet paper.

"Please... where is my son?"

The question slipped from Orin's lips in a choked whisper, his voice trembling. He took a step back, legs quaking as the man's other hand twisted and pulled. Flesh split, and blood spurted in thick streams until the nail slid free with a horrible, squelching noise.

The figure's arms hung limp for a moment, the cross creaking ominously behind him. And then, with a violent shudder, the wood began to splinter, crumbling in on itself as his body slumped forward. He fell, knees bending at unnatural angles, folding grotesquely beneath him in a twisted mockery of a bow.

He hit the ground with a dull thud, and for a heartbeat, everything went still. Then his form dissolved, unraveling into a swirling mass of black mist that spread like a stain across the earth, seeping into the soil.

"Papa, I'm here!" Cal's voice rang out, faint but clear, cutting through the horror that had rooted Orin to the spot.

His knees buckled as he staggered forward, tears blurring his vision. "Cal!" he choked out, forcing himself to keep moving, pushing through the suffocating mist. "I'm coming. I'm coming!"

His breath hitched, the ground beneath him slick with the remains of whatever that thing had been. "Cal!" he gasped, stumbling forward as a shape began to coalesce from the murk.

His hands shook uncontrollably, outstretched and desperate to touch his son, to hold him. But as the fog melted away, what emerged was not Cal.

It was a nightmare.

The boy's body twisted grotesquely, joints bent at unnatural angles, bones jutting out beneath ashen skin that hung loose and mottled. His face, once so full of life and warmth, was now a ghastly mask: gray and rotting, with patches of decayed flesh peeling away to reveal raw muscle beneath. His eyes bulged, obscenely large and bloodshot, barely anchored by ragged threads of sinew. Thick, black blood seeped from the corners, streaming down his face.

"Papa, save me," he whimpered, his voice a wet, garbled mess that made Orin's stomach lurch. "Please, Papa… I want to go home. I—I don't feel so good."

"No… no, no, no." The words tumbled out, broken and breathless, as Orin reached for him, his hand trembling so violently he could barely keep it steady.

In response, Cal just stood there, his chest rising and falling in shallow, shuddering gasps.

"Thump… thump… thump."

A deep, rhythmic pounding reverberated through the stillness, shaking the ground beneath Orin's feet. He staggered, his gaze snapping away from Cal, heart racing as he searched frantically for the source.

"Papa!"

Cal's scream tore through Orin like a knife. High-pitched and shrill, it was the sound of a child trapped in unimaginable pain. "Papa, help me!"

"Cal!" Orin lunged forward, but the mist swirled around him, thickening, coiling like a living thing. It wrapped around his legs, yanking him back as if the darkness itself had claws.

"Thump... thump... thump."

The pounding grew louder, each beat rattling his bones, making the earth tremble beneath his feet. He twisted, fighting against the pull, fingers stretching out, so close to Cal's mangled form he could almost feel the cold of his skin.

"Cal, please!" he screamed, tears burning hot trails down his cheeks. "I'm here! I'm—"

"Thump. Thump. Thump."

The ground shuddered violently, the mist tightening around Orin in a suffocating grip. He was being dragged away, feet sliding across the dirt, his outstretched hand just inches from Cal's. He fought against it, screaming his son's name, but it was no use.

Cal stared at him, eyes glassy and hollow, lips pulling back in a hideous, broken grimace.

"Papa... don't leave me," Cal whispered, voice fragile and fading.

And then, he crumbled. His form disintegrated into a cloud of black ash, scattering into the wind as if he'd never been there at all.

"Cal!" Orin cried out again, the word tearing from his throat as he lurched forward.

The mist swallowed the sound, the pounding fading into a dull, distant echo. "Thump. Thump. Thump."

"Orin, wake up." Shira's voice sliced through the lingering haze of his sleep, soft yet edged with urgency. "Someone's at the door. Make them go away."

Groggy, Orin blinked into the dim morning light, struggling to claw his way out of the nightmare's grasp. Jagged fragments of fear and desperation tangled in his chest, refusing to release their hold. He turned his head, and the familiar world slowly bled back into focus. The warmth of their bed enveloped him, Shira's scent—like wild honey—filled his senses, and the steady rhythm of her breathing beside him offered a moment of comfort. She lay sprawled across the mattress, one leg tangled in the covers, the other stretched out and bare to the morning chill.

Sunlight filtered through the green-tinted window, casting dappled patterns across her pale skin. Her hair spilled over the old pillow, catching the light as if each strand were spun from molten gold. Orin reached out, letting his fingers hover just above her cheek, almost afraid to touch and shatter the quiet beauty of this moment.

But then a sharp, insistent thumping shattered the calm. He flinched, the sound reverberating through the stillness, jerking him fully awake. His gaze snapped to the door, now echoing with impatient knocking. The noise was loud, desperate even. Outside, the world seemed to hold its breath. No birds sang. No fairies danced in the dawn light. Instead, a murmur of anxious voices drifted through the open window, rising and falling like a tide. The clatter of hurried footsteps on cobblestones sent a shiver of unease skittering down his spine.

Shira moaned softly beside him, squeezing her eyes shut as if she could will the noise away. She burrowed deeper into the worn quilt, its red and white flowers faded and fraying at the edges. "Go away," she mumbled, her voice thick with sleep.

"I'll handle it," he murmured.

Leaning over, he brushed a kiss against her cheek, the soft curve of her lips twitching into a drowsy smile. "I love you," he whispered.

"Mmm... love you too," she sighed, already drifting back into sleep.

The knocking pounded on, insistent. Reluctantly, Orin pulled himself from the bed, the cool morning air wrapping around him like a cold hand. His bare feet hit the wooden floorboards, and he winced at the bite of the cold, each step a reminder of the world outside, waiting.

He crossed the room to where Cal's old chair sat in the corner, its uneven legs creaking under the weight of his best shirt and brown leather vest. The chair wobbled as he tugged the shirt free, his fingers lingering for a moment on the worn wood, a small smile tugging at his lips despite the turmoil brewing outside.

Thump, thump, thump! The pounding at the door grew louder, each knock more urgent than the last. He felt another chill skittered down him, but he pushed it aside. Whoever stood on the other side was bringing more than just a wake-up call.

The warmth of their small space faded as he stepped into the living room, the chill biting against his skin like an unwelcome guest. The hearth was nothing but a pile of lifeless ash, gray and cold, and shadows clung to the corners, thick and unmoving. He rubbed his arms, goosebumps prickling along his skin. The house seemed to hold its breath, and with every creak of the floorboards beneath his feet, the silence pressed in heavier, as if it sensed something was amiss.

"Thump, thump, thump!"

The pounding at the door reverberated through the room, sharp and demanding. The sound grated on his nerves, sparking a flare of irritation.

"All right, all right. Coming!" he snapped, hurrying to the door.

Whoever was out there better have a good reason for dragging him out of bed at this unnatural hour. He yanked the door open, expecting to see some flustered villager with a petty complaint, but the sight that greeted him made his stomach tighten.

Upon opening the door, he saw Ferkin, slouched against the doorframe, his broad shoulders hunched forward, his face a splotchy shade of red. A grin stretched across Ferkin's unshaven face, and the thick, bitter smoke from the huken leaf clenched between his teeth swirled lazily around his head. The stench of stale dandle beer and sweat assaulted Orin's nose, making him grimace and step back.

"Morning, beautiful. Sleep well?"

Ferkin's smile widened, revealing a row of yellow-stained teeth, and he tipped his head back, releasing a plume of smoke that curled around them like a noxious fog. His bloodshot eyes, rimmed with exhaustion, glinted with a wild, manic energy.

"Ferkin, what in the spirits are you doing here?" Orin demanded, waving away the smoke.

He caught sight of the street beyond Ferkin—villagers moving hurriedly past, their faces drawn tight, tension etched in every line. "What's going on?" he asked, his confusion deepening as more people rushed by, their steps quick and uneasy.

Ferkin let out a low, throaty chuckle, but there was no humor in it. His laugh scraped across the porch, raw and hollow. "You don't know?"

He took another long drag from the huken leaf, the end flaring bright red, then blew out a cloud of acrid smoke. "That wife of yours must've shown you a really good night."

Heat crept up Orin's neck despite himself. "Ferkin—"

"Everyone's headed to town hall," he interrupted, his grin fading as his gaze flicked nervously over his shoulder. "Elders called a meeting. They say it's urgent."

A knot of unease twisted in Orin's gut as he watched Ferkin, his friend, stand at the threshold. The man's jovial demeanor felt out of place, a mask that couldn't quite hide the tension lurking beneath. Orin sensed something was wrong, but before he could press for answers, the front door burst open with a bang. Cal came barreling out, his shaggy hair bouncing wildly around his freckled face. Orin couldn't help but feel a fleeting warmth at the sight of his son, so full of life and energy.

"Uncle Ferkin!" Cal cried, launching himself at the man with all the force of a small hurricane.

Ferkin barked a laugh, the sound booming as he crouched to catch the boy. Orin felt a swell of affection as he watched their reunion. "Ahh, you little shit!" Ferkin said, swinging Cal up effortlessly before setting him back down with a playful ruffle of his unruly hair. "What're you doing out here in your nightgown, huh? You'll catch your death."

Cal's innocent question about breakfast contrasted starkly with the tension crackling in the air. Orin noted the shift in Ferkin's expression, the grin wavering slightly as his gaze flickered towards him, laden with unspoken worries.

"Maybe next time, little man," Ferkin replied softly, ruffling Cal's hair again, but the gesture lacked warmth, shadowed by his unease. "Right now, we need to head to town. Come on, Orin, you need to see this."

The urgency in Ferkin's voice set Orin's nerves jangling. He instinctively rested a hand on Cal's shoulder, squeezing a bit tighter as if to shield him from the world outside. "Go on, Cal. Get dressed and tell your mother we need to leave," he instructed, his voice steadier than he felt.

Cal nodded, his smile fading as he sensed the tension. Orin watched him dash back inside, the small footsteps echoing through the quiet house. As the door closed behind him, the silence felt heavier.

"What's going on, Ferkin?" Orin demanded, his voice low and rough. Anxiety pulsed beneath his skin, thrumming like a distant storm. "Why the sudden meeting?"

"I don't know, Orin," Ferkin murmured, eyes darting toward the restless crowd beyond their doorstep. He seemed to shrink under the weight of his worries, shoulders tense and wary. "But it's not good."

Orin's stomach churned as Ferkin leaned closer, dropping his voice to a whisper. "You didn't tell anyone about—"

"No," Orin interrupted sharply, the word cutting through the air like a blade. He glanced around, the lie tasting bitter on his tongue. "I haven't said a word about yesterday."

Relief flickered in Ferkin's eyes, his posture loosening slightly. "Good. Because if they found out—"

"They won't," Orin bit out, his words clipped and firm. His gaze swept the street, scanning the villagers' anxious faces as they rushed by, fear etched into every line. "We'll meet you there. Shira wouldn't want me to go without her."

"Fine," Ferkin said, already turning away, shoulders hunched as if bracing for the worst. "But don't dawdle, Orin. Whatever this is, it's bad."

He watched as Ferkin wove through the crowd, his figure swallowed by the mass of bodies moving toward town hall. A heavy knot formed in his gut, twisting tighter with every step Ferkin took away from the house. Whatever had Ferkin rattled wasn't something small.

The door creaked behind him, and he turned to see Shira standing in the hallway, brush poised in midair, eyes wide and searching. "Orin?" Her voice trembled, barely more than a whisper. "Cal said Ferkin stopped by and that we needed to leave. What's going on?"

"There's a meeting at town hall," he replied, forcing his voice to steady even as his heart hammered against his ribs. "We should go."

"Is it about what you saw yesterday?" Her gaze locked onto his, fear shimmering in the depths of her eyes.

"I don't know." He admitted quietly, glancing away. "But we'll find out soon enough. Just... get dressed."

She nodded slowly, her movements stiff, deliberate, as if any sudden motion might shatter the fragile tension hanging between them. He turned back toward the window, watching the villagers funnel down the cobblestone path like a river of uneasy faces and hunched shoulders. He gripped the doorframe tightly, the wood creaking softly beneath his fingers, every instinct screaming that something was about to change forever.

The village pulsed with a restless energy as they stepped onto the main street. Normally, mornings unfolded in a gentle chorus—birds warbling, dixin fairies flitting through the sunlight, and the great sefmores whispering secrets in the breeze. But today, the air was thick with unease, broken only by the occasional creak of branches, as if the woods themselves sensed the shift.

Orin's gaze flicked upward as a streak of brilliant red cut through the green canopy. He barely caught the flash of a Londor bird's massive wingspan, its crimson feathers shimmering like molten metal. The sight sent an uneasy shiver down his spine. He had scoffed at omens before, but today felt different.

"Papa, look!" Cal's shout broke through Orin's thoughts.

The boy bounced on his toes, pointing at a small figure darting across the street. "Noro!" Cal called, his joy infectious as he spotted the other boy.

The two collided in laughter, their exuberance a stark contrast to the anxiety clawing at his insides. For a brief moment, the weight of the day faded, replaced by the lightness of childhood innocence.

Trailing behind them, a woman swept forward, her gait stiff and measured. Orin observed her closely, noting how she moved like a tightly coiled spring, wound so tight that the slightest misstep might send her snapping. The lace-trimmed red dress clung high around her neck, pinching the flesh into a ring of creases, while her black hair was pulled into such a severe bun that it made her skin draw taut, highlighting every line etched by years of frowning.

"Kerra," Orin muttered, keeping his voice low. "Queen of pompousness herself."

Shira nudged him with her elbow, her lips twitching as she tried to smother a laugh. "Be nice, Orin. She's not that terrible."

He snorted but bit back a reply as Kerra's gaze swept over them like a hawk circling prey. Shira stepped forward, a smile gracing her lips, the expression holding just the right touch of courtesy.

"Good morning, Kerra. How are you today?" she asked.

Kerra's eyes flicked down at Shira, one brow arching slightly. "Morning," she answered crisply, her mouth pulling tight in what might have been an attempt at a smile. Orin could only describe it as more of a grimace.

Kerra's gaze drifted over Shira like a farmer inspecting a stubborn mule, her lips thinning as if the mere sight of her threatened to sour her morning tea. "Very well, my dear," she finally sniffed, her tone clipped. "But you'd better hurry and change, or you'll be late for the meeting... unless, of course, that's what you're planning to wear."

Her chin lifted ever so slightly, a subtle movement that somehow dripped with disdain. Orin watched Shira's eyes drop to her own dress, a rose-red gown that shimmered softly in the sunlight, its color deepening against the gold of her hair. He thought it made her look radiant, like a flame caught in a breeze. "Oh, my dear Kerra, as always, your sense of fashion is simply... unmatched," Shira replied, her syrupy sweetness barely veiling her sarcasm.

Kerra blinked slowly, the sarcasm skimming past her like water off a duck's back. "Oh, my dear, you mustn't blame yourself. I was just fortunate to marry into the right family." Her gaze flickered Orin's way, sharpening like a blade unsheathing. "Tenison—spirits rest his soul—always appreciated the finer things. I suppose that's why he chose a wife with sophistication and beauty."

She flashed a smile, her teeth gleaming like a predator's under the crimson stain of her lipstick. "Yes, that must be right, Kerra," Shira murmured, the muscles around her mouth twitching as if restraining the urge to bare her teeth. "How lucky you were to be blessed by the spirits with such things us ordinary folk can only dream of."

The corner of Orin's mouth twitched. "And that extra chin you have? I bet that was a special gift from the spirits, too."

The words slipped out before he could think better of it. Shira's laughter exploded, a startled burst that she quickly smothered with her hand. Kerra's face deepened to an angry shade of crimson, her eyes blazing. "Mr. Arator," she spat, voice low and trembling with barely leashed fury. "How is life... doing whatever it is you do?"

Orin straightened, affecting the most serious expression he could muster. "Why, I'm doing splendidly, Kerra. In fact, just the other day, if you'd believe it, I spotted a kerontha."

Her brows knitted together, confusion flickering in her gaze. "You saw a... what?"

"A kerontha," Orin repeated, deadpan. "Surely, a woman of your sophistication knows what a kerontha is."

Kerra's eyes darted to Shira, who was now hunched over, shoulders shaking violently in a struggle to contain her mirth. "Well," Kerra said stiffly, her voice tightening. "The simple lives of tree healers and what they see are sometimes lost on me. What exactly is a... kerontha?"

"Oh, it's a rare beast," Orin said solemnly, leaning in as if sharing a treasured secret. "Quite loud. Most people prefer to steer clear of it. But the easiest way to spot one is by its enormous, sagging chin."

Shira trembled beside him, her fingers digging into his arm so tightly that her knuckles turned pale. Kerra's face, flushed a furious crimson, seemed to swell as she drew herself up, towering over them like a storm cloud poised to unleash.

"Well, I must say your manners are severely lacking," she snapped, her words slicing through the air like a whip.

Before Orin could retort, Shira slipped smoothly between them, her smile tight but placating. "Yes, I'm sure my husband's humor is lost on many, Kerra." She murmured with a sigh, shooting Orin a look that warned him to keep quiet. "Do forgive us. We're just a bit... on edge, with all this talk of meetings and such."

Kerra's rigid stance softened, if only a fraction, though her chin remained proudly tilted as if she had to hold herself above the very idea of forgiving them. "I understand," she said, drawing out the words as if weighing them. "These meetings can be... unsettling for some people."

Her eyes swept disdainfully over their modest home—the moss-covered stone walls, the sagging roof, and the weather-beaten gate that leaned like a drunken sentinel. Orin clenched his fists at his sides, anger boiling just beneath the surface.

"But I wouldn't worry too much, Mr. Arator," she continued airily, turning her gaze back to him with a condescending smile. "I imagine this is just about the elders wishing to… improve some of the lesser structures in the village."

A sharp reply burned on his tongue, but Shira jumped in, her voice smooth as silk. "Yes, Kerra, you're probably right. This village could certainly use a bit of cleaning up."

Kerra's gaze lingered on their home a moment longer, her lips pursing in faux sympathy. Then she turned back to Shira, her eyes gleaming with thinly veiled malice. "If you ever want to… upgrade, dear, I'm sure my new husband could find something for Mr. Arator. Perhaps a position as a ground's cleaner. Something… not too difficult."

Orin's jaw clenched, fists itching at his sides. "Thank you for the offer," he bit out, the words tasting like ash.

"Of course, dear." Her smile stretched wider, sharp as a blade slipping between ribs. "Just thought I'd mention it." She snapped her fingers, her movements crisp and practiced. "Noro, darling, we're leaving."

The boy darted to her side, cap bouncing as he trailed after her like an obedient puppy. They swept around the corner, and Shira let out a long, shaky breath, shoulders sagging.

"That woman," she muttered, shaking her head as if to fling off the weight of Kerra's presence.

"You're radiant, my love," Orin murmured, leaning down to press a kiss against her forehead. "That pompous bitch wouldn't know a nice dress if it smacked her right in her smug chin."

Shira's laughter burst out, light and bright. Orin turned to Cal, who had edged closer, eyes wide with excitement. "Did you and Noro have fun?" he asked.

"Yes, Papa!" Cal crowed, bouncing on his toes. "I smacked one of the Dixin fairies right on the head!"

Orin glanced over, spotting one of the tiny creatures perched on a nearby branch, its wings buzzing indignantly as it rubbed its head. "Try not to hurt them too much, alright? We need their help keeping the garden in order."

"Okay, Papa," Cal mumbled, scuffing his shoe against the dirt, shoulders hunched.

137

7
Unwelcomed News

The village, usually as quiet as a still pond, now buzzed like a stirred-up sting hive. The dirt-packed streets, typically sparse and sleepy, were alive with a surge of restless bodies, all pushing toward the looming shape of the town hall. From wrinkled elders leaning on their walking sticks to wide-eyed younglings clutching at their parents' hems, it seemed every soul had been pulled from their homes and into this unexpected huddle.

Shira's fingers dug into Orin's arm as they rounded the corner and faced the heaving tide of people. "Seems the whole village turned up," she whispered, her voice tight with nerves.

Her eyes darted over the crowd—wide, concerned—reflecting the pale morning light like twin moons. Orin followed her gaze, seeing a sea of heads bobbing and shifting, all making their way up the broad stone steps to the Town Hall doors. The scene was a swirling mess of colors—cloaks and tunics in earthy browns, dark greens, and bold flashes of crimson and gold—all flapping in the crisp morning wind.

Voices rose and fell around them, a tangled mess of excitement and worry. Folks leaned in close, murmuring, while others snorted and shook their heads, caught between fear and frustration.

"Wouldn't drag us here 'less it's bad news...""Heard whispers 'bout shadows in the woods... the Dixin fairies been sayin'...""Probably just another tax—bloody elders and their coin pouches..."

High above, a Londor bird—the same one that had been circling when Orin left the house—swept through the sky, its red wings cutting the air clean like a blade through silk. Its shadow passed over them, a flicker of darkness against the noise and movement. The sight of it twisted Orin's gut, but he shoved the feeling down, trying to ignore the crawling chill along his spine.

"I don't like this, Orin. I've never seen the elders call a meeting this big," Shira muttered, almost drowned out by the clamor.

She pulled herself closer to him, shoulders tight, her face lined with unease. The crush of villagers was staggering. Men, women, and children all squashed together, necks craning, eager to get a look at the stone beast of a building rising before them.

It was the only structure in Terra built entirely from stone. It towered above them, its gray bulk a stubborn reminder of days long gone when the old tribes ruled these lands. The front steps, cut from the same ancient stone, stretched out like a giant's staircase, each one etched with winding vines and twisted shapes of animals that were symbols of the clans that once lived and died on this soil. Time had smoothed the carvings, wearing them down like river rocks, but they still whispered of a past that no one dared to remember out loud.

"It'll be fine," Orin lied, though even he could hear the hollowness in his voice. He tried to force a grin, but Shira just pressed in tighter, as if bracing against a storm. His thoughts drifted back to the shadow he had seen skulking in the forest, a figure too dark and too fast to be anything good. Could this all be linked to that? The thought coiled tight in his belly, but he pushed it aside.

They trudged up the worn stone steps, swept along by the crowd. Each footfall seemed to echo in the hollow air, heavy and uneasy, like the ground was holding its breath. Orin glanced at the carvings again. These were stories of what came before them. A warning, maybe. Or a promise. But today, the only story that mattered was the one waiting for them inside those heavy, iron-bound doors.

Cal's eyes were as big as saucers, darting every which way like a kid turned loose in a sweetshop. He jabbed a finger toward the iron tide trees, their twisted silver branches clawing at the sky like the hands of some old giant woken from a deep sleep. Lined up at the square's edge, their gnarled limbs sagged under the weight of thick, iron chains tethering beasts—Snores—from far-flung places. The massive creatures pawed at the ground, nostrils flaring, legs stomping restlessly as their thick-scaled hides shimmered like armor. Each of their tusks curved long and sharp, nearly the length of a man's arm, and their dark, keen eyes swept over the crowd with something almost... knowing.

"Look, Papa! The snores!" Cal exclaimed.

His tugging nearly pulled Orin's sleeve clean off. The boy's face lit up, a grin wide enough to split, but there was a flicker of unease beneath the surface. Orin ruffled his hair and started to talk when a flash of Cal looking fleshless and rotting pushed its way into the forefront of his consciousness. He quickly reached out, grabbing Cal's shoulder, heart racing out of his chest.

"Papa?" Cal's voice brought him back, and he noticed the somewhat frightened look on the boy's face and the puzzlement on Shira's.

"Sorry, just a bad dream… left me a little shaken," Orin said, releasing Cal's shoulder. Shira nodded in understanding.

"Bad dreams will do that." She reached out to take his hand and started to lead them on. "Luckily for you, I can make them all go away."

As they pushed through the crowd toward the entrance, the doors rose up to meet them; they were intimidating, great hulking slabs of dark wood, polished and gleaming like some fierce old warrior's shield. Each door, hewn from the heart of a great Sefmore tree, was as wide as a cart and twice as tall, and every inch of it was covered in carvings: warriors locked in battle, grand feasts, and rituals lost to time. But it was the Emerald Lady that snatched Orin's gaze—a shimmering figure set in delicate gold inlay—split down the middle between the doors. When they were shut, she stood whole and proud, eyes glinting like jewels in the sun. Now, with the doors thrown wide, she was fractured, broken.

As they stepped through the yawning archway, the hum of voices swallowed them whole, bouncing off the stone walls like a thousand murmured secrets.

The air was damp and thick with the scent of old water and must, clinging to the cracks and crevices. The hall stretched up and out, a cavern of shadows and light, the ceiling arching so high it made Orin's head spin just to look at it.

"Papa, look!" Cal's voice was a squeak of wonder.

Orin tipped his head back and felt his breath whoosh out of him. Above, painted across the entire ceiling, was a mural so grand it seemed to shift and breathe with life. Eight lands spread out in a dazzling circle: Terra's forests, rich greens and browns twisting through valleys and hills; Aquam's shimmering oceans, blue and deep like endless sky; Ballator's jagged peaks, the mountains standing stark and proud; Caprale's wild marshlands, dark and teeming with life; Caelum's soaring heights, the Skylands bathed in pale blues and grays; Cavatio's winding tunnels, the underground city glowing with the faint light of a thousand lanterns; Secretum's mist-shrouded woods, swirling with hidden shapes; and Devoro's barren wastelands, red and cracked under a cruel sun.

At the center of it all, painted in vivid, pulsing colors, was the Emerald Lady with her arms stretched wide, embracing the world in a silent promise.

Light poured in through towering stained-glass windows, each pane a riot of reds, greens, and blues, the colors dancing like fire as sunlight splintered across the hall. The floor was awash in a kaleidoscope of hues, the light twisting and turning, casting strange shapes that seemed to flicker and dart across the stone like restless spirits.

Ahead, the great balcony loomed high and broad, its stone edge jutting out like the prow of some ancient ship. Three enormous chairs sat perched there, each carved with symbols of old bloodlines and power, the stone worn smooth by time and memory. Behind them, a grand tapestry hung, threads of gold and emerald weaving a picture of the Great Mother, her hands resting protectively over Terra, while the other lands curled around her like wayward children.

Two staircases wound down from either side of the balcony, spiraling gracefully to the hall below, where thick velvet curtains hid shadowed doorways. Everything about the place seemed to whisper secrets and stories untold, of power and promise... and of things best left undisturbed.

"What's down the steps, Papa?" Cal's little voice piped up, his tiny hand gripping Orin's so tight he thought he might never let go.

Cal's gaze was locked on the dark creep of the stairway, eyes round and locked, peering down into the black that swallowed the lower hallways. "Those? They're the catacombs. Where the ancients are buried. Where the secrets of Terra sleep."

Cal shivered, clutching tighter. Shira's head whipped around, her eyes sharp like Orin had said a curse word in a temple. He shook his head, giving her a look that meant not now. The place thrummed with a strange energy, a prickling under his skin that wouldn't quit. This wasn't a time for curiosity. Not today. Not when it felt like even the stones under their feet were holding their breath.

"C'mon now," Orin muttered, glancing over the sea of faces, some pale and drawn, others flushed with the thrill of whatever news was about to break. "Let's find us a seat."

They wove through the crush of bodies, elbows and shoulders jostling as folks shoved and scrambled for a spot. Voices buzzed around them, thick and heavy with rumors, like the hum of bees ready to swarm. Shira gripped Cal's hand so tight her knuckles went bone white. Cal's eyes darted about, wide with that mix of fear and wonder only a child could manage, soaking up every whispered word and anxious glance as they pushed toward a sliver of wooden bench Shira had spotted, somehow still empty amidst the jostling tide.

"There, over there!" Shira shouted, nodding her chin toward the tiny patch of wood.

Orin lowered his shoulder and pressed forward, clearing the way with a few apologetic grunts as murmurs rose and fell around them, words flying quick and sharp like sparrows in the rafters.

"Heard the Ferums are massin' troops—gettin' ready to invade, they are," a hunched old woman whispered behind them, her voice thin and brittle, fingers digging into the arm of the man beside her like claws.

"Rubbish!" the man shot back, snorting. "Ballatorians've no taste for Terra. They'd sooner eat dirt. Nah, it's thieves, I'm telling you. Raiders have been seen in the outer woods. This meeting'—it's a trap to flush them out, mark my words."

Orin glanced at Shira. Her face was pale as bone, lips pressed so tight they'd nearly disappeared. She caught him looking and tried for a smile, but it flickered and died before it even reached her eyes.

"Easy now, Shira," he murmured, squeezing her hand just once.

But he could feel his own pulse hammering, that uneasy, jittery feeling crawling up his spine. Whatever this was, it wasn't going to be good news. The elders didn't summon the whole village except for the big things. And big things? They never went down easily.

"It'll be alright."

He lied, and she knew it. But what else could he say? Cal looked up at him with those wide eyes, trust shining clear as a summer sky, and all he could do was squeeze Shira's hand a little tighter.

"Better be," she muttered, her voice low and tight. "Better be."

They slid onto the bench, the wood creaking like it might snap under the weight of worry alone. Cal wriggled in beside Orin, his gaze fixed still on the mural above.

He tugged at Orin's sleeve, voice low. "Papa... what's gonna happen?"

As he glanced down at Cal, a surge of protectiveness swelled within him, a fierce urge to shield the boy from whatever darkness lay ahead. "Don't know, my boy," he murmured softly, his heart aching. "But we'll find out soon enough."

He couldn't shake the feeling that whatever awaited them had the potential to tear their world apart. Cal's eyes were lost in the colors dancing across the ceiling, nearly causing his father to overlook the grating sound of a voice that made his skin crawl. "Oh, I've no doubt this is just a ploy to clean up the village!"

The words boomed across the hall, slicing through the crowd like a whip crack. Tension coiled in his body as he turned slightly to see the speaker, standing tall and rigid as a post, looking down his nose at the world. His vest gleamed like polished oak, and his shirt—so crisp and spotless it might as well have been made of snow—radiated arrogance.

The man's mustache, thin and waxed, curled at the ends like sneering question marks, giving him the appearance of a rooster dressed for a ball. He puffed out his chest, his eyes flicking around the hall as if he were a king surveying his domain. "Yes, yes," he continued, his voice loud enough for half the room to hear. "A cleanup indeed. High time, too. Things have gotten quite... messy." He glanced around expectantly, as if waiting for applause, his smug grin nearly splitting him in half.

Orin clenched his jaw, forcing himself to look away from the man who had a talent for burrowing under one's skin. Beside him, Shira leaned in close, her breath tickling his ear. "I love our house just the way it is," she whispered, her voice low yet fierce.

He turned to her, and the look in her sharp, unyielding eyes made his heart swell. "I know, love." He murmured, pressing a kiss to her brow. "Wouldn't change a single thing."

Before she could respond, movement at the front of the hall caught his attention. The massive wooden doors began to swing shut, groaning like a beast being put to rest. Eight guards stepped forward. There were four on each side, boots striking the stone floor in perfect rhythm. Their leather armor gleamed in the dim light, swords hanging heavily at their sides, long enough to slice a man clean in half. Each guard moved with the stiff, deliberate grace of a coiled spring.

The murmurs from the crowd died away, giving way to a thick, uneasy silence as the doors slammed shut with a bone-jarring boom. The sound echoed off the stone walls, and Shira gasped beside him, her breaths coming quick and sharp. He squeezed her hand, pulling it against his chest. "It's alright," he mouthed, hoping she could read the reassurance in his eyes.

Yet the silence pressed in like a weight, making it difficult to breathe. Then, from deep below, the faint creak of another door opening rippled through the quiet, sending a shiver down his spine. He felt Shira's fingers clamp tightly around his, her nails biting into his skin. Cal's small voice, nearly lost in the tension, broke through. "Papa, look."

He followed Cal's gaze, his heart racing as three figures emerged from the shadows beneath the balcony. The first was an old man, his hair and beard a waterfall of white cascading down his back. He moved like a ghost, his robes of white and gold rippling around him as he glided up the steps. Light caught the fabric, making it shimmer as if alive.

"That's Belma," he murmured to Cal, leaning close. "One of the elders."

Belma's sharp, cold gaze swept the room before he took his seat at the far end of the balcony. Behind him shuffled a woman, leaning heavily on the wall. She was ancient—older even than Belma—her face a map of deep creases and untold stories. Her short white hair was nearly swallowed by a wide-brimmed hat, the emerald band around it the only splash of color.

"Who's that?" Cal whispered, his eyes glued to her.

"Celica," he breathed. "Head of the elders."

She made her way to the center, sinking into her chair with a soft sigh. The room seemed to hold its breath as she settled, her frail hands gripping the stone arms of her seat like she was holding the world together by sheer will.

The last figure stepped into the light, and something about his stride twisted his stomach. He was younger than the others—maybe fifty—but hard to determine with his close-cropped gray hair and the lines etched deep into his face. Unlike Belma and Celica, he wore no robes, just a rough leather vest and a knee-length kilt, sandals laced tight around his legs. A broad sword, scarred and battered, hung low at his hip, and he moved with the ease of someone who knew exactly what that blade could do—and had done it many times before.

Cal tugged at his sleeve. "Who's he, Papa?"

"That's... well, he's not an elder. Just their... enforcer," he muttered, his gaze locked on the man's face. "That's Maraco, leader of the Terra Guard."

Maraco stood at the edge of the balcony, his gaze sweeping over the crowd like a hawk eyeing its prey. Then, without a word, he stepped back, hands clasped behind his back, and Celica slowly pushed herself upright.

A hush fell over the room, thick and suffocating, every pair of eyes locked on her frail form as she sat there, small and trembling against the vast stone backdrop. But when she finally spoke, her voice cut through the silence like thunder.

Orin let out a small cough right as Celica began to speak, a sharp voice hissed behind him. "SHHHH!"

He whipped his head around, only to meet the pinched face of a stern-looking woman, her eyes narrowed to slits. Lips pressed tightly together, she glared as if he had just spat in her stew. He stared back, irritation bubbling within him, but the woman held his gaze, her jaw set hard. With a sigh, he turned away, biting back the urge to mutter something sharp. Focus, this was no time for petty squabbles.

Up on the balcony, Maraco strode forward, boots thudding against the stone floor like a drumbeat. His gaze swept over the room—cold and assessing—measuring each soul packed into the hall. The set of his shoulders was stiff, his face drawn tight. Whatever he had to say, it wasn't going to be good.

He shifted on the bench, leaning forward with his heart thumping like a trapped rabbit. Shira's hand remained in his, icy and tense. He glanced at her, noting her wide, unblinking eyes fixed on the balcony, her breath coming shallow and quick.

Behind him, the stern woman shifted again, rustling like a dry leaf caught in a stiff wind. Her gaze felt like needles digging into his back, but he ignored her. Every fiber of his being strained toward the front of the room, where the elders waited like statues on that high perch, carved from the very stone they leaned against.

As the crowd hushed, murmurs faded into a tense, brittle silence. Celica leaned forward in her massive chair, the lines of her face deep and shadowed in the dim light. She appeared so small up there, almost swallowed by the cold, gray stone. When she finally spoke, her thin, wavering voice rang out like a bell, cutting through the silence.

"People of Ithicel!" The words echoed off the high ceiling, bouncing back to fill the room with their weight.

Every eye turned toward her, the hall so quiet that one could've heard a leaf hit the floor. "I have troubling news. Yesterday, a group of our finest scouts were attacked..." She paused, her chest heaving with the effort.

A murmur rippled through the room, fear flickering in the eyes around him. Shira's fingers clamped tighter around his, nearly crushing his hand, but he barely felt it; all his attention was fixed on Celica.

"One scout," she breathed, voice trembling under her age. "One scout, who was mortally wounded, made it back. Before his soul passed, he told us... he told us that they were attacked. It started as seeing a prophet. But as soon as the prophet's soul spilled, a loud shriek sound came after."

Her voice broke on the name, the word ringing out like a curse. "An army... of Fleshers."

The crowd erupted. Gasps and cries of shock crashed like a tidal wave, fear spreading in a heartbeat. Shira's nails dug into his skin, her face as white as a sheet, eyes wide with terror.

"Fleshers?" The word escaped his lips unbidden.

Monsters, pure and simple, creatures that lived only to consume. Before his time, entire villages had been lost to their endless hunger. And now... now they were here?

"Papa...?" Cal's small voice trembled beside him, eyes straining as he clutched his arm.

He swallowed hard, forcing his voice steady. "It's... it's gonna be alright, Cal." He murmured, though the lie tasted bitter on his tongue.

He glanced up at the balcony, at Celica's bowed head and the heavy weight of Maraco's grim stare. The words struck like a punch to the gut, knocking the wind clean out of him. For a heartbeat, the hall held its breath, then—

All hell broke loose.

Shouts erupted from every corner, voices crying out in disbelief, twisted and raw with fear. Bodies crashed together as people stumbled back, clutching at sleeves and shoulders as if trying to keep from drowning.

"NO!" Someone bellowed, the sound tearing from their throat like a wounded beast. "No! It can't be true! They can't be here!"

"QUIET!" Maraco's roar slammed into the chaos like a thunderclap, booming over the madness.

The crowd froze, shuddering like a herd of spooked Tigar deer, the echoes of his shout ringing in the rafters long after his mouth closed. He stepped forward, eyes blazing, jaw clenched as if holding the whole place together by sheer will alone. "You will be silent and listen!" He thundered.

The weight of his voice seemed to pin everyone in place. Slowly, grudgingly, the uproar died down to a low, fearful murmur.

"Thank you, Maraco." Celica whispered, her words soft as falling snow in the hush that followed. "You may sit."

Maraco nodded, stepping back with slow, wary grace, his eyes never leaving the crowd. Celica breathed deeply, shoulders sagging with the effort. She looked out over them, her gaze heavy and sad. "It's come to our attention," she said, voice trembling just a touch. "That the flesher hordes have changed direction... toward Terra."

The words landed like stones in a pond—small, quiet splashes—but the ripples tore through the room. Heads jerked up, eyes wide and staring. Someone gasped, sharp and high.

"How many?" A voice rang out—some man near the front, his tone hard as steel. "How many?"

It was a demand, the kind that came from a man needing to know, even if it would shatter him. Celica's eyes fluttered shut for a moment, her lips moving silently as if begging for strength. "Over twenty-five hundred." She whispered, barely more than a breath.

The hall erupted.

Screams tore through the air, cries of terror mingling with desperate, angry shouts. Mothers yanked their children close, shielding them with trembling arms, faces contorted in fear. Men roared back and forth, voices tangled and wild, some spitting disbelief, others steeling themselves for battle. It was as if the ground had cracked open, the fear pouring from every soul packed into that hall, churning together until the very walls seemed to shudder under the weight of it.

"No!" A woman shrieked, tears streaking down her face as she clung to the man beside her. "We'll all be killed! They'll butcher us—"

"What about the children?" A man's voice cracked, rising above the din. "What'll happen to them?"

"Please, my family—my—"

The crowd surged like a living beast, voices crashing together in a tide of anguish and dread. He felt it all slam into him, washing over him in waves so strong he thought he might be swept under, pulled down into the madness.

But then he looked at Shira.

Shira, was shaking like a leaf in a storm. Her face was pale, cheeks streaked with silent tears that glimmered in the colored light. He could see the desperation in her wide eyes, and in that moment, she seemed so small, so fragile. A deep twist formed inside him at the thought of her being lost, of her being ripped away from him.

"No," he breathed, pulling her close, wrapping his arms around her as if he could shield her from the very world itself. "No, it'll be alright."

Leaning in, he pressed a kiss to her cold lips, trembling with the need to make it true. "I promise, love. Everything'll be alright."

Nearby, Cal's gaze was fixed on the ceiling, wide and dazzled, soaking in the colors of the mural above like he had no care in the world. His moment of fear lost as the shining lights stole his attention. He was lost in the swirl of paint and light, the figures dancing across the stone, his mouth hanging open in a small, dreamy smile. The screams, the cries, the wild panic buzzing through the air seemed to him like mere whispers of wind rustling through the trees.

And Orin envied him for it. How he wished Cal could remain in that blissful ignorance. The child had no idea what was happening, no inkling that the world was teetering on a knife's edge.

And Orin would give anything to keep it that way.

"WE WILL HAVE ORDER!" Maraco's roar split the air, cracking like a whip. "SILENCE! EVERYONE WILL BE SILENT AND LISTEN!"

The hall shuddered as panic shrank back, folding in on itself as people fell quiet, one by one. The sobs and wails dwindled to a low murmur, but never altogether vanished, but any shout was swallowed up by the weight of Maraco's fury. He stood tall and unbroken, a granite pillar in a sea of fear, daring anyone to defy him with his piercing glare.

"Thank you, Maraco." Came Belma's voice, soft yet steady, like the rumble of distant thunder.

Though his frame was bent with age, his presence was unyielding, and his words resonated with a power that stirred the very air. His gaze swept across the crowd, calm yet piercing, as if he could see into the depths of every soul before him. "People of Ithicel, and all who have journeyed from distant Terran villages to stand with us today, hear me now. Never—not once in the long history of our proud land—have we bowed to invaders. And I swear to you, with every fiber of my being, we will not falter now. This is our home, our legacy, and together, we will defend it with the will and spirt of the Great Mother."

A murmur rippled through the crowd, softer this time, hushed and uncertain, but with a hint of something almost like hope.

Belma raised a thin, withered hand, and the whispers faded away. "We are calling every able-bodied man and boy who can swing a sword or draw a bow. One hour from now, gather by the Serpent's Arch," Maraco declared, his voice like iron; Fear was gone from his face, replaced by something hard and unbreakable. "Scouts are rallying the nearby villages. Messages have gone out to summon the great Nephilim's."

He paused, letting the words sink in, his gaze sweeping over the crowd, daring them to look away.

"we will not just defeat the Flesher horde—we will crush them. We will grind their darkness into dust and scatter it to the winds. This is our stand, our moment, and history will remember the day we rose as one and said, 'No more!'"

The crowd stood still, breaths held, as if the whole room was on the edge of a cliff, teetering. A low, deep rumble started somewhere near the front. A cheer began to swell, like the first roar of a coming storm. It spread, growing louder until it burst forth in a deafening howl of defiance. Men and women shot to their feet, fists pumping. The noise rolled through the hall like thunder, raw and fierce, a sound that made the blood sing and skin prickle. The fear that had gripped them moments before melted away, replaced by something wild and hot. A battle cry shook the stone walls, ringing out like the roar of a beast awakening from slumber.

"LOW-LANDERS, PREPARE FOR BATTLE!" Maraco bellowed, thrusting his sword high.

The blade flashed in the light, a gleam of steel reflecting the light. The crowd erupted again, shouts and cries spilling over one another in a chaotic rush, a wild frenzy.

Orin turned to Shira, his heart a tangled mess of fear and love. She looked up at him, face pale but set, her eyes wide and bright. He squeezed her hand, feeling the warmth of her skin against his. "Stay strong," she urged.

Even as she spoke, he could feel her trembling, could see the doubt flickering in her gaze. Then the doors swung open, and the hall emptied in a rush. Bodies pushed and jostled, a tidal wave of villagers spilling out onto the street. Orin tightened his grip on Shira's hand, pulling Cal close with his other arm as the noise hit them; a chaotic roar of shouts, cheers for the coming battles, sobs, and panicked cries, all tangled together in a deafening din.

Outside, the street was a writhing mass of people, faces pale, eyes wide. Some ran, clutching children, pushing through the crush as if their very lives de-pended on it. Others stood frozen, mouths agape, staring blankly as if the world had split open at their feet. Men barked urgent orders to one another, while women snatched up their little ones, fingers clamped tightly around tiny hands, scanning the faces around them like scaled Bracken wolves sensing the air for danger.

"Let's get home. Quickly," Orin shouted, leaning close to Shira's ear.

His words were nearly swallowed in the chaos. They pushed through the crowd, shoulders bumping, Cal pressed tightly against his side, his small fingers gripping Orin's sleeve. Everywhere there were voices crying, shouting, and pleading. Faces twisted with fear, eyes darting around as if they expected death to come stomping through the village at any second. The lingering fear was thick and choking, wrapping around them and turning the air sour.

Orin pulled Shira closer, wrapping his arm around Cal's small shoulders. "C'mon, stay with me!" He shouted, but even as they shoved through the crush of bodies, he couldn't shake the feeling that something had already changed—something deep and dark—like the ground beneath their feet had shifted, setting everything just a little off-kilter.

"Orin, we should've left sooner!" Shira's voice came out tight and choked, her eyes darting around the square like a trapped rabbit, flitting from one frightened face to another.

There wasn't time to talk, not now. All Orin could do was push forward, shoving through the crush of bodies.

"Papa?" Cal's small voice piped up, so close yet nearly swallowed by the noise around them. His grip on Orin's arm was like a vise, tiny fingers clinging for dear life. "Can I come with you to fight, Papa?" His eyes, round and trusting, peered up at him—completely oblivious to the weight of what he was asking.

Shira's breath hitched beside him, her face going bone white as she shook her head, lips pressed so tight they turned bloodless.

Orin dropped to one knee, scooping Cal up, holding him close against his chest. "You, my brave son," he murmured into Cal's ear, his voice low and steady. "Have the most important job of all. You're going to protect your mama, understand?"

Cal's brow furrowed for a second, then smoothed out, a tiny flicker of pride lighting up his little face. He nodded solemnly, resting his head on Orin's shoulder, as if that small promise had made everything right again.

But it hadn't. Not by a long shot.

All around them, the square was boiling over, voices clashing and crashing against each other in a tangle of despair and desperate bravado. "My boy!" A plump woman near them wailed, fat tears rolling down her cheeks as she clung to her son's arm, like she could keep him anchored by will alone. "They're gonna take my little boy to war!"

Her sobs tore at the emptiness, raw and hopeless. Men were shouting over each other, some puffing up their chests with big, brave words that rang hollow in the rising panic.

"To arms! We'll show those Fleshers what it means to mess with Terra!" roared a burly fellow, swinging an old, rusted sword high above his head.

A few around him took up the cry, raising fists and cheering; Though Orin could still see it in their eyes—the flash of fear they couldn't quite smother. Others were already slipping back, edging away with pale faces and tight lips.

From the far end of the square, a high, thin shriek ripped through the din. "We're all gonna die!"

Orin craned his neck, squinting through the throng, and there—clinging to a low-hanging branch of an old tree—was a wild-eyed man dressed in filthy rags, his hair a matted tangle. His eyes rolled in their sockets as he swung back and forth, arms flailing. "No one will survive! Death's comin' for us all!"

His voice was a harsh rasp, cracking with desperation, slicing through the crowd's fear like a blade. "Shut up, old man!"

A young soldier, barely more than a boy himself, shoved at him, but the old man clung on, stubborn as a barnacle. "Run, you fools! Run while you still can!" He shrieked, his words breaking, wild. "Run!"

The crowd flinched back, recoiling as if they'd been slapped. A ripple of unease spread out from him like a stone dropped into a pond. Whispers and fearful glances darted around, the panic creeping back in, slithering around the edges of the bravado.

"Let's go," Shira whispered, her voice thin and strained as her fingers dug into Orin's arm, nails biting into his skin. "We need to get away from here. Away from this... Madness."

He nodded, pushing them through the press of bodies, slipping through gaps where they could, squeezing past as best they could. The air felt thick and sour, the noise roaring in his ears like a thousand buzzing flies. Ahead, the edge of the street beckoned like a lifeline.

Finally, they burst free of the crowd, the din fading to a dull roar behind them. Orin glanced back, just in time to see two guards dragging the old man down from his perch. He fought like a demon, limbs flailing, eyes wide and darting. "We're all doomed! Doomed!" He kept screeching, even as they hauled him off.

"Come on," Orin muttered to Shira, squeezing her hand as they hurried down the street. He tried for a smile, tried to sound steady. "Let's get home."

The village blurred as they walked, everything twisted and strange, like a bad dream. Flowers bloomed bright and cheerful along the roadside, their colors almost garish against the fear all around them. The sweet scent of them hung heavy, too sweet, cloying. It made his stomach turn. The Dixin fairies flitted about in tight, frantic circles above their heads. Their tiny voices buzzing like alarm bells, sharp and panicked.

Shira kept glancing back, her eyes wide and glassy. "Will... will anything ever be the same?" She murmured, almost too soft to hear.

Orin didn't know what to say. He just pulled her closer.

They reached the house in silence, the sight of their little gate bringing a flicker of relief. But as Orin shoved through the front door, the latch splintering under the force, that relief turned to ash.

"Get to your room Cal!" He barked, harsher than he meant to. "Now."

"But Papa—"

"No buts!" Shira's voice wavered, tight and shaky. "Go on, do as your father says!"

Cal's face crumpled, but he turned, shoulders slumped, and shuffled down the hall, casting one last sulky glance back before slipping into his room. Shira followed Orin into their bedroom, her face drawn, eyes dark with worry. "Orin, what are you doing?"

"I'm getting ready." He said simply, yanking his father's old armor from the chest at the foot of their bed.

The leather creaked as he lifted it, the familiar sound wrapping around him like an old friend. How many times had he listened to his father's stories, watching him polish this very breastplate? How many battles had he seen in it?

His hands fumbled with the straps, shaking.

"Orin, stop," Shira pleaded, stepping closer, her voice cracking. "You're not a warrior. You don't have to do this."

Orin whispered, his throat tight, "I do. I must defend us. Defend you. Defend Cal. Our home."

Shira's fingers trembled as they brushed over the old, worn leather of the armor. "But... what if you fail? What if... what if you're killed?" Tears glistened in her eyes, spilling over. "What if I lose you?"

Her words hit him like a punch. For a moment, he stood frozen, the weight of her fear pressing down on him. Then, dropping the armor, he wrapped her in his arms, holding her tight as she shook against him. "In this life and the next." He whispered fiercely, burying his face in her hair. "You'll never lose me. Never."

"Promise?" she breathed, looking up at him, her eyes wet and desperate.

"I swear." He murmured, cupping her cheek and brushing away the tears with his thumb.

She sagged against him, the fight draining out of her. They clung to each other, as if they could hold back the storm together. After a deep, shuddering breath, she stepped back, her gaze steady now, filled with a quiet, terrible resolve. "Let me help you prepare." She whispered.

Orin managed a small, strained smile. "Of course."

Though her hands were still trembling, Shira helped him fasten the straps of the armor, her touch lingering on the old leather as if she were trying to pour all her hope into it. When he reached for his father's sword, she took his hands in hers.

"Take it." She murmured, pressing the blade into his grip. The cool metal of the hilt felt solid and comforting. "May it protect you... as it did him."

He nodded, sliding the sword into the sheath at his side. Turning to her, he stood there in his father's armor, feeling more like a scared boy than a man ready for battle. But when she looked at him, there was something fierce in her gaze that made his chest tighten.

"My warrior," she whispered, so soft it was almost a breath.

8
Ferkin

Her pale green dress was bunched up around her waist, and her hair spilled down in wild, tousled waves. She barely noticed the creak of the floor or the muted voices beyond the door; there was only the heat of the moment, raw and consuming.

"Yes... yes, Ferkin—don't stop," she murmured, her voice thick with anticipation. She felt his hand reach over her shoulder, fingers tangling into her hair, pulling her head gently but firmly back toward him. The world outside dissolved, leaving just the rhythm of their movement and the heady scent of aged wood and warm skin.

He leaned over her, drawing a deep breath, his body taut with restraint. The air between them was buzzing, the connection palpable. As he gathered the last of his strength, he held himself there, wanting to make this moment linger just a heartbeat longer.

"Oh, Sindri!" Ferkin cried out.

And then, in the quiet that followed, her voice cut through the haze, bringing him back. "Ferkin?" she whispered, her tone cool, distant, as if reminding him of the walls that had now returned around them.

"'Yes, Sindri?' He looked at her, his heart racing as she tried to catch his eyes.

"Sindri is my sister."

Startled, the woman leaned back, pushing him off and pulling her skirt back down. "You fucking prick!"

Ferkin stared at her in surprise. She looked just like Sindri. "Wait, you're not Sindri?"

"'No, I am not Sindri!" Her voice rose, frustration spilling over. "I'm Lorna, her sister!"

She threw her hair back over her bony shoulders and began to storm out the door. "Wait, wait, wait!" he called after her.

She turned, catching him in the act of pulling up his trousers. Her face snapped back in disgust. 'What?'

"'If I make it back from this fight alive, maybe you and Sindri can come by and visit me together. We can talk about this whole thing."

He flashed his best boyish grin, the one that always made the girls smile. Lorna hesitated, a flicker of a smile creeping onto her lips. "Oh, Ferkin, baby," her words fell from her lips like spun sugar. "You won't need to worry about that. You're going to be far too busy being some flesher's plaything."

She laughed and walked out the door. Ferkin raced to the door, calling after her. "Yeah, well, all you whores look alike. Your sister was better anyways!"

Two men at the end of the hall erupted in laughter at the sight of Lorna walking away or perhaps at Ferkin, standing there with his trousers only up to his knees. Slamming the door behind him, he lazed back in an old wooden rocking chair in the corner of his room.

"Huh, sister," he muttered to himself, a laugh bubbling up as he gazed out the window of the old pub.

The hour was almost up. A group of twenty men rode past the old, shackled tree, their leather armor creaking as they moved, seeming almost too fat for their snores to carry them.

Reaching over, Ferkin grabbed his mug of mostly empty stale dandle beer and chugged it. A sinking feeling washed over him, a sensation he hadn't felt since he was a boy watching his father get killed. Shaking off the daunting memory, he stood up from the rocking chair and began putting on his armor.

Soon enough, he found himself walking out of the small room, making his way down the old, rickety stairs to the pub. As he stepped into the now-empty space, full of knocked-over chairs and the stench of liquor, he noticed a woman behind the counter staring at him.

"Well, I guess you're my last customer today, Ferkin," she said, offering a sad smile. "I guess they're all gone."

"Aye, they are. I guess so shall you be."

"'Selice, if I don't make it back—"

She shot him a fierce look. "You will make it back! I lost Mom and Dad; I'm not losing my big brother too.'"

"'Do you think anything could best your brother?" He smiled, trying to lighten the mood. "And besides, you need someone to fill that room upstairs, and who better than family?"

Selice wiped the tear from her eye. "I will have three jugs of dandle beer here for you when you get back."

She walked out from behind the bar, wrapping her short arms around him. "You come back and don't keep me waiting alone here long."

He leaned down and kissed her forehead. "You stay safe and keep the doors locked until I return."

After one more embrace, he turned and walked out the door. The streets were starting to empty, the final few men heading toward the Serpent's Arch. Women and children made their way to pray to the Emerald Lady for protection. Approaching the pole where his Snore was tied, he fastened the saddle tight and mounted.

Ferkin took great pride in the scars on his Snore; she was the toughest in the land, proving it with every battle. He spoke to her gently while stroking her neck. "Come on, girl. Let's go and kill some fleshers."

The Snore grunted in response, as if she understood and agreed. The streets of the village were nearly deserted as Ferkin and the others marched steadily toward the Serpent's Arch. Aya shifted beneath him, her muscles taut, sensing the tension in the air. Even the faint whispers of families saying their goodbyes—the tearful farewells of children clinging to their fathers—seemed far away, like echoes from another life. The rhythmic crunch of boots on gravel and the low, restless grunts of snores beneath their riders were the only sounds that tethered him to the present. Everything else felt distant, as though they were moving through a dream. Or a nightmare.

Ferkin swung up into the saddle, and Beastly shifted again beneath him, her weight a reassuring, solid presence. Her scales glinted dully in the dim light, the once-vibrant greens and blues muted by dust and neglect. He ran a gloved hand along her thick neck, feeling the tension in her muscles. She let out a deep, throaty rumble that vibrated through him, her massive frame bunching as if she knew the battle that lay ahead. "Steady, girl," he whispered, trying to sound more confident than he felt. "Long day ahead of us. You know what we're up against."

The village behind them looked like a shell of itself, hollowed out by the impending weight of it all. No laughter, no market chatter, no children playing in the streets, just silence broken only by the occasional soft sobs and the tramp of feet. The life had been sucked out of Ithicel, leaving it desolate, as if it had already accepted its fate. As if it were waiting to be buried.

He couldn't help but think of what this place used to be. Flashes of memory came unbidden, images of brighter days: bustling streets filled with vendors hawking their wares, the smell of fresh Turpin bread and herbs in the air, the sound of music and conversation flowing freely. He remembered the days when they were young, when Ferkin and Orin would race their snores through the fields until their lungs burned and their beasts were lathered with sweat, daring each other to hold on for just one more heartbeat. But those were different times. Today wasn't a day for nostalgia. There was no room for it now.

Ahead, the Serpent's Arch loomed, towering above them like a dark omen. Its twisted stone columns reached skyward, casting long, skeletal shadows over the gathering soldiers. The carvings that lined the ancient pillars seemed to shift and writhe as if the serpents etched into the stone were coming to life, watching them as they marched toward an uncertain fate. Ferkin had always hated the Arch—its oppressive presence, its grim history—but today it seemed even more sinister, as if the stones were whispering of death.

Underneath the arch, chaos reigned. Men and beasts swarmed in a frantic blur, leather armor chuffing, blades flashing in the light. Commands were barked, orders shouted, but it was barely controlled madness. Snores, with their armored hides and razor-sharp claws, shuffled nervously under their riders, snorting and stamping as if sensing the unease in their human companions. The air was thick with fear, but no one spoke of it. They all knew what awaited them beyond the Arch, and yet, they pressed forward.

A knot of fear tightened in Ferkin's gut. This was it. The Fleshers were coming. He wanted to believe, to hope that the stories were just that—wild tales meant to scare them. But deep down, in the pit of his stomach, he knew better. Fleshers didn't just kill: they consumed. They ripped apart flesh, bone - everything. They left nothing behind. They were just resources, like animals hunted. The fear etched into every face around him confirmed it. They weren't facing an army. They were facing annihilation.

He scanned the chaos, his eyes locking onto Lundor near the Serpent's Arch. Lundor's towering figure was unmistakable, even amidst the swirl of movement. Ferkin urged Beastly forward, weaving through the crowded streets. Dismounting beside him, he felt the earth shift beneath him as the beast settled. Lundor's face was as hard as the armor that encased him, lined with scars from battles long past. His expression gave nothing away, but the tension in his jaw told Ferkin that he felt the same dread curling in his gut.

"Didn't expect to see you here, Lundor," Ferkin called out, his voice strained, barely audible above the noise.

Lundor turned his head, his eyes locking on Ferkin's with the same intensity he always had. He gave a brief nod. "Didn't expect to see you either, healer. But these days, it seems we're all needed."

Ferkin opened his mouth to respond, but a voice rang out from behind him, cutting through the clamor. "Ferkin! About time you showed up!"

He managed a nod in acknowledgment, but before he could say anything, Beastly jerked beneath him, nearly unseating him. He stumbled off, his cheeks burning as he heard laughter erupt around him. "Good with herbs, not so much with beasts, eh?" Ferkin's own laughter boomed, slicing through the grim atmosphere like a knife.

Ferkin stifled a laugh as he watched Orin stumble off his snore, his cheeks burning with embarrassment. The snore, oblivious to the situation, snorted and flicked her tail, as if she hadn't done a thing wrong.

Before Ferkin could tease Orin further, a warning shout pierced the air. "Orin, move!" Lundor's voice cut through the chaos with urgency.

Ferkin's attention snapped to Orin, who spun around, heart racing. Just in time to see a massive sotto ant scuttling up his arm, its pincers snapping dangerously close. Ferkin winced as Orin hissed, slamming his arm against a nearby tree in an attempt to dislodge the creature. But the ant's grip only tightened, and Ferkin could see the pain ripple across Orin's face as the venom surged through his veins.

In a flash, Lundor was there, his knife gleaming in the dim light. With swift precision, he pinned the ant against the bark, ending its threat in a brutal strike. But the damage was done; Orin winced, the venom already spreading.

"You alright?" Lundor asked, his tone surprisingly amused.

Orin clenched his jaw, flexing his hand. "I've had worse," he muttered, shaking out his arm as the pain settled into a dull ache. "Can't seem to stay out of trouble, even out here."

Lundor chuckled, sheathing his knife. "Good thing you've learned how to get out of it just as fast."

Ferkin watched as Orin tested the movement in his hand, flexing his fingers. The sting was a stark reminder of the dangers lurking in the wilderness, even before the fleshers arrived. Ferkin couldn't shake the feeling that this was just the beginning of their troubles.

Suddenly, the horns blared—a shrill, bone-chilling sound that silenced everyone in the camp. The air grew heavy, a shroud of unspoken fear settling over them. Ferkin turned to see Maraco, astride his snore, commanding attention. The beast was a reflection of its rider's steely resolve, muscles rippling beneath its glossy hide. Maraco's armor gleamed in the pale light, every plate shining like a beacon. With his sword raised high, the blade caught the weak sunlight and glinted ominously. His voice boomed across the camp, striking deep into the hearts of every man present.

"Men of Terra!" Maraco began, his voice a thunder-clap that echoed across the thick tree-lined forest . "Look around you. Look at the faces of your brothers, your comrades, your kin. Remember them. For today, we stand not as individuals, but as one—one force, one will, one unbreakable spirit. And today, we stand at the edge of darkness."

The silence that followed was heavier than the fear that had come before. Every eye was fixed on Maraco, every breath held. He lowered his sword slightly, the blade still gleaming, and his voice dropped to a growl, each word sharp as a dagger.

"The Fleshers are not like any enemy we have faced. They do not come for land, for glory, or for conquest. They come to consume. To devour. To erase us from existence. They are the void, the end of all things, and they will not stop until there is nothing left but silence and ash."

He paused, letting the weight of his words sink in. The men shifted uneasily, their hands tightening on their weapons, their eyes darting to the horizon as if expecting the Fleshers to emerge at any moment. Maraco's gaze swept over them, fierce and unyielding.

"But!" he roared, and the sudden force of his voice made every man snap to attention. "But we are not prey. We are not beasts to be slaughtered. We are the men of Terra! We are the flame that burns in the darkest night, the shield that stands against the tide of oblivion! We are the ones who say *no more*!"

The air seemed to crackle with energy as Maraco's voice rose, his words igniting something deep within every soul present. He raised his sword again, the blade catching the light like a star in the gloom.

"They will come," he said, his voice steady now, a low rumble that carried across the camp. "They will come with their teeth and their claws, their hunger and the hate of their father. They will come to break us. But they do not know us. They do not know what we are made of. They do not know that we would rather die on our feet than live on our knees!"

A murmur of agreement rippled through the ranks, growing louder, fiercer. Maraco's eyes burned with a fire that seemed to leap from man to man, kindling their courage.

"Today, we fight not for ourselves, but for those who cannot fight. For the mothers who kissed their children goodbye, for the fathers who taught us to hold a sword, for the lovers and whores who whispered promises we intend to keep. We fight for the future. For the light that still burns, even in the darkest corners of this world."

His voice softened, but the intensity of his words only grew. "And if we fall, we fall as heroes. But if we stand—if we stand, we will send the Fleshers back to the hell they crawled from! We will show them that Terra is not a feast for the taking, but a fortress that will never fall!"

The roar that erupted from the men was deafening, a primal cry of defiance that shook the very earth. Ferkin felt it in his chest, in his bones, a fire that could not be extinguished. Maraco's voice rose above the tumult, a clarion call that pierced the chaos.

"So I ask you, men of Terra—will you stand with me? Will you fight not for survival, but for victory? Will you show the Fleshers that they have made their last mistake?"

The response was instantaneous, a thunderous "YES!" that seemed to split the sky. Maraco's lips curled into a fierce smile, and he raised his sword one final time, the blade shining like a beacon of hope in the gathering darkness.

"Then let them come," he said, his voice a whisper that carried the weight of a thousand storms. "And let them learn the price of defiance. Let them learn the pain of following the one they call Father, Him, Almighty, the One."

The men erupted into cheers, their fear replaced by a blazing determination. Ferkin felt his heart pounding, his grip on the reins tightening as he looked at Maraco, a figure of unyielding strength and resolve.

In that moment, he knew—they would not lose. They could not lose.

Ferkin glanced over at Orin, their eyes locking for a moment. Orin gave a sharp nod, determination etched on his face. He was ready, as always, to charge into whatever hell awaited them. He saw him there, a boy, barely nine or ten, with a helmet too large for his head. The child's small hands trembled on the reins of a massive snore that towered over him, the beast fidgeting with unease.

Ferkin's heart sank at the sight of the boy. So young and fragile, thrust into the nightmare unfolding around them. But there was no time for sentiment; they had to focus on the impending battle.

He watched as Orin urged his Snore closer to the boy, his voice low and firm. "What's your name, boy?"

The child looked up, fear evident in his wide eyes. "L-Lamar, sir," he stammered.

"Lamar, have you ever fought before?" Orin asked.

The boy shook his head, his lips trembling. "No, sir."

"Listen to me, Lamar. You stay close to the others. If anything happens—if you get separated—you run.

Do you hear me? You run back home. Don't look back. Just run."

Lamar nodded, gripping the reins tighter, knuckles white with fear. "Yes, sir."

Orin gave him a final nod, the weight of unspoken words heavy in the air. As the army began its march, the sound of hooves and boots filled the forest with tense energy. Maraco led the way, his snore surging forward like a battering ram, clearing a path through the dense woods. Ferkin followed closely behind, flanking Orin, with Lundor just ahead. The trees loomed high above them, their shadows stretching long as daylight faded. The deeper they ventured, the more the forest felt oppressive and watchful, as if it held its breath, waiting for the inevitable clash.

No one spoke as the hours dragged on. The silence hung thick and unbreakable, interrupted only by the steady thudding of hooves and the rustling of leaves. It felt as if the forest itself demanded quiet, daring anyone to disturb the fragile balance of fear and foreboding that enveloped the air. As the group pressed deeper, the atmosphere grew heavier, stifling, as though something ancient and malevolent lurked just beyond sight.

Suddenly, Maraco's hand shot up, fingers spread wide in a signal to halt. The army came to an abrupt stop, Snores snorting in protest, their muscles tense and trembling beneath their riders. The air thickened with an unseen menace, and Ferkin's pulse quickened, a familiar cold knot twisting in his gut. He scanned the trees, searching for any sign of movement, but there was nothing but the eerie stillness that cloaked the woods like a suffocating fog.

"We're close," Maraco muttered, his voice low as his eyes narrowed, raking over the darkened forest ahead.

A cold shiver crept down Ferkin's spine, prickling every nerve. The Fleshers were out there, lurking in the shadows, waiting for the perfect moment. He could feel it in his bones, a visceral knowing that gnawed at his insides. His hand instinctively moved to the pouch at his belt, fingers brushing against the dried herbs and salves he carried. As a healer, he had faced death many times, in various forms. But this...this was different. The fleshers didn't simply kill; they devoured everything. The stories spoke of them leaving nothing behind but bones, ash, and a hollow, gut-wrenching emptiness.

"Orin," Maraco's sharp voice cut through the swirling thoughts, pulling Ferkin back to the present. His gaze was fixed on Orin, hard and unyielding. "You're a healer. If you see anything—anything out of the ordinary—you let me know. Immediately."

Orin swallowed, his throat tight. "Yes, sir."

The silence swallowed them again as they pressed forward, the darkening woods around them growing more twisted and gnarled with every step. The trees seemed almost alive, their thick branches reaching across the path like skeletal fingers, blotting out what little light remained. Ferkin's snore grew restless beneath him, her ears flicking nervously as she pawed at the ground, sensing the danger lurking ahead.

Then it came: a subtle shift in the air, almost imperceptible at first, a faint whisper on the wind, like a breath too soft to hear. Ferkin strained his ears, convinced it was merely the creak of a tree or the rustle of leaves. As they moved deeper, the whisper grew louder, more distinct—urgent, pleading.

"Help me…"

The words were barely audible, but they sliced through the stillness like a knife. Ferkin's heart pounded in his chest as he looked around, trying to pinpoint the source. The voice seemed to drift from everywhere and nowhere, carried on the wind, growing more insistent with each passing moment.

"Help me…" it repeated, a desperate, haunting plea.

Her Cries

A snore let out a grunt. "Come on, Orin, move your beast!" Smifen's voice grated, low and breathless as he wrestled the reins of his own mount, the beast's snout quivering as they picked their way down the jagged slope. "Can't afford to lose a step now."

Orin's snore—stubborn as a boulder—snorted in response, claws scraping loose pebbles down the cliffside in a harsh cascade. Aya shifted uneasily under him, ears flicking at the shrill cries echoing through the ravine. He leaned forward, squinting past the twisted branches that clawed the sky like skeletal fingers. A bitter stench curled around them, rank and heavy like meat gone to maggots, churning his gut.

Smifen's beast stumbled, causing him to curse under his breath. "You smell that, Orin? Smells like a battlefield. Or worse.""Worse," Orin muttered, keeping his gaze ahead.

The cries—those desperate, keening wails—cut through the silence, bouncing off the crumbling cliffs around them. No other sound answered. No bird calls. No skitter of life in the underbrush. Just... emptiness. Hollow and still."Something's dead wrong here," Maraco growled from beside him, his fingers twitching restlessly at the hilt of his axe. He cast a wary glance around, brow furrowed. "Orin, you're the one always sticking your nose in the dirt and whispering sweet nothings to trees. What's happened here?"

Orin shook his head, staring out at the blighted land stretching before them. Trees were stripped bare, their bark cracked and splintered, branches hanging limp as if the life had been sucked out of them. "I... I don't know, sir. I've never seen anything like it."

Maraco's gaze bore into him, sharp and probing, but before he could press further, another voice chimed in, tight with fear. "I have."

Heads turned. Tidal, one of the youngest among them, sat stiff in his saddle, face pale, eyes wide and strained. His hand gripped the hilt of his sword like a lifeline. "This... this is Gullveg.""Gullveg?" Maraco's tone dropped, dangerous. "You think Gullveg did this?"

The name seemed to hang in the air, thick and heavy. Orin could see the tension tightening around the others, faces hardening.Tidal nodded frantically, swallowing so hard they could see his Adam's apple bobbing. "Y-yes, sir. It has to be. The stories say—""Enough with your damned stories!" Lundor snarled, spurring his Snore closer. He loomed over Tidal, eyes flashing. "Gullveg's a fable. A ghost story to scare children into bed. Get a grip, boy, or you'll skewer yourself on that blade before we even reach the cries."

Tidal flinched, loosening his grip, but his gaze still darted around, nervous as a cornered hare. "But, sir, the land—"

Lundor cut him off with a harsh bark of laughter. "How thick-headed are you, boy? Gullveg's just a tale for old men to spin over a fire, nothing more." He spat, lips curling in disdain.

"Aye, nothing but smoke and nonsense," Ferkin agreed, slapping Tidal on the back so hard the lad almost toppled from his saddle. "You listen to too many fireside tales, pup. Next thing, you'll be shivering at shadows, thinking every flicker's a wraith coming for your blood."

Tidal flushed, fists clenched tight. Orin bit back a grim chuckle. The lad was green, true enough, but he wasn't wrong about one thing—whatever had touched this land wasn't natural.

"Enough!" Maraco's shout cracked through the air like a thunderclap, cutting through the low murmur of mocking laughter. He yanked his snore around, eyes blazing. "We're here to track the source, not squabble over campfire stories!"

He wheeled on Tidal, seizing the front of his tunic and yanking him forward until they were nose to nose. "You think you know what's out there, boy? Then let me tell you something. Gullveg's a shadow—a ghost. Nothing more. Speak that name again, and I'll have your tongue for a trophy. Understood?"

Tidal's eyes went wide, breath hitching. He nodded jerkily, the color draining from his cheeks. "Y-yes, sir."

"Good." Maraco shoved him back roughly, wheeling his beast around. "Now keep your wits about you. If something's alive out there, it's not Gullveg. It's something real." He paused, casting a steely gaze over the rest of them. "And real things bleed."

The silence that followed was thick, heavy. Even the cries had quieted, fading into the eerie stillness. Orin swallowed, glancing sideways at Smifen. He raised a brow, a grim smile tugging at his lips. "Looks like we're in for a long day, eh, Orin?"

Orin nodded, gripping his reins tighter. "That we are, mate. That we are."

Tidal's face drained of color, his cheeks a stark, sickly white beneath the grime of travel. His wide eyes darted frantically between the others, silently begging for someone to step in, to stop Maraco's crushing grip. But the men stood stone-still, faces impassive, the threat of their captain's wrath hanging thick. Maraco didn't relent, his knuckles taut as he held the boy's vest tight. Only when Tidal gave a small, jerky nod—more out of instinct than any real agreement—did Maraco shove him back into his saddle. "The next man who dares—"

"HELP ME!"

The scream tore through the trees, raw and desperate, cutting Maraco's words short. It jolted through them like a blade scraping along bone, yanking every head around. For a heartbeat, they stood frozen, the breath stolen from their lungs. The voice had shifted; no longer a distant wail, it was so close it seemed to reverberate from the very earth beneath them. "Help me... please..."

A woman's voice emerged, weak and shuddering, broken.

"Move!" Maraco's bark shattered the spell, and they lurched into action, kicking their beasts into motion.

Branches lashed at them as they crashed through the underbrush, tearing toward the hollowed-out valley beyond. Orin's heart hammered as he fought to keep up, eyes scanning wildly, lungs burning with each gulp of the stifling air.

"There!" he shouted, his voice cracking.

He threw his hand forward, pointing to the dry riverbed. A small, crumpled form lay sprawled amidst the lifeless stones, as still as the corpses of the trees surrounding her.

They skidded to a halt, beasts snorting and stamping. Orin's snore pawed at the ground, claws scraping against the loose gravel. The others fanned out, forming a loose ring around the figure. It was a woman—gods—what was left of her, at least. Orin slid off his mount, legs shaky beneath him as he inched closer.

Her body was mangled, twisted at unnatural angles, flesh hanging in tattered strips. Blood seeped sluggishly from gaping wounds, dark and viscous, pooling in the dirt. Lofen flies—those bloated, buzzing demons—swarmed thick around her, crawling through the open sores, their wings a sickening drone. Her face... gods above, he had to look away. Her skin had been peeled back in places, flayed to the bone, as if she'd been torn apart and put back together by a butcher who didn't care about keeping her whole.

"By the gods..." Ferkin staggered back, a hand clamped over his mouth as he doubled over. He retched, choking on bile.

No one moved to help him. They were all locked in place, horror clawing up their throats.

"This—this isn't..." Smifen's voice trailed off, strangled. He shook his head, eyes wide.

"Not just an attack," Maraco murmured. His voice was quiet, barely audible. He swung down from his mount, dropping to a knee beside the woman's body. "This... this is Him's converting."

"What happened to you?" Lundor whispered, leaning in, his voice trembling despite his forced calm.

He tilted his head, ear brushing dangerously close to the woman's torn lips. She wheezed, breath rattling like dry leaves in a dead wind, her mouth working soundlessly as if grasping for words that wouldn't come. Then her eyes began to change.

The white of her sclerae darkened, ink spilling across the surface like a stain spreading through fabric, a pulsing blackness that seemed to swell and grow until her entire gaze was swallowed by that dark void. Orin's skin prickled, a shudder running down his spine. The air thickened, growing heavy, dense with something that tasted like copper and ash. His heartbeat roared in his ears, a frantic thrum that seemed to match the rhythm of that eerie darkness swirling in her eyes.

"Lundor," he croaked, the sound barely more than a choked rasp.

He wanted to tell Lundor to pull back, to put distance between himself and whatever she'd become. But the words stuck, frozen on his tongue.

Lundor didn't move, didn't blink. He just leaned closer. "What did this to you?" he asked again, voice low and strained.

She blinked once, slowly, her breath stuttering in shallow gasps. Then her head turned, bones creaking, mouth cracking open with a grotesque, jerking motion. The blackness in her gaze seemed to writhe, something vile and ancient staring back at them from the depths of her ruined soul. Her lips twisted, peeling back in a grotesque parody of a smile.

"Death is here," she hissed.

The words seemed to ripple through the air, slithering along their nerves like a thousand cold, slimy fingers. Ferkin let out a low, strangled curse, stepping back, his sword trembling in his grip. Smifen froze, eyes wide, lips parted in a silent gasp. A shudder ran through the group, the kind that digs deep, down to the marrow. And then... the sound started.

There was a series of sharp, sickening cracks, like wood splintering under immense pressure. The woman's body convulsed, her spine arching violently. They watched in horrified silence as her ribs bent inward, bone and flesh twisting and contorting, the sound of snapping cartilage filling the air.

She screamed—a shriek that wasn't human. A keening wail of pure, unadulterated pain. It tore from her throat, raw and jagged, echoing through the ravine, bouncing off the cliffs around them. It was a sound that shouldn't have been possible, a sound that seemed to reverberate in the hollow spaces of their chests, setting every nerve aflame.

"DEATH IS HERE!" she wailed, the words a chilling, guttural roar.

"Gods—" Tidal staggered back, nearly dropping his sword.

His face was a mask of horror, eyes wide, pupils blown. He gasped, breath coming in harsh, erratic bursts, his gaze flicking around wildly as if expecting something to lunge at them from the shadows. "What—what is this?!"

The woman's body convulsed again, spine bowing so sharply that Orin could see the jagged curve of bone through her torn flesh. Blood splattered across the ground, her abdomen tearing open with a sickening rip. Dark, glistening entrails spilled out in a wet, slithering heap, pooling around her twisted form. She didn't scream, didn't react. Just lay there, trembling, her mouth opening and closing in a grotesque mimicry of speech.

And then, she spoke again.

"I... I want to go home," she whimpered, voice thin and high-pitched—the tone of a child lost and frightened.

Orin's heart clenched painfully. It wasn't her voice. Couldn't be. There was no way that sound came from the mutilated wreck before them. Her mouth didn't make any movements. It was as if the words just poured out. "Please... please, take me home. I want... I want my Mommy...Please, someone phone my mom-my!"

Then she twisted her head, eyes locking onto Orin—soulless, blackened—"Now I am become Death, the destroyer of worlds."

Her voice was that of a man speaking through her. The woman's grin widened as she locked eyes with Ferkin. "Nothing is possible unless one will com-mands, a will which has to be obeyed by others, begin-ning at the top and ending only at the very bottom."

Then locking eyes with Smifen, she said, "And in those days shall men seek death, and shall not find it; and shall desire to die, and death shall flee from them."

"Gods above," Smifen breathed, his voice cracking. He took a half-step back, his face ashen. "What the fuck...?"

"No... gods, no..." Orin whispered, the words slipping out unbidden.

His vision blurred, tears welling in his eyes as he stared at her, at the broken, sobbing thing she'd become. She shouldn't be alive. She shouldn't be able to speak, to beg like that. But she was. And the words... oh, gods, the words...

"Mommy... please, Mommy, take me home..."

The wailing rose, louder, higher, until it seemed to pierce through Orin's skull. He pressed his hands to his ears, biting down hard enough on his lip to taste blood, but it did nothing. He could still hear her, hear that desperate, aching cry.

"Mommy, take me home..."

"Stop it," Maraco growled, stepping forward. His face was twisted, his mouth drawn in a tight line. "Stop it!" His voice was raw and trembling as he stared down at her, tears glistening in his eyes like shattered glass.

"Please... Mommy..."

With a roar of anguish, Maraco yanked his sword free and drove it down with all the force he could muster. The blade punched through her skull with a sickening crunch, the sharp edge splitting bone and flesh in a spray of dark blood. Her body spasmed once, a violent jerk that sent more blood splattering across the ground... and then she went still.

The silence that followed was absolute, crushing. Orin stood there, his heart hammering, chest heaving, staring down at her lifeless form. The blackness in her eyes dimmed, fading away until there was nothing left but empty, hollow sockets staring sightlessly up at the sky.

"Maraco..." Tidal's voice was thin and trembling. "What... what was that? And how do you 'phone'?"

Maraco didn't answer. He just stared at her, the blade still buried in her skull, shoulders heaving. Slowly, he tore his gaze away from her, looking up at the rest of them. His face was pale, his eyes hollow.

"She's... she's at peace now," he murmured, his voice hollow and distant.

He wrenched his blade free with a sharp tug, the sound of metal scraping against bone sending a shiver down Orin's spine. Maraco turned away from her, looking to the rest of them—his men, his brothers. They were all pale, every one of them. Faces drawn and sickly. And the fear, oh gods, the fear that flickered in each of their eyes.

"Back to the group," Maraco ordered quietly, sheathing his sword with a trembling hand. "We need to rejoin the others."

"Maraco..." Tidal stepped forward, his hands trembling. His face was a sickly gray, his eyes wide and wild. "We're... we're all going to die, aren't we?"

Maraco's gaze shifted, locking onto Tidal's. For a long moment, he didn't speak. He just stared at the younger man, his expression unreadable.

"We're not going to die," Maraco said quietly, though there was no conviction in his voice. "Not if we move. Now."

The others hesitated, then began to mount up, their faces pale and drawn. But Tidal just stood there, shaking his head, lips trembling.

"We're going to die," he whispered again, his voice high and wavering. "We should run... we should hide..."

"Tidal—" Orin started, but Maraco cut him off with a sharp look.

"Mount up," he barked, his voice harsh. "Now."

Orin swallowed, his gaze lingering on Tidal for a heartbeat longer, then nodded slowly. "Yes, sir."

Before any of them could move, Ferkin roared, a snarl tearing from his throat as he lunged forward. His hand shot out and cracked against Tidal's cheek with vicious force. The sound of a brutal smack that sent Tidal sprawling, his body hitting the blood-soaked ground with a sickening thud echoed through the ravine.

"You cowardly shit!" Ferkin spat, looming over him, his broad shoulders heaving with each ragged breath. His face twisted, eyes blazing with something wild, something raw and jagged that Orin realized, with a jolt, was fear. "May the spirits take you, you miserable wretch—curse you and every damned kin you've got, you worthless—"

"ENOUGH!" Maraco's voice cracked through the air like a whip, raw and jagged.

The force of it silenced Ferkin mid-rant, his mouth snapping shut, rage flickering to something almost like shame. Maraco stood stiff in his saddle, chest heaving, his eyes blazing as he stared down at the pair of them. "I said enough."

Ferkin recoiled, stepping back, his gaze dropping to the dirt. Tidal lay there, curled up in the muck, blood and tears streaking his face, a low, pitiful sob escaping his lips. He looked... small. Broken. A child caught in the wrong place at the wrong time.

"Get up," Maraco growled, his voice low, trembling with barely contained fury. He didn't dismount. Didn't move. Just glared down at Tidal, his jaw clenched tight. "Get up, and join the back of the line. Burn the body."

Tidal flinched, a keening whimper breaking free as he struggled to push himself up. His limbs shook, knees buckling beneath him, but he staggered upright, his face smeared with dirt and blood, shoulders hunched. He kept his gaze locked on the ground, not daring to look at any of them.

Orin glanced away, his jaw tightening. The others shifted, their eyes flicking anywhere but at Tidal; the tension coiled around them like a suffocating fog. The world around Orin felt... off. Twisted. As if something were watching, lurking just beyond the edges of his vision. He forced himself to look up, his gaze drifting to the woman's mangled corpse in the center of the ravine. Her body lay crumpled, entrails glistening wetly in the flickering light of the dying fire. The hollow sockets of her eyes stared blankly up at the sky, empty, lifeless.

Or were they?

A shiver crawled down his spine, a cold, sickening sensation settling deep in his gut. For just a moment—just a heartbeat—he thought he saw something shift. Something dark and endless, flickering deep in those empty eyes. A shadow. A presence.

He blinked, his heart thudding painfully against his ribs. But there was nothing. Just the corpse, still and silent, its eyes vacant.

"Orin, move out," Maraco snapped, his voice strained.

Orin tore his gaze away, swallowing hard as he nudged Aya forward. The others followed, the line forming as they began to make their way out of the ravine, the beasts' hooves crunching softly against the frost-bitten ground.

But the chill lingered, clawing at his skin, digging into the marrow of his bones. Even as they rode away, leaving the broken remains behind, he could feel it like a cold, invisible hand resting on the back of his neck.

He glanced over his shoulder once, twice, scanning the tree line, the shadows.

There was nothing. No movement. No sound.

But the feeling didn't leave. The sensation of being watched, of something dark and hungry tracking their every step, burrowed into their very souls. He clenched his teeth, hunching his shoulders against the phantom weight of it.

"It's still out there," he whispered, the words swallowed up by the silence.

Smifen shot him a sharp look, his face pale, drawn tight with worry. "What was that, Orin?" he murmured, voice low. His beast snorted beneath him, ears flicking nervously.

"Nothing," Orin muttered, shaking his head. "Just... keep moving."

Smifen didn't press, but Orin noticed the way his gaze kept drifting to the rear, to where Tidal rode, slumped and silent. Tidal's shoulders trembled with each step of his beast, his eyes fixed on the ground.

"We'll die like a crazed bitch," Tidal whispered suddenly, the words soft, trembling, barely audible. "Like fodder, in the dirt..."

Ferkin's head snapped around, a growl rising in his throat, but Maraco shot him a warning glare, silencing him with a look.

"We're not going to die," Maraco said quietly, his eyes hard. "We're going to find whatever did this. And we're going to kill it."

Tidal's gaze lifted, hollow and empty, meeting Maraco's. "But it's not a thing," he murmured, voice thin and quivering. "It's a curse. A shadow. It's—"

"Quiet," Maraco barked, his voice like a blade. "Not another word. Do you understand me?"

Tidal flinched, his mouth snapping shut. He nodded shakily, his eyes dropping back to the ground.

The rest of the ride was steeped in silence. No one spoke. No one even breathed too loudly, the weight of what had happened pressing down on them like a heavy shroud. Orin's fingers ached where they gripped the reins, the cold biting through his gloves. And still... still, he felt it. That presence, hovering just beyond the edges of his awareness. Staring. Waiting.

"Orin," Smifen murmured again, his voice a strained whisper. He leaned closer, eyes darting nervously around. "You think... you think it'll come for us?"

Orin shook his head slowly, his throat tight. "It's already here, Smifen."

Smifen went pale, his lips pressing into a thin line. They didn't speak again. They just rode, the silence thick, choking, as the forest closed in around them.

The ride back up the ravine felt like a slow, grinding crawl, the weight of what they'd seen trailing behind them like a dark shadow. The men moved in silence, eyes darting to the tree line as if expecting something—anything—to lunge out from the darkness. Each snap of a twig, each murmur of wind through the dead leaves sent ripples of tension through their ranks, shoulders tensing, hands tightening on reins. Tidal lagged, drifting aimlessly at the rear, his gaze distant, lips moving in a frantic murmur that none of them could catch. It was as if he were barely tethered to the present, floating somewhere far away.

Orin glanced back at him, a chill prickling at the nape of his neck. The lad looked like a ghost—pale, trembling, a stark reminder of the horror they'd left behind in that cursed ravine.

"Tree healer, you're with me," Maraco barked, his voice cutting through the stillness like a blade.

His tone brooked no argument. He caught Orin's eye, face set, jaw clenched tight. There was something simmering beneath his stony expression, a storm of emotions held just beneath the surface.

Orin nodded, nudging his snore forward to fall into step beside Maraco. The rest of the men shifted, shuffling their mounts back into formation with weary, jerky movements. The snores snorted and stamped, picking up on the tension, the unease. With a quick flick of his wrist, Maraco signaled, and the convoy began to lurch forward, a slow, ponderous march through the tangled undergrowth.

Ferkin drew up beside Orin, his breath hot and ragged against Orin's ear. "Well, that was a fucking sight, eh?" he muttered, a strange, twisted grin spreading across his face.

Orin blinked, taken aback. He turned his head to stare at Ferkin, disbelief tightening his chest. "What's so funny about it?" he snapped, his voice sharp with the anger that bubbled up, sudden and vicious.

How dare he laugh after what they'd seen—what they'd done? "What's funny, Ferkin?"

Ferkin met his gaze, eyes wild, shining with something feverish. His grin stretched wider, teeth bared in a manic parody of humor. "What's funny?" He let out a short, jagged laugh, a sound so out of place it sent a shiver down Orin's spine.

"What's funny is—"

But the words died on Ferkin's lips. His face crumpled, the grin shattering, twisting into something raw and desperate. He doubled over in his saddle, shoulders shaking as a hoarse, choked sob ripped free. The laughter turned into something else—something ragged and broken—a sound that tore at the edges of Orin's nerves. He clenched his teeth, fists tightening around the reins as he struggled to keep his own emotions in check.

"What the fuck is wrong with you?" Orin growled, the anger flaring again, hot and sharp. He saw it—the glisten of unshed tears in Ferkin's eyes—the way his shoulders hunched inward, trembling. Whatever had twisted Ferkin's mind, it wasn't humor. It was pain. Something deep, something old.

Lundor glanced over, brow furrowing as he caught the exchange. His gaze flicked nervously between them, confusion and unease etched across his features.

The laughter stopped abruptly, cut off as if a string had been severed. Ferkin bowed his head, his chest heaving with each shuddering breath. When he finally spoke, his voice was low, hoarse, and haunted.

"That woman's name… was Shyla," he whispered, the words almost lost in the rhythmic creak and sway of the convoy. He didn't look up, didn't meet Orin's gaze. Just stared down at the ground as if the dirt held all the answers. "I used to chase after her when I was a boy. I thought I was in love with her. Hell, I was in love with her."

He swallowed hard, throat bobbing. "Always told her I'd marry her one day. But she…" He let out a short, bitter laugh that was more sob than sound. "She used to throw rocks at me. Said she'd rather die than marry an idiot like me."

The words hung there, heavy, sinking into the silence like stones dropped into still water. Orin stared at him, the anger leeching away, leaving only a hollow ache in its place. He opened his mouth, but no words came. What could he say to that? What could anyone say?

"I guess she got what she wanted," Ferkin murmured, voice breaking. He lifted a trembling hand to swipe at his eyes, smearing dirt and blood across his face. "She's dead. She's... gone. And I..." He shook his head slowly, shoulders slumping. "I couldn't... I didn't..."

Orin reached out before he could stop himself, placing a hand on Ferkin's shoulder gently. "I'm sorry, Ferkin," he said quietly. The words sounded empty, hollow. Useless. But what else was there? "Are you okay, my friend?"

Ferkin didn't respond. He just stared blankly ahead, eyes red, unfocused. Then, slowly, he straightened, his expression hardening, mouth setting into a grim, thin line.

"No," he said simply. Then, more fiercely, each word a vow carved in stone: "I'm going to kill every last Flesher bitch. I'll make them suffer the same way. I'll make them beg for death."

There was nothing left of the laughing, joking man Orin had known. Only this—this raw, festering rage.

Orin opened his mouth to say something, anything to offer some kind of comfort. But the words stuck, caught in his throat. What could he say to a promise like that?

He glanced over at Lundor, hoping for help, for some sign of how to handle this. But Lundor looked just as lost, his gaze fixed firmly ahead, jaw clenched. There was no help there. No words that could ease this.

As the convoy trudged on, Orin let his gaze drift to the others, searching their faces. They were pale, drawn, eyes flicking back and forth nervously. And then he caught Lamar's gaze. Lamar gave him a small, tight nod, lips quirking in a strained attempt at a smile. But behind his eyes, Orin saw it. The same fear that twisted in his gut. The same shadow that darkened all their thoughts.

For a moment, Orin's mind drifted to Cal back home, his face lit up with excitement as he begged Shira for more stories, more tales of adventure and danger. Cal's voice rang in his ears, breathless and eager: "When can I fight with Father? When will I be old enough?"

The darkness wrapped around them like a heavy cloak as they trudged through the woods. Their leader's sharp command snapped everyone back to attention, and the weight of their experiences hung heavily in the air. The atmosphere was thick with shadows, the landscape transforming into an oppressive gloom, and the rhythmic sounds of the saddles creaking and hooves clopping provided a haunting backdrop to their journey. As the trees loomed taller and darker, their twisted branches reached out like clawing hands, draped in the unsettling crimson glow of the setting sun.

Among them, Ferkin remained motionless, his silence unsettling. He sat hunched over in his saddle, eyes cast downward, the simmering rage within him like wildfire waiting for the right moment to erupt. The others felt the tension emanating from him, an unhealed wound that festered beneath the surface.

"Hold!" Maraco's voice sliced through the stillness, commanding immediate compliance. The men halted abruptly, shifting nervously in their saddles, the horses snorting and pawing at the ground. Ears perked up as they strained to detect what had caught Maraco's attention.

A faint sound, almost imperceptible, began to reach their ears. It was the clash of metal, the low growl of men engaged in combat. A chill ran down their spines, and instinctively, hands tightened around the hilts of their weapons. Without hesitation, Maraco raised his horn to his lips and blew two long, mournful blasts that echoed through the trees, a call that felt both desperate and urgent.

The seconds stretched unbearably, each heartbeat amplifying the tension. Then, from deep within the woods, the response came—three short, sharp blasts that stirred a rush of relief.

"Move on!" Maraco bellowed, his stern demeanor softening into an uncharacteristic smile.

Beside him, Lundor's face lit up with disbelief. "More men," he whispered, as though the word held the promise of hope. "We might just have a chance, Orin. We might just survive this hell."

But the weight of unspoken fears kept their gazes fixed ahead, where flickering lights danced amid the dark trees. As they drew nearer, the sounds of voices mixed with the restless movements of beasts hidden in the shadows.

Suddenly, a hulking figure emerged from the darkness. He towered over them, a giant of a man with broad shoulders and thick arms. His wild hair, streaked with gray, framed a face marked by a deep scar running down his neck. Sharp, dark eyes swept over the group, assessing each weary face and haunted gaze.

"Maraco," he rumbled, his voice deep and resonant, echoing like a growl through the forest. "Dear little brother of mine."

In one fluid motion, Maraco dismounted, striding forward with a grin that momentarily lifted the heavy atmosphere. The two men embraced, the roughness of their connection a testament to the battles they had faced.

Yet, as they pulled apart, the smile faded from the older man's face. His gaze shifted, lingering on the hollow expressions and dried blood caked on their armor. "You look like hell, brother," he murmured, concern evident in his tone. "What happened out there?"

Maraco's expression darkened. "We have much to discuss, Jessup," he replied quietly, casting a glance back at his men.

His eyes rested on Ferkin, still simmering with unexpressed rage, then drifted to Tidal, who remained slumped at the rear, ghostly pale. Understanding passed between the brothers, but Jessup's focus shifted to Lundor. "Lundor, is that really you?"

Lundor's grin returned, wide and genuine. "Aye, it's me, you old brute," he replied, emotion thick in his voice.

Jessup's booming laughter erupted, echoing joyfully through the clearing. It was a sound so incongruous with the oppressive silence that it seemed to banish the shadows. "Too many years, my friends!" he roared, the joy infectious. "Too many damned years since we've hunted in these woods together."

With an expansive gesture, he beckoned them forward. "Come! You've had a long journey, brother. There's food and fire waiting. Rest, and in the morning..."

But as his expression shifted, something fierce and unrelenting took its place. "In the morning, we finish this."

The convoy rumbled into the camp, stirring up dust and the pungent scent of charred wood. All around, fires blazed fiercely, casting long shadows against the crimson-streaked sky, nearly obscuring the setting sun. The air was thick with the aroma of roasting rabbit, the fat dripping and sizzling over the open flames, mingling with the unmistakable scent of dixin fairy pies—golden, flaky pastries filled with spiced fruits. Rough-hewn tents were pitched in staggered rows, their faded colors blending seamlessly with the encroaching darkness of the forest, stretching back as if merging with the looming tree line.

Men clustered around the fires, their goblets sloshing with dark ale, voices rising in hearty, guttural song. Old battle hymns echoed off the tree trunks, filling the camp with an infectious energy. Women in tattered skirts or bare from the waist up straddled the laps of their partners, laughing and singing along, their high, merry voices adding to the chaos. The camp buzzed with a frenzied atmosphere, reminiscent of a festival, yet there lingered a darker undertone—an unspoken awareness that each breath, each bite of meat, and each stolen kiss could be their last.

"I see your men are in good spirits, brother," Maraco called, his voice barely rising above the din.

Jessup turned, a grin spreading across his face. The firelight danced across the scars crisscrossing his broad nose, and broken teeth flashed in his smile. "Yes, yes," he nodded eagerly. "A good night's feast, a whore to warm their beds, and a cup of strong ale does wonders. It makes for strong-spirited fighters on the battlefield."

Maraco chuckled, shaking his head in amusement. "I'm glad to see nothing has changed over the years."

Yet, Jessup's smile faltered, his gaze drawn to a large tent at the center of the encampment. Its canvas walls, stitched from the tanned hides of fallen Snores—enormous beasts whose pelts were sought after by kings—loomed ominously. The tent towered over the others, adorned with bone totems and fluttering red tassels that swayed gently in the evening breeze. The sight tightened Jessup's stomach; this was no ordinary war camp but a staging ground for something far more significant.

"Come, brother," Jessup urged, his voice lowering. "We need to speak of tomorrow's battle." He glanced over his shoulder, his expression shifting with seriousness. "Lundor, you should come as well. I value your opinion greatly."

Lundor stepped forward, a silent shadow beside Maraco. Towering over both men, he possessed an imposing presence, his long hair tied back in a single warrior's braid that hung down to his waist. He gave a stiff nod, his expression unreadable, yet his eyes gleamed with a mix of anticipation and resolve.

10
Squabble

The command tent buzzed with tension, the low murmur of soldiers preparing for battle outside creating an undercurrent of urgency. The canvas walls shivered in the night breeze, carrying in the mingled scents of iron and smoke. Maraco stormed to the center of the tent, his heavy boots thudding against the floorboards. The maps scattered under his sweeping hand as he glared across the table.

"We cannot let this intrusion into our land go unpunished!" he roared, slamming his fist onto the sturdy oak.

Goblets trembled and sloshed, and for a moment, the entire tent seemed to reverberate with his fury. His gaze, sharp as a blade, locked on Jessup. "We must do more than just win this battle. Devoro's been a thorn in our side for too long."

Jessup shifted, leaning forward. His brow furrowed, shadows dancing in the creases. "And you think we won't win?" His voice was low, measured—a challenge hidden within the words.

Lundor, perched lazily in his chair at the edge of the table, exhaled a stream of smoke. "What makes you so certain?" he drawled, barely lifting his gaze from the glowing embers of his pipe.

The chair creaked as he leaned back, the soft leather molding to his frame. "All I see is bloodshed and a fool's hope."

Jessup's eyes narrowed. He jabbed a finger into the table, right over the clustered marks of enemy formations. "We have the numbers. We have a strategy. And the Nephilim are with us." His voice grew taut, knuckles whitening on the map's edge. "Do you doubt our strength?"

Maraco's gaze flicked between them, his expression caught somewhere between impatience and concern. "Lundor's right about one thing—confidence is not a strategy. We need something decisive." He glanced at Jessup, his tone softening slightly. "Something that will make this more than just another skirmish."

A slow smile curled on Jessup's lips, something dangerous lurking behind it. "Oh, we'll have more than just strategy."

He leaned back, the atmosphere in the tent seeming to thicken around him. "We'll have a force that Devoro won't expect."

Lundor's brow furrowed. He shifted forward, the legs of his chair scraping against the floor. "What are you on about, Jessup?" His voice dropped low, suspicion edging each word.

Jessup's smile widened, teeth flashing like a predator scenting blood. "We're summoning Kronac."

The tent fell silent. Lundor's chair crashed to the ground as he surged to his feet, face twisted in rage.

"You *stupid* fool!" He rounded on Jessup, nostrils flaring. "The Kronac can't be controlled!"

"And why is that, old friend?" Jessup taunted, his calm demeanor unshaken by Lundor's outburst. "You're afraid of a weapon we can't tame?"

"A *weapon*?" Lundor spat, voice trembling with fury. "It's no more a weapon than a storm is! You can't wield it! You can only pray it doesn't destroy *everything*!"

Maraco stepped between them, his expression hard, eyes flicking uneasily to Jessup. "The scrolls are clear, brother. Kronac was created for war, but it answers to no master. Summoning it could be our undoing."

Jessup's grin didn't falter. He waved a dismissive hand. "Legends. Old wives' tales meant to keep lesser men from seizing real power. We'll bind it with the blood rites, as the ancients did."

"Blood rites?" Maraco's tone was sharp now, his fists clenching at his sides. "Those same rites left cities in *ruin*. You'd risk—"

"A chance at absolute victory?" Jessup interrupted, his voice silk over steel.

He glanced at Maraco, then Lundor, eyes glittering with ambition. "Yes, I would. Devoro won't know what hit them."

Lundor shook his head, his face pale beneath the heavy smoke. "You're mad," he whispered, stepping back as if the very idea tainted the ground where they stood. "Mad and blind. Kronac *will* turn on us."

"And if it doesn't?" Jessup's voice was soft now, almost coaxing. He leaned across the table, hands splayed as if to draw them in. "If it doesn't, we'll have a power that can crush Devoro once and for all."

Maraco exchanged a look with Lundor. Doubt flickered across his features, but beneath it, something else—a sliver of temptation. He shook his head, as if to dispel it. "And if it does? If Kronac turns?"

"Then we die," Jessup said simply, his smile fading. "But if we do nothing, we lose everything anyway."

He straightened, a steely determination settling over his features. "The question, my brothers, is whether we'll risk death for a chance at victory... or sit idle and watch our land burn."

The silence stretched, heavy and suffocating, until Lundor broke it with a soft, bitter laugh. "You always were a reckless bastard," he muttered. "Fine. Summon your beast. But know this, Jessup." He jabbed a finger at him, voice low and fierce. "When it comes for us—and it *will*—I'll put you down myself."

Maraco's jaw clenched, a flicker of resignation in his eyes. "Then it's settled," he murmured. "But we'll need more than blood rites to keep it bound. There are wards, chains—"

"There's *me*," Jessup interrupted, a gleam of something wild in his eyes. "I'll hold it."

"What a load of shit," Jessup spat, his hand slamming down onto the table's edge. The sudden movement sent the goblets clinking and the flame of the lanterns flickering. "Maraco, tell me you don't buy into these old wives' tales like Lundor does." His eyes locked onto Maraco's, blazing with a demand for support.

Maraco didn't respond immediately. His gaze dropped to the table, tracing the lines of the map absently, as if hoping the answer would reveal itself among the scattered terrain markings. He inhaled slowly, weighing each word before releasing them. "I don't put much stock in legends," he said at last, lifting his gaze to meet Jessup's. "But neither do I trust the

Kronac." His voice lowered, tense. "Such power…
it could be beneficial—if we're desperate enough.
But that's exactly why I'm urging caution, brother.
Summon him only if we have no other choice."

Lundor grunted, the sound more like a derisive
laugh than agreement. He rocked back in his chair,
arms crossed. "Did you hear that, Jessup? 'Only if we
have no other choice.' Even Maraco doesn't want to
dance with your monster."

Jessup's lips twisted into a snarl, his hand twitching toward the hilt of his sword before he stopped
himself. "I hear him just fine," he muttered. "But I
don't see either of you offering better solutions."

His voice dripped with frustration, but after a
long, tense moment, he exhaled sharply and nodded, though his eyes still burned with defiance.
"Fine. We'll leave it be—*for now*."

Lundor gave a heavy, exaggerated sigh, as if finally
putting down a burden. "Good. That's settled, then."
He reached down, hauling his chair upright and dropping into it with a creak of wood and leather. "Now," he
growled, grabbing the nearest jug of wine and splash-

ing the dark liquid into his cup. "Let's talk about a strategy—one that doesn't involve waking up nightmares."

Jessup watched him, fingers still toying with the hilt of his sword, the muscles in his forearm taut beneath the flickering torchlight. A slow smirk tugged at his lips. "Agreed," he murmured, though there was a glint in his eyes that spoke of defiance. "But if all else fails, it's good to know we have something... unpleasant in our back pocket." His smirk widened. "Just in case."

Maraco leaned back, shoulders easing as the tension slowly drained from the air. He raised his own cup, taking a long pull before setting it down with a firm clink. "Let's just hope it doesn't come to that," he said, shooting Jessup a pointed look. "For all our sakes."

Jessup held up his hands in mock surrender, his smirk never wavering. "Hope all you want. But plans change."

"Then we'll plan *better*," Lundor interjected sharply. He set his goblet down with a hard thud, leaning forward over the table. "Now, what do we have in terms of positioning? And someone get us more damn ale," he barked suddenly, his voice cutting through the thick, smoke-laden air.

The flap of the tent burst open, and a young squire stumbled inside, cheeks flushed and eyes wide. "Yes, my lords," he stammered, clutching a fresh jug of ale to his chest like a lifeline. He fumbled with the goblets, nearly dropping one in his haste as he poured.

"Careful, boy," Maraco muttered, reaching out to steady the jug. "There's no need to rush yourself into an early grave."

The squire blinked rapidly, nodding so hard his helmet wobbled on his head. "Of—of course," he breathed, filling each cup to the brim.

Lundor's face softened just slightly as he leaned back. "Good lad. Now, run along."

The squire scurried out, and the three commanders turned their eyes back to the maps, their earlier argument receding like a storm that had passed, but not entirely forgotten. The shadow of Kronac's name loomed over the table, unspoken yet tangible, like the scent of blood in the wind.

Maraco cleared his throat, his gaze still dark with lingering unease. "We'll push from the east," he said, tapping the map with a calloused finger. "The Ironwood line will give us a good vantage."

"And the river?" Jessup asked, his focus shifting sharply. "What of Devoro's forces there?"

"Scouts report they're reinforcing their position," Maraco answered. "But that could work in our favor. They won't be expecting us to break the dam and flood the pass. They'll have no other choice but to come along the Ironwood Line. There, we will set the Age's upon them"

Jessup's lips curled slightly, the earlier tension easing into something more calculating. "I see. We draw them in, giving us the upper hand—"

"Then crush them," Lundor finished with a satisfied grunt. "Force them into a slaughter." He took a deep drink from his goblet, eyes glinting over the rim. "Just like old times."

"Just like old times," Maraco agreed, a ghost of a smile tugging at his lips. He raised his goblet high, nodding toward his brothers-in-arms. "To strategy."

"To victory," Jessup corrected softly, his voice thick with a dangerous, almost feral edge

The camp roared with life around Orin—a chaotic symphony of warriors' shouts, the crackling of firewood, and the occasional sharp clang of metal on metal. Men bumped shoulders as they laughed and hollered, the gleam of their armor reflecting the dancing flames. A few clung to each other drunkenly, swaying like trees in a storm, while others sang bawdy songs that reverberated across the campsite.

Orin spotted Ferkin sitting alone, a shadow amidst the revelry. Usually, he would be in the center of it all, guffawing with a wench on each knee or tumbling with the lads in a rowdy mock fight. But tonight, he looked... broken. His shoulders sagged, and his gaze was distant, fixed on something unseen beyond the fire's reach.

"Hey!" Orin called out, striding over to him. "Why don't you come have a drink with me by the fire, old friend?"

Ferkin blinked, as if waking from a trance. His eyes, once sharp and full of life, seemed dull and clouded.

He stared at Orin blankly for a moment, then gave a slow, reluctant nod. Orin pulled himself off Aya, who was snorting softly as she shifted her weight. Her scales were thick with dust from the long march, and her heavy hooves left deep prints in the ground.

They found a spot near one of the larger bonfires, where a stout man sat with a flagon in one hand and a nearly naked woman perched on his knee. His bald head gleamed in the firelight, and his stomach jiggled with each chortle. The woman—a slip of a thing with long brown hair and a worn expression—sat stiffly, a forced smile plastered on her face.

The man squinted up at them, his small eyes narrowing suspiciously. "Well, now," he slurred, his gaze flitting between Orin and Ferkin. "What do we have here?" He belched, and the thick stench of sour beer rolled over them.

He wiped his chin with a thick hand, smearing drool across his tangled beard. "Orin," he said, keeping his voice light as he offered a smile. "And this here is Ferkin."

"Kefnop," the man grunted in return, his beady eyes lingering on Ferkin's hollow expression. "You look like a man in need of a drink," he said, a slow grin spreading across his face.

Before they could reply, Kefnop's fist tightened in the girl's hair, yanking her head back. She gasped, her eyes wide with pain. "Fix my friends a drink," he growled, his grip digging in until tears sprang to her eyes.

The girl managed a strained smile. "Of course," she whispered, her voice quavering.

"More for me too, sweetheart?" Kefnop sneered, his grin broadening.

"Of—of course," she stammered, prying herself from his grasp.

Orin saw the tear slip down her cheek, glistening in the firelight before she turned away, hurrying toward the supply tent, her bare feet whispering against the dirt.

Kefnop watched her go, chuckling. "Pretty little thing, isn't she?"

Ignoring him, Orin stared into the flames. The fire here burned blue, a strange, ghostly light that sent eerie shadows dancing across the campsite. "Charweed," he murmured, recognizing the peculiar glow.

Only the marshfolk to the south used such kindling. It made the flames brighter, hotter... and far more dangerous.

"Orin?" He glanced up sharply, spotting Lamar hovering at the edge of the firelight. The boy looked small and lost. His hands twisted nervously around the hem of his tunic. "Ferkin told me to stick close to you," he murmured.

Kefnop's gaze shifted, his grin widening. "What's this, then? A whelp among us horrid beasts?" He leaned forward, beady eyes gleaming with malicious glee. "How old are you, boy?"

Lamar straightened, trying to puff out his chest. "Nine," he answered, though his voice wavered.

"Nine!" Kefnop boomed, drawing the attention of the nearby soldiers. "Nine, and already running with killers?" He laughed, a cruel sound that grated on Orin's ears. "Tell me, boy—have you ever killed a man?"

Lamar's eyes darted to Orin's, pleading silently for help. "N-no, sir," he whispered.

"Ah, I see." Kefnop rubbed his beard thoughtfully, his grin turning sharp. "How about a whore then? Ever bedded one?"

Lamar shook his head, trying not to look directly at him.

Kefnop staggered to his feet, his right hand starting to unfasten his slacks. "Well then boy, let me teach you. You be the boy whore...I'll be the hard fuck from behind. What do you say? Only just got tonight."

The boy's face flushed crimson. He looked back at Orin, wide-eyed and trembling. But before Orin could speak, Ferkin moved. Slow and deliberate, like a flame meeting air. His hand dropped to the hilt of his sword, the blade gleaming faintly in the fire's eerie light.

Kefnop saw it, and his grin faltered. He leaned back, spreading his hands. "Come now, I'm only jesting—"

Ferkin's fist shot out, a blur of motion. The crack of bone against bone rang out, and Kefnop's head snapped back as he toppled over, crashing to the ground in a heap. Before he could even groan, Ferkin was on him, the tip of his sword pressed against the fat man's throat, drawing a thin line of blood. "Your shriveled cock touches anything tonight... I'll cut it off."

"You do talk after all," Kefnop wheezed, his lips curling into a bloody smile. He spat out a tooth, laughing hoarsely. "Go on then, finish it."

"Ferkin!" Orin shouted, stepping forward. "He's not worth it."

Ferkin's gaze flickered, the fire in his eyes dimming just a fraction. He looked around, noticing for the first time the silent ring of soldiers watching. Lamar stood at the edge of the circle, small and frightened.

"Do it, you coward," Kefnop spat, his voice thick with fury. "I dare you."

For a heartbeat, Orin thought Ferkin would do it. His jaw clenched, his grip tightened on the hilt of his sword, but then, slowly, he stepped back. "You're not worth the stain you'd leave on my blade," he muttered.

Kefnop staggered to his feet, clutching his bleeding nose. "Curse you!" he roared, spittle flying. "Curse you and your bastard children! You'll regret this!"

Before he could say another word, his foot caught a root, and he went sprawling face-first into the dirt. Laughter erupted around the camp, loud and raucous. Even Lamar, despite himself, giggled at the ridiculous sight of the once-proud Kefnop flailing on the ground.

"Call it a night," Orin said, still chuckling as he wiped a tear from his eye.

Kefnop scrambled up, his face a mask of rage. "This isn't over," he snarled, pointing a trembling finger at Lamar. "You won't always have your friends around, boy."

He turned and stormed off, limping and muttering curses under his breath.

Orin turned to Ferkin, still grinning. "It's good to have you back, old friend."

Ferkin merely grunted, rubbing his knuckles absently. He glanced at Lamar, his expression softening. "Stay close, boy. If I'm not around, stick with Orin."

Lamar nodded, a tentative smile breaking through his fear. "Thank you," he whispered.

"For what?" Ferkin grumbled. But as Lamar's smile widened, Ferkin's lips twitched into the closest thing to a smile Orin had seen from him in a long time. "You'll be fine with us, boy," he murmured.

And for the first time that night, Lamar's smile seemed genuine.

11
Nephilim

Early morning began with a warm, wet slap across Orin's face. He jolted awake, eyes wide, just as a thick, slobbering tongue dragged from his chin to his forehead, leaving a trail of gooey slime in its wake.

"Ugh! You stupid beast!" he grumbled, wiping the sticky mess off with his sleeve.

Aya snorted in what he could only describe as amusement. Her shaggy, mud-streaked hide twitched as she shook her head, sending droplets of muck flying. Then, with a cheerful huff, she bounded off, her heavy hooves thudding as she lumbered around the camp.

Orin sighed, rubbing the last of the muck from his eyes. The tent was small and cramped, the thin canvas barely holding off the morning chill. Beside him, Lamar was still curled up under his threadbare blanket, looking more like a lost goshen hopper than the man he pretended to be. In sleep, all the fear and defiance drained from his face, leaving him small and fragile. His fists were tucked under his chin, and a faint smile played on his lips.

"Sleep well, little one," Orin murmured softly, reaching out to gently tug the blanket higher over Lamar's shoulders.

Outside, the camp was already coming alive, the low hum of voices and clanking metal creeping through the thin tent walls. Orin took a deep breath, feeling the weight of the day ahead settle over him like a heavy cloak.

He slipped out quietly, pulling his own cloak tighter as a sharp wind cut through the clearing. The morning sun strained to pierce the dense Ironwood canopy overhead, casting long shadows that seemed to flicker like ghostly fingers over the rough-hewn tents and supply carts. Smoke from last night's campfires twisted lazily into the sky, the embers all but extinguished.

His stomach rumbled, a reminder that he hadn't eaten since midday yesterday. He glanced around, watching a few of the men crouched around the remaining coals, eagerly cramming their mouths with foraged mushrooms and the wriggling larvae of flies. The sight of them crunching through those squirming bugs made his insides twist.

"Blech. No, thank you," he muttered under his breath, swallowing back bile.

Movement caught his eye. There, half-hidden behind a splintered log, was a half-eaten dixin fairy pie. He hesitated, his nose wrinkling in distaste. The crust was hard and cracked, the filling probably on the edge of turning. But compared to a handful of wriggling larvae? He shuddered. Desperate times...

Orin crouched down, pulling the pie free from the dirt. The first bite was tentative, his teeth sinking cautiously into the crust. But to his surprise, the meat inside was still good, savory juices bursting across his tongue. He let out a quiet, relieved breath and tore into it, crumbs flying.

"Good morning to you too," came a low, familiar voice.

Orin looked up, still chewing, to see Ferkin looming over him. His grin stretched wide beneath the scraggly mess of his beard, mischief dancing in his eyes. "Didn't think you'd be so eager to eat dirt, Orin."

Orin swallowed hastily, raising an eyebrow. "I trust you had a more refined breakfast, then?" he shot back, gesturing to the empty flask hanging from Ferkin's belt.

Ferkin barked out a laugh that seemed to shake his whole frame. "If by 'refined,' you mean a swig of whatever swill I found in the bottom of that keg last night, then yes!" He dropped down beside Orin with a thud, his huge hand snatching up a chunk of pie. "But hells, this might be our last meal. Might as well enjoy it."

He bit into the stale crust, tearing through it like it was fresh bread. As he ate, Orin noticed the way Ferkin's fingers trembled, just slightly. To most, Ferkin was a mountain of a man, unshakable, unbreakable. But Orin knew better. He saw the fear lurking beneath the surface, the doubt Ferkin tried so hard to hide.

Their eyes met. Orin didn't say anything, just offered a small, knowing smile. "Me too," he murmured softly, trying to chase away the unease building in his chest.

They ate in silence, the quiet broken only by the camp coming to life around them. Men stumbled out of their tents, blinking against the pale dawn light. Armor clanged as buckles were tightened, straps adjusted. Voices hummed low and uncertain, edged with tension.

Orin took a swig from his flask, wincing at the taste. "Dandle beer's gone flat," he muttered, grimacing.

"Still better than no beer," Ferkin quipped, his grin turning wry. He nudged Orin's shoulder, then nodded toward Lamar, who was poking his head out of the tent, blinking sleepily. "Your shadow's up."

Orin turned, raising a hand in greeting. "Morning, Lamar. You hungry?"

The boy's face lit up briefly, but before he could answer, a rough, gravelly voice interrupted them. "You boys awake?"

They looked up to see Lundor standing there, his broad frame casting a long shadow across them. His face was lined with exhaustion, dark circles etched deep under his eyes. The grim set of his mouth made Orin's stomach twist.

"Yes, sir," Orin answered quickly, scrambling to his feet. "What's the news?"

"Scout news came in." Lundor jerked his thumb over his shoulder, toward the thick treeline that loomed like a wall at the edge of camp. "Scouts spotted movement. We break camp in an hour."

Ferkin's grin vanished. He set down the last of the pie, his shoulders straightened. "What kind of movement?" he asked, voice low and dangerous.

"Fleshers," Lundor growled, his gaze flicking to each of them in turn. "And more than we expected."

A cold chill swept through Orin. "How many?" he asked quietly.

Orin watched Lundor's mouth tighten, the old soldier's demeanor signaling the gravity of the moment. "Enough." The word hung in the air, heavy and suffocating.

"What's the plan?" came Ferkin's voice, a tightness evident in his jaw.

Lundor sighed, rubbing a hand over his weathered face. "Gather the men, break camp. We can't let them know we've spotted them. Until we break the dam and push them towards the Ironwood line."

"And if they find out?" Ferkin's voice was edged with concern.

"Then we fight." Lundor's tone was flat, eyes hardening with determination. "But we'll be damned if we go down without a plan."

Orin glanced at Ferkin, noting the humor that had vanished from his friend's face. "You heard him," he murmured, urging Ferkin to action. "Let's get moving."

"All right," Ferkin replied, though the gravity of the situation lingered between them.

"You must get your things together. We head out in ten minutes," Lundor ordered curtly, turning his back to them.

Ferkin's scowl deepened as he tossed the remaining crust of pie into the dirt. "Do you think we could at least take a moment to enjoy what might be our last meal before you start barking orders, old man?" His voice attempted levity, but the tension behind it was palpable.

Lundor didn't flinch. He glanced over his shoulder, his gaze distant as if he were peering through the canvas walls of the command tent where Maraco and Jessup were likely still locked in a debate over maps and strategies. "Ten minutes, and then we leave," he repeated softly, but the steel in his tone left no room for argument.

Orin swallowed hard, his appetite vanishing. He observed Lundor's hands, knotted and weathered, skin stretched tight over protruding veins. Yet those hands remained steady, more so than any man Orin had seen in camp.

"We must push the Flesher horde back to the pits they crawled out of...before worse comes," Lundor murmured, more to himself than to them.

His eyes drifted to a small, gnarled barken tree at the edge of camp, where an ancient, frail Snore lay nestled in its roots, wheezing heavily. "Delilah," he whispered softly.

The Snore's ears twitched, laboriously lifting itself upright. Nearby, a few men chuckled as it staggered, shaking its brittle tusks.

"Only you would name a beast after a temptress from the old tales," Ferkin scoffed, shaking his head.

Lundor ignored the comment, stepping forward to rest a hand against Delilah's snout, his expression softening. "Any great warrior deserves a name," he murmured. "And you, girl, are one of the greatest."

With a shudder, the Snore knelt with a groan, bowing its massive head. Lundor climbed onto her back with an agility that belied his age, straightening to fix them with a stern, unyielding gaze.

"Nine minutes," he said quietly, urging Delilah forward down the narrow path toward the camp's edge, his posture ramrod straight, shoulders squared as if he bore the weight of the world.

Ferkin stared after him, brow furrowed. "What in the spirits is he talking about?" he muttered, confusion creasing his features.

Orin shook his head, brushing the last crumbs from his mouth. "I don't know, but we'd better get ready.

When Lundor says, 'nine minutes,' he means nine minutes."

Ferkin's scowl faded, a mischievous grin taking its place. "Nine minutes, huh? Well, hells, I can make that work." With a quick nod, he spun on his heel and marched off toward his tent.

Taking a deep breath, Orin ducked back into his own small tent. "Lamar," he whispered, crouching beside the boy and giving his shoulder a gentle shake. "We have to go."

Lamar blinked up at him, eyes bleary with sleep. "Sister?" he mumbled, instinctively reaching out with his small hand.

"No, it's Orin," he said softly, smoothing the frayed blanket over the boy. "We're leaving soon. Get your things."

Lamar nodded slowly, rubbing his eyes and yawning, stretching his thin arms overhead. Orin straightened and stepped back out into the clearing.

The once-quiet camp had erupted into a frenzy of activity. Men stumbled into mismatched pieces of armor, cursing as buckles snagged or refused to latch. The sharp scent of sweat and fear mingled in the cool morning breeze as soldiers hurried to pack away the remnants of the camp. Women who had accompanied the army began filing out, clutching small bundles of coin as they headed toward the safety of the villages.

Orin glanced toward Ferkin's tent just as a shrill scream cut through the chaos.

A girl stormed out, cheeks flushed red, and Ferkin staggered after her, struggling to yank his trousers up around his hips. "Baby, wait! I was in a hurry!" he called, desperation creeping into his voice.

She spun around, eyes blazing. "Maybe next time, you can get it stiff!" she spat, hands on her hips.

Laughter erupted around them, loud and raucous. Even the nearby soldiers, struggling with their gear, paused to chuckle at Ferkin's plight. He flushed scarlet, yanking his trousers up as he glared at the camp.

"Shut up, all of you!" he snarled, stalking past the jeering men, his ears burning.

Orin bit back a grin, shaking his head as Ferkin stormed over. "Didn't even last nine minutes, did you?"

"Fuck it, Orin," Ferkin growled, though the corner of his mouth twitched.

Before Orin could reply, a long, low horn blast silenced the camp. All eyes turned toward the main path as Maraco and Jessup rode into view, their armor polished to a blinding sheen in the pale morning light. Maraco's helm caught the sun's weak rays, casting long, jagged shadows across his face, while Jessup's expression remained grim beneath his visor.

"Men!" Maraco's voice rang out, strong and commanding. "You have gathered here today to fight for this land of ours…"

His words echoed through the clearing, each syllable heavy with purpose. "We face a horde unlike any we've fought before. A mindless, ravenous force that will not stop until we are ground to dust beneath its heel." He paused, allowing the weight of his words to settle. "But I look out at you, at all of you, and I see strength. I see courage. I see men willing to stand against the darkness and drive it back!"

A murmur rippled through the gathered soldiers. Some nodded, while others clenched their fists around the hilts of their weapons. Jessup leaned forward in his saddle, his gaze hard and unflinching. "And when the Fleshers break upon us, when the battle is at its fiercest, remember that we do not fight for power or gold." He raised his sword high, the blade gleaming in the morning light. "We fight for each other!"

A roar erupted from the men, a sound that shook the very camp. Ferkin bellowed along with them, his earlier embarrassment forgotten, his face flushed with battle lust. Orin, too, raised his voice, caught up in the rising tide of emotion. The roar swelled, a great, living thing that surged forward, hungry and unafraid.

Jessup's voice boomed across the clearing, cutting through the clatter of armor and the low murmurs of the men. Every head turned; every grumbling word and nervous joke died in their throats. "We are faced with a threat that has no claim in Terra." Jessup's eyes swept over the sea of soldiers, lingering on the youngest recruits struggling to mount their unruly Snores, then shifting to the veterans whose hard gazes spoke of too many battles fought and survived. "I expect nothing less than the utter annihilation of this vile horde."

Another roar erupted from the men. The snores stamped and pawed, tossing their heads as if they understood the command. The soldiers buzzed with an electric energy—a volatile mix of fear, rage, and raw anticipation that sent shivers down Orin's spine. The camp seemed to surge, like a beast waking from a long, restless slumber.

Jessup turned slightly in his saddle, glancing back at his brother, who stood behind him, his face as unreadable as ever. "Maraco, some words of encouragement before we set out?" he asked, raising an eyebrow.

The camp fell silent again as Maraco rode forward. His Snore, a dark, twisted creature with a single gnarled tusk and eyes that glowed eerily in the low light, shifted beneath him. The beast snorted, its muscles rippling under its coarse scales as it came to a stop beside Jessup. Maraco looked around slowly, taking his time as his gaze roved over the men.

"We will meet this threat at the Ironwood Tree line," he began, his voice low and steady. "When the fight starts, you will stand your ground. Do not break formation."

The soldiers exchanged uneasy glances. This wasn't the fiery battle cry they had been expecting—the kind of speech to make hearts pound and blood sing. Instead, Maraco's words were clinical, almost detached, like a healer laying out the steps of a gruesome operation.

Jessup leaned closer, a bemused smile tugging at his lips. "I meant some encouragement, brother," he murmured.

Maraco's eyes flicked to him, a faint spark of amusement in his gaze. "Encouragement?" He turned back to the men, cleared his throat, and raised his voice. "It is written in the stone before stones that our greatest ancestors before our age began were stagnant in their quest for knowledge. They did not believe in the great spirits or our Mother. Instead, they were plagued by false writings from a book written by man himself."

A ripple of confusion swept through the crowd. Men shifted uneasily in their saddles, some frowning, others scratching their heads.

"This book, written by man, caused them to wage war on their own brothers, who followed yet another book, written again by man for man. It is said they fought to the bitter end with the powers of the great mushrooms that once covered all Irada." Maraco's voice was calm, almost contemplative, as if he were discussing history with a group of scholars instead of rallying troops for war.

Orin caught Jessup sighing loudly, shaking his head. "I think you're starting to bore them, not excite them, brother."

But Maraco didn't falter. His eyes blazed with sudden intensity. "Our lost ancestors fought, murdered, and died for dusty old books riddled with hatred and lies. They tore each other apart for nothing but the hollow promises of false gods. But we—" He paused, sweeping his gaze over the men again, and this time they leaned forward, their attention caught by the force of his words. "We know the truth. Our Mother is great and powerful. We see her eye day and night, growing larger each day as she feeds on the sun and moon. She watches over us from the cosmos, and she will help us defeat this evil horde of Fleshers."

A murmur rippled through the crowd, confusion giving way to something warmer: hope. Maraco drew his sword, the blade gleaming like molten silver in the morning light.

"We will send them to the dirt," he shouted, his voice rising to a fierce crescendo. "With the strength and might of the Lowlanders and our great Mother's bless-ing. We will not perish today! We will not show mercy to Him's vile creation today! We will be written into history so that your Bastards, bastards, bastards will tell his little sons of whores that their blood showed Lowlander rage this day."

This time, the roar that went up was deafening. Men slammed their swords against their shields, Snores bucked and growled, and the earth itself seemed to tremble under the force of their cries. Orin's heart surged, pounding in time with the rhythm of the war drums. Even he found himself caught up in the fervor, the rush of emotion like a tidal wave sweeping him along.

Maraco turned sharply, sheathing his sword with a decisive motion. "Move out!" he ordered, his voice cracking like a whip.

The camp erupted into a flurry of activity. Men leapt into their saddles, Snores huffed and pawed at the ground, and armor clanked as weapons were hoisted and shields secured. Jessup shot a look down at Lun-dor, who sat stiffly atop Delilah, his gaze fixed on the Tree line ahead.

"Keep an eye on them, old friend," Jessup murmured softly. "We'll need your steady hand before the day is done."

Lundor nodded once, his face as grim and unyielding as stone. "I'll do what I can."

With a final nod, Jessup and Maraco spurred their Snores forward, riding to the head of the column. The men followed in a chaotic rush, some barely managing to control their mounts as the beasts snorted and stamped, sensing the rising tension in the air.

"Stay close," Orin whispered to Lamar as he lifted him onto his Snore's broad back. The boy clung to the reins, his knuckles white and eyes wide with fear. Orin swung up behind him, wrapping a protective arm around his trembling frame. "I won't let you fall."

Lamar glanced back at him, his face pale. "Promise?"

"I promise," Orin murmured, squeezing his shoulder gently. "I'll be right here."

A shout drew Orin's attention. Behind him, a thin man wrestled with his own Snore, the creature bucking and shaking its head as he struggled to mount. His armor—an ill-fitting mishmash of plates that looked as if they'd been scavenged from a dozen battle-fields—rattled with each jolt.

He finally managed to swing himself into the saddle, panting heavily. "By the spirits, I've never seen such a force!" he called, catching Orin's eye. His grin was strained but determined. "Truly, we will be victorious!"

Orin forced a tight smile, nodding. "Let's hope so," he replied, but a cold dread coiled in his gut.

The men might be fired up now, ready to charge headfirst into the fray, but he couldn't shake the un-easy feeling that, before the day was done, they'd all be swallowed by the dark tide lurking beyond the tree line.

The hours dragged by as Orin trudged through the dense woods, the weight of what awaited them press-ing down like the thick mist curling at their feet. The early morning light, which had barely managed to pierce the canopy's thick weave, now streamed through in bright, broken rays, splashing fragments of sunlight onto the forest floor. Lamar squinted against the harsh contrast, his small frame shifting uneasily atop his Snore.

"Look up there," Orin murmured, tapping the boy's arm gently and gesturing ahead.

Lamar blinked, his gaze following Orin's finger until it landed on what lay before them—a tightly woven barrier of ironwood trees. Their gnarled trunks and massive limbs bent and twisted together, forming a seamless wall of living wood. From where they rode, it appeared almost solid, like an impenetrable fortress stretching endlessly in both directions, blocking any view of what lay beyond.

"What is that?" Lamar whispered, his voice tinged with awe as he took in the colossal structure.

Sunlight glinted off the dark bark, casting long, shadowy fingers that seemed to writhe and shift on their own. "This," Orin murmured, keeping his tone low as if speaking too loudly would shatter the spell of the place. "Is the last line of defense for the Lowlanders. Beyond this point, only the bravest of our scouts dare to venture."

Lamar swallowed hard, his small hands tightening on the reins. "Why is it... why does it look like that?"

Orin glanced up at the interwoven branches, their twisted shapes blocking out most of the sky. "It was grown this way, woven and shaped over centuries by understanding. It keeps us safe... and keeps what's out there from coming in."

A rustling to their left made them both turn. Ferkin, riding his massive, armored snore, approached slowly, his beast's tusks clicking as it snorted. He leaned forward in his saddle, pointing toward a small clearing just off the path. There, a group of eight figures stood in a loose circle, shrouded in deep green cloaks trimmed with crimson lace. Their hoods were pulled low, shadowing their faces, and what little skin showed was hairless and smooth, like pale, polished marble.

"What in the spirits are they doing?" Ferkin asked, his tone edged with suspicion. His gaze flicked between the eerie group and the looming ironwood wall ahead of them.

"I believe… they're the Ages," Orin muttered, his eyes locked on the men as they began to move in slow, deliberate patterns.

Every step seemed to resonate through the forest, as if the ground itself recognized their presence. "The Ages?" Ferkin echoed, frowning. "Weren't they supposed to be some kind of—"

"Guardians," Orin interrupted softly. "Protectors of the border."

Ferkin grunted, but Orin could see the unease in his eyes. The Ages spread their arms wide, fingers splayed as they tilted their heads back, necks craning painfully. The eldest—a man whose face was creased and lined like withered parchment—opened his mouth and began to hum, a deep, resonant sound that seemed to vibrate through Orin's very bones. One by one, the others joined in, each voice matching the note perfectly until the air buzzed with their eerie harmony.

"What is this?" Lamar whispered, his eyes wide.

The sound grew, swelling until it seemed to fill the entire forest. Then, abruptly, the hum broke, replaced by a sharp, rhythmic chant that sent a chill racing down Orin's spine: "Veni vocare nos tibi defensiva tutores, Veni vocare nos tibi defensiva tutores."

The words echoed in the clearing, each syllable charged with a strange, almost physical energy. The earth beneath the Ages shuddered, dirt and leaves trembling as if something massive stirred below. A pale yellow light—sickly and unnatural—began to glow at the center of their circle. It started as a faint pulse, then flared brighter, spilling out from the cracks in the soil like molten gold.

The ground buckled and caved inward, a pit opening in the center of the clearing. From its depths, a blinding radiance erupted, searing the air with its intensity. Then, a roar—deafening and primal—burst forth, shaking the trees around them. The ironwood wall trembled, the massive trunks groaning in protest.

"Nephilim!" Ferkin's shout was nearly lost in the chaos as he yanked his sword free, eyes wild.

From the pit, a beast began to rise. It clawed its way up, massive shoulders rippling with an ancient power. The creature towered over them, dwarfing even the largest Snore. Its hide was black and coarse, covered in jagged ridges like the hardened skin of some forgotten monster. Thick veins glowed a sickly yellow beneath its fur, pulsing like molten lava.

Twin suns of malevolent light burned where its eyes should have been. They swept over Orin and Lamar, locking onto their small forms with a gaze so intense it felt like a physical weight pressing down on Orin's chest. Aya shifted nervously beneath him, and he tightened his grip on the reins, heart pounding.

The beast reared up, its roar tearing through the forest like a physical blow. It crashed back down, sending a shockwave through the earth that nearly unseated Orin. He heard Lamar cry out, felt him flinch as the creature loomed over them, its breath hot and fetid.

"We summon thee to defend," the Ages intoned, their voices calm and steady even as the ground cracked and splintered beneath the beast's massive weight.

The Nephilim' gaze shifted to them, its eyes narrowing. It lowered its head slowly, a low, rumbling growl vibrating through the clearing.

"Stand back!" Orin hissed, pulling Lamar closer. "Keep still!"

The boy's breath hitched, but he didn't move, his eyes glued to the monstrous figure before them. Orin could feel him trembling, every muscle in his body taut with fear.

Orin watched as Ferkin's Snore stamped the ground, nostrils flaring. "In all the spirits… that thing, I thought they were not actually real!" he growled, but Orin couldn't answer. He was too focused on the beast, which radiated menace with every movement.

"Veni vocare nos tibi defensiva tutores," the Ages chanted again, their voices merging into a single, resonant note.

The Nephilim hesitated, lowering its head slowly—almost reluctantly. The light in its eyes dimmed, and the harsh, savage edges of its form began to blur and soften. It folded its limbs, crouching low until its belly touched the ground, gaze fixed on the Ages.

"We summon thee to defend," the eldest member repeated softly, stepping forward.

A rumble escaped the beast's throat, a sound reminiscent of distant thunder. It turned its head slightly, eyes flicking toward Orin and Lamar before returning to the Ages.

"Protect us," the man whispered, his voice barely audible over the crackling energy that buzzed in the air. "Guard us from the darkness beyond."

Slowly, the beast nodded. A low, guttural growl escaped, but it held still, waiting.

Orin let out a breath he hadn't realized he was holding. "They've tamed it," he murmured, half in disbelief.

Ferkin snorted in reply. "Tamed?" He shook his head, eyes never leaving the beast. "No... they've bound it."

Though the tension in the atmosphere didn't fade, it shifted, settling into something dark and simmering, like a storm held at bay. The Nephilim watched them with eyes gleaming like molten gold, a silent threat lurking in its depths.

"Let's keep moving," Orin urged, nudging Lamar's Snore forward. "Whatever that thing is, I don't want to be here when it decides to break free."

Ferkin grunted in agreement, casting one last wary glance at the hulking beast. "Aye... let's go."

The ground around the yellow pit seethed and bubbled, the soil writhing as if it were alive. Another monstrous head broke free of the earth, then another—two more Nephilim clawed their way up from the glowing abyss, each as nightmarish as the first. They shook themselves, sending clods of dirt flying as they stretched and roared, their cries blending until the forest itself trembled.

"Well, I never in all my life," came a voice dripping with arrogance—Jessup from the town hall. He shoved his way forward, his Snore grumbling irritably as it shouldered past the tightly packed ranks.

"Yes, yes, what do you think, little brother?" Jessup prodded, eyes alight with excitement.

He leaned forward, gaze flicking to Maraco, who sat rigid in his saddle, slack-jawed, staring at the titanic beasts. Before Maraco could respond, Lundor's no-nonsense voice cut through the tension. "I believe, Jessup, that we should prepare for battle."

Maraco blinked, as if waking from a spell. "Prepare for battle!" he roared, his voice booming across the clearing.

The camp erupted into motion. Soldiers snapped into formation, their Snore mounts jostling and grunting as they shifted into tightly packed ranks. Tusks clashed as the beasts snorted and stamped, their massive heads swinging into place. Archers scrambled up the trees, nimble as cats, disappearing into the thick foliage above. The creak of bowstrings being drawn echoed through the woods as they took their positions, arrows ready.

The Ages, their ritual complete, moved silently to the base of the ironwood wall, resuming their eerie, resonant hum. The sound vibrated through the trees, blending with the guttural growls of the pacing Nephilim.

"Lamar, stay close!" Orin shouted, twisting in his saddle to find the boy amid the chaos.

"Yes, sir!" Lamar called back, voice trembling yet steady.

He maneuvered his Snore beside Orin's, eyes wide as he flicked between the towering beasts and the men assembling around them.

"Nothing to worry about, kid," came a gruff voice from behind.

Orin turned to see Tidal pushing his way forward, his Snore snorting softly as he brought it to a stop beside them. His face was flushed with determination, the lines of tension in his shoulders tight, but his eyes were clear and steady.

"Nice to see you've decided to join us again," Ferkin quipped, one brow arched.

Tidal's cheeks darkened, but he squared his shoulders. "I lost my calm before, but I assure you, it won't happen again."

His jaw set, and despite the chaos, he looked almost defiant. Orin leaned over, clapping him on the shoulder. "These are hard days, Tidal. We need men like you."

Orin glanced around at the younger soldiers nearby, boys not much older than Lamar, all pale-faced and trembling. They watched Tidal, eyes darting nervously from him to the massive Nephilim and back. He raised his voice just enough for them to hear. "I- I- I think we keep going, no matter what."

Murmurs of agreement rippled through the group, small nods and stiffened backs. He caught a few of them straightening, shoulders squaring as they exchanged glances. Fear still clung to them, but something else brewed beneath the surface.

Lundor, standing tall atop his Snore, surveyed the assembled ranks. His voice rang out, calm and firm, carrying over the clamor. "Our scouts report that the Fleshers will reach us before the last light fades."

The men fell silent, every eye turning to him. Seven hundred soldiers, their faces grim and set, armored and armed. Some were warriors, scarred veterans of a dozen skirmishes. Others were farmers, bakers, and craftsmen who'd never held a blade before today. But every one of them looked up at Lundor, their gazes hardening as they waited.

Orin listened intently as Lundor spoke, his voice strong and resonant. "We are from all walks of life," he declared. "Warriors, bakers, farmers—yet today, we stand together."

A cheer erupted from the gathered soldiers, rough and wild, surging through the camp like a breaking wave, raw and fierce. Orin felt the energy in the air, an electrifying mix of hope and determination.

Beside Lundor, Jessup rose in his saddle, standing tall. "In years to come, when your bastard children ask of your deeds, you'll tell them of this day!" He raised his sword high, the blade gleaming in the pale light. "The day when evil dared cross our borders and was met with fire and rage!"

The cheer transformed into a deafening roar. Men beat their chests, swords clanged against shields, and Snores bucked and stamped, shaking the very ground beneath them. Orin noticed Lamar's eyes shining, his chest puffed out with something resembling pride. Even Tidal, his face still flushed, joined the cacophony, his voice hoarse but fierce.

Orin opened his mouth to join the rallying cries when something caught his eye. A shape, small and hunched, lurked just beyond the edge of the clearing. His blood ran cold as he recognized the twisted, gaunt figure half-hidden in the shadows of the ironwood wall. It was Kefnop. The man watched them with that same oily smile, his eyes fixed on Orin. A shiver crept down his spine as Kefnop tilted his head, grinning wider.

"Orin, what's wrong?" Lamar's voice was small, strained, pulling him back to the present.

Orin shook his head, forcing a tight smile. "Nothing, kid. Just... just stay close."

But as the men roared their defiance, their voices echoing through the forest, Kefnop's smile only widened. He took a slow, deliberate step back, his gaze never leaving Orin's, then another, and another, until he melted into the shadows.

Orin's heart pounded—not from the fervor of the rallying cries but from a sense of foreboding. What was Kefnop doing? He knew the man was a coward, trouble waiting to happen, yet there was something unsettling in his smile that made Orin's skin crawl.

"Stay alert," he murmured, barely audible over the din. "Eyes sharp."

Ferkin glanced at him, brow furrowing with concern. "What's the matter?"

Orin shook his head again, eyes still fixed on the spot where Kefnop had disappeared. "I don't know," he muttered. "But I've got a bad feeling."

"Of course you do," Ferkin grumbled, but his gaze sharpened, scanning the tree line.

Around them, the men prepared for battle, unaware of the dark figure that had watched from the shadows. Even as they shouted their defiance, Orin couldn't shake the nagging feeling that Kefnop had seen something they hadn't—something that could turn their cries of victory into screams of terror before the day was through.

12
They're Here

Time crept slowly forward as the men stood vigil, straining their ears for any sign of the approaching enemy. The quiet stretched on, every minute dragging like a weight, while the weary Terra soldiers shifted restlessly in the shadows. Aya, sensing the unease, began to fidget, her massive form stirring as she ground her tusks against the ironwood roots, sending up a spray of bark and splinters. One of the men reached out to soothe her, murmuring softly.

"Maybe they decided to turn back?" a voice rang out, shattering the tense silence. It was bold, filled with the brittle edge of impatience.

"Maybe we're in the wrong place?" another man called, this time softer, tinged with doubt and hope.

Their whispers turned to low murmurs, and soon the men were grumbling openly, talk of abandoning the vigil spreading like a ripple across a pond. Observing them, the tension began to fray at the edges of their discipline. But more than that, Ferkin stood out. He hadn't joined in the chatter. Instead, he sat stock-still, eyes wide and darting about as though searching for something invisible. His silence was a warning, one that others heeded with a growing knot of unease.

"What's wrong with you?" someone hissed, leaning closer.

Ferkin didn't answer. His hands were clenched in his hair, fingers digging into his scalp as if trying to claw something out. His chest rose and fell in ragged gasps.

"Ferkin!" another man snapped, shaking him by the shoulder. "What's going on?"

"They're coming," he breathed, the words trembling on his lips. "I can hear them in my head—thousands of them."

His voice was hollow, laced with a terror never heard from him before. The men glanced around, their hearts pounding. The forest was silent. Nothing moved among the ironwood's twisted roots, no sound stirred the air save for the men's soft mutterings.

"I don't hear anything," one said sharply. "Pull yourself together."

"It's not out here," he whispered, clutching at his chest as though something within him was tearing apart. "It's inside me. They're in my spirit, Orin. Tugging and screaming."

Eyes began to turn their way, the men's conversations fading into uneasy silence. Fear was spreading, rippling out from Ferkin like a plague. He was shaking now, his face pale and slick with sweat, eyes wild and unfocused.

"Don't you hear them?" he moaned, louder now, his voice cracking. "Oh spirits, they're so loud... they're calling my name."

"Ferkin, stop!" came the bark, glancing around at the others. "You're scaring the men. There's nothing there—"

"Yes!" he shrieked, hands clamping over his ears. "Yes, I hear you!" His voice surged, a rising crescendo of agony. "GET OUT OF MY HEAD!"

With a choking sob, he crumpled forward, slumping over the saddle. Panic surged in the chest of one nearby, but before they could react, a shrill scream tore through the dawning light.

"They found me! There are so many of them!" The cry came from one of the lookouts, high in the branches.

Men scrambled, hands going to weapons, eyes darting wildly. Maraco tried to rally them, shouting for calm, but another scream split the remaining calm, then another. The camp unraveled into chaos, soldiers shouting and stumbling back as if the very shadows were attacking.

Lundor surged forward, grabbing Maraco's arm. "Sound the horn! They're here!"

The signal blast echoed through the ironwoods, a desperate call that seemed to resonate with the terror gripping every heart. In that moment, it was clear Ferkin's cries weren't madness; they were a sickening greeting. And they had not been willing to say hello.

Before Maraco could lift his horn for a second blow, an ear-splitting screech erupted from the depths of the darkened tree line, slicing through the stillness like a blade. The shriek reverberated through bone and marrow, making even the air vibrate in agony. The men instinctively clasped their hands over their ears, grimacing and bending at the waist, but no gesture could shield them from the onslaught. The sound was a visceral force, raw and relentless, searing through their skulls like a fiery needle.

The snores growled and reared, stomping furiously, their own bellows drowned by the monstrous shrieking. They clashed back and forth in confusion, tossing their massive heads as they snapped their thick jaws. Even the Ages, who stood at the periphery of the forest, weaving their chants into the ground, swayed uneasily. Their rhythmic humming faltered, slipping into discord as they clutched their temples, mouths contorting in silent pain.

"Oh, Great Mother, they're here," Ferkin wheezed, voice strained and eyes wide with dread.

His fingers dug into his chest, grasping at the fabric as if trying to tear something free from beneath his ribs. A new pressure surged behind the eyes of those nearby. There was a brutal, unyielding force that swelled with each heartbeat. It felt as if a hand had gripped their skulls, squeezing tighter and tighter, the pain blooming like a white-hot fire that threatened to split their heads apart. They clenched their eyelids shut, hoping to contain the sensation, but it was like trying to hold back a tide.

Suddenly, as abruptly as it began, the noise ceased. The silence that followed was jarring, thick and heavy, as if the world itself had taken a breath and forgotten to release it.

The men staggered, their faces pale and smeared with rivulets of blood. They blinked sluggishly, as if waking from a nightmare, wiping their ears with trembling fingers. The snores quieted, panting heavily, their eyes rolling in their sockets.

"Get back here!" Lundor bellowed, his voice raw and frantic. A few of the men had turned and were sprinting away, abandoning their posts, their weapons clattering uselessly to the ground as they fled toward the closest village.

Maraco, still kneading his earlobes in a vain attempt to quell the persistent ringing, turned to face Lundor, who was yanking on his snore's reins, trying to urge the massive beast around to pursue the deserters. "Let them go, my friend," Maraco said, his tone steady despite the chaos.

Lundor's gaze snapped to Maraco, wild and desperate, his eyes bulging. He looked every bit the cornered animal. "We need them all to fight!" His voice was high-pitched, verging on hysteria.

Maraco stepped forward, his presence like a bulwark against the storm, and slapped a heavy hand on Lundor's back. "No," he said softly, his words calm but ironclad. "We only need the ones who won't die easily."

Lundor's panic flickered, then dimmed as he slowly nodded. He swallowed hard and turned his gaze toward the hulking figures of the Nephilim who were roaring and charging into the darkness of the woods, their massive feet churning the earth into mud. He absently ran his fingers over the coarse, raised lines of the scar across his chest, the mark of an old, near-fatal wound. His expression hardened as he turned back toward the line of men who remained.

"They're coming!" a voice cried out, high and sharp, echoing through the trees.

The line of the forest seemed to ripple, the dark silhouettes of the ironwood branches shuddering as if alive. The massive limbs, normally as unyielding as iron bars, snapped and twisted like brittle twigs under an unseen force.

Maraco's eyes narrowed. He turned sharply toward the Ages, who had regrouped, their pale faces strained but resolute. He took a deep breath and shouted, "Now! Do it now!"

In unison, the Ages shifted their chant. The low, harmonious hum gave way to a new rhythm, words spilling from their lips in a powerful cadence: "Arbor spiritu tuo uti tuerentur terra vestra."

Their voices carried a primal authority, resonating deep within the soil and bark. The ironwood trees responded, their branches creaking and groaning as they intertwined, wrapping and twisting around each other with serpentine grace. A shiver ran down Maraco's spine as he watched the trees bend and sway, forming an impenetrable wall of wood and thorns. On the other side of the barricade, shrieks and snarls erupted viciously with desperate sounds of creatures caught in a trap.

The area grew thick with the smell of blood and burning flesh. A dense, black mist rose from the far side of the ironwood barrier, swirling and coiling upwards like a sinister bloom. It spread rapidly, darkening the sky, its inky tendrils writhing as if alive.

"What in the—what is that?" an arrogant man, Duoslum, gasped, his eyes wide and uncomprehending as he took a step back.

"Bits and pieces of finely ground fleshers," a man nearby shouted, his voice tinged with something that might have been hysteria or grim satisfaction. "Carried up by the wind."

Jessup gripped his sword tightly in his left hand as the sound of screeching and shrieking filled the bound wall, growing louder and more menacing with each passing minute. Every nerve in his body was taut, his muscles coiled, ready to spring at the first sign of a breach. The air smelled of sweat, dirt, and the sickly-sweet rot of the fleshers' stench. He cast a sidelong glance at Maraco, whose posture was as stiff as the great ironwood trees. His eyes locked on the quivering branches above.

"Do you think this will hold them back, brother?" Jessup's voice was low and tight, edged with a worry he dared not show the men.

Maraco's lips twitched into a brief, thin smile, more a ghost of reassurance than a true expression. "I think the Great Mother watches over us this day," he replied softly, though the confidence in his words wavered, betraying a flicker of doubt.

His fingers tightened on the hilt of his own blade, knuckles bone white. The sun hung lower in the sky, its light filtered through the dense canopy above, casting a web of dancing shadows across the battlefield. Each fleeting movement seemed to mock the men's efforts, teasing at unseen terrors lurking just beyond their reach. And still, the fleshers came in waves of twisted, nightmarish forms; their distorted limbs clawed desperately at the walls of the spellbound barricade that shimmered faintly in the dim light. The wall itself seemed to breathe, vibrating with each impact, tendrils of crackling energy lashing out as if in pain or fury. Every few minutes, the men would retreat a step as the barrier leaned dangerously, groaning under the relentless assault, only to surge forward again, reinforced by the chanting of the spellweavers hidden behind the ranks.

Maraco could only imagine the horrors on the other side. He envisioned creatures with hollow eyes and teeth like jagged shards of bone, driven by a hunger that knew no end. He shuddered, unwilling to let his mind dwell too long on what might break through if the wall finally fell.

"Push forward!" Jessup bellowed, his voice cutting through the din as another wave smashed against the barricade with such force that the entire structure buckled, the top bowing down like a tree caught in a hurricane wind.

The men at the front row gritted their teeth, ramming their shoulder braces against the wall's base to keep it from collapsing. Wood and metal groaned in protest; the spell-bound carvings etched into the timber glowed fiercely as they strained under the pressure.

"Alright, you sons of rotting whores, PUSH!" Jessup roared, a savage grin twisting his lips as he spurred the men on.

The soldiers responded like one creature, the beasts tethered to the rear—massive snores, hulking creatures of muscle and sinew—digging their iron-shod hooves into the earth, straining against their harnesses. The ground trembled beneath their feet as the creatures let out bellowing cries, their immense strength adding weight to the men's desperate efforts. The wall shuddered, its bending arc straightening ever so slightly.

"Hold it! Hold it!" one of the voices screamed as the fleshers on the other side shrieked and wailed, their bony limbs tearing at the wood with frantic, clawing motions.

The barrier pulsed with a sickly green light, and Lamar, a young charge of the group, edged forward, his eyes wide with fear and determination. "Where are you going, boy?" the older figure growled, grabbing the leather straps around the neck of Lamar's snore and jerking it back.

"I was going to help push," Lamar said, his voice trembling but earnest.

His face was set, stubbornly resolved despite the terror etched in his wide eyes. "Not today." The older figure tightened his grip on the reins and leaned in close, staring hard into Lamar's face. "You'll have your chance to fight, Lamar."

He released the straps and instead laid his hand gently on the boy's shoulder. Lamar's pulse thumped wildly beneath the older man's fingertips. "But now is not the time for young ones like yourself to take the risks of men. You'll hold back until I say otherwise."

Lamar's gaze met his, a flicker of rebellion flashing in the green depths of his eyes before he lowered his head, nodding slowly. "Will today be the day I fight?" he asked, his voice soft.

The older man exhaled, casting a quick glance over Lamar's shoulder to where the wall still strained against the weight of the attacking hordes. "Perhaps. But not until I give the word."

He released Lamar and looked back at the battle line. Jessup and the others were still pushing, sweat streaming down their faces, every muscle straining. The roar of the fleshers grew louder, more desperate, and the wall pulsed again, bending inwards under the relentless onslaught.

The sounds of battle raged around them, the screams of the fleshers mingling with the shouts of the men. In the distance, a figure briefly moved amidst the chaos before disappearing, swallowed by the crush of bodies and flashing steel, leaving only the echo of its presence behind.

The older man's skin prickled. Whatever came next, he knew in his gut it would be worse than anything they'd faced so far. "Mother protect us," he muttered, gripping his sword tighter.

The wall buckled, creaking like the spine of some great beast as the fleshers' grotesque forms pressed and scraped against it. The men's faces were drawn and pale, shadows cast deep into their hollowed eyes by the guttering torchlight. Each agonized moan from the other side clawed at their sanity, echoing through the bones of the wall like the wails of the damned. Every shudder of the timbers, every tortured groan, seemed to whisper that it was only a matter of time before the hellish horde would burst through.

With a hoarse cry, Jessup barked commands, his voice fraying at the edges. Sweat and blood smeared his face, and his eyes darted nervously between the men and the ever-bending barrier. The wall seemed to sway as though it had a heartbeat of its own, a sick, unholy pulse. And with every push, every desperate lunge, the timber groaned louder, its cries merging with the tormented shrieks from beyond.

The older man glanced back at Lamar, whose knuckles were white around his weapon. His face was a mask of anxiety. "I believe no one will have to fight or die today," he whispered, though even as the words left his lips, they tasted bitter and hollow.

An hour dragged on, each minute a lifetime, until the fleshers' strikes began to slow. Their wails became fainter, choked as if something monstrous were devouring their very voices. The men around the older man straightened, hearts daring to beat a little faster as a ripple of cautious optimism passed among them. The wall—no longer quivering like a terrified animal—stood taller. The last of the horde let out a series of rasping, ragged cries, a death rattle that sent shivers racing down the men's spine.

"We did it, we won!" Jessup's shout shattered the uneasy silence.

He drew his sword high, its blade catching the dying light. The men roared in response, laughter breaking free from tight throats. The relief was tangible, intoxicating, and even the older man found himself smiling as a wave of release washed over him. Lamar's grin stretched wide, the first genuine smile he had seen on the boy's face in what felt like ages.

The older man turned to Ferkin, who still stood rigid, clutching at his chest. The haunted look in Ferkin's eyes sent a chill through his heart. "My friend, it is over now," he murmured, trying to offer comfort.

Ferkin shook his head violently, his gaze locked on the distant tree line. "No! It has not yet begun," he rasped, his voice hollow and broken.

The deadness in Ferkin's eyes made the older man's hands tremble, the flicker of unease inside him blooming into full-blown dread. Something unnamable slithered beneath his skin—a crawling sensation, as if unseen eyes were watching them from the darkness.

Jessup, oblivious to the growing terror, turned to the men, his laughter booming. "Men!" he bellowed. Faces lit with euphoria turned towards him, anticipation shining bright in their eyes. "Drinks and whores are yours tonight!"

The roar of approval drowned out the growing whispers of fear. Jessup raised his voice even louder, letting the joy flood back in. "Let no man today—"

A deafening rumble cut him off, deep and resonant, as if the earth itself had opened its jaws to growl. The trees beyond the wall shivered, leaves falling in a flurry as a shadow unfurled. Silence fell like a shroud over the men, cheers strangled in their throats. The Nephilim began to snarl, hackles raised, and the men's faces drained of color.

Ferkin's gaze was locked on the trees, his face now ghostly white. He swallowed hard, his voice a whisper barely audible above the stilling breeze. "It's not over yet, my friend. But we will get through this."

Before Jessup could react, a piercing roar erupted from the forest. The trees trembled, shattering and splintering as something massive crashed through. Out of the dense darkness emerged a nightmare given form: a towering, hulking creature with dark gray skin like blighted stone. Its twin heads were crowned with curling, jagged horns that scraped the heavens, eyes glowing red like embers in blackened sockets. Each head let out a guttural bellow that reverberated through the clearing, and the very ground seemed to tremble in fear.

"Again, do the chants again!" Maraco's voice cracked with terror, and the Ages scrambled to their positions, their voices rising in a panicked, discordant chant.

Before they could complete the incantation, the beast charged, moving at a speed that belied its monstrous size. The impact was cataclysmic. Shards of splintered ironwood exploded outward, a deadly storm of wooden shrapnel that ripped through men and Nephilim alike. Screams filled the woods as bodies were skewered, blood splattering the earth in dark arcs. The beast crashed into the nearest Nephilim with a bone-jarring force, its horns puncturing deep into the creature's side. The Nephilim bellowed, the sound full of pain and finality, as the dark monstrosity drove it back into the forest, slamming it against the ancient trees. Timber cracked and shattered, the mighty trunks splintering down to their roots.

Archers tumbled from their perches as their screams were swallowed by the roaring chaos. The Nephilim let out one last, feeble moan as the beast wrenched its massive head back, dark ichor spraying in thick, noxious streams. Its golden eyes dulled, fading to a lifeless black as the veins beneath its skin pulsed and darkened.

With a sickening crunch, the creature lifted one massive foot and brought it down in a brutal stomp. The Nephilim' skull caved in, bone and brain matter bursting forth like overripe fruit. The ground beneath seemed to recoil as yellow-gray matter oozed out, spreading like a vile stain.

Silence hung in the aftermath, thick and suffocating. The men stood frozen, horror etched into their faces as the beast straightened, its twin heads turning slowly toward them. The red eyes burned with malevolence, lips peeling back to reveal rows of jagged, blood-stained teeth. It took a step forward, the earth shaking beneath its weight.

Maraco's voice was strained but commanding as he shouted to the remaining archers still perched high on the ironwood branches. "Bring it down, bring it down!" The words echoed through the forest, desperate and urgent.

The archers released a volley of arrows that whistled through the air like a swarm of locusts. Each one struck the beast's thick, hardened grey hide, only to bounce off harmlessly, splintering like dried twigs. Not a scratch, not even a dent. The creature lifted its foot, a monstrous appendage the size of a wagon wheel, crusted with mud and darkened blood. One man stared up, breath freezing in his lungs, as its shadow enveloped him completely.

"I love you, my beautiful wife," he whispered, a breathless prayer to the woman he would never see again.

Shouts came from every direction—men crying out for Orin to run, to flee—but there was nowhere to go.

The beast's foot loomed above, casting its dark, heavy shadow. The ground quaked as it began its descent, a rumbling growl reverberating from its throat like a tremor from the depths of the earth.

Then, a blur of fur and muscle slammed into the beast's leg. The Nephilim roared, their growls filling the surrounding area. One, the larger of the two, clamped its powerful jaws onto the creature's thick neck, teeth gnashing, fur bristling with rage. The other Nephilim, leaner but no less fierce, lunged at the beast's raised leg, its jaws working feverishly, tearing into the thick hide as if possessed. The beast stumbled, its focus shifting from the men to the snarling attackers, giving them a precious heartbeat to move.

One man broke into a sprint, lunging out from the shadow, his legs burning with the effort. He barely had time to breathe before he collided with Tidal. The force knocked them both to the ground in a tangle of limbs.

"Spirits, Orin! That was a close one!" Tidal gasped, his breath hitching as he struggled to rise.

The two pulled each other up and turned in unison to the sounds of frenzied shouts from the trees above.

13
The Thick

essup's voice cracked as he scrambled down the trunk, exclaiming, "They're coming, they're coming!"

He pointed frantically at the widening gap in the ironwood wall. Beside him, Maraco's expression darkened as he stared into the broken tree line, where shadows writhed and twisted.

He ran a shaking hand through his hair, his sword gleaming in his fist. "This is it?" he wheezed, his voice hoarse with disbelief. "This is how it ends?"

"I don't know!" Jessup squealed, his gaze locked on the massive tunnel the beast had carved through the ironwood barricade.

In the yawning darkness, shapes began to emerge, hunched figures swarming forward with an eerie, twitching grace. Lundor, perched on a lower branch, stared in horror, his mouth opening and closing like a dying fish. "Fleshers!" The word escaped him as a broken whisper, a single utterance of terror.

At that moment, a figure rode forward, blocking Lamar's view. His face had gone ashen, his eyes wide and glassy as if he were seeing his own death. The figure reached out, gripping his shoulder tightly.

"Look at me!" came the command. Slowly, Lamar's gaze shifted, meeting the figure. "Do you remember what I told you?"

Lamar swallowed hard, his throat bobbing, and nodded. "We will get through this, Lamar," the figure repeated, voice steady despite the fear coursing through him.

A shrill, piercing horn blasted through the forest, drowning out the cries of men and beasts alike. The figure turned sharply, heart hammering in his chest. From the shattered tree line, they came. There were hundreds of them, a writhing mass of bodies that seemed to move as one. They spilled out from the darkness, claws gleaming, eyes glowing with malice. Fleshers advanced, creatures of nightmare, their skin patched and sewn together like some monstrous tapestry.

Tidal, still on horseback, leaned back in his saddle, tears streaking down his dirt-streaked face. "Great Mother, this is it," he murmured.

The fleshers hit their lines like a tidal wave, crashing into the men with a frenzied hunger. They moved in a twitching blur, faster than anything anyone had ever seen. Bodies flew, screams erupted, and men were torn apart, shredded under the fleshers' onslaught. The sounds of bones snapping, flesh ripping, and the sickening squelch of blood drowned out all else.

"Push back, push back!" Maraco roared, swinging his sword in a wide arc.

He turned just as a towering flesher leapt, clearing the sea of bodies and landing directly in front of him. It stood over nine feet tall, its frame grotesquely muscular, each limb bulging with unnatural strength.

Its skin was a horror, a patchwork of decayed flesh and darkened muscle, stitched together with crude, blackened threads. Age had turned the hide as black as midnight, a darkness that seemed to swallow the light. Its eyes burned a furious red, two orbs of fire set deep in its skull. The face was a twisted mask of malevolent glee, with three long, jagged bones jutting from each side of its skull, curling like the gnarled branches of a cursed tree.

The creature's grin stretched impossibly wide, revealing teeth that gleamed like blackened steel, stained with the blood of countless victims. It loomed over Maraco, head tilting slowly, studying him as if deciding where to bite first.

Maraco gripped his sword tighter, muscles tensed. "Come on, you ugly bastard," he spat, raising his blade.

The flesher's grin widened further, lips peeling back until they split, dark blood oozing from the corners of its mouth. Then, with a snarl that shook the very ground, it lunged.

"Brother, move!" Jessup roared, his voice drowned by the chaos as he watched Maraco freeze for a heartbeat too long.

The warning came too late. A massive force crashed into Jessup, knocking him back against the sinewy remains of a dead snore. Bones crunched, and blood splattered across his vision as he fought to steady himself. He looked up just in time to see Maraco stagger, his sword swinging free of its scabbard as the hulking flesher loomed overhead, its blackened skin glistening like polished obsidian, the vile stench of rot thick around it.

With a desperate cry, Maraco thrust his blade upward, burying it deep into the creature's distended gut. The weapon pierced flesh and sinew, and a thick stream of inky blood gushed forth, staining the ground in a spreading pool of foul ichor. Maraco grimaced, his face a mask of determination as he tried to lock eyes with the beast. But the flesher merely grinned, its expression an eerie caricature of glee.

The thing seemed to revel in the pain, its fading eyes glowing with malevolent delight.

"Maraco, get out of there!" Jessup bellowed, swinging his sword furiously to carve a path through the thrashing melee.

The battlefield was a sea of bodies and blood, the gauntlet of enemies between them unyielding. Every step he took felt like a lifetime, every swing of his blade an eternity. He could see Maraco struggling, the flesher's clawed hand descending like a vice around his brother's torso. A sickening sound, like wet parchment tearing, filled the air as those claws punctured deep into Maraco's sides.

Maraco gasped, feeling the searing pain as his skin peeled away, his flesh unraveling like a shroud being torn from bone. But as the agony mounted, something else shifted inside him—his fear drained away, replaced by a strange, surreal calm. The world slowed. His vision blurred and then sharpened again, capturing the battlefield in stark, crystal clarity.

Screams and the clash of weapons mingled in a discordant symphony of war, but Maraco's gaze wandered beyond the fray. He watched arrows sail gracefully through the sky, arching in a perfect arc before plunging into the dark forms of the enemy. He saw his men fighting with desperate valor, their armor glinting like polished mirrors. Then, he noticed the leaves and their delicate green tendrils trembling in the breeze, their vibrant emerald color contrasting sharply against the dull carnage. The last few rays of sunlight filtered through the canopy above, casting dappled patterns on the ground below. The sweet fragrance of sweeden flowers wafted on the gentle breeze, incongruously beautiful amid the chaos.

Jessup's voice broke through the haze, raw and ragged with despair as he shouted, "Maraco! NO!"

But he was too far away, too late to intervene. With a single, practiced motion, the flesher tightened its claws and broke free of the armor. In the same fluid movement, it ripped Maraco's skin away, leaving behind a horrific, fleshless form that crumpled to the earth like a discarded puppet. The creature tossed the sagging remains into the ravenous horde surging forth from the ironwood treeline, where grotesque figures tore at Maraco's body like starved jackals.

Jessup's vision blurred red with fury. It exploded through him, burning away everything else. He lunged forward, heedless of pain and his own survival. All that mattered was the creature standing before him and that infuriating smile. The flesher still grinned down at him, stretching Maraco's skin over its own body as if trying on a new coat.

With a wordless howl, Jessup broke through the remaining fighters, his blade a whirling tempest of rage. He saw neither friend nor foe and cared not at all. He carved a path of carnage, cleaving through flesh, bone, and steel alike. When he finally reached his brother's killer, the creature was still smiling that damned smile. Time seemed to slow as Jessup raised his blade high, his muscles coiling tight with murderous intent.

The flesher looked up at him, amusement dancing in its dull eyes. It cocked its head mockingly, and then—snap. Jessup brought his sword down with every ounce of strength he had, connecting with the creature's skull and biting deep. For a moment, the flesher merely blinked, its smile widening as it raised its bloody claws and dropped Maraco's skin to the ground.

"Die, die, die, DIE, DIE, DIE!" Jessup screamed, his voice thick with hate.

With a savage twist, he yanked his sword free and swung again. This time, the blade swept clean through the creature's neck, severing its head from shoulders. The flesher's grin never wavered, even as its head toppled to the dirt and rolled to a stop at Jessup's feet, lying there face up with that grotesque smile fixed in place.

Breathing hard, Jessup stared down at the dismembered creature. He could feel blood pounding in his ears, his heart hammering against his ribs. Slowly, he turned his gaze to the pile of flesh at his feet, what remained of Maraco. The saggy, loose skin looked like a discarded garment, limp and hollow.

"Damn you," Jessup whispered, his voice breaking. He fell to his knees, clutching the remnants of his brother's skin to his chest. "Damn you..."

Lundor, one of Jessup's closest comrades, paused mid-strike, locking his gaze on Jessup as he held the fragile, ruined skin in trembling hands. The battle raged around them, but for a moment, everything else seemed to fade.

"May your soul pass in peace, brother," he murmured softly, bowing his head. "And may we be together again soon."

Jessup's grief twisted into something darker, more dangerous. He raised his head, his eyes blazing with a deadly resolve as he looked toward the ironwood treeline. The horde still poured forth, endless and unrelenting.

"Orin, HELP!"

Lamar's desperate cry pierced through the chaos, drawing attention amid the carnage. He appeared as a small figure in a sea of violence, cut off and pushed toward the front lines, where fighting swirled like a boiling cauldron of steel and blood.

"Go get him!" Ferkin shouted as he barreled past, swinging his axe in a wide arc that sent a flesher reeling.

"Ride, girl, ride!" Orin urged Aya, feeling the snore's muscles coil beneath him, her nostrils flaring as she sensed the urgency in his voice.

With a fierce roar, Aya reared back on her hind legs before crashing forward, her hooves pounding the earth like war drums. With a surge, they charged through a knot of gnarled fleshers, their twisted bodies flying like ragdolls under the weight of the beast. Lamar's face lit up as Orin hurtled toward him, but relief was short-lived.

"Watch out!" Orin bellowed.

Lamar spun around, only to find three fleshers stalking toward him. They moved like flickering lights, shoulders low, claws tapping against the ground, grinning with wide, malicious smiles that split their grotesque faces in half.

Lamar's snore bellowed, its head jerking wildly as it tried to keep the attackers at bay. The young beast's tusks glinted in the dim light, slashing as the fleshers darted in and out, taunting him with their slit red eyes glowing with malevolent glee.

"Orin, hurry!" Lamar's voice cracked with fear just as his snore shrieked and reared up.

He barely had time to cry out before one of the fleshers grabbed a tusk and yanked, toppling the beast over. The ground shook as the young snore collapsed, its scream tearing through the battlefield. Two fleshers pounced, seizing its flailing head. Their claws flashed, stabbing into the snore's eyes and throat with brutal precision. Blood sprayed, dark and thick, as the creature's struggles weakened.

"LAMAR!" Orin roared, spurring Aya onward, but he was still too far away.

With a heart-wrenching thud, the beast fell, trapping Lamar beneath its massive weight. His leg twisted awkwardly, pinned under the creature's bulk. He bit back a scream as the snore's spiked hide dug into his flesh, the pain sharp and immediate. Straining against the weight, he found that every movement sent agony shooting through his trapped limb.

Around him, the battlefield raged in a storm of chaos with steel clanging, beasts roaring, and men screaming as they were torn apart. The acrid stench of blood and fear filled the air, thick and suffocating.

"Get up... get up," he whispered frantically to himself, hands scrabbling at the ground, fingers digging into the dirt in a desperate attempt to pull free.

But it was no use. Panic clawed at his chest, squeezing the breath from his lungs as he looked up. The three fleshers had climbed onto the snore's corpse, crouching over him like crows over carrion. Their mouths split into wide, toothy grins, sharp fangs glistening as they watched him struggle.

"Please... no..." Lamar whimpered, his voice barely audible.

One of the fleshers let out a shrill, ear-splitting squeal that made him cringe, hands flying up to cover his ears. He squeezed his eyes shut, trembling all over.

Cold, bony fingers slick with the snore's blood brushed against his cheek. He froze, a shudder running down his spine as one of the fleshers traced a claw down his face, leaving a thin, stinging line of blood. He flinched, but the flesher's grip tightened, forcing him to look up.

The creature's breath washed over him; it was hot, rancid, thick with the stench of decay. Lamar gagged, his stomach twisting as the foul smell threatened to overwhelm him. Tears streamed down his face as he turned his head, desperately trying to escape the fetid breath invading his senses. But the flesher leaned closer, its grin widening.

"Lamar!" Orin's shout cut through the haze of terror, and the fleshers' heads snapped up.

He was almost upon them. Aya let out a furious roar, muscles bunching as she leaped forward. They crashed down, the impact shaking the ground beneath them.

With a snarl, she lunged, jaws snapping shut around two of the fleshers. They shrieked as her teeth closed in, and she shook her head violently, their twisted bodies flailing helplessly in her grip. Orin felt her savage delight as she crushed them, the sound of bones breaking like thunder.

He leaped off his snore and charged the third flesher, its skeletal figure gleaming in the dim light. The creature, with sinew-stretched skin and a sickening array of misshapen bones, sprang from the fallen snore, landing before Orin with a guttural hiss. He tightened his grip on his sword, knuckles white. With a roar, he hurled it forward, the blade stretched out.

The flesher twisted its spine, arching impossibly high, its elongated limbs creaking and shifting. Its grotesque face contorted into a grin, rows of jagged teeth glistening. An unholy chuckle bubbled from its throat as its black, hollow eyes bore into his, unyielding and menacing. Orin's breath hitched. For a heartbeat, he stood frozen, caught in the towering creature's shadow, fear scraping at the edges of his resolve.

But fear was quickly eclipsed by the heat of something far more primal: rage. A rage so deep it almost drowned him, fueled by the sight of his fallen friends scattered across the blood-soaked earth. Rage for the family he might never see again. And, more than anything, a fury surged with every pulse of that damned, mocking grin.

With a surge of adrenaline, he threw his sword again, this time with every ounce of strength and desperation left in his battered frame. It whistled, the blade flashing in the gloom like a bolt of lightning. The flesher's grin faltered, just for a fraction of a second, before the sword drove through its skull, the force splitting the creature's head like a shattered melon.

The beast collapsed with a sickening crunch, its body crumpling like a marionette with severed strings.

"Even in death, they grin," he muttered under his breath, the bitterness heavy in his voice.

"I!" Lamar gasped, relief flooding his face as the grotesque form hit the ground with a resounding thud.

Blood trickled down Lamar's legs, pooling around his waist, staining the earth a deep crimson. The boy was pinned beneath the body of a fallen snore, his face pale and strained. He dropped to his knees beside Lamar, slipping his arms beneath the boy's shoulders and carefully pulling him free. Lamar's limbs trembled violently, his breaths ragged.

"I told you to stay close," he said, his voice softer now, though worry crept in at the edges.

He could feel Lamar's fear seeping into him like a chill. Tears welled in Lamar's eyes, his shoulders shaking as he finally broke down, sobbing against his chest. He held him tight, one arm wrapped protectively around the narrow shoulders. "It's okay, just stay close. And this time, don't wander off. There's a battle going on, you know."

A small, forced smile tugged at Lamar's lips, but it was thin and fragile, his wide eyes still shadowed by the horrors he'd witnessed. Behind them, Aya snorted impatiently. Her great head swung around, nostrils flaring as she tried to swallow the last of the remaining fleshers, jaws snapping with a sharp, bone-crushing sound.

"Come on." He tried to inject some levity into his voice as he scooped Lamar up, cradling him against his side. The boy clung to him, his small hands clutching his armor. His weight was a reminder of how young he really was, how fragile.

The battlefield around them was still alive with the clamor of war, the screams of men, the roars of beasts, and the unholy shrieks of the fleshers. But for a moment, it all faded, the chaos muted. He glanced down at Lamar, his tear-streaked face resting against his shoulder.

"We'll get through this," he murmured, more to himself than to the boy.

As they stepped back to Aya, his foot snagged on something soft, sending Lamar and him sprawling onto the ground. Pain shot through his ribs as he scrambled to right himself, glancing back to see what had tripped him. His breath caught in his throat.

Duoslum lay splayed on the ground, his once-proud frame reduced to a crumpled mess. Blood poured in thick rivulets from a gaping wound in his neck—a wound too clean, too precise to be anything but the work of a blade. He gurgled with every shallow breath, spitting crimson froth. He'd seen all manner of battlefield injuries: flesher bites, arrows protruding from limbs, even limbs severed by catapults, but a sword wound? That was something different. It whispered of treachery amidst the chaos. As he knelt beside him, Duoslum's glassy eyes slowly turned to meet his.

"I... would very much... like to see my love... just one last... I have to... home... She's waiting... I can't keep her wai..."

His words faltered, drowned out by wet coughing, then he was gone. His eyes, once full of life, faded to a lifeless stare before he could finish.

Orin's heart clenched. He glanced down at Duoslum's clenched fist, where something crumpled was hidden in his death grip. Carefully, he pried the fingers open to reveal a drawing of Duoslum's wife, smiling up from the parchment, radiant and happy. Hastily, he crinkled it back up and placed it gently in his hand, folding his fingers over it.

"Are you okay?" he asked, his voice tight, glancing back at Lamar.

The boy was clutching his leg, eyes wide with a mix of fear and bewilderment as he stared at the corpse. He didn't answer. He didn't need to.

"Come on, let's get you back up."

"Are you going to fight this whole battle on your knees?" a gruff voice barked.

He glanced up to see Ferkin looming on his snore, blood dripping from a deep gash along his bicep.

"I see you went and got yourself another scar to show off to the girls, then?" he forced a grin, trying to steady his voice.

Ferkin snorted but didn't respond. Instead, his gaze drifted past him to the shattered battlements and the flood of fleshers pouring in like a black tide. He sighed heavily, the weight of it tangible. "I never thought we'd actually lose this thing."

He shared a quick look with Lamar then back at Ferkin. "The battle is not lost, not while you're still standing with only a small scrape to show for it."

Even as he said it, he knew he was lying to him and to himself. The walls were crumbling, their men falling faster than he could count.

"What a fucking day this turned out to be," Ferkin grumbled, his voice low.

He nodded grimly, his gaze sweeping over the chaos unfolding around them. Fleshers swarmed over the broken ramparts, scaling the tall sefmore trees with unnatural speed, their grotesque limbs lashing out and ripping archers from their perches. The screams of the dying mingled with the wet, sickening sounds of flesh being torn from bone.

"Do you see that cluster of sefmore trees in the distance?" he murmured to Lamar, pointing to a small grove standing tall amidst the carnage.

The boy nodded shakily, too scared to speak.

"Hide behind one of those. You'll be safer there. "The words felt hollow as they were spoken, but it was the only thing he could offer. Ferkin looked at Lamar, a strange softness in his eyes. "You fought well, boy."

Lamar blinked, managing a tight, trembling smile before limping off toward the trees. They watched him go, neither speaking. Around them, the battle raged on, men being ripped from their saddles, fleshers swarming over their prone bodies like ants on carrion. The screams, once sharp and piercing, now formed a constant backdrop to the sound of steel on bone and the guttural snarls of the beasts. "You ready for this, my friend?" Ferkin asked quietly, his eyes fixed on the seething horde before them."Ready as I'll ever be."In the distance, he saw Tidal and a few others sprinting away from the fight, abandoning their posts. His jaw tightened. "Cowards!" Ferkin spat, disgust twisting his features.He wrapped his fingers tightly around the reins, knuckles turning white. "Let's finish this." They charged headlong into the mass of fleshers, trying to force them back. Jessup's voice rang out somewhere to the left, barking desperate commands to rally what remained of their forces. But it was no use. The fleshers were relentless, clawing at the legs of their snores, dragging the massive beasts down with frightening ease. "Come at me, you ugly little fuckers!" Ferkin roared, swinging his blade with a savage joy that only he could muster.

Amidst the blood and death, he was grinning. That mad, reckless grin that had been seen a thousand times before—the grin that usually meant he was about to do something incredibly stupid. But that smile vanished when he saw it—the dark, twisted shape of a flesher slithering up behind Ferkin, its sword-like claws poised to strike. "Ferkin, look out!" he screamed.

The creature lunged, its claws biting deep into the spine of Ferkin's snore. The beast let out a tortured bellow, legs buckling beneath it. Ferkin twisted, blade flashing, but he was too slow. The flesher wrapped its spindly arms around his waist, pinning him in place.

"No!" He threw his sword with everything he had, the blade spinning through the air like a comet, but the flesher ducked, the blade grazing one of the twisted bone spurs protruding from its skull.

He could only watch, helpless, as the creature tightened its grip. Ferkin's snore sagged, its back legs dragging uselessly. The flesher's grotesque face loomed over Ferkin, its empty eyes boring into him.

"You are dark," it hissed, its voice like a thousand knives scraping together. "Darkness runs in your spirit, a spirit that has no place in the light."

"Ferkin, no!"

His voice was raw and frantic as he struggled to reach him, but the fleshers were closing in, blocking his path. The flesher leaned in closer, its claws slicing open Ferkin's throat in one swift motion. Blood sprayed, hot and red. He screamed, yanking at the reins, desperate to get to him, but the creatures were everywhere, their twisted forms closing in around him.

The flesher dipped its hand into the gash in its own chest, scooping out a handful of thick, black blood. It forced the ichor into Ferkin's mouth, the crimson of his wound darkening as the vile substance mixed with his own blood. The creature stepped back, a sick smile twisting its lips as Ferkin's body convulsed. "You will be purified," it whispered. "Purified by the Father of old."

Ferkin slumped forward, his chest heaving as the black blood seeped from his mouth. The flesher unwrapped its claws and leapt back into the horde, grinning now, its teeth gleaming in the dim light. There he sat—Ferkin, his friend, his brother—motionless in his saddle, head bowed, blood running in black rivulets down his chest. His heart pounded, fury and despair warring within him.

"FERKIN!" he roared, but Ferkin didn't move.

He was gone, swallowed by the darkness, just like the battle they were losing.

14

Summoning

Fleshers surrounded Jessup, their rotting mouths hanging open, dripping saliva and blackened ichor. The ground beneath them squelched with each step as they moved in unison, driven by the scent of fresh flesh. Shadows writhed in the periphery, and the grotesque creatures twisted and contorted, their limbs jerking unnaturally as if puppeteered by some unseen malevolent force.

In the distance, the towering figure of the last Nephilim staggered, massive legs faltering as hundreds of the fleshers clung to its side like a swarm of starving leeches. The beast's roars became strained and desperate, its voice cracking with each attempt to shake free. Razor-sharp claws raked at its throat, slicing through thick scales to expose the vulnerable red muscle beneath. As its lifeblood poured out, steam rose into the chilling night breeze, carrying with it a metallic scent that stung the nostrils.

The Nephilim' final groan was a sound of despair; it was a creature bred for battle, now brought to its knees. It swayed once more before collapsing in a bone-rattling crash that echoed across the battlefield, sending a tremor through the land. The ground quaked violently as if recoiling from the horror unfolding, and then the beast lay still, its body vanishing beneath a writhing mass of pale, grasping hands and snapping jaws. The fleshers tore into it, feasting on its warm flesh, their screeches of hunger mixing with the Nephilim' dying moans as its massive frame shuddered and fell silent.

Jessup let out a bestial roar, swinging his blood-stained sword with ferocious strength. The blade cleaved through the neck of a flesher, sending its decapitated head rolling across the ground. Black blood splattered across his face and mingled with the crimson that trickled from his own wounds. His body was a tapestry of shredded skin and exposed muscle, his armor hanging in tatters. But still, he fought on, his breath ragged and filled with defiance.

"Which bastard is next?!" he bellowed, eyes wild as he drove his sword into the heart of another flesher.

The creature convulsed violently, its mouth stretching open in a silent scream as thick black blood spilled out, pooling in the dirt like oil. Its death was brief, but its suffering lingered like a dark promise of what awaited them all.

Lundor, his robes drenched in sweat, glanced over at the remaining Ages. The protective spells, once shimmering shields of light, were failing. Each Age fell in quick succession, their bodies convulsing as the power within them ruptured, unleashing a terrible burning light that scorched their flesh. One by one, their souls—brilliant orbs of white—burst forth from their corpses, only to be torn apart by invisible claws. The wailing spirits clawed at the sky, their screams merging into a deafening chorus of agony before vanishing into the thinning canopy above.

"I believe now it's time!" Jessup's voice cut through the chaos as he turned to face Lundor, eyes blazing.

He pointed his sword toward the last dying Nephilim, where fleshers swarmed over its body, their jaws snapping at its throat, tearing chunks of meat with each bite. "No! We can still win this!" Lundor's voice was a desperate plea, trembling with hollow hope. "We just need more time!"

But his words were swallowed by the roar of the fleshers and the agonized cries of the dying. Jessup did not respond; his gaze was fixed, unblinking, on the last Age—the one who had not yet fallen. "Summon the Light Bringer!" Jessup's voice boomed, each syllable resonating with grim finality.

The Age, a frail figure cloaked in shadows, turned slowly. His eyes met Jessup's, and in that moment, the expression of acceptance on his face was more terrifying than anything the fleshers could conjure.

Lundor stumbled forward, bile rising in his throat. "No, Jessup! Don't do this!" he shouted, but his cries were drowned out again as the Age began to chant, his voice low and reverberating with an unearthly echo.

"Facere tamen non fiet motus." The words dripped with forbidden power, and as they spilled from the Age's lips, the world seemed to shudder.

Fleshers froze mid-lunge, their limbs locked in place, jaws agape in twisted snarls. Everything thickened, pressing down on them all with an unbearable weight. "No!" Lundor screamed, his voice breaking.

He reached out, but a searing pain tore through his stomach. Looking down, breath hitching, he saw three long, jagged claws piercing through his abdomen. He could feel each icy point tearing at his flesh, sending waves of cold pain radiating through his body. A deep, guttural chuckle reverberated behind him.

"Maraco..." Lundor whispered, his vision blurring. He glanced up at the canopy above, a faint smile ghosting his lips as memories of running through sun-dappled woods with his old friend flashed before his eyes. "I will be with you now."

The flesher behind him let out a gurgling hiss and plunged another set of claws into his chest. Lundor gasped, his body convulsing as the beast twisted its claws, wrenching his torso apart. "Don't... summon the—"

His voice cut off with a sickening wet crunch as the flesher ripped him in half, his blood spraying in a crimson arc across the battlefield. Jessup didn't even flinch. He watched as the last Age stepped forward, pulling a gleaming dagger from his belt. The blade's handle was encrusted with green jade and gold, inscribed with runes that glowed faintly in the gloom. With a slow, deliberate motion, the Age sliced open his wrist, letting his blood pour out onto the ground in a steaming torrent. The crimson liquid hissed as it hit the dirt, pooling around him to form a perfect circle.

The Age knelt, his chanting voice rising in pitch. "Egredietur de tenebris lucem vocare nos tibi."

His eyes rolled back, leaving only the whites visible as he took the blade to his own throat. With a grim smile, he drew it across his skin, the blade parting flesh effortlessly. Blood gushed forth, and the ground seemed to drink it greedily.

The circle of blood began to glow, spinning faster and faster. The Age's body trembled violently, a bright light emanating from within. His soul, a shimmering orb, started to tear free. Instead of ascending, it was caught and bound to the circle, trapped in a vortex of agony. The soul let out a wail, a sound so filled with torment that even the fleshers recoiled.

The battlefield fell silent as the soul, once pure and white, began to darken, twisted by some malevolent force. It clawed at the edge of the circle, eyes wide with terror, screaming as it was dragged down into the swirling blood, clawing and begging to escape, pleading to be set free. Its cries echoed across the forest, a chilling lament that resonated deep in the bones of every creature that heard it.

Jessup watched, unblinking, as the soul was consumed by the blood, its final, desperate scream lingering long after it had vanished. The ground inside the circle bubbled and split, a blackened hand clawing its way up from the depths of the earth.

The Light Bringer had been summoned.

"What have I done?" Jessup whispered, voice trembling as the soul disappeared beneath the swirling circle of blood.

The atmosphere thickened, suffused with a silence that seemed to weigh heavier with every passing heartbeat. Everything—the last of the men, the fleshers, even the trees—stood in an unnatural stillness, as if held captive by some unseen force.

Then, the circle shuddered, the blood within roiling faster. The quiet broke as a low, guttural hum resonated through the ground. Jessup felt it first as a subtle tug, like a whisper brushing the edges of his consciousness. Then, the pull grew stronger, yanking at his very bones, threatening to drag him into the maw of that infernal vortex.

"Get back!" he bellowed, the words torn from his throat as a wave of force erupted from the circle.

It was too late. With a sickening whoosh, everything—every blade of grass, every leaf, every shred of flesh—was wrenched from its place and hurled toward the blood-red spiral.

Jessup's heart hammered as he drove his sword into the thick trunk of a nearby sefmore tree, the blade biting deep into the bark. His knuckles whitened as he clung to the hilt, muscles straining, every nerve in his body screaming. Around him, men and fleshers were lifted like ragdolls, their screams swallowed by the growing roar of the circle. They twisted in midair, limbs flailing, eyes wide with primal terror as they spun faster and faster. Flesh tore from bone with sickening wet sounds, mingling with the agonized howls of the damned.

Jessup's feet left the ground. Panic flared in his chest as he felt his body being lifted, gravity warping beneath the pull of the vortex. He gritted his teeth, holding on with all his strength. But the creaking of the sefmore tree grew louder, its roots groaning in protest as they began to tear free of the earth. Even the trees were not safe. His grip slipped, his hands slick with sweat and blood. "No!" he shouted, voice drowned by the cacophony of destruction.

His arms trembled, muscles burning as he fought against the relentless force. His fingers—one by one—began to loosen.

Ahead, through the maelstrom of flesh and debris, he saw the remains of his men. Their bodies were no longer whole, shredded into grotesque pieces that twisted and writhed, pulled apart by the centrifugal force. He could see their faces, twisted into expressions of eternal horror, mouths agape in screams that would never end. Blood sprayed in crimson arcs, spattering his face as the ground beneath the circle cracked and split, revealing the black void beneath.

The sefmore tree splintered with a deafening crack. The last of Jessup's grip gave way, and he was flung toward the heart of the storm, spinning out of control. He howled as his arms were nearly torn from their sockets, the force stretching him, pulling him apart. The pain was indescribable; he twisted in midair, the world blurring around him, until he was face-to-face with the circle.

It was no longer just blood. Faces—hundreds of them—pressed against the surface, their eyes empty and soulless. They mouthed silent screams, their expressions locked in eternal torment. Limbs protruded from the swirling mass, hands clawing desperately at the air, pulling at whatever was near—flesh, bone, or soul.

His legs snapped, shattering as they were pulled in different directions. He cried out, a ragged, desperate sound, feeling his tendons stretch and tear. Blood filled his mouth, the metallic taste choking him as the force began to twist his torso. The pain was maddening, beyond comprehension. Still, the circle pulled.

In his final moments, Jessup's gaze locked onto the center of the vortex. The blood parted, revealing s omething... something worse than death. A maw of darkness yawned wide, lined with twisting remnants of time, an abyss that stretched into infinity. From its depths, shadowy forms slithered and writhed. These were things that should not exist, that defied all reason and sanity. Within a second the life of every trapped soul lived within him. Countless ages of birth and death filled his mind.

Jessup's consciousness was a fragile thread, stretched across the fabric of existence, woven into the tapestry of every atrocity ever committed. He was not merely a spectator; he was a participant, a vessel forced to endure the cumulative horrors of history, each moment more grotesque and unbearable than the last. His mind, once his own, was now a battleground for the worst of time, a theater of suffering where every act of cruelty played out in excruciating detail.

As the formation of existence unfolded before him, Jessup felt the searing heat of the sun's birth, its nuclear fury scorching his skin, peeling it away layer by layer. He was there when Irada—dust and chaos—coalesced into a planet, its molten core churning beneath him, his body sinking into the liquid fire, his screams swallowed by the void. The beasts that roamed the primordial earth tore into him, their teeth sinking into his flesh, their claws ripping him apart, over and over, a thousand, a million times. He felt every bite, every shred of muscle torn from bone, every sinew snapped like a frayed rope.

When the great rock fell, cleansing the earth of the beasts, Jessup's body was incinerated, his flesh seared to ash, only to reform and burn again, an endless cycle of agony. The fractured land masses of Irada tugged at him, pulling him apart, his limbs stretched to their limits, his bones cracking under the strain. He pleaded for death, for release, but it never came.

He was trapped, a prisoner of time, forced to endure every moment of suffering that followed.

The dawn of man brought no respite. Jessup felt Cain's brutal blow against his head, the crack of his skull echoing in his mind. He felt every punch thrown in anger, every sword raised in war, every arrow loosed, every musket fired, every bullet that tore through flesh, every bomb that leveled cities. He felt the sting of the whip, the sear of the brand, the weight of chains. He was the slave, the prisoner, the condemned. He felt every rape, every violation, every act of cruelty inflicted upon the innocent. He was the victim of every lynching, every hanging, every burning at the stake. He felt the hands raised in violence, the fists clenched in hatred, the fingers that pulled triggers and lit fuses.

When the mushroom clouds rose, Jessup was there, his body consumed by the heat, his skin blistering and peeling away, his lungs filling with the acrid smoke of a dying world. He felt the boils rise on his flesh, the sickness spread through his veins, the radiation eating him from the inside out. He saw the planet dying, its rivers poisoned, its forests burned, its skies darkened by the greed and folly of men. He heard the cries of the innocent, the wails of the starving, the screams of the dying. He felt their despair, their hopelessness, their pain.

And then he saw them—the eyes, glowing with a malevolent hunger, fixing on him as he hurtled toward them. They were the embodiment of every atrocity, every act of cruelty, every sin ever committed. They were the collective suffering of humanity, and they wanted him. Jessup tried to scream, but no sound came out. His throat was raw, his voice gone. His eyes bulged, the flesh around them bubbling and melting as the darkness reached out, tendrils of shadow coiling around his broken body. He felt his bones snap, one by one, shattering to dust within him. The pain was unbearable, a white-hot agony that consumed him, that left no room for thought, for breath, for existence.

He was no longer Jessup. He was nothing but pain, a vessel for the suffering of the world, a witness to the horrors of history. And as the darkness closed in, as the tendrils of shadow tightened around him, he knew there would be no end, no release, no peace.

He would endure, forever, a prisoner of the worst that time had to offer, a living testament to the depths of its cruelty.

And still, the eyes watched, hungry, unblinking, waiting. The pain so intense he could no longer think, no longer breathe. He could no longer be.

The forest was thick with smoke and the scent of charred wood, searing through Lamar's lungs as he desperately fought to stay hidden. The ground trembled underfoot, sending small pebbles skittering like fleeing insects. From his perch behind the twisted trunk of a sefmore tree, Lamar's red-rimmed eyes widened, fixated on the chaotic horror that unfurled before him. He had wept all he could, his body too parched and exhausted to muster more tears. All that remained now was a deep fear that made his skin prickle with icy dread.

The battlefield was a sea of bodies, shattered weapons, and grotesque creatures surging forward like a tide of nightmares. The sky above fractured with a deafening crack as ancient trees were wrenched from the earth, roots dangling like exposed veins. And then, the earth split in a hiss of molten fury. A pair of massive, flaming horns began to pierce through the circle of runes that smoldered in the center of the clearing, their heat so intense that it shimmered and warped around them.

Lamar's heart thundered against his ribs. Panic seized him, raw and electric, and he turned to run. The moment he moved, however, something solid and brutal crashed into his face. Pain exploded through his skull as he was hurled to the ground, his body folding like a rag doll.

"Where do you think you're running to, you little shit?" Kefnop's voice was a guttural snarl, dripping with a venomous pleasure.

Lamar blinked up through his bleary vision, his senses reeling. Kefnop loomed over him, his grotesque form silhouetted against the inferno of battle. His face was smeared with dirt, caked in a mixture of dried blood and mud, and his leather armor hung in tatters around his bulging, distended belly. His leg, slick with oozing blood from a gaping wound, looked like it should have made standing impossible—but the hatred blazing in his eyes seemed to numb him to pain.

Kefnop's boot slammed into Lamar's ribs, the impact sending shards of pain lancing through his chest. Lamar gasped, his vision blurring at the edges. Another kick. Then another. The sickening crunch of breaking bones echoed in his ears, and Lamar's world shrank to a small, dark place filled only with agony.

"You think you can make a fool of me?" Kefnop bellowed, his voice a feral roar. "Who's laughing now, huh? Who's going to save you now, you pathetic little worm?"

Kefnop's eyes glittered with something dark and unhinged, but Lamar's gaze shifted past him, and his blood ran colder than the grave. Kefnop's rage twisted his face into a grotesque mask of malice as he drew his sword, raising it to deliver the final blow. He sneered, but then froze. The air around him changed, thickening with a presence that clawed at the senses like the chill of a crypt. Slowly, Kefnop turned, his sword trembling in his grip.

A figure stood behind him, cloaked in shadows that seemed to bleed into the very fabric of reality. Ferkin. Or what was left of him. His form was warped and wrong, as if something had torn him apart and crudely stitched him back together. His skin, once pale, had blackened and cracked, resembling obsidian that had been shattered and melted back together. The outlines of his skull were faintly visible beneath the stretched, taut skin of his face. But it was the smile—oh, gods, that smile—that made Lamar want to claw his own eyes out. It stretched impossibly wide, splitting his face into a grin filled with jagged, glistening teeth that looked like shards of polished bone.

Ferkin didn't speak. He didn't need to. The low, rumbling chuckle that reverberated from his chest sent every instinct in Lamar's body screaming in terror. Kefnop's hand jerked, his sword slashing wildly at the abomination in front of him.

But Ferkin moved with an inhuman swiftness. His clawed hand shot out, catching the blade effortlessly. Metal groaned and twisted as his fingers clenched. Then, with a flick of his wrist, he sent the sword spinning away like a discarded toy. Kefnop staggered back, his eyes wide with horror. But before he could turn to run, Ferkin lunged.

The world slowed. Lamar's breath hitched as he saw Ferkin's claws tear through Kefnop's belly, the flesh parting like wet paper. For a heartbeat, there was silence. Then, Kefnop looked down. His hands trembled as they reached for his abdomen, as if trying to hold in the tangled mess of his own guts that spilled onto the ground in a sickening, steaming heap.

"You... you little..." Kefnop's voice was a wet gurgle, his words cut off by a hideous, wheezing sound.

Ferkin's arm, still embedded in his body, flexed. With a horrible, wet squelch, Ferkin tore his arm free, and with it came a chunk of Kefnop's insides. Kefnop crumpled to his knees, eyes wide, mouth opening and closing in a silent scream.

But Ferkin wasn't done. He reached down, claws digging into Kefnop's flesh, and began peeling. Inch by inch, strip by strip, he skinned the man alive. Kefnop's shrieks—high-pitched, animalistic—cut through the chaos of the battlefield, each one a raw, primal cry of agony. Lamar tried to turn away, tried to shut his eyes, but he couldn't. He was paralyzed, forced to watch as

Ferkin reduced the man to a writhing, skinless thing, the crimson ruin of his flesh glistening in the firelight.

Lamar's head swam. Blood dribbled from his nose, his vision swimming in and out of focus. The pain in his ribs flared with each ragged breath, and he felt consciousness slipping away.

But then—Ferkin turned.

Lamar's heart stopped. The creature's eyes, burning pits of malevolent fire, fixed on him. That smile—gods, that smile—widened.

Ferkin stepped forward, each movement slow and deliberate, savoring the fear that radiated off the boy in waves. His claws, dripping with Kefnop's blood, twitched in anticipation. Lamar's limbs refused to obey him. He could only watch as Ferkin crouched beside him, his skeletal form looming like a harbinger of death.

"Hello, little one," Ferkin murmured, his voice a sibilant whisper that slithered into Lamar's ears and coiled around his mind. "Time to now see."

Lamar's world went black.

Orin paused, breath hitching as he saw the horns, like twin spires of hellfire, rising slowly from the depths of the churning pit. They glowed a baleful crimson, radiating waves of searing heat that set the very air ablaze. With every inch they rose, the earth around the pit shuddered, cracks splintering outward, steam hissing violently from the ground.

"Kronock!" a voice thundered behind him, raw with awe and terror.

A chorus of wild cheers erupted from the last few men around him, a frenzied roar of admiration and fear as the monstrous being hauled itself from the abyss. Lava erupted around it, gushing over the ground in molten rivers, consuming everything it touched. His stomach clenched as he looked upon the Light Bringer, Kronock. With a powerful heave, Kronock dragged his massive form up from the seething chasm and planted one clawed foot upon the solid earth. The men's chants grew louder, swelling into a primal rhythm that made his skin crawl.

Kronock's gaze swept over the battlefield, molten eyes gleaming like twin suns, a god surveying the ants that dared to summon him. He towered over them, immense and terrible, his form wreathed in flames and smoke. Fleshers poured from the tree line, shrieking their war cries. Kronock arched his back and stretched, the sound like a mountain groaning as it shifts. Every movement rippled with power, the sheer presence of him warping everything around the timeless beast.

How long had it been since he last walked the earth? How long had he festered in that fiery prison, shackled and starved? The years of captivity had turned his hunger into a savage hatred, his fury palpable as it radiated off him in waves of scorching heat. His horns blazed brighter, hotter, until he could hardly look at them. They were the very embodiment of wrath, and he was the harbinger of doom. His gaze settled on the men—his men—the ones who were not of his Father's creation. Rage twisted his monstrous features as he watched them cut down the fleshers, spilling their foul black blood upon the soil.

He stumbled backward, sweat streaming down his face as Kronock's hand stretched out, and a whip of pure flame burst into existence, crackling and writhing like a serpent eager to strike. The heat it cast was unbearable, scorching even from a distance. Fire poured from Kronock's eyes, and his skin—if it could be called that—seemed formed of molten rock, eternally melting and reforming in a hellish cycle. The trees around him withered and ignited, the forest aflame within seconds.

Kronock tilted his head back, opening his mouth, and what came forth was no mere roar. It was a sound of unbridled rage and triumph, a shaking bellow that reverberated through the earth, shattering stones and deafening all who heard. It was the sound of freedom—and death.

"Run!" Orin screamed, but the men did not listen.

They stood transfixed, still chanting Kronock's name as though caught in some fevered dream. Panic surged through him, and he turned and fled, feet pounding against the scorched ground. The heat from Kronock's wings seared his back as he sprinted, the vast appendages of fire and blackened stone unfurling behind him like a phoenix reborn from the ashes of a world destroyed.

"Run, damn you!" he shouted over his shoulder, but the men continued to cheer, oblivious to their doom.

He forced himself to look forward, breath ragged, lungs burning as he dashed for the tree line. Behind him, the air shattered with the crack of Kronock's whip, and he heard the men's joyous chants turn into horrible, agonized screams as the blazing lash tore through them, leaving nothing but ash and cinders in its wake.

He didn't dare look back. He didn't need to. He could hear the sound of flesh and bone turning to dust, the cries of men being ripped apart by the frenzied fleshers. Blood, black and red, soaked the earth, mingling with the molten rivers that flowed from Kronock's pit. The trees around him were ablaze, the forest a sea of flames, and the sky darkened as ash began to fall like snow. His heart hammered wildly in his chest, terror driving him forward.

He had to get home, he thought desperately, every muscle screaming in protest. Please, let this be a nightmare. Let him wake up.

"Lamar!" he gasped, the name tearing from his throat as he stumbled through the undergrowth.

He's still waiting. He has to be. He pushed on, blind to the branches whipping at his face, to the smoke choking him. Ahead, the meeting place loomed, just beyond the burning trees.

"Almost there!" he rasped, but as he burst into the clearing, a shadow loomed before him.

A hand, cold and cruel, clamped around his neck, lifting him off the ground as though he weighed nothing. He struggled, kicking out blindly, but the grip only tightened. Behind him, the flesher laughed, a hideous, rasping sound that made his blood run cold.

It threw him down, and the world spun. Pain flared through his skull as he hit the ground, stars dancing before his eyes. He tried to rise, but the flesher stepped forward, grinning down at him, its too-wide mouth split into a grin that stretched ear to ear. It crouched low, its breath hot and fetid against his face.

"Your Mother won't save you now," it hissed, voice a guttural rasp that sent a shiver of revulsion down his spine.

Its claws curled around his waist, lifting him effortlessly. Agony ripped through him as the talons dug deep, pinning him like a butterfly on a collector's board.

"The meek will not inherit the earth," it whispered, its forked tongue flicking out to drag slowly up his face, leaving a slick trail of slime. "And you, little one, are so very meek."

It chuckled again, the sound low and malicious, and he squeezed his eyes shut as its teeth—jagged, yellow, and far too many—gleamed in the firelight.

"And now," it purred, jaws gaping wide. "You're mine."

Pain exploded through him as its mouth closed over his head, teeth sinking deep, and everything—the fire, the screams, the terrible laughter—faded into darkness.

15

No Time

Adelicate voice echoed through Orin's mind—a sweet, haunting whisper that reverberated through every part of him. "Find me, Orin."

The words lingered, a siren's call searing itself deep into his subconscious. They pulsed within his thoughts, as if the voice itself were woven into the fabric of his soul. He could feel droplets gliding down his face and arms, a mixture of sweat and the early morning dew that clung to the scorched earth like nature's tears. A cool breeze whispered across his skin, each gust playfully stirring the fine hairs on his arms, making them sway in the soft caress of the wind. Despite the horror around him, a fleeting smile tugged at his lips. A memory of Shira shimmered in his mind's eye as he envisioned the way the sun bathed her fair skin in a radiant glow, making her seem otherworldly, like a spirit of light untouched by darkness.

Then the thought struck him. An icy dagger of dread twisted in his gut. Was it a dream? The scent of ash and decay filled his nose, choking him as his lungs struggled to breathe in the fetid air. He forced his eyes open, fighting against the gritty weight of soot and scorched flesh clinging to his lashes. His vision blurred, the world swimming in a haze of red and gray. A ragged cough tore through his chest, each hacking gasp raking through his throat until he spat out a mouthful of blood and ash.

"I'm alive," he croaked, the words like a curse on his lips.

Pain radiated through his limbs as he tried to push himself up, his legs trembling like those of a new-born foal. He swayed, unsteady, and the world tilted around him. His gaze swept over the desolation; there was a charnel house of corpses, charred and skinless, piled upon each other in grotesque heaps. Some still writhed, their mouths open in silent screams as the last vestiges of life clung stubbornly to their ruined bodies.

Above him, the sky stretched clear and blue. It was cruelly beautiful against the stark devastation below. The last blackened remains of the once-vibrant forest toppled around him, clearing away the green canopy that had shielded them. His eyes were drawn upward, captivated by a glimmering bird that glided across the sky; this was not a living creature, but a sleek metal form with unmoving wings that carved trails of white in the sky. It looked like a real cloud maker from his dreams. But, he was not dreaming. He blinked, and the image wavered like a mirage, vanishing into the blinding expanse of sunlight. He shook it from his mind and tried to take a deep breath to relax.

Then, a sound broke through the stillness: a low, mocking chuckle that slithered, sinking deep into his ears. It was a dark melody, dripping with malice, igniting something raw and primal within him. Rage flared in his chest, a savage beast clawing at his insides. Trembling with fury, he stumbled forward, grabbing a large, half-burned branch smoldering with dull embers. With a guttural roar, he swung it wildly, the heavy limb cutting through the ash-filled air.

Nothing. The laughter continued like a phantom sound that gnawed at his sanity. He looked down and froze. A creature lay before him. There was a flesher, mangled and grotesque. Its legs had been severed at the waist, entrails spilling out in a glistening black tangle across the scorched ground. Yet still, it breathed. Still, it stared up at him with those hellish red eyes, a twisted grin spreading across its bloodied face. Each exhale forced a spray of black blood through its clenched teeth, splattering in a grotesque mockery of life. Orin trembled, his entire body vibrating with the force of his rage. Without thinking, he raised the branch high above his head and brought it crashing down onto the flesher's skull.

Again. And again. The creature's laughter rang out, even as its bones splintered and flesh tore. The twisted mirth continued until, with a final shudder, it fell silent, and its eyes darkened to empty pits, its grin frozen in a ghastly rictus. But he didn't stop. He couldn't stop. He swung the branch until it crumbled in his hands, until the flesher's head was nothing but a pile of charred, pulverized dust.

He stood over the remains, chest heaving, arm trembling with exhaustion. His breaths came out in ragged sobs, each one scraping his throat raw. Then the sobs turned to cries, and the cries into screams of anguish and rage. He dropped to his knees, clutching at his head as images of the battle seared through his mind. Blinding flashes of light, the sounds of screams, the sickening crunch of bones and flesh all repeated over and over. It all came rushing back, each memory a shard of glass digging deeper into his psyche. His stomach lurched, and he doubled over, vomiting up black ash and blood.

Weak and disoriented, he collapsed onto his side. His vision swam, the world spinning in a nauseating whirl of colors and shadows. But he forced himself to move. He had to move. Crawling on bloodied hands and knees, he dragged himself away from the carnage. His body screamed in protest, every muscle burning with the effort, but he kept going. He clawed his way over the broken, dismembered bodies of those he had once called friends, their lifeless eyes staring blankly into nothingness. The sun's rays pierced through the swirling ash, casting harsh light onto the skinless corpses, their flesh sizzling in the heat. The smell of rot and death clogged his lungs until every breath felt like poison.

His fingers slipped in the mixture of blood and ash, leaving dark red streaks in his wake. Each inch he gained felt like a victory and a defeat all at once. With every pull, every ragged breath, he tried to block out the faces of the fallen, the cries of the dying. But the memory of that voice lingered—soft, sweet, and filled with yearning.

"Find me, Orin..."

And so, Orin crawled.

Things began to clear as he dragged himself farther away from the charred, death-riddled wasteland. Each desperate pull moved him one painful inch away from the nightmare he had left behind. His breathing steadied, the ragged gasps of ash-choked agony giving way to slow, deep breaths. Sweet, clean air filled his lungs, loosening the tightness in his chest. In the distance, he heard the faint murmur of water running over smooth river stones, the sound like a song of hope in the stillness. The soft babbling of a brook rang through his ears, and with the promise of water, he found strength where there had been none. He dug his fingers into the dirt and pushed forward, driven by that single, clear sound cutting through the oppressive silence.

The rush of the water grew louder, the melody swelling as he quickened his crawl. His throat felt like coarse stones grinding together, and his tongue stuck dryly to the roof of his mouth, cracked and parched like the leather armor clinging to his back. Pain shot across his lips as they split open, blood seeping from the raw wounds. But the air turned cooler, wetter, and tinged with a sweet scent. The promise of water—cool, life-giving water—pulled him forward until he reached the bank of a small brook.

A movement caught his eye. Three tiny figures peeked out from behind a cluster of vibrant, star-shaped sweeden flowers. He blinked, struggling to focus on the strange creatures. Little more than a few inches tall, they looked at him with wide, curious eyes. Delicate wings shimmered on their backs, catching the dappled sunlight. Dixin fairies, he realized. They hovered cautiously, their fragile wings beating like hummingbirds, watching him as if he were some sort of bizarre intruder.

He locked eyes with the largest of the trio, her eyes a deep shade of violet. She whispered something to the others, and in a flurry of iridescent wings, took off, disappearing into the underbrush. The other two hesitated, still peering at him, but he paid them no mind. His thoughts shifted abruptly, a jarring reminder of his purpose. He needed to get back to his village to warn them of what had happened. They had lost the battle. Everyone... gone.

But home was far away, and his body was still weak, trembling from exhaustion. He needed rest if he was ever going to make it back. With renewed resolve, he stripped off his soiled armor and clothes, the smell of blood and smoke clinging to the fabric. He slid into the cool embrace of the brook, submerging himself fully beneath the water. The stream rushed over his bare skin, soothing the deep aches in his muscles. His body floated, weightless, as he let the water carry away his pain, his fear.

Why was he still alive? He could still feel the flesher's claws digging into his flesh, the weight of its body crushing him. Everyone else had been skinned alive, and yet he was here. Why?

The thought clawed at his mind, each question a fresh wound that throbbed behind his eyes. He shut his eyelids tight, trying to blot out the memories. Slowly, too slowly, he drifted into a restless sleep.

When he awoke, the sun had shifted, its rays cutting through the thick canopy above, warming his skin despite the chill of the water. He stirred, groggy, the world around him still hazy with fatigue. And then he heard a voice, high and scratchy, just above him on the bank.

"I think it's dead."

He kept his eyes closed, heart pounding as he strained to hear.

"It really is an ugly thing," a second voice chimed in, softer but still laced with uncertainty.

"Yes, it is ugly. And very dangerous," the first replied, voice hushed.

His curiosity piqued. He blinked his eyes open, ever so slightly. Two tiny figures stood at the water's edge, creatures covered in thick, brown and white fur. They looked almost like small, upright hares, with large ears that twitched and swiveled at the slightest sound. One was taller, its whiskers twitching side to side in agitation, while the smaller one—barely six inches tall—seemed almost timid in comparison.

"Wooden Gobels," he breathed, the realization hitting him like a jolt of lightning.

The creatures froze, wide eyes fixing on his.

"Yes," the taller one said, his tone thick with disdain. "And you have no fur on."

Orin blinked, taken aback by the bluntness of his words. The creature looked him up and down, nose wrinkling in disgust. He laughed, a choked, humorless sound that seemed to surprise them. But before he could speak, they bolted, tiny bodies disappearing into the underbrush in a blur of fur and whiskers.

"Wait! Come back!" he shouted, stumbling to his feet.

They were gone, the undergrowth swaying in their wake. He sighed, stepping out of the brook. His muscles still ached, but the soreness had faded to a dull throb. The blood was gone from his hands, the grime washed away, leaving raw, reddened skin in its place. He glanced at his discarded clothes, which were torn and stained with blood and ash. The mere thought of putting them back on made his skin crawl. The stink of death clung to the fabric, a reminder of the horrors he had barely escaped. He scooped them up and dunked them into the stream, watching as the water turned red, swirling with the blood that had soaked so deeply into the cloth.

A sharp crack echoed through the forest.

He froze, every muscle tensing. His heart hammered in his chest as he spun around, eyes darting to the shadowy tree line.

"Who's there?" he called out, voice wavering.

Fear coiled in his gut. It wasn't a flesher; if it was, he'd have heard their high-pitched squeals by now. But something—or someone—was out there.

He held his breath, listening. The forest was silent, heavy with anticipation. Slowly, he reached down and pulled his clothes from the water, never taking his eyes off the darkened trees.

"Keep it together," he whispered to himself, his voice barely audible over the soft gurgle of the brook beside him.

He shook his head, trying to force away the feeling that he wasn't alone. Maybe it was just his mind playing tricks after everything he had seen. Maybe he was imagining it all. He glanced around one more time, the unease growing like a parasite inside his chest.

Still, there was nothing. No movement, no sound except for the murmuring brook and the gentle rustle of the leaves overhead. But that didn't stop the sensation of unseen eyes fixed on him, burrowing into his back.

He sucked in a breath and turned back to the task at hand. Slowly, he dressed, his fingers stiff and clumsy. The cold, damp clothes clung to his skin as he struggled to pull them on. They still reeked of smoke and blood, the acrid scent mingling with the wet fabric and making his stomach churn. He shivered as the soaked fabric pressed against his wounds, sending a jolt of pain through his sore muscles. But it was the best he could do. He had no choice.

"Shira..." he murmured, her name like a talisman on his lips.

Guilt twisted inside him as he thought about how much time he had wasted. Every second spent lingering by the brook felt like an eternity stolen from her. He clenched his fists, anger simmering beneath the surface. He needed to get back. He needed to warn them.

The sun climbed higher, its golden light piercing through the treetops. He glanced up, cursing himself for wasting precious daylight. He couldn't afford to waste more time. With a deep breath, he steeled himself and began the long trek back to the village.

The forest stretched out before him, familiar yet unsettling. The leaves were no longer vibrant emerald; their color was muted and pale, like sickly flesh. The trees stood silent, their bark dull and lifeless, their branches hanging limply. Even the mighty oaks, once so proud, seemed to sag under the weight of some unseen burden. The sight sent a shiver down his spine, but he pushed the thought away. There would be time to worry about the forest later. For now, he had to focus on getting home.

Every step was agony. His body screamed in protest, each muscle quivering with exhaustion. He longed for

Aya to quicken the journey. The image of riding her, her rhythmic gait carrying him swiftly across the land, filled him with longing. But there was no Aya. Only the endless path stretching out before him and the dull, throbbing pain radiating through his limbs.

His thoughts wandered as he trudged onward. He pictured Ferkin's face, wondering if he had made it back. Ferkin had been so full of fire and fight—surely, he had survived. And Lamar… he begged the Great Mother he'd escaped. Lamar needed to return to his sister. He pictured his home, the warmth of the hearth, the smell of Shira's cooking. The memory wrapped around him like a warm blanket against the chill creeping into his bones. He could almost taste the fresh turnip bread she should have in the fire right about now. A hunger twisted in his gut, but it wasn't just for food. He hungered for the safety of home, the feeling of her arms around him.

The day slipped away too quickly, the sun sinking lower and lower until its light was nothing but a distant glow on the horizon. The sky deepened, shifting from a bruised purple to a star-drenched black. The pale, ghostly glow of the full moon washed over the landscape, turning everything silver. His legs trembled beneath him, each step heavier than the last.

He stumbled, knees buckling under the weight of exhaustion. Pain flared up his spine as he collapsed onto the ground, gasping. The cold earth bit into his skin, the sharp edges of rocks and roots pressing against him. His body began to shiver violently, the night breeze clawing at him with icy fingers. A sharp, stabbing pain twisted in his gut, making him curl in on himself. He clutched his abdomen, teeth clenched as the agony tore through him.

He tried to push himself up, but his arms gave out. Darkness danced at the edges of his vision. He could barely breathe, his chest tightening as if something were squeezing the life out of him. A sound drifted through the stillness—soft, almost imperceptible. Footsteps?

No... not footsteps. Pattering. Like tiny paws skittering across the ground.

His eyes fluttered shut, the cold seeping into him. His clothes, still damp with the brook's water, began to freeze against his skin, each breath a painful rasp. He needed to make a fire. He needed to move. But he couldn't. He couldn't even muster the strength to lift his head.

The last thing he heard before slipping into unconsciousness was a soft, high-pitched voice.

"I found it."

A sudden weight pressed onto his chest, and he forced his eyes open, blinking sluggishly. A small creature stood on top of him, peering down at his face with a look of concern. Its fur was a mix of brown and white, its ears twitching with curiosity. A Wooden Gobel.

"It is definitely dead this time," another voice said—deeper, raspier.

"Look, it's blue around its mouth, Kellop." The smaller Gobel—no more than a handful of inches tall—bounded onto his stomach, sniffing at his armor. "At least he has fur on this time," he added, pawing at the leather straps.

The larger one, Kellop, leaned down, pressing his ear against Orin's chest. "I think it's still alive."

The small one looked up with wide eyes. "Can we kill it?"

Kellop's lips curled into a smirk. "No, Flup. We cannot kill it."

Flup jumped off him, his tiny paws skittering across the ground. He sniffed around the clearing, his nose twitching furiously.

"What are you doing?" Kellop asked, tilting his head.

"If we can't kill it, we may as well stop it from dying," Flup muttered, digging into the dirt. He unearthed a tangle of roots and bulbs, yanking them free. "It can eat these when it wakes up."

Kellop's gaze flicked back to Orin, lingering on his blue-tinged lips. "I don't think it's going to wake up. Its hide is changing color."

Flup glanced at Orin, brow furrowing. His small paws pressed against Orin's forehead. "I know," he whispered softly, as if reassuring himself.

Then, with a determined nod, Flup gathered a pile of sticks and twigs, arranging them carefully a few feet away. He chanted softly, his tiny voice barely audible. "Hoc igitur dico, dominum ignis."

The sticks flared, glowing red before bursting into flames. The warmth licked at Orin's skin, and he felt a flicker of life return.

"Let's go, in case it wakes up," Kellop murmured nervously, eyeing Orin warily.

Without another word, the two wooden gobels darted off into the underbrush, their tiny bodies disappearing into the shadows.

Orin was alone again, the fire crackling softly beside him, its gentle warmth chasing away the chill. He lay still, staring up at the stars, the memory of those small voices lingering.

The night bled slowly into morning as the first hints of dawn crept over the horizon, painting the sky with soft hues of gold and crimson. Orin stirred, the ache in his muscles pulling him reluctantly from the dark abyss of sleep. Rolling onto his side, he blinked the world into focus, feeling the chill of the dew-soaked ground beneath him. The fire beside him sputtered weakly, a few feeble flames flickering against the encroaching light, their glow fading as the early morning mist settled over the embers.

"Morning, beautiful," he murmured, the words slipping from his lips automatically as he turned, reaching out for Shira, but his hand met only empty space, brushing against cold earth.

Reality slammed into him with the force of a hammer, the brief, warm dream of home shattering around him. Shira wasn't here. He wasn't home. The cruel reminder brought a hollow pang to his chest. He sat up slowly, staring at the remnants of the fire and the small pile of edible roots neatly stacked beside it. Confusion washed over him. He didn't remember starting a fire. He didn't remember gathering any food.

He shook his head, pushing the thought aside. There was no time to waste pondering small mysteries. He grabbed a handful of the roots, shoving them into his mouth and chewing greedily. The bitter, earthy taste coated his tongue, but he forced them down, ignoring the unpleasant flavor. His stomach rumbled, a ravenous beast eager for sustenance, and each bite seemed to breathe new life into his weary body. Slowly, the gnawing hunger faded, replaced by a small measure of strength.

Swallowing the last mouthful, Orin stood, wincing as the stiff muscles in his legs protested. He stretched, feeling the tendons pull and release, the soreness easing ever so slightly. With a low sigh, he glanced around, catching sight of dew glistening on the leaves like tiny jewels. He wandered over, tilting his head to catch the droplets on his tongue, savoring each cool bead of moisture. The fire, the roots... they must have been his doing, something he'd managed before collapsing from exhaustion. But why couldn't he remember?

He strapped on his belt, fastening it tight around his waist, and set off again, his footsteps heavy but determined. The forest around him seemed even more lifeless than before. The leaves drooped, their color faded to a pallid, sickly green, as if drained of vitality. The deep, rich browns of the bark had turned to a rotting black, the trees themselves withering under some unseen blight. The sight unnerved him, a hollow unease spreading through his chest. But that was a mystery for another time. There were more pressing matters.

He pushed onward, each step bringing him closer to the trail that connected the villages. Relief and dread warred within him as he finally stumbled onto the familiar path, its surface scarred and broken. He froze. A chill ran down his spine as he stared at the ground. The dirt was churned and torn, gouged with hundreds—no, thousands—of overlapping footprints. Large, clawed impressions meshed in chaotic patterns, the unmistakable mark of flesher tracks. They stretched out in both directions, disappearing down the trail.

Panic clawed at his throat. He dropped to his knees, running his fingers along the torn earth, his mind racing. There were too many. Too many to count. And they were heading straight for the villages.

"No," he whispered, the word barely a breath.

A sickening fear roared to life inside him, burning away any lingering fatigue. With a choked cry, he scrambled to his feet and sprinted down the trail, the world blurring around him. His heart pounded, each beat echoing like thunder in his ears. He didn't care about the pain in his legs, the sharp sting of branches whipping against his face as he ran. He had to get there. He had to see it for himself. The sight that greeted him when he reached the first village stopped him cold.

Bodies lay strewn across the ground, their flesh torn and mangled, scattered like broken dolls at the entrance of the village gates. Blood soaked the earth, a dark, sticky sheen that glistened in the early light. His breath hitched, the air turning thick and cloying with the stench of rot and decay. He staggered forward, his vision blurring with tears. His friends, his people...

The fleshers had been here.

The grating, guttural grunts of something alive jolted him from his daze. He forced himself to look, following the sound past the lifeless bodies. Beyond the gates, amidst the carnage, a snore thrashed wildly, its massive frame jerking and convulsing. Its thick, muscular tail was pinned beneath a fallen black thorn Sieran tree, the wicked spikes of the tree's bark embedded deep into its flesh. Blood—black and glistening—oozed from the gashes, soaking the ground around the exhausted beast.

The ground was littered with the remains of the battle. Shredded flesher limbs lay scattered at the snore's feet, their foul blood staining the beast's tusks. The sight was almost surreal—the snore had fought to protect the village, perhaps even saving a few before it was trapped. But there was no one left to save now.

Another snore lay at the base of the fallen tree, its body broken and lifeless. A pang of sorrow welled up in Orin's chest. The dead snore's massive form must have been the reason the tree had toppled, pinning the other in its deadly embrace. He pressed his hands against the gnarled trunk, closing his eyes.

"Cinis cinerem, vita ad pulverem," he whispered.

A faint green mist began to swirl around the jagged veins of the tree, glowing softly in the dim light. The knowing hummed through him, a gentle vibration that spread down his arms. Slowly, the tree began to whiten, the bark turning brittle under his touch. The mist pulsed one last time and then faded.

With a roar, the snore jerked forward, the brittle wood shattering into a cloud of fine, white dust. Orin threw himself backward, landing hard on the ground as the beast's tail whipped around, narrowly missing his head. For a moment, he lay there, panting, heart racing. The snore turned, its massive body casting a long shadow over him.

It stared at him, its great dark eyes wide and wild. And then it charged.

Orin scrambled to his feet, but pain exploded in his ankle as he twisted it, sending him crashing back to the ground. The snore loomed over him, its breath hot and wet against his face. He squeezed his eyes shut, bracing for the impact.

But instead of crushing him, a rough, wet tongue swept across his cheek, smearing saliva down his face. He opened his eyes slowly, disbelief warring with relief. The snore was licking him, its powerful tail thrashing as though it were a playful child.

"Bo?" he whispered, trying to think of a fitting name. The beast grunted, snorting loudly as if to confirm. Laughter bubbled up in his chest, half-hysterical. "Come on, Bo," he murmured, reaching up to grab one of its massive tusks.

With a grunt of effort, he pulled himself up, the sharp pain in his ankle flaring with every movement. But he ignored it. He had to. Clenching his teeth, he swung onto Bo's broad back, the familiar feel of the thick hide beneath him grounding him in the chaos.

"Let's go," he breathed, tightening his grip on the reins that still hung around Bo's neck.

Bo snorted, shaking his massive head, and then reared back, his powerful legs kicking off the ground. They charged forward, Bo's enormous frame crashing through the forest like a juggernaut. The trees blurred past them, and Orin leaned forward, urging him on. They had to reach the next village before it was too late. He couldn't fail again.

He kept off the path, knowing the fleshers were using it. Each detour through the dense under-growth weighed heavily on him, but it was the only way to stay alive. Without Bo, he had no choice but to cover the ground on foot, every aching step pounding into his already worn body. The hours dragged by a grueling march through a world that seemed to wither and die around him. The trees that had once stood tall and proud were losing their luster, their bark pale and cracked like bones stripped of life. The soft, green glow that used to fil-ter through the forest canopy was gone, replaced by a stark, almost blinding light that pierced through the leaves, forcing him to squint against the harsh-ness.

Everything was changing. The ferns that once car-peted the forest floor were shriveled; the flowers' vi-brant colors faded to dull browns as their petals scat-tered like ashes in the wind. Even the comforting hum of dixin fairies and the gentle buzz of lofen flies—creatures that used to dance in the air—had vanished, leaving only a hollow silence in their place.

The top of the Serpent's Arch came into view, its shadowed silhouette rising ominously in the distance. Orin urged Bo onward, pushing him hard despite the weariness gnawing at them both. The snore's heavy breaths matched his own, its thick hide gleaming with sweat. Suddenly, a piercing cry tore through the quiet, shattering the unnatural stillness. He jerked his head up, scanning the treetops. The cry echoed again, shrill and desperate, reverberating through the canopy.

A glowing shadow passed over them, its shape twisting and writhing as it circled back, swooping low. Bo reared up, eyes rolling in panic. Orin gripped the reins, struggling to hold on as the snore thrashed beneath him. Then the shadow burst through the trees, revealing itself to be a massive londor bird, its feathers wreathed in roaring flames, a living comet hurtling straight toward them.

"Bo!" Orin screamed, but there was no time.

He threw himself off the snore's back just as the bird collided with a rattling crash. The impact sent a shockwave through the ground, and he hit the dirt hard, pain lancing up his injured ankle. Through a haze of agony, he watched helplessly as flames erupted around Bo, swallowing him in a furious inferno. His death throes echoed through the forest, a guttural bellow of pain and fear. His skin sizzled and cracked, the scent of burning flesh thick and nauseating.

"Shira!" The scream tore from Orin's throat, raw and desperate.

She was all he could think of. The realization hit him like a hammer to the chest—the fleshers were already at the village. He had failed.

Ignoring the pain, he forced himself up, every step sending fresh agony shooting through his ankle. He stumbled toward the village, each breath a struggle against the suffocating stench of rot and smoke. The arch loomed ahead, a twisted shadow against the morning light. As he drew closer, the smell of death thickened, clawing its way into his lungs.

The thorny passage that once stood proud and strong was slick with blood, dark rivulets trickling down the thorns, staining them crimson. The iron gates, once a symbol of security, lay crumpled and broken on the ground, twisted into grotesque shapes by some unimaginable force. His gaze fell on a small rocking chair, its rhythmic motion slow and deliberate as it swayed in the breeze. Next to it, a half-finished embroidered cloth lay discarded—the delicate image of a blooming tiradill flower staring up at him from the dirt.

His heart hammered painfully against his ribs as he moved past the chair, fighting to keep himself together. He pushed onward through the village square, stepping over the bodies scattered like discarded dolls. Some lay sprawled across the dirt path, their limbs twisted at impossible angles, their skin torn away. Others hung grotesquely from windows, draped over the frames as if they had been thrown there—skins flayed, muscles exposed. Blood pooled around the entrances of shops, dark and sticky, mingling with the dirt to form murky puddles that splashed against his legs as he moved through the carnage.

The wooden doors of the town hall came into view, standing tall and unbroken amidst the ruin. A flicker of hope flared in Orin's chest as he stared at the unshattered stained-glass windows. Maybe... maybe they were inside. Maybe they had hidden away, safe from the slaughter. He limped up the stone steps, the once-imposing structure now looming like a mausoleum in the pale light. Bodies of the village guards lay strewn across the steps, their faces twisted in frozen agony. Orin swallowed against the bile rising in his throat, forcing himself to step over them.

"Please, let them be here," he whispered, his heart pounding as he shoved against the heavy wooden doors.

They groaned open, the eerie creak reverberating through the empty hall. A gust of cold wind rushed out, wrapping around him like a shroud. The mural that once adorned the ceiling had shattered, fragments of paint and plaster scattered across the stone floor. The long wooden benches stretched out before him, empty and silent.

"Hello!" he called, his voice echoing through the vast, hollow space.

His eyes fixed on a lone figure seated at the front, unmoving. Relief and fear battled within him as he staggered forward. "Are you okay?"

The figure didn't respond. He moved closer, his pulse roaring in his ears. As he approached, the details came into focus: a green ring around a white hat, a familiar symbol. His blood ran cold. "Celica?" he whispered, his voice trembling.

There was only one person in the village who wore that hat. Something was wrong. Her skin, usually flushed with life, was pale. Her chest, unmoving. He reached out slowly, his hand shaking as he grasped her arm.

"Celica?" he pleaded, the name a desperate prayer on his lips.

No response. He touched her shoulder, and her head lolled forward, a lifeless marionette. His breath caught in his throat as he saw the dark stain spreading across her chest—a stab wound, deep and precise. In her hand, a knife glinted faintly in the dim light, its blade slick with dried blood.

He swallowed hard, his gaze shifting to her clenched fist. A crumpled piece of parchment was clutched tightly in her grip. Gently, he pried her fingers open, dread coiling in his stomach as he smoothed out the bloodstained note.

"I believed in you. Why have you forsaken us?"

The words blurred through his tears, struggling to understand why she would have left a note. Who did she intend to read it? Who would even be left alive? His heart twisted painfully, each word a knife driven deeper into his soul. A sob escaped him, raw and broken. He crumpled the note, crushing it in his fist as if he could erase the words, erase the pain. But there was no erasing this. He had failed her. Failed them all.

A tear traced a path down his cheek as he leaned over her, brushing a hand gently over her lifeless eyes to close them. "I'm sorry," he whispered, his voice choked. "I'm so sorry."

He turned away, the note slipping from his fingers to the cold stone floor. He couldn't stay there. He had to keep moving. Shira... Cal... maybe, just maybe, they were still out there.

With a deep breath, he pushed down the grief, the rage, the despair. He straightened, forcing himself to walk away from Celica's lifeless form.

His ankle throbbed relentlessly with every faltering step, each one like a jagged blade slicing through flesh, but he pushed forward. He had to keep moving. The pain didn't matter. Nothing mattered except reaching them in time. He stumbled past the village pub, his breath hitching as the familiar sight came into view. Selice—strong, fiery Selice—was pinned against the outer wall of her own establishment. Her eyes, wide with terror, stared vacantly ahead, forever frozen in that moment of agony. A flesher's claws were buried deep in her chest, its twisted grin still etched in its mangled face. But Selice had fought back—her sword was driven straight through the creature's skull, its blade jutting out the back in a final, desperate act of defiance.

Orin choked on a sob and tore his gaze away, forcing himself to keep moving, to keep running. The bodies began to thin as he left the heart of the village, but the dread only deepened. His leg dragged behind him, the pain blurring into the background as sheer willpower drove him forward. He dropped to his knees, tears streaming down his face as he crawled, clawing his way up the hill toward the small house that had once been their haven.

The stone wall surrounding their yard was in ru-ins, the neatly stacked stones he had gathered with his father as a boy now scattered and broken. The gate—the white gate that Shira used to paint every spring, laughing as she brushed on a fresh coat—was gone. Ripped from its hinges and tossed carelessly into the street like a piece of trash. He looked at the path, the path they had built together, stone by stone. The pathway where Cal used to race ahead, pretending to be a brave warrior protecting them from imaginary monsters, was gone. It was ruined now, the stones they had so carefully laid shattered and strewn like broken memories.

The vibrant red and white nordor bushes Shira loved, the ones she had tended to so diligently, were torn from the earth, their roots exposed and dangling, left to wither and die. Their beautiful, sturdy front door—stained with Tiran tree nuts to match the rich warmth of the surrounding forest—lay in splinters. He fell to the ground, his hand trembling as he reached for the twisted black metal handle that had once been a proud adornment. His fingers brushed over the scratched family crest branded into its base, and a wave of pain crashed over him, so deep it stole the breath from his lungs.

He bowed his head, gasping as a dull pressure began to build at the base of his skull, spreading upward until his vision blurred. But he couldn't stop. Not now. Not when he was so close. He pushed through the agony, crawling inside. The living room was a wreck; blood stained the soft sponge floor that had once been so comforting, the fibers soaked through and darkened. The fireplace, always warm and inviting, was cold and dead, the lingering scent of charred wood now mixed with something fouler. Their two rocking chairs—the ones passed down from Shira's parents, the chairs they had sat in so many times, holding Cal between them, dreaming of the future—were smashed to pieces, their broken frames tossed carelessly against the walls.

Orin turned to the kitchen, dread squeezing his heart in a vise. And there she was.

Orin's knees buckled, and he collapsed beside Shira, his breath hitching painfully in his chest. She lay crumpled on the floor, draped in the white dress he loved—the one with green stripes down the sides and delicate lace patterns wrapping around her arms. The dress she wore on special days, for him. A golden band encircled her wrists, and the soft, cloudy white of the lace covered half of her delicate hands. Her legs, her beautiful legs, were torn and shredded, the flesh ripped away, and her throat—oh gods, her throat was a gaping wound, blood pooled thick and dark around her lifeless form, soaking into her long, golden hair.

"Shira..." he breathed, the word breaking on a sob. He gathered her into his arms, cradling her head in his lap. Her skin was ice-cold, the warmth of life long gone. "No, no, no... please, no..."

His hands trembled violently as he stroked her hair, the silken strands matted with blood. He cupped her cheek, his fingers brushing over her parted lips, willing them to move, to speak. "Wake up," he pleaded, nudging her gently. "Shira, please... please wake up. You have to... please, I'm begging you..."

But she didn't move. Her head lolled lifelessly in his arms, her body limp and broken. He shook her gently, then harder, desperation clawing at his insides. "Please, please... Shira... just open your eyes, just say something, please... anything..."

But there was nothing. No smile. No warmth. Just cold silence.

"Shira!" he screamed, the sound ripping from his chest, filled with all the anguish and hopelessness that had been building inside him since the moment he'd found her.

He clutched her close, rocking back and forth like a child, sobbing into her hair. His tears soaked her dress, mingling with the blood. He hummed her favorite lullaby, the one that used to make her smile so beautifully, even on the darkest of days. He hummed and hummed, but she didn't move, didn't stir. She was gone.

"Papa..."

The word was faint, barely more than a whisper, but it sliced through the fog of grief like a knife.

"Cal?" he gasped, his heart lurching painfully.

He gently laid Shira's head down, his hands trembling as he stumbled to his feet. Ignoring the pain, he staggered down the hall, pushing open Cal's door with a frantic shove.

"Papa, you're home..." the boy whispered, his voice so thin, so fragile.

Cal lay on the floor, his tiny frame curled around a picture of his grandfather standing beneath the spirit tree. His little chest… gods, his chest… the flesh had been stripped away, his ribs stark white against the raw, exposed muscle. Each breath was a struggle, his ribs rising and falling weakly. Orin dropped to his knees beside him, his hands hovering helplessly.

"I'm here, son. Papa's here," he whispered, tears streaming down his face as he reached out to stroke his hair.

Cal's eyes were wide and glassy, his face ghostly pale. "Grandfather didn't come, Papa," he murmured, his voice a broken, shattered thing. "I called… but nobody came."

Orin's heart shattered. "Shh, shh… I'm here now, Cal. I'm here. I heard you, and I came home."

Cal looked up at him, a tiny smile trembling on his lips. "I… I was brave, Papa."

Orin bent down, resting his forehead against Cal's, holding him as gently as he could. "You were so brave, my boy. So very brave."

Cal's little hand reached up, brushing against the wooden pendant hanging from Orin's neck. "Do you… like it, Papa?" he whispered, his breath hitching painfully.

Orin swallowed, nodding fiercely. "I love it, Cal. It's... it's the best thing anyone has ever given me."

Cal's smile faltered, his fingers slipping from Orin's. His eyes dimmed, his breaths coming slower and slower until they finally stilled.

"Cal?" Orin whispered, shaking him gently. "Cal, no... no, please, don't go... stay with me, please, Cal..."

But he was gone.

A broken sob tore from Orin's throat as he gathered Cal into his arms, holding him close, rocking him back and forth just like he had when he was a baby. "My brave boy... my sweet, brave boy..." he murmured, pressing a kiss to his tiny forehead.

The hours slipped by unnoticed, the world darkening as the moon rose high overhead. The sweet scent of Garling flowers was gone, the glow of lofen flies nowhere to be seen. Orin held his son close, his tiny form curled against his chest, and he closed his eyes. He imagined them outside, on a sunny day, Shira's laughter filling the air as they played by the stream. He imagined gathering stones with Cal, just like he had with his father.

And in that broken, bittersweet memory, Orin drifted into sleep, clutching his son's lifeless body as if he were only sleeping. As if they were still a family. As if they were still with him.

16
Just A Nightmare

The first rays of dawn pierced through the gaps in the tattered curtains, casting slender beams of golden light across Orin's face. He stirred, groggy, his mind still clinging to the remnants of a fractured dream, but the familiar scent of woodsmoke cocooned him. It wrapped around him like a protective shield, warding off the darkness. Blinking, Orin's eyes slowly adjusted to the soft glow of morning.

Confusion settled over him, thick and disorienting. For a moment, he couldn't place where he was or why. Memories of ash, blood, and death flickered like distant embers, far removed from this moment, this reality.

"Morning, sleepyhead," a soft voice murmured beside him, pulling him further into wakefulness.

He froze, breath catching in his throat as he turned toward the voice. His heart clenched painfully in his chest, and he was sure it would stop. There, beside him, was Shira, her lips curved in that playful smile. Her golden hair spilled over the pillow, catching the morning light in a way that felt perfect.

"Shira?" he whispered, the name barely making it past his dry lips, as if saying it might break the fragile illusion.

She laughed, a light, airy sound that sent a wave of warmth through Orin, something deep and familiar stirring in his chest. Reaching out, she brushed a lock of his hair back from his forehead, her fingers soft and cool against his skin. "Who else would it be?" she teased, her hand lingering as though she, too, found comfort in the contact.

Orin couldn't stop himself. His hand moved of its own accord, fingers trembling as they brushed against her cheek, the warmth of her skin jolting him. His breath hitched. She was here. She was alive. Tears prickled at the corners of his eyes, and his throat tightened. "You're here," he croaked, his voice unsteady.

The lump in his throat grew as the weight of disbelief pressed down harder. Her brow furrowed slightly, eyes narrowing with concern. "Of course, I am. Where else would I be?" There was a pause, a shift in her expression. "Are you feeling alright?" she asked, her tone soft and gentle, as though afraid to push too hard.

Orin opened his mouth, but no words came. How could he explain the nightmare he had been living? The image of her lifeless body, the blood, the cold emptiness that had swallowed him whole. It felt like a nightmare from which he had just woken, the lines between dream and reality blurred beyond recognition. Had he imagined the horror? Or was this a dream?

Before he could respond, a small whirlwind burst through the door, dragging Orin's attention away from the confusion that swirled in his head.

"Papa! You're awake!" Cal's voice rang out, bright and full of energy as he launched himself onto the bed.

His small body collided with Orin, who gasped, catching the boy in his arms. Cal's laughter bubbled through the room, cutting through the fog that threatened to consume him.

Orin hugged him tightly, pressing his face into Cal's hair. The scent of earth, grass, and something distinctly Cal washed over him. He closed his eyes, holding his son close, and for the first time in what felt like an eternity, he let the tears fall. "My brave boy," Orin whispered, his voice breaking as he spoke. He clung to Cal as though he were the only thing anchoring him to this world.

Cal pulled back just enough to look at him, face bright and alive, eyes wide with excitement. "Come on, Papa! There's so much to do! The storm knocked down the big sefmores, and Mama says we can build a playhouse!"

His enthusiasm was infectious, his small hands tugging at Orin's arm as if he couldn't wait for the day to begin. Beside him, Shira sat up, her smile soft but amused as she watched them. "He's been planning since dawn," she said, teasing yet filled with warmth.

Orin looked between them, first at Shira, alive and breathing beside him, and then at Cal, filled with life and energy. It all seemed too perfect, too real. But wasn't this what he had been dreaming of for so long? A second chance? He swallowed the rising doubts, forcing them down. Whatever had happened before didn't matter now.

"Well then," Orin said, his voice stronger, a smile tugging at the corners of his mouth. "We best get started, hadn't we?"

Cal leaped off the bed with a cheer, disappearing out the door in a flurry of motion. Shira's laugh followed him, her eyes meeting Orin's as she leaned in, brushing her lips softly against his cheek. "He's missed you," she said softly.

Orin reached for her hand, squeezing it gently as he held her gaze. "I've missed both of you more than you can imagine," he replied, his voice thick with emotion.

She smiled, leaning in to kiss him—soft, warm, and grounding. For a moment, everything felt right. The world felt whole again. Whatever nightmare he had endured, it was gone. This was his reality now. This was real.

The rest of the morning unfolded in perfection. Orin and Cal ventured outside to the yard, the massive sefmore tree lying across the grass like a fallen giant. They worked together, chopping wood, stacking logs, preparing for the playhouse that Cal had so meticulously planned. Hours passed in a blur of work and laughter, the kind of peace Orin hadn't known in years.

Shira joined them in the afternoon, bringing baskets of Cain's berry bread and poplar jam, her laughter mingling with Cal's as they ate together in the rays of sunlight now exposed by the fallen tree. The warmth of the day, the sounds of their voices, the feel of their presence—it all felt so... right.

As dusk settled, casting the sky in soft hues of gold and purple, Orin returned to the cottage with Shira and Cal. The scent of Shira's cooking filled the small space, and Cal, full of excitement, chattered endlessly about the playhouse they had worked on throughout the day. The evening had been peaceful, almost perfect, and now, as the fire crackled low in the hearth,

Shira curled up beside Orin, resting against him with a sense of ease.

Her voice, soft and filled with affection, broke through Orin's thoughts. "Promise me you'll stay this time," she whispered, her eyes searching his with a quiet intensity.

Orin's heart skipped a beat, a sharp pang of guilt sweeping through him, though he couldn't quite identify its source. He nodded slowly, pressing a kiss to her temple. "I promise," he whispered, though the words felt heavy, tasting like ash on his tongue.

They kissed, losing themselves in each other for a moment, and Orin allowed the doubts to slip away. The fire flickered low, and outside, the world was still and quiet.

In the days that followed, time seemed to blur for Orin, each moment flowing seamlessly into the next. He and Cal threw themselves into building the new playhouse, their work accompanied by the sound of hammers, saws, and bursts of laughter. The scent of sawdust and earth clung to the air, and the old sef-more tree creaked under the weight of their efforts.

Nearby, Shira tended to the garden, her soft humming mingling with the natural sounds around them.

One particularly warm afternoon, the sun hung high in the sky, its heat pressing down as Orin and Cal labored away. Sweat dripped from Orin's brow, and Cal's cheeks were flushed from the exertion, though his enthusiasm never waned. They finally paused for a break, collapsing in the cool shade beneath the sprawling sefmore trunk.

Shira appeared not long after, carrying a pitcher of dandle beer, condensation trickling down the cool mugs in the heat. Her face glowed in the afternoon light as she handed them their drinks, a soft smile playing on her lips.

Cal, always full of energy, barely took a sip before leaping to his feet. "Look, Papa!" he exclaimed, holding up a small wooden carving. "I made a londor bird!"

Orin took the carving from his son's eager hands, turning it over with a smile. The wings were uneven, the beak too long, but Cal's pride in his creation made any imperfections invisible. "It's wonderful," Orin said warmly. "Maybe it'll bring us some good luck."

Cal beamed, his eyes sparkling. "I'm going to hang it in the playhouse!" he declared, already planning where it would go.

Shira laughed softly, ruffling Cal's hair with affection. "At this rate, your playhouse will be the envy of the entire village," she teased gently.

But as she spoke, Orin noticed a brief shadow pass across her face—a flicker of something unreadable. It vanished almost as quickly as it appeared, leaving Orin uneasy, though Shira's smile soon returned.

"Maybe we should invite some of the other children once it's finished," Orin suggested, hoping to lighten the mood.

Cal hesitated for a moment, his enthusiasm dimming slightly. "Maybe," he mumbled, his fingers fidgeting with the hem of his shirt.

Orin glanced over at Shira, noticing how her posture had subtly stiffened, though her smile remained. "We'll see," she said softly, her tone carrying a weight that Orin couldn't quite place. "For now, let's just focus on making it perfect for you."

The tension hung in the air for a moment longer before Cal bounced back, eagerly resuming his plans for the playhouse. Orin joined in the conversation, laughing with his son, though the earlier unease lingered in the back of his mind.

That evening, as the sun sank below the horizon and the cottage grew dim, the scent of Shira's stew filled the room. The rich aroma wafted through the air as they sat down to dinner, but something caught Orin's attention. Shira was wearing a dress he didn't recognize—a deep, shimmering blue that seemed to catch the light from the hearth in an almost ethereal way.

"Is that new?" Orin asked, gesturing to the dress with a curious look.

Shira glanced down, her brow furrowing slightly. "This old thing?" she laughed lightly. "I've had it for ages."

Orin frowned, certain he had never seen it before. "Are you sure? I don't remember ever seeing it."

Shira waved a hand dismissively, her smile turning playful. "You men never notice anything," she teased, though there was a guarded edge to her voice.

Before Orin could press the issue, Cal interrupted, his voice brimming with excitement. "Papa, can we go fishing tomorrow? There's a spot by the river where the Lumen fish glow at dawn! Please?"

Orin turned to his son, smiling despite the tension in the room. "That sounds like a wonderful idea, Cal."

As they ate, however, Orin couldn't shake the feeling that something was off. It wasn't just the dress. The entire room felt different. The table seemed to be positioned at an odd angle, the curtains appeared a shade lighter than he remembered, and every time he tried to focus on these details, they slipped away from him like water through his fingers.

Later that night, after Cal was tucked into bed, Orin stood in the dim light of the bedroom, still feeling unsettled. He hesitated, then turned to Shira with a frown. "Shira, did you move the table?"

As dusk descended, casting the sky in hues of gold and purple, Orin led Cal back inside the cottage. The scent of Shira's cooking filled the air, and Cal chattered excitedly about the playhouse they had been working on and the adventures he planned for it. The day had been perfect, with the fire crackling low and Shira curled against him by the hearth.

Shira's soft voice broke through Orin's thoughts, full of love but tinged with something deeper. "Promise me you'll stay this time," she whispered, her eyes searching his.

For a brief moment, Orin's heart seemed to stop. Guilt—sharp and cold—washed over him, though he couldn't quite place why. He nodded slowly and pressed a kiss to her temple. "I promise," he murmured, though the words felt like ash on his tongue.

They kissed again, losing themselves in the warmth of each other's embrace, and for a while, Orin allowed his doubts to slip away. The fire burned low, and the world outside remained still, wrapped in quiet.

In the days that followed, life settled into a comfortable rhythm of simple pleasures and hard work. Orin and Cal threw themselves into building the playhouse, hammering and sawing as they laughed together. The massive fallen sefmore tree groaned under the weight of the growing structure, and the smell of sawdust and earth filled the air. Shira was always nearby, tending to her garden, her soft humming a constant melody blending with the sounds of nature.

One afternoon, as the sun hung high in the sky and the heat bore down on them, Orin and Cal took a break beneath the shade of the sefmore's trunk. Shira appeared soon after, carrying a pitcher of cool dandle beer, droplets of condensation running down the mugs. She smiled, radiant in the afternoon light, as she handed them the refreshing drinks.

Cal, ever energetic, barely took a sip before jumping to his feet. "Look, Papa!" he exclaimed, holding up a small wooden carving. "I made a londor bird!"

Orin took the carving, turning it over in his hands. The wings were uneven, the beak too long, but Cal's joy made its imperfections disappear. "It's wonderful," Orin said with a smile. "Maybe it'll bring us some good luck."

Cal's chest swelled with pride. "I'm going to hang it in the playhouse!" he declared, already plotting its place.

Shira laughed softly, ruffling Cal's hair. "At this rate, your playhouse will be the envy of the entire village."

But as she spoke, Orin noticed a shadow pass across her face—a brief flicker of something unreadable in her eyes. Before he could dwell on it, her smile returned, and the moment passed as quickly as it had come.

Later that evening, they gathered for dinner, Shira's favorite stew filling the cottage with its rich aroma. As they sat down to eat, Orin noticed Shira was wearing a dress—a shimmering blue gown he had never seen before. It flowed gracefully around her, catching the flickering light of the hearth.

"Is that new?" Orin asked, gesturing to the dress.

Shira glanced down at herself, a playful smile on her lips. "This old thing? I've had it for ages."

Orin frowned, struggling to recall if he had ever seen it before. "Are you sure? I don't remember it."

"You men never notice anything," Shira teased lightly, though there was an edge to her tone, something defensive. Orin opened his mouth to question further, but Cal's eager voice interrupted, asking about a fishing trip the next day.

After dinner, Orin couldn't shake the nagging feeling that something was off. Not just the dress, but the entire cottage—the table seemed to be at an odd angle, the curtains a shade lighter than he remembered. Each time he tried to focus on these details, they slipped away, elusive and fleeting.

Later that night, as they prepared for bed, Orin finally voiced his concerns. "Did you move the table in the dining room?" he asked, the question hanging in the air.

Shira looked at him, puzzled. "The table? Orin, you're imagining things. You're probably just tired."

She smiled warmly, but Orin's unease only deepened. As they lay in bed, he stared up at the ceiling, trying to trace the familiar patterns of the wooden beams. Even they seemed off, somehow.

"You're tense," Shira whispered, resting her hand on his chest. "What's bothering you?"

"I just... I feel like something's off," Orin admitted, struggling to put his thoughts into words. "Little things. I don't know how to explain it."

Shira offered him a comforting explanation—stress from the recent storm, perhaps—but Orin wasn't convinced. Her words made sense on the surface, but the gnawing doubt remained. She kissed him softly. "Try to rest. Tomorrow will be better."

The next morning, Orin and Cal set off for the river, hoping to spot the Lumen fish glowing at dawn. But as they ventured deeper into the forest, the usual sounds of wildlife faded, replaced by an oppressive silence. The further they walked, the quieter it became, as though the forest was holding its breath.

"Papa, look!" Cal's excited shout snapped Orin from his thoughts.

He was crouched by a tree, marveling at a cluster of glowing mushrooms. Orin smiled, kneeling beside him. "They say if you make a wish on one, it might come true," Orin said, his voice low.

Cal's eyes lit up, and after making his wish, they continued toward the river. But soon, a thick fog rolled in, cold and heavy, obscuring the path. Orin's nerves were on edge as they pressed forward, visibility dropping to mere feet.

"This isn't normal," Orin muttered, gripping Cal's hand tightly.

The path that had been clear moments before now twisted and buckled, unfamiliar and unsettling. "Papa..." Cal's voice quivered with fear.

"It's alright," Orin said, trying to stay calm. But even as he spoke, panic gnawed at him.

A haunting melody drifted through the mist—familiar, yet wrong. It was the lullaby Shira used to sing to Cal, but distorted and warped. Orin's breath caught as a soft whisper followed, barely audible but chilling.

"Time's undone, Orin..."

Orin stopped in his tracks, heart hammering in his chest. "Who said that?" he called out, spinning in a circle. But the fog consumed everything beyond a few paces, leaving him feeling small and isolated. Cal tugged on his hand, his brow furrowed with confusion.

"Papa?" the boy's voice trembled, barely more than a whisper.

Forcing a smile, Orin tried to calm his rising fear. "It's nothing, Cal. Let's keep moving."

His words felt hollow, but he needed to reassure his son. Together, they pressed forward, though Orin's mind raced, replaying the strange whisper over and over. Something was wrong, and with each step, the landscape seemed to shift subtly, warping as if it were alive. The trees grew closer, and the ground beneath them seemed to buckle and twist.

Just as Orin began to fear they were hopelessly lost, the fog thinned. Familiar landmarks emerged through the mist, and relief washed over him as the cottage came into view. But something wasn't right. The bushes, which had been torn apart by the storm only days before, now stood tall and vibrant, their red and white blossoms in full bloom. Orin slowed his pace, his eyes narrowing in disbelief.

"Did Mama replant these?" he muttered under his breath, more to himself than to Cal.

"They've always been there, Papa," Cal replied, looking up with innocent confusion.

Orin's heart sank. No—they hadn't. He remembered clearly seeing the storm ravage the garden. Before he could say more, Shira appeared at the cottage door, waving cheerfully.

"There you two are!" she called out, her smile bright. "I was starting to worry."

Orin approached her slowly, his mind clouded with unease. "Did you fix the garden already?" he asked, trying to keep his voice steady.

Shira laughed lightly, her eyes sparkling. "What do you mean? The garden is fine."

He glanced back at the bushes, then at her. "But after the storm, they were destroyed..."

She placed a gentle hand on his arm, her touch warm yet unsettling. "You must be tired, Orin. Come inside, I've prepared lunch."

He allowed her to lead him in, though the inconsistencies gnawed at him. The strange fog, the whisper in the woods, the garden—it all swirled in his mind, pressing on the edges of his sanity. As they sat down to eat, something else caught Orin's attention. Shira was wearing a different dress—a bright yellow one, pristine and almost too new, contrasting with the deep blue gown he was certain she had worn the night before.

"You're wearing a different dress," Orin said, trying to sound casual, though his mind was far from calm.

Shira looked at him, her expression slightly puzzled. "I've had this dress for years, Orin."

He shook his head, his voice firm. "No, you were wearing blue earlier today. I'm sure of it."

Her smile wavered, but only for a moment. "Perhaps you're remembering wrong," she said gently, though something cold flickered behind her eyes.

Turning to Cal, Orin sought validation. "Cal, do you remember what dress Mama was wearing this morning?"

The boy looked up from his bowl, uncertainty clouding his face. "I... I don't know," he mumbled, quickly looking down again.

Shira reached across the table, taking Orin's hand in hers. "Let's not worry about that now," she said softly, her thumb brushing his skin. "Eat your soup before it gets cold."

Orin stared down at the steaming bowl, the scent of herbs and vegetables filling the small room. It looked delicious, but his stomach churned with unease. He couldn't bring himself to take a bite. The nagging feeling that something was terribly wrong had only grown stronger.

"Orin," Shira's voice cut through his thoughts, gentle yet firm. "Everything is alright."

He wanted to believe her. He wanted to dismiss his doubts as nothing more than stress. But the mounting inconsistencies, the whispers, and the shifting world around him wouldn't let him rest. That night, sleep refused to come. Orin lay in bed, staring up at the ceiling, tracing the familiar beams that now twisted in the shadows. The darkness stretched on, and even the sound of Shira's soft breaths beside him felt distant, disconnected from the world.

"Can't sleep?" Shira's voice broke the silence.

Orin glanced over, finding her watching him, concern etched in her face. "Just restless," he muttered, running a hand through his hair.

She reached out, her fingers grazing his arm. "Do you want to talk about it?"

He hesitated. Voicing his fears might make them more real. "I just... I feel like something's wrong," he finally admitted. "Like things aren't the way they should be."

Her expression softened, and she sat up beside him, her touch comforting. "Orin, our minds play tricks on us, especially after the storm. It'll take time for everything to feel normal again."

Orin met her gaze, searching for reassurance, but the doubt gnawed at him. "I keep having these memories—or dreams—of losing you."

Shira smiled, a soft, almost sad smile. "I'm right here. I've always been here."

As she lay back down, rolling over to face away from him, she added softly, "Get some sleep, Orin. You have a busy time undone ahead of you."

Orin's mind swirled with confusion at her words. But before he could dwell on them, exhaustion overwhelmed him, and he passed out.

Orin moved through the following days in a surreal blur, where everything seemed perfect on the surface but carried an undercurrent of unease. He and Cal finished the playhouse, its wooden beams solid, nestled deep within the trunk of the ancient sefmore tree. Cal's laughter filled the clearing as they hammered in the final nails, his joy lighting up the space. Shira kept busy in the kitchen, baking Orin's favorite pastries, their scent mingling with the earthy aromas outside the cottage. In the afternoons, Orin and Cal would head to the river, skipping stones across the water and attempting, unsuccessfully, to catch Lumen fish.

One afternoon, as Orin sat down for lunch, his eyes fell on the painting above the mantel. It had always been a serene depiction of the Spirit Mountains, but now, something was wrong. The once-bright peaks were now shadowed, dark tendrils creeping across the sky. His brow furrowed in confusion.

"Did you alter the painting?" Orin asked, a hint of uncertainty in his voice.

Shira glanced up, her expression calm and unbothered. "No," she replied simply, her tone so neutral it felt dismissive. "It's always been like that."

Orin frowned, shaking his head slowly. "No, it wasn't. It was brighter before, more peaceful."

Shira offered a patient smile, the kind she used when she thought Orin was overthinking things. "Perhaps you're remembering it differently," she said gently.

Unsatisfied, Orin rose from the table and moved closer to the painting. The brushstrokes were familiar, but the colors had darkened, the once-peaceful scene now ominous. His eyes locked onto a figure in the distance, barely noticeable but distinctly wrong.

"Papa, come sit!" Cal's voice interrupted Orin's thoughts, bringing him back to the moment. "The food is getting cold."

Reluctantly, Orin returned to the table, forcing a smile. "Of course," he said, though the unease gnawed at him.

As they ate, Orin's gaze flicked between Shira and Cal. Cal's stories about catching giant fish were wild and enthusiastic, and Shira's laughter was warm, her eyes soft with affection. It should have been enough to calm Orin, but out of the corner of his eye, he noticed something unsettling: Shira's dress. She was now wearing a deep red gown with intricate gold embroidery. It shimmered in the candlelight, a striking contrast to anything Orin had seen her wear before.

"That's a beautiful dress," Orin remarked, his tone cautious as he watched her closely.

Shira glanced down at the fabric, her fingers brushing it as though she hadn't noticed it before. "Thank you," she replied smoothly, her voice unreadable.

"Is it new?" Orin pressed, the knot of unease tightening in his stomach.

Her gaze met his, guarded and distant. "I've had it for some time," she said, her voice calm but her eyes betraying nothing.

Orin nodded slowly, choosing not to push the matter, though the tension settled deeper within him. That evening, long after the sun had set and the cottage was bathed in the soft glow of the hearth, Orin found himself wandering outside. He sought solace in the night air, lighting his pipe filled with Turpin root, hoping the familiar habit would calm his racing mind.

The sky above was a brilliant tapestry of shimmering green twinkles, the moon casting its silver light across the landscape. But as Orin stared up at the constellations, he realized something was wrong. The stars were misaligned, the patterns unfamiliar, as though the very heavens had shifted.

"The Eye of Mother... it's so much bigger," Orin muttered to himself, dread creeping into his thoughts.

"Enjoying the view?" Shira's voice floated over his shoulder, startling him despite its warmth.

Orin turned to see her standing behind him, her presence serene yet unsettling. "Something feels off," he admitted, unable to keep the words in. "The Eye—it's bigger. And the moon... it's being swallowed."

Shira stepped closer, slipping her hand into his. Her touch was cool, but her grip steady. "You're overthinking again," she said softly, her voice soothing but carrying an undercurrent of something Orin couldn't place.

"Maybe," Orin conceded, though the feeling of unease only deepened. "But it's like pieces of the world have shifted, moved in ways they shouldn't."

She smiled gently, squeezing his hand. "The world is always changing, Orin. We have to change with it."

Orin searched her face, looking for reassurance. "Promise me this is real," he whispered, his voice betraying his growing desperation.

Her smile faltered, just for a moment. Her eyes flickered with something unreadable. "What else would it be?" she asked softly, though the question felt more like a challenge than comfort.

Orin took a deep breath, his heart heavy with doubt. "A dream," he murmured. "Or worse."

Shira stepped even closer, guiding his hand to her chest, pressing it against the steady rhythm of her heartbeat. "Feel this," she whispered, her voice a calming murmur. "I'm here. With you."

The steady thrum of her heart beneath his palm grounded him, yet the doubts refused to leave entirely. Even as Orin closed his eyes, trying to let go of the unsettling feelings, a part of him remained convinced that something, somewhere, was terribly wrong.

The night pressed down on Orin like a suffocating weight as Shira's words rang in his ears, firm yet distant. "You won't," she had assured him, her voice steady. "Come inside. It's getting cold."

Inside the cottage, the warmth of the hearth felt false. The fire crackled softly, casting flickering shadows across the walls, but there was an odd chill creeping into the room. Orin sat at the dinner table, staring at the hearty stew before him. Its rich aroma of meat and spices should have been comforting, yet it was cloying, oppressive. His stomach churned as he glanced around the room, feeling a strange sense of disconnection.

Across the table, Cal sat in silence, his small hands resting beside his untouched meal. The boy stared intently at his food, his focus unsettling. Shira, sitting beside him, moved mechanically as she ate, each movement too precise, her spoon tapping rhythmically against her bowl.

"Did you enjoy your pipe?" Shira's soft voice broke the silence, though there was something unnatural about her tone, like she didn't expect a response.

Orin hesitated. The words caught in his throat as the unease from earlier gnawed at him. "It was... very pleasant," he finally replied, though it felt like a lie. His mind was still fixated on the stars, on how wrong they had seemed. He glanced at her, forcing a smile. "Just observing the stars."

"Oh?" she replied, a thin smile curving her lips, though her eyes didn't quite meet his.

The tension in the room mounted, the shadows along the walls seeming to stretch and darken. Orin's sense of being watched grew unbearable, the sensation prickling at the back of his neck.

Then, Cal dropped his spoon. The sharp clatter against the bowl cut through the quiet like a blade. Orin flinched, his heart leaping in his chest. He turned to his son, but Cal remained rigid, unmoving, his wide eyes staring straight ahead, unfocused and distant.

"Cal?" Orin called, his voice tight with concern.

There was no response. Cal's lips parted slightly, a shallow breath escaping, but no words followed. The chill in the room deepened, a cold that seeped into Orin's bones.

"Cal?" Orin's voice grew louder, laced with fear.

Shira's head snapped toward their son, her eyes narrowing. "Is everything alright, darling?" she asked, though her words were hollow, like they were being recited from memory.

Cal's lips moved, parting just enough for a faint whisper to slip through. "Time is lost," he murmured, barely audible, yet the words struck Orin like a hammer.

Orin froze, his heart pounding in his chest. "What did you say?"

Cal didn't look at him, simply repeated the phrase with slightly more force. "Time is lost."

A cold wave of dread washed over Orin. His gaze darted to Shira, seeking reassurance, but her face remained neutral, as if none of this was unexpected.

"Cal, eat your dinner," Shira said, her voice soft yet disturbingly detached.

But Cal didn't move. Instead, his voice grew louder, repeating the phrase with an eerie insistence. "Time is lost. Time is lost. Time is lost."

Orin's heart raced, panic surging through him. "Cal, stop that," he said, trying to sound firm, but his voice wavered with fear.

Cal's voice crescendoed into a near scream, his words filling the room like a twisted chant. "TIME IS LOST! TIME IS LOST!"

"Cal, enough!" Orin shouted, his pulse quickening. But his son didn't hear him. Cal's wide eyes, pupils blown, seemed to gaze into some unseen horror, his small body trembling as he stood on his chair, now screaming, "TIME IS LOST! TIME IS LOST! TIME IS LOST!"

Orin turned to Shira, panic rising in his throat. "Shira, what's happening?"

But when he looked at her, the air around her shifted. Something in Shira had broken. Her wide eyes locked onto Orin's, her mouth twisting into a grotesque smile that didn't belong on her face. And then she began to laugh—a soft, unsettling giggle at first, but it quickly escalated into a wild, uncontrollable cackle that echoed around the room.

Orin's stomach churned in terror. "Shira! Stop!" he cried, leaping from his chair, his hands trembling.

But she didn't stop. Her laughter grew, a maniacal sound that bubbled up from her chest as she clawed at her own sides, raking her nails down her arms, drawing thin lines of blood. Crimson welled up, spreading across her pale skin.

"Shira!" Orin begged, rushing toward her, but she jerked away, still laughing, tears streaming down her face.

And then, without warning, a deep, jagged gash opened across her throat. Blood poured from the wound, soaking the front of her dress, but she didn't seem to notice. She just kept laughing, her manic cackle filling the room as the blood spilled down her chest, staining everything in its path.

"SHIRA!" Orin screamed, stumbling back, his mind unable to process the horror before him.

And then, Cal's voice pierced the chaos once more. "TIME IS LOST! TIME IS LOST!" His small frame shook as he stood on the chair, his screams now otherworldly.

Orin's world spun as he looked between his son and his wife, the terror overwhelming him. "What is happening?" he whispered, his voice barely audible, his body trembling as the nightmare unfolded before his eyes.

Both of them stopped then, their laughter and screams cutting off abruptly. In eerie unison, Shira and Cal turned their heads toward Orin, their eyes hollow, devoid of life, as if whatever humanity they once had had been extinguished. Their voices joined together in a guttural, nightmarish shriek.

"You didn't save us!"

The words hit Orin like a physical blow, reverberating through his skull. His knees buckled under the weight of it. They stepped toward him, their movements unnatural, jerky, and then, as if made of ash, their bodies began to disintegrate. Pieces of them flaked away, their skin turning to dust, collapsing in on itself as they dissolved before his eyes.

Orin watched in horror as they crumbled, the ash swirling around him, their haunting accusation lingering in the air.

"You didn't save us!" they screamed, even as their forms disintegrated, the dust scattering across the floor like remnants of a nightmare.

Orin stood frozen, trembling, unable to move or breathe. The room fell into a deafening silence. The fire in the hearth was now cold, its once warm glow replaced by an icy void. The weight of the empty room pressed in on him, suffocating in its stillness.

"Shira? Cal?" Orin whispered, his voice cracking. But there was no answer.

Stumbling backward, he collapsed into a chair, his hands shaking violently as he buried his face in them. The truth crashed over him like a tidal wave. This wasn't a dream. The memories came rushing back—the battle, the destruction, the cold, lifeless bodies of his wife and son lying in the ashes of their home.

This was the illusion.

Tears streamed down Orin's face as sobs wracked his body. The crushing weight of his grief was unbearable. He cried for them, for everything he had lost, for the cruel trick his mind had played on him. The suffocating despair of their absence settled over him like an anchor, dragging him deeper into a void he couldn't escape.

And as he sat there, alone in the cold, hollow room, Orin realized there was no waking from this nightmare.

419

17
Feral

A soft voice whispered through Orin's mind, "Come to me, Orin."

It was a sweet, aching echo that made his heart wrench. He shook his head violently, pushing it away, refusing to listen. His hands trembled, fingers caked with soil and blood as he packed the last of the overturned dirt. He didn't care about the grit coating his skin or the sweat dripping from his brow. The sun punched through the dying canopy, blinding and harsh, but Orin barely noticed. His face was streaked with dirt, tears mingling with dust and drying around his beard in a crusty mask. He didn't care.

All he could think about were the two mounds of earth before him.

Orin stumbled to a nearby tree, ripping off a wide tiran leaf and using it to smooth the dirt around the freshly dug graves. The motion was automatic, mechanical—something to keep his hands busy, to keep his mind from shattering completely. But no matter how hard he tried, he couldn't escape the truth staring back at him from the ground. He kept waiting—hoping, pleading—that at any moment he'd wake up from this nightmare. That he'd open his eyes to Shira's soft voice calling him to breakfast or the sound of Cal's little feet tapping excitedly down the hallway. That he'd feel Shira's warm hand on his shoulder, her laugh filling the room as she teased him for falling asleep in the backyard again.

But the yard remained empty and silent. The sun climbed higher, burning away the last remnants of the cool morning breeze. The house stood desolate behind him, every window a dark, hollow eye staring out at nothing. He kept glancing over his shoulder, hoping—begging—to see someone, anyone, walking up the path. But no one came. No one ever would.

Orin finished the graves, placing them side by side under the oldest sefmore tree in the yard—the same place where he'd buried his parents all those years ago. He used to think it was a peaceful spot, where the roots of the great tree reached deep, protecting those who rested beneath. Now, it felt like a cruel mockery, a place that had become a tomb for everyone he had ever loved.

He looked at the house—their home—the place where they had built a life, shared laughter, and made plans for a future that would never be. There would be no more lively chatter in the marketplace. No more butcher's shop filled with the smells of fresh meat and spices. No more evenings at the pub where Ferkin would crash after drinking too much, bragging about some nonsense while they all laughed. Everything was gone, reduced to dirt and ash in the span of a few days.

His hands were numb as he twisted together brittle vines from the torn bushes, forming them into a crude wreath. A thorn bit deep into his palm, and blood trickled down his wrist, but Orin barely felt it. The wreath had no real purpose, no meaning. But every sixth day, Shira would sit in the kitchen for hours, weaving flowers and vines into beautiful wreaths to brighten up the house. She would smile, that soft, secret smile of hers, and say, "When I die, I hope you'll put one of these on my grave."

His chest tightened painfully. He placed the thorny wreath gently atop her grave, then another beside it, for Cal. They looked pitiful, haphazard, like the kind of thing he would've done as a boy and shown to her with pride, only to have her laugh and kiss his cheek, promising to teach him how to do it right.

A memory surfaced of his mother's voice, soft and full of sorrow, telling him that time heals all things after his grandfather died. It was a lie. A cruel, stupid lie.

"What a load of shit," he muttered bitterly, staring at the mounds of dirt that now served as his family's resting place.

Anger coiled in his chest, a dark, twisting serpent of rage that made his hands shake. He could see it in his mind—their last moments. Shira's screams, Cal's cries of terror. The fleshers ripping them apart, laughing as they tore into his wife and son. A snarl escaped him as he imagined himself there, slashing at those monsters, tearing them apart limb by limb until there was nothing left but a bloody mess.

His vision blurred. He reached up, clutching the wooden necklace around his neck that Cal had made for him, his tiny hands working so hard to carve the little spirit tree. Orin could almost hear his son's voice, the way Cal had called his name, so full of fear.

"Cal!" Orin screamed, the sound tearing from his throat, raw and broken. He fell to his knees, clutching the pendant so hard it bit into his skin. "I should have been there! I should have saved you!"

His voice cracked, the words splintering under the weight of his guilt. It was his fault. He hadn't been there. He hadn't protected them. He should've been at home, not at some pointless town hall meeting. Ferkin had told him to go, convinced him that it was important. But it wasn't. It was a stupid, meaningless waste of time, and now his family was dead.

"I believed in you!" Orin screamed up at the sky, his voice hoarse and ragged. "I trusted you to watch over us and keep us safe!"

The necklace burned against his chest, a reminder of every broken promise, every vow he'd failed to keep. With a snarl, he ripped it from his neck and hurled it. "How could you?!" he roared, fists pounding against the dirt. "How could YOU?! They were my family!"

His knuckles split open, blood mixing with the dirt as he slammed his fists again and again into the ground. He cursed the Great Mother's name until his voice was nothing but a strangled rasp, until his arms were weak and trembling. He collapsed onto his side, ribs screaming in pain, gasping for breath. "Shira... I'm sorry," he whispered brokenly. "Please, please come back. I'll do better next time. I swear it. I—I won't leave you alone again. Please, just... just come back..."

But there was no answer. No soft voice. No gentle touch. Only silence.

Orin waited, curling in on himself, desperately listening for the whisper he longed for. But as the minutes stretched on and the day slipped by, the silence remained unbroken. His chest ached, the hollow inside him yawning wider with every passing second. He pulled his knees to his chest, curling up in the dirt beside the graves, letting the sobs consume him—great, wrenching sobs that tore through his chest, leaving him breathless and broken.

"I'm sorry," he whimpered again and again, the words fading into the wind. "I'm so sorry..."

The day dragged on, the sun climbing high overhead and then slipping away, its light replaced by the pale, cold glow of the moon and the eye of the Great Mother. Orin lay there, curled in the dirt like a child, wanting nothing but to be loved, to be held. He closed his eyes and imagined Shira's arms around him, Cal's laughter echoing through the yard as they played by the stream. He pictured them gathering stones together, building something beautiful.

No more than an hour passed before the tears finally dried, leaving his eyes raw and aching. His head pounded with every beat of his heart, each pulse a sharp, blinding throb behind his temples. He blinked against the pain, forcing himself upright. His legs felt like stone, his entire body protesting as he stood and faced the sky.

"You are no mother of mine, and I am no child of yours!" he snarled through gritted teeth, the words ripping from his throat like a curse.

All the stories he had been told as a child, the tales of the Great Mother's wisdom and mercy, seemed like mockery now. He had never questioned them, out of fear that doubt would bring her wrath, that to question was to invite eternal damnation. But now? Now he had nothing left to lose. Now he stood among the shattered remains of everything he loved, and the faith he had clung to all his life felt like a cruel, empty lie.

He scoffed bitterly and turned away from the empty sky. The necklace that Cal had made lay glinting dully in the dirt, a reminder of his rage and failure. With a sigh, Orin bent down and picked it up, threading it back around his neck. Guilt twisted his gut. He had thrown away the last gift his son had made for him, something the boy had poured his tiny hands and hopeful heart into crafting. What kind of man was he to discard it so thoughtlessly?

As he turned back toward the graves, the pain swelling fresh in his chest, a sound froze him in place.

A small, brittle crack echoed—a creak of wood shifting, like the sound of a vase shattering. Orin knew that sound. His heart clenched as the memory of Cal breaking Shira's favorite vase rushed back. The sharp noise echoed in his mind, mingling with the sound he'd just heard. But this wasn't a memory. This was real. He whipped around, his heart hammering wildly, eyes darting to the house.

Something—or someone—was inside.

His hand flew to his sword, gripping the hilt so tightly his knuckles turned white. Adrenaline surged through him, every nerve alight. Blood pounded in his ears as he rushed toward the house, his body moving on pure instinct. Any pain, any exhaustion, was forgotten, replaced by a blinding need for revenge. He would make the monsters who did this pay. He would cut them down, one by one, until he stood knee-deep in their black blood.

He burst through the back door, the wood splintering under the force, and sprinted down the hallway.
His sword was drawn, the blade gleaming in the faint
light as he rounded the corner into the living room. He
could see the dark shadow stretched across the far
wall, a twisted silhouette, and he let out a roar—his
vision blurring with fury as he swung at the figure.

The shadow leapt away, crashing into the cold fireplace. A cloud of gray ash exploded around the room.
Orin coughed, waving a hand to clear the dust as
he raised his sword again, ready to strike. But then
he heard it—a small, pitiful cough, so soft it barely
reached his ears.

He hesitated, blinking through the haze. Slowly, cautiously, he stepped forward, peering into the cloud of
dust. A small shape began to emerge—a frail form
hunched against the soot-stained hearth.

His breath caught.

A little girl's face stared back at him from the dust,
her red-tinged hair tangled and matted, partially cov-
ering her thin, skeletal features. Soot smeared across
her cheeks, her lips twisted back in a snarl that bared
pale yellow teeth. Her eyes, impossibly wide and

bright blue, blazed with a feral intensity, watching him like a cornered animal.

She hissed, the sound low and menacing, her lips curling back as if she meant to bite. Freckles dotted her gaunt face, disappearing into the dirt and grime that clung to her skin. Beneath the dirt, he could see just how malnourished she was—nothing more than skin and bones wrapped in ragged clothes.

"What's your name?" Orin asked softly, lowering his sword slightly.

She didn't move, didn't blink. Just stared at him with those piercing eyes, her body coiled like a spring, ready to lash out. He forced a smile, trying to look less threatening, but the girl lunged at him with a snarl, clawing at his face.

"Hey!" he yelped, grabbing the back of her black tunic and flinging her across the room.

She crashed into the kitchen table, knocking it sideways, but before he could even draw breath, she scrambled to her feet, still hissing, eyes locked on him like a predator sizing up its prey.

Orin held up his hands in a gesture of peace. "I can help you!" he shouted, his voice calm despite the tension in the air.

The girl leapt onto the edge of the turned-over table, crouching like a wild animal. Her eyes darted around the room, restless and full of suspicion. Then, they locked onto something behind him. Slowly, Orin turned, following her gaze. The roast—Shira's last meal—still sat on the counter, stale and hardened, forgotten in the chaos.

"Are you hungry?" Orin asked gently, taking a cautious step closer.

Her eyes remained fixed on the roast. The hunger in her expression was unmistakable—she was starving. Orin took another step, trying to ease the tension between them. "My name is Orin," he said softly, making his voice as soothing as possible. "What's your name?"

The girl's eyes flicked back to him, wary and mistrustful. He could see the internal struggle—whether to trust him or grab the food and run. She looked half-wild, a child thrown into a world of horrors and left to fend for herself. Slowly, ever so slowly, she lowered her guard.

"I'm Maurelle," she whispered, her voice barely audible, strained as if she hadn't spoken in a long time.

"Maurelle," Orin repeated softly. "That's a lovely name." She said nothing, her gaze still locked on the roast, licking her cracked lips.

"How about I fix you some food?" Orin offered, taking another step closer. "You can eat as much as you want, and maybe... maybe you can tell me about yourself?"

Maurelle didn't respond. Slowly, she stepped off the table, her eyes never leaving him. She shrugged off the black cloak, revealing her thin, battered frame wrapped in patched leather armor. Her trousers were old and tattered, and the leather was frayed at the edges. A crudely hammered bronze chest plate covered her torso, the straps hanging loosely around her thin shoulders. Her midriff was bare, the skin marred by scars and bruises. Her arms, wrapped in ill-fitting leather braces, hung at her sides, tense and ready.

Orin's heart ached at the sight. She was just a child, alone and afraid, left to scavenge and survive in the ruins of a world torn apart by monsters. Slowly, Orin sheathed his sword and held out his hands to show he meant no harm.

"It's okay, Maurelle," he murmured, keeping his voice low and calm. "I won't hurt you. You're safe here."

But as he spoke, a chilling thought struck him. She shouldn't be here. The fleshers had torn through the village and killed everyone. No one should have survived. How had she?

"Maurelle," Orin asked quietly, his heart pounding in his chest. "Where did you come from? How... how did you get here?"

She hesitated, her eyes flicking to the door and then back to him. Her tiny fists clenched, and for a moment, Orin thought she would bolt.

But then, softly, she whispered, "I hid."

Something in her voice, in the haunted look in her eyes, made Orin realize—she wasn't hiding from the fleshers. She had been hiding from everyone.

His stomach twisted at the thought. A street kid, alone and battered, who had somehow survived while everyone else perished. His gaze fell to the emblem on her chest—an unfamiliar design he'd never seen in their village or any neighboring ones. But her vivid red hair, tangled and wild, marked her unmistakably as a Lowlander, one of the last of their people to carry the old blood.

Maurelle moved with surprising ease, lifting the table and dropping into a seat with a sense of impatience, as if humoring him by staying. Orin watched her warily as he moved to the kitchen and pulled out two plates. But the moment his hand reached for a knife, Maurelle froze. Her eyes went wide with fear, her body tensing like a cornered animal.

"Hey! I'm not going to hurt you!" Orin blurted out, panic tightening his chest.

The knife wavered in his grip as he held it up for her to see, his hands trembling slightly. "It's just for the roast. That's all."

Maurelle's eyes remained fixed on the blade as Orin sawed through the dry meat. The roast was so tough it felt like cutting through old leather, but he managed to pry off a piece and slide it toward her.

Before Orin could set it down, she snatched it up, tearing into it with feral intensity. Her teeth sank into the tough meat as if it were nothing, chewing and swallowing with a speed that left Orin speechless. She devoured the first piece before he had even cut another. Stunned, he carved another portion and slid it over, but she wolfed it down just as quickly, her jaws working like a beast.

"How...?" Orin murmured, half to himself.

The roast had been left out for days, dry and hard enough to make his own jaw ache just thinking about biting into it. Yet, Maurelle tore through it with an ease that seemed unnatural. Orin shook his head, watching her in disbelief.

"Where are you from?" he asked softly, trying to understand this strange girl who had appeared in his home.

But she didn't respond. She didn't even look up, her eyes fixed on the next piece of meat like a starving dog guarding its meal. Frustration simmered in Orin's chest. Shira would never have tolerated this kind of behavior, and neither would he.

Orin cleared his throat loudly, the sharp sound cutting through the quiet room. "I said, where are you from?" he repeated, his voice firmer, laced with irritation.

He expected her to flinch, to show some sign of remorse. But instead, Maurelle turned her gaze toward him, her eyes flat and emotionless. "Around," she muttered dismissively.

Orin clenched his teeth, fighting back the angry retort that threatened to escape. They stared at each other for a long, tense moment, and then, with deliberate defiance, Maurelle reached out and grabbed the entire roast. Snarling, she bit into it, tearing off a chunk and chewing loudly.

Orin's hands tightened into fists, but he forced himself to remain calm.

Orin watched as the girl let out a growling burp, wiping her mouth with a careless swipe of her sleeve. Her eyes, finally breaking from the food, wandered around the room until they landed on the bloodstains darkening the floorboards.

"Who died?" she asked casually, her tone as indifferent as if she were inquiring about the weather.

Orin's stomach twisted at her words. He followed her gaze to the dark stain on the floor, where Shira had fallen, her life spilling out into the cracks of their home. His throat tightened, struggling to keep his voice steady.

"My wife," he managed, the words heavy with grief. "She was killed by fleshers. I couldn't get to her in time."

A flash of pain crossed his face as the memory of Shira's broken body resurfaced, the blood soaking her golden hair. Rage bubbled up inside him when he noticed the faintest flicker of a smile on Maurelle's lips. His fists clenched, but then he realized it wasn't a smirk; her expression was distant, detached.

"Time," she murmured, an eerie smile creeping across her face. "I couldn't do anything with time."

Orin frowned in confusion. "What are you talking about?" he snapped, frustration seeping into his voice.

"I never had enough time," she whispered, eyes unfocused, as if lost in another world. "But I always had too much." She let out a hollow, almost eerie laugh. "My mother used to say that."

Orin muttered under his breath, rubbing his temples in frustration. "What does that even mean?"

She didn't answer, only smiled as if she knew something he couldn't grasp. Letting out a sigh, Orin realized pressing her for answers was pointless. She wasn't going to tell him anything she didn't want to. He watched as Maurelle pushed away from the table, her small frame slipping past him into the living room. Orin followed, keeping a wary eye on her.

She stopped in front of the wall where his family pictures used to hang. The faded, broken frames lay shattered, their contents long gone. Her fingers brushed lightly over a spot of blood smeared across the wood, her expression thoughtful.

"What's this?" she asked, pointing to the crimson stain.

Orin stepped closer, eyes narrowing at the dark blotch. "It's... blood," he said quietly, his throat tightening again.

"Why is it doing that?" Maurelle's voice suddenly sharpened.

Orin's heart raced. The blood—what little remained—seemed to shift ever so slightly, moving beneath a faint breeze drifting through the shattered door. It slid across the wood, almost alive, before vanishing into the grain.

He leaned in closer, his pulse quickening. "What...?" His fingers brushed the wood, feeling the roughness of dried blood, but in the still-wet spots, the surface was smooth, almost glossy.

A shiver ran down his spine.

"We need more blood," he whispered, the realization hitting him like a bolt of lightning.

There was something here—something hidden, something vital. Without thinking, Orin turned and rushed past Maurelle, his mind spinning. He had to know more. He had to understand what was happening.

As he reached the door, he threw a glance over his shoulder at the strange girl who stood watching him, her head tilted to one side. "Don't steal anything," he muttered, his voice firm.

Maurelle raised an eyebrow, a faint smirk playing on her lips. "Where would I put it?" she asked dryly, gesturing to her tattered clothes.

Orin shook his head and stepped outside. The wind whipped across his face, carrying the scent of blood and ash. The world outside was withering. Trees once lush and green were now browning at the edges, their leaves curling and falling in a deathly cascade. The forest, once vibrant, was collapsing, drained of life, as though a curse was spreading through it.

Through the dying trees, Orin's eyes were drawn to the Great Spirit Tree. Once hidden by the dense canopy, it now stood stark and skeletal, its branches stripped bare, its mighty trunk gaunt and exposed.

His heart clenched. The Spirit Tree had never been visible before—something was deeply wrong. He had no idea what was causing the decay, but deep down, he knew. It had to be the fleshers. They were a plague, a poison corrupting everything they touched.

Orin's gaze swept the streets, searching desperately. He needed more blood. The stench of decay filled his nostrils as he stepped forward, past bodies strewn across the ground. Then, he saw it—a small figure lying crumpled in the dirt not far from his house.

His breath caught in his throat as he approached, heart pounding. He knelt beside the body, using his sword to gently roll it over.

It was a child. His skin had been stripped away, leaving raw muscle exposed. His face was barely recognizable, but beside him, a pointed black hat and a torn green vest lay in the dirt. Orin's heart froze.

The hat... the vest... His mind reeled.

Orin stared down at the small body, his chest tightening painfully. There were no more tears left to shed, no grief able to surface. He felt hollow, empty, numb. But a flicker of something—surprise, confusion—flickered through the void. Noro should have been safe. Orin had seen him and his mother, Kerra, heading into the forest after the town hall meeting. Why was he here? How had he ended up back in the village?

Shaking his head, Orin struggled to make sense of the questions swirling unanswered in his mind. Slowly, he lowered his sword, using the blade to roll the small body onto its side. His stomach churned as Noro's limp form shifted, lifeless. Gritting his teeth, Orin pressed the tip of his sword into the child's chest. The blade pierced muscle, and thick, dark blood oozed out sluggishly, like sap. Orin clenched his jaw, watching as the crimson liquid trickled down the blade. Carefully, he lifted Noro's black hat, catching the blood as it dripped, the hat slowly filling.

Orin's hand shook as he straightened, staring down at the lifeless form of his son's best friend. A child. Noro should have been playing in the woods, laughing and running free—not lying dead, skinned, on the streets of their broken village. Nausea twisted in his gut, but he swallowed it back, turning away.

Then, something else caught his eye. A small figure rested at the base of a sefmore tree. Hesitant, Orin squinted through the gray morning light. As he drew closer, he saw that it was a dixin fairy, its tiny body curled up against the tree's roots. Orin knelt down, his heart aching at the sight. The fairy looked so small, so fragile. Its delicate skin had turned a sickly gray, and its once-bright wings were now dulled and lifeless.

He reached out, brushing his fingers lightly over its tiny cheek. Cold. The fairy was dead. A lump rose in Orin's throat as he noticed the tiny sword clutched in its hand, crudely carved from a black wood branch. It seemed the fairy had tried to defend itself in its final moments.

"Poor little thing," Orin whispered, shaking his head sadly.

Suddenly, the fairy moved.

Orin jerked back, heart pounding in his chest. The tiny mouth opened, and its dead, milky eyes rolled back in its skull. Then, it began to scream.

The sound was shrill and piercing, sending shivers down Orin's spine. He stumbled back, horrified, as the dead fairy let out that terrible, unearthly wail. Its face twisted in agony, the sound raw and desperate, like a soul trapped in unending torment.

"What...?" Orin breathed, his voice trembling.

The fairy was dead—cold and lifeless—yet it screamed. The noise tore through the air, making Orin's ears ring and the hairs on his arms stand on end. He stood transfixed, unable to move, unable to breathe.

The scream went on and on, unbroken, unrelenting.

Minutes passed, but the fairy didn't stop.

Orin had no idea what kind of horror could make a creature scream even after death, but the sight and sound of it felt like a knife twisting in his gut.

"What are you doing?" Maurelle's voice rang out, snapping Orin from his trance.

He flinched, turning sharply to see her standing in the doorway of his house, her expression impatient.

Orin looked back at the fairy, at its tiny, twisted face, before turning away, his hands shaking. He headed back toward the house.

"Did you get lost or something?" Maurelle demanded, tapping her foot as Orin approached. "You took forever."

His jaw tightened, anger flaring hot in his chest. Biting back a retort, he brushed past her, ignoring the sharp look she shot him as he stepped into the living room. She followed, hovering close behind.

"So, what now?" she asked, her voice grating against his raw nerves.

Orin didn't answer. His gaze was fixed on the wall, on the spot where the blood had moved. Taking the blood-filled hat, he flung it at the wall. The dark liquid splattered across the wood, and slowly, it began to trickle down, soaking into the floorboards. But some of it didn't. In certain places, the blood seemed to catch, pooling and spreading, forming strange, jagged lines.

Symbols began to appear—etched into the wood as if the blood were revealing something hidden beneath the surface.

Maurelle's eyes widened, her mouth dropping open slightly. "What... what do they mean?" she whispered in awe.

Orin leaned closer, squinting at the symbols. They were crude, almost childlike, but something about them tugged at a distant memory. They weren't from Terra. He'd seen something like them once, long ago, in an old book about the neighboring kingdoms.

"I think they're Ballatorian," Orin murmured, tracing one of the lines with his finger. "This one... it means 'Great Spirit.'" He moved his hand to another. "And this... I think this one means 'Risen.'"

An excited grin spread across Maurelle's face. "Risen?" she repeated, breathless. "Then what are we waiting for?"

Orin blinked, taken aback by the sudden intensity in her eyes. "What...? What do you mean?"

"Let's go to Ballator, to the Great Spirit Rock!" she urged, her gaze flicking back to the symbols. "If they have an army, they can help us. We can't stay here."

Her voice grew soft, almost wistful, as she glanced out the window at the dying trees. "There's nothing left here, Orin. It's all gone. Everything."

Orin glanced around the room, the stillness wrapping around him like a suffocating shroud. For a brief, fleeting moment, he could almost hear the soft patter of Cal's little feet racing down the hallway, his son's laughter echoing through the house. The scent of Shira's cooking seemed to drift through the air—turpin root bread baking in the oven, the rich aroma of dandle beer brewing on the table. His mind filled in the missing pieces, painting a scene of warmth and life. For just a heartbeat, everything felt normal, like it always had been. As if he only needed to step into the kitchen to see Shira humming softly to herself, her hair tied back as she cooked. As if Cal would come barreling around the corner, giggling, his little face flushed with excitement.

But it wasn't real.

Maurelle's voice sliced through the fragile illusion, shattering it like glass. "So, what do you think?" she asked, her tone casual.

The sound yanked Orin back into the cold, empty present, dragging him out of that brief escape. He flinched, the warmth of the memory replaced by a rush of anger and grief.

"No!" Orin roared, the word exploding from him before he could stop it.

Maurelle jumped back, her eyes wide with shock. "This is my home!" Orin shouted, his voice breaking. "I'm not leaving my family!"

His chest heaved, desperation clawing at him, his heart feeling torn between the need to hold on to what was left and the painful truth that it was all gone. Each word was like a plea to the universe to let him stay, to let him keep this one thing when everything else had been taken away.

He turned sharply, shoving past Maurelle, not caring that he nearly knocked her over. Rage and grief blurred his vision as he stormed down the hallway, his footsteps echoing loudly in the silence. He threw open the door to his bedroom, slamming it shut behind him.

The moment Orin stepped inside, his knees buckled. The bed stood there, untouched, the quilt still rumpled from that last morning. Shira's pillow—her favorite, soft and floral—still bore the faint imprint of her head. The scent of her perfume lingered, light and delicate, wrapping around him like a cruel reminder of what he had lost. His legs gave out, and he collapsed onto the bed, crawling into the same spot where he had slept beside her for seventeen years. He reached for her pillow, pulling it close, clutching it desperately as if holding onto it could somehow bring her back.

"I miss you," Orin whispered, his voice cracking as he buried his face into the fabric. It still smelled like her—faintly floral, with a hint of the spices she used in the kitchen. "I miss you so much."

He shut his eyes tight, holding the pillow close, willing himself to feel her warmth, to imagine her lying beside him. The illusion was fragile, slipping through his fingers like sand no matter how tightly he clung. "Please," he murmured, his voice muffled against the pillow. "Please, just... just come back. Let me hear your voice again, just once."

But there was nothing. No answer. No comforting touch.

The harder he tried to hold onto her memory, the further away it seemed to slip. Even the scent of her perfume felt like it was fading, turning into something distant and unreachable. He clutched the pillow tighter, his body trembling with the effort of holding back the sobs that threatened to tear him apart.

"Please come back," he begged, the words breaking into a silent sob. "Please... I can't do this alone."

The silence pressed down on him, heavy and suffocating, smothering the last flicker of hope. Time blurred, slipping by unnoticed as he lay there, clutching the pillow like a lifeline. The sun dipped lower, the room growing darker, the shadows stretching long and cold. Orin felt the day slipping away, felt the world turning without him.

"Orin."

The sound of Maurelle's voice pulled him back, distant and muffled through the closed door. "Are you coming out?" she called, the faintest hint of impatience in her tone. "Or should I wait a little longer?"

Orin rubbed his eyes, blinking against the dim light. Slowly, reluctantly, he loosened his grip on the pillow and pushed himself up. It felt like letting go of Shira all over again, a fresh stab of pain that left him hollow. He turned, glancing one last time at the rumpled bed, at the ghost of her presence.

And then he forced himself to walk away.

He opened the door, his gaze falling on Maurelle leaning against the doorframe. She glanced up, fiddling absently with her hair. Her expression shifted, softening slightly as she looked at him.

"So... I guess I might have been a bit rude before, huh?" she muttered awkwardly, her eyes flicking to his red, puffy face.

Orin didn't answer. He didn't trust himself to speak. He brushed past her, moving stiffly down the hall and into the living room. The cold night blew in through the broken door, carrying the sharp stench of rot and decay. He inhaled deeply, the putrid smell burning his lungs.

"Thank you for tidying up," Orin murmured, glancing at the small pile of shattered wood and debris she had swept together.

Maurelle's eyes brightened, a faint, pleased smile tugging at her lips. "Well, you did feed me."

Orin turned, following Maurelle's gaze as she peeked out the doorway. "The smell's getting worse," she said, wrinkling her nose. He stared out into the darkened street, his eyes narrowing at the sight.

"Everything is dead or dying," Orin muttered, his voice rough with a mix of grief and exhaustion.

The street that had once been full of life had transformed into a barren wasteland. The vibrant colors of the flowers had disappeared, replaced by a sickly gray. The luminescent blooms that once lined the path were now withered and blackened, their petals curling inward. Dead leaves lay scattered across the ground, piling up against the lifeless bodies strewn along the road.

"It's all very strange," Maurelle murmured softly, her gaze distant as if she were trying to understand what had caused the sudden decay.

The usual sounds that filled the air were gone. The cheerful music of the fairies had faded into an eerie silence, and the once-bright glow of the lofen flies had vanished. The world felt as if it had stopped, holding its breath in anticipation.

Orin sighed deeply, the weight of everything settling heavily on his shoulders. "Start the fire," he muttered. "I'll fix the door."

Maurelle nodded and turned back inside, leaving Orin to face the crumbling world alone. He stepped outside, running his hand along the bark of the house's trunk. It felt brittle, cracked, and weak, as though the house itself was succumbing to the same fate as the land. He pulled a long, splintered strip of bark free, awkwardly wedging it into place to seal the broken doorframe.

"This place won't stand much longer," Orin said quietly, mostly to himself as he forced the bark into place.

Maurelle's soft voice drifted from inside, carrying a heavy question with it. "Do you think the Great Mother has cursed the land?"

Orin paused, glancing up at the dark, starless sky. "I don't think the Great Mother is even up there anymore," he murmured, his voice thick with doubt.

Stepping back inside, he lit the fire, using the last remnants of embers to drive away the night's biting cold. The warmth spread slowly, though it did little to ease the emptiness he felt. His gaze flickered toward the bedroom, and grief tightened his chest. He couldn't bring himself to sleep in there—not without her.

He crossed the room, pulling the floral quilt from the bed, along with the two pillows. Silently, he laid them beside the fire. "We'll sleep out here tonight,"

Orin said, his voice low, avoiding Maurelle's eyes. "It's warmer."

She nodded, saying nothing, though her expression carried an unreadable weight.

They settled in near the fire, the crackling flames providing the only sound in the stillness of the house. Orin's stomach growled faintly, as did Maurelle's, but there was nothing to eat. The strange symbols on the walls seemed to flicker in the firelight, their shapes twisting in the shadows.

Orin watched Maurelle as she slowly drifted off to sleep, her small frame curled up against the warmth of the fire. She looked peaceful, as though the chaos outside didn't touch her dreams. A surge of envy washed over him—how could she sleep so easily when everything around them was falling apart?

He lay back, his fingers brushing the wooden pendant that Cal had made. It felt rough against his skin, but familiar, grounding him as his eyes fluttered shut.

A sudden sound jolted him awake.

"Orin, wake up!" Maurelle's urgent voice cut through the fog of sleep as she shook him. "There's something outside."

Orin's heart leapt into his throat as he sat up, straining to hear the noise. *Thump. Thump.* The ground seemed to tremble with each impact. The sound grew louder, closer, shaking the very walls of the house.

"Stay here," Orin whispered, creeping toward the door. He pressed his eye to the narrow gap, peering out into the oppressive darkness. The pounding was right outside now, heavy and ominous.

"What is it?" Maurelle whispered, her voice quivering with fear.

Orin turned to hush her, but it was too late.

The pounding stopped.

Every muscle in Orin's body tensed, his breath caught in his throat. He looked back at Maurelle, eyes wide with fear. She stared at him, her face pale, her voice small and trembling. "What is it?"

Dread clawed at Orin's chest. He swallowed hard, his mind racing.

"Run!" Orin shouted, his voice raw with panic as he lunged for Maurelle.

Her eyes widened in confusion, frozen for a moment as the reality of the situation sank in. "RUN!" he screamed again, the terror clenched in his voice.

<h1 style="text-align:center">18
It's All Gone</h1>

Orin screamed, his voice tearing through the chaos as the beast—a hulking mass of scales and flesh crowned with three jagged horns—thundered toward the house, its hooves ripping the earth apart. The ground shook under the onslaught, and the walls trembled as if they, too, feared the beast's wrath. Maurelle jolted up from the floor, her face pale, and the two of them sprinted down the hallway, adrenaline fueling each desperate step. Orin kicked open the back door just as the creature's bulk slammed into the front of the house, splintering wood and glass, sending a storm of debris cascading around them.

"Go, go, go!" Orin roared, shoving Maurelle through the doorway.

As he turned to follow, he froze. A shrill, spine-chilling screech echoed through the carnage. His eyes locked on the beast, now standing in the ruins of his home. It roared, a guttural, rattling sound that shook the air. Its eyes, burning with a furious electric blue, glowed like twin fires, casting eerie shadows across its armored skin. The tail lashed violently, slicing through the air like a sharpened blade.

Then Orin saw it. Perched on the beast's back was the rider—a flesher. Its skeletal form was draped in tattered black cloth, skin stretched tight over sharp bones like something clawed its way out of a nightmare. Its skull was an obsidian void, eyes pits of searing crimson that blazed as it met Orin's gaze. A horrible, rasping laugh escaped its lipless mouth, the sound twisting in his ears, filling him with primal dread.

Maurelle screamed at him to run, her voice nearly drowned out by the beast's roar and the sinister cackle of the flesher. But Orin's feet wouldn't move. This thing—it had to be the monster that killed his family. Rage and fear churned inside him, and his hand drifted to the hilt of his sword. The beast lowered its head, muscles bunching beneath its thick hide as it prepared to charge.

With a thunderous bellow, it lunged down the narrow hallway, the walls crumbling like paper in its wake. Orin raised his blade, knowing it was useless, knowing he was about to be crushed into dust. He clenched his teeth, bracing for the end.

Suddenly, he felt a sharp tug at his hair, and the world spun as Maurelle yanked him backward. They hit the ground hard as the beast crashed past, exploding through the back door, wood and glass splintering in every direction. The flesher's cruel laughter echoed above the chaos.

"Get up!" Maurelle shouted, grabbing Orin's arm.

They scrambled to their feet, stumbling into the dark, dead forest behind the house. The beast roared in fury, its massive form shaking the ground as it swung its head, searching for them. Then it locked onto them, nostrils flaring, and charged, its hooves pounding the earth like thunder.

"It's catching up!" Orin yelled, his heart pounding as they sprinted through the twisted underbrush.

The thundering footfalls grew closer, the beast's breath hot on his neck. They leaped over fallen trees and dry, cracked stream beds, their lungs burning with effort. Orin risked a glance back just as the three horns plowed into his side. The world tilted as he flew, slamming into a tree with bone-jarring force. Pain exploded through his ribs, and he crumpled to the ground, gasping for breath.

The beast loomed over him, drool dripping from its slavering maw, fangs gleaming like scythes in the moonlight. Each jagged tooth was as long as Orin's forearm, stained with the blood of countless victims. Its eyes locked onto him, promising pain beyond death.

"Feast on your prey," the flesher hissed, its voice a chilling whisper of death.

It leaned forward, skeletal fingers clawing at the air as if it could already feel Orin's flesh tearing under its claws. He tried to move, tried to lift his sword, but his limbs felt like lead. Helpless, he stared into the maw of the beast as it opened wide, its rancid breath filling his nostrils.

But then—*thwack*—something small and hard struck the side of the creature's head. It snarled, jerking back.

"Hey, ugly!" Maurelle's voice rang out.

She stood atop a fallen tree, eyes blazing with defiance. Another stone flew from her hand, striking the flesher square in the chest. It hissed, a sound like nails on a chalkboard, and turned the beast to face her.

She glanced at Orin, panic flaring in her eyes. "Okay, that's my plan. Now what?"

Orin forced himself to sit up, pain screaming through his body, and muttered a chant, half-re-membered words from a battle long ago. *"Arbor spiritu tuo uti tuerentur terra vestra."*

The earth shuddered beneath him, and roots—thick, gnarled roots—erupted from the ground. The beast reared back, bellowing in rage as the roots twisted around its legs, squeezing tight. It bucked and thrashed, trying to tear itself free, but the roots held firm.

The flesher leapt from the beast's back, landing lightly despite its skeletal frame. It moved toward Orin, crimson eyes blazing with malice. But he kept chanting, the words flowing from his lips like a spell.

"Over here!" Maurelle screamed, waving her arms.

The flesher didn't even glance her way. With a snarl, it leapt high, claws outstretched, aiming straight for Orin's throat.

The roots surged forward, a black tendril shooting up like a spear. The flesher's eyes widened in shock as the root impaled it mid-leap, bursting through its chest with a sickening crunch. It hung there, skewered, dark ichor oozing from the wound as it writhed and thrashed.

Orin sagged back against the tree, gasping for breath. "You... you didn't have to come back," he managed, looking up at Maurelle as she hopped down from the fallen tree and extended her hand.

Orin didn't think much of it when Maurelle flashed him a grin, but her smile quickly faded. "You almost got me killed back there," she muttered.

Guilt twisted in Orin's gut as he winced. "It won't happen again."

"Damn right, it won't," Maurelle replied under her breath, glancing up at the dangling flesher. Her eyes widened in horror. "What in the spirits...?"

Orin turned to see what had caught her attention, and his heart dropped. The flesher's bony fingers wrapped around the root, slowly pulling its mangled body free. Black, pitch-like blood oozed down the root, but the creature didn't stop. Inch by inch, it dragged itself towards the ground.

"They don't know when to quit," Maurelle growled.

Without hesitation, she yanked a dagger from her belt, the blade gleaming in the moonlight. With a flick of her wrist, she sent it spinning through the air. The dagger embedded itself in the flesher's skull with a sickening crunch. The creature's head snapped back, its body twitching—but still, it smiled. Its lips curled into a gruesome, blood-stained grin, dead but not defeated.

"Burn it," Maurelle whispered, her voice trembling with fear. "Burn it, and let's get the hell out of here."

"We need to get out of Terra." The words came out raw and bitter from Orin's mouth. He hadn't realized until now how deep the pain of leaving cut him—the pain of knowing he would never see his home again. The last tie to Shira, the last piece of a life he could barely remember, was gone. He drew a deep breath, trying to steady the storm within, and brushed dead leaves from his clothes, as if that could rid him of the weight of loss.

Maurelle glanced over at him, her eyes softening with sympathy as she offered a faint smile. "I'm sorry about your house, really. But the best thing we can do now is warn the Ferums and seek asylum before that thing comes back."

The mention of the Ferums sent a shiver down Orin's spine. Warriors who knew no fear, no pain, they were legendary even in the darkest bedtime stories. Orin had heard only fragments of their tale, mostly from his father, who described their land as surrounded by a stone wall so high it seemed to claw at the stars. If anyone could face the horrors stalking Terra, it would be them. Maybe they even held the answers to the symbols etched into the walls of Orin's shattered home.

"Damn!" Orin swore, frustration bubbling up. "I forgot to copy the markings on the wall."

Maurelle let out a soft laugh and pulled out a small scrap of bark parchment from her pouch. "You mean these markings?" she asked teasingly.

Orin snatched the parchment from her hand, heart racing as he saw all twenty-two symbols carved into it, smeared with coal from their old fireplace. The sight of them made his skin prickle. How had she—?

"Maybe I really do need you," Orin muttered, managing a smile despite the tension.

"Maybe just a little," Maurelle quipped, grinning before her smile faded as the shadows around them deepened.

The fog thickened, tendrils of mist curling around their legs, cold and clammy like a corpse's touch. Every now and then, the crack of a rotten branch echoed through the silent forest, as if the land itself was crumbling. They trudged westward, deeper into the woods, the fog masking treacherous roots and jagged rocks.

"This is how I die," Maurelle groaned, dragging her feet. "Starving to death in the middle of nowhere with you of all people. I was better off before I met you, you know."

"Then feel free to leave," Orin snapped, kicking aside a fallen branch. The stench of rot was thick in the air, suffocating. "There's no reason for this," he muttered more to himself than to her, crumbling a branch from a nearby tiran nut tree into dust. "The whole land is dying, and I can't figure out why."

"Maybe the land is starving, like we soon will be." Maurelle's voice was edged with darkness, brittle and tired.

Orin spun around, eyes blazing. "If you're that hungry, go find some giggle beetles to eat. I hear they're a delicacy."

Maurelle glared at him, then held out her hand, revealing the crumbling remains of three green giggle beetles. Their chitin was split and rotting. "They're dead, too," she spat, hurling the beetles to the ground with a vicious flick. "Everything is dead."

Orin turned away, his chest tightening. The smell of death clung to everything, even here, miles from the ruins of his village. As they walked, he glanced skyward, locking his gaze on the eerie glow of the Eye of Mother in the night sky.

"Why did I ever believe in her?" he whispered bitterly.

"What are you saying?" Maurelle's voice cut through his thoughts.

"Nothing important," Orin muttered, shaking his head.

The bitter taste of doubt gnawed at him. Had he truly been so naive to think the gods were watching over them? The fog grew thicker, wrapping the world in an opaque shroud. Orin glanced back to check on Maurelle, only able to make out the faint glimmer of her belt buckle in the mist.

"We should stop for the night," he called out, a sudden fear tightening around his heart.

What if they got separated in this cursed fog? What if something—or someone—was out there waiting for them? Maurelle didn't respond. She sank into the fog, vanishing into the swirling gray. Orin hesitated for a moment before settling against the rough bark of a dying sefmore tree. His body ached, exhaustion seeping into his muscles, but sleep seemed impossible. The mist crept closer, cold and damp, wrapping around him like a living thing.

Above them, the night sky shimmered through a break in the fog, the stars burning brighter than Orin had ever seen them. It felt wrong, almost mocking; the beauty of it was a cruel contrast to the death spreading across the land. He stared up at the stars, his eyes drawn to the towering form of the Great Spirit Tree in the distance, still standing tall, still clinging to life.

"What a lie," he whispered bitterly.

The Spirit Tree was supposed to be a symbol of hope, a promise that the land would heal. But looking at it now, all he saw was a dying giant, its branches twisted and gnarled, struggling against the inevitable. With a sigh, he closed his eyes, letting the creaking of the dead trees and the faint rustling of leaves lull him into a restless half-sleep.

He awoke the next morning, jolted by the piercing stab of white light against his eyes. He blinked rapidly, trying to shake off the harshness of it. It made him miss the soft, emerald glow of the sun filtering through the lush canopy that used to surround them. But that canopy was gone now; the fog had lifted, revealing only barren trees standing like empty sentinels.

Glancing down, he found Maurelle nestled against his chest, her face peaceful as she slept, her breath rising and falling softly. Despite the stiffness in his body, he didn't want to wake her. But they couldn't afford to rest any longer.

Gently, he shook her shoulder. "Hey, time to get up."

Maurelle stirred, blinking the sleep from her eyes before jolting upright, a flash of embarrassment coloring her cheeks. She quickly averted her gaze as if she'd been caught doing something she shouldn't.

"Comfy sleep?" he teased, hoping to break through the awkwardness with a grin.

She just rolled her eyes, a small smirk tugging at her lips, and stood up. She began wandering around, scanning the barren landscape for something, anything, to eat. After a few minutes of futile searching, she turned to him, hands on her hips. "So, what's for breakfast?"

He glanced around, hoping for some miracle. "We'll find something along the way."

With that, they began their trek toward Ballator, eyes fixed on the ground as they walked. Hours melted together as the sun rose higher, bringing with it a heat that clawed at their throats. Orin's tongue felt like sandpaper, and every swallow seemed to scrape at his throat. If they didn't find food or water soon, they wouldn't make it much further.

Suddenly, Maurelle paused, her ears perked up. "Do you hear that?" she whispered, her voice bubbling with sudden excitement.

Orin strained his ears. "I don't hear anything..."

But she was already smiling. "Water—I hear water!"

Before he could even react, she took off like a blur, her laughter trailing behind her as she sprinted through the dead forest. "Wait, hold up!" he shouted, running after her.

As he chased her, the faint sound of water trickling over rocks finally reached his ears. Everything felt wet—moist—changed, cooling down, and he caught the familiar scent of fresh, flowing water. The trees and shrubs seemed to come alive the closer they got—lush greenery breaking through the barren wasteland. The buzzing of tiny lofen flies filled the area, and soon enough, he burst through the foliage, breathless, to see Maurelle standing at the bank of a pristine lake.

"It's beautiful," she murmured, staring out over the shimmering water.

The lake stretched out endlessly, its clear blue surface mirroring the sky above. Wildflowers painted the banks in splashes of yellow and white, their sweet fragrance mixing with the earthy scent of the woods. Red-spotted cofen toads leaped between the reeds, their tiny bodies gliding effortlessly before disappearing with a soft plop into the water.

"Race you in!" Maurelle's voice rang out as she kicked off her boots, the excitement in her eyes contagious.

Orin grinned, already pulling off his clothes. He couldn't help but notice the bare skin of her back as she unfastened her chest plate, the bronze armor dropping with a soft thud. Scars crisscrossed her shoulders, stark against her pale skin, each one telling a story she hadn't shared.

"Hurry up!" she called, snapping him out of his thoughts.

She wriggled out of her leather pants and darted into the lake. He tossed his clothes aside and plunged into the water after her. The coldness hit him like a shock, quenching the burning heat that had wrapped around his body. He took a deep breath and submerged himself. Beneath the surface, the world transformed. The water was crystal clear, revealing schools of scamper eels darting past, their bright pink and blue bodies flashing like tiny beacons. The lakebed was covered in a blanket of soft, pale sand, so pristine it seemed almost surreal. For a moment, the pain, the exhaustion, the fear—it all washed away.

Maurelle's hand brushed against his foot, and he turned to see her floating beside him, her red hair fanning out like a fiery halo. She was grinning wildly, her eyes sparkling even underwater. Neither of them cared about being bare-skinned; the only thing that mattered was the chill of the water, the thrill of life coursing through them once again.

They resurfaced together, laughing, and made their way back to the bank. They collapsed on a thick bed of flipper grass, their toes still trailing in the cool water, the sun warming their skin. Orin reached over and plucked a few lakedale bulbs from a nearby cluster.

"Here, try these." He handed her a handful of the purple bulbs, and they bit into them together, sweet juice spilling down their chins.

They laughed, savoring every drop. Time seemed to stand still as they lounged there, soaking up the sun and the moment of peace. As the sky turned from brilliant blue to deepening gold, they got dressed reluctantly, knowing they couldn't stay forever.

Orin built a small fire by the bank and gathered more lakedale bulbs while Maurelle slipped off to hunt some toads. They ate until they couldn't take another bite, their bellies full and the tension that had weighed on them for days finally easing.

As they lay on their backs, staring up at the stars twinkling against the inky blackness, Orin found his thoughts drifting back to the scars on her back.

"What happened to your back?" he asked quietly.

Maurelle's gaze remained on the sky, but Orin noticed her jaw tighten. "My mother and I... we didn't have the best of relationships." Her voice was soft, each word heavy with a history he couldn't yet grasp.

He hesitated, unsure of how to respond. "Is that why... why you don't seem to get upset about anything? Why I haven't seen you shed a single tear?"

She turned her head to look at him, her expression distant. "I did all my crying a long time ago."

Rolling over, she faced away, her silence a clear signal that she was done with the conversation. Orin stared up at the sky, watching the trails of light from passing comets streak across the darkness until sleep finally claimed him.

Orin jolted awake, the soft sound of a woman's humming drifting through the trees like an eerie melody. The forest seemed to hold its breath, the low, haunting tune wrapping around them, making his skin prickle. His heart was already pounding as he scrambled up, reaching for his sword. Maurelle was beside him in an instant, her dagger glinting in the dim fire-light.

"Who's there?" he shouted, his voice echoing through the silent woods.

There was no response, only that unsettling song.

"There!" Maurelle hissed, pointing into the shadows.

Orin turned and saw her stepping out from the trees like a ghost. A woman draped in a tattered blue dress that might have once been beautiful approached, a white necklace dangling down and vanishing between the silver-edged fabric that clung to her frail frame.

"Are you... are you alright?" Orin asked cautiously, noting the woman's bare, filthy feet as she swayed closer, humming all the while.

The woman stopped, her face breaking into a smile that made the hair on the back of his neck stand on end. "Oh, we're just fine. Yes, yes, just fine, aren't we, dear?"

She glanced down at what looked like a swaddled baby wrapped tightly in brown cloth. Her ribs jutted out sharply beneath her dress, and her matted brown hair twisted with dead leaves and twigs. She looked like she'd been wandering the woods for weeks... months, even.

"We... we have some food, if you're hungry," Maurelle offered hesitantly, her eyes wide as she took in the woman's skeletal frame.

The woman's smile stretched wider. "Well, aren't you a sweet one?" She glanced down at the bundle in her arms, her voice dripping with a kind of warped affection. "You hear that, my beautiful girl? These kind people are going to help us. What kind, kind people they are."

Orin shot a confused look at Maurelle, who shrugged, clearly just as unsure about what to make of this bizarre encounter. His eyes lingered on the woman's swaddled 'baby.' Something didn't feel right.

"Can you be a dear and pass us some food?" she asked sweetly, lowering herself to sit by their fire.

He swallowed hard and handed her the last of the lakedale bulbs. She took them eagerly, slowly sucking the juices as if savoring a rare delicacy. "What's your name?" he asked quietly, unable to tear his gaze away from the strange emptiness in her eyes.

She looked up at him, smiling that unsettling smile. "I'm Lena," she said softly, her gaze dropping to the bundle cradled in her lap. "And this is my beautiful little girl, Tiriella."

The hair on Orin's arms stood on end as he and Maurelle watched her rock back and forth, humming a lullaby that made his stomach twist.

"Mommy loves you, yes she loves you. No one else will ever have you. You are mine, yes all mine. And I will love you till the end of time. Sleep well through the night. Don't let those bad dreams bite. Sleep well through the night. I'll be with you till you die."

"Well, that's... cheery," Maurelle whispered into his ear.

Orin forced a weak smile, but every nerve in his body was on edge. Something about Lena felt... off. More than off. She looked shattered, hollowed out from the inside. What horrors had she endured to become this?

"Where are you from?" Maurelle asked gently, trying to ease into conversation.

Lena didn't look up. "Oh, here and there, dear."

"Are you from one of the villages?" Maurelle pressed, her tone soft.

The woman's smile faded. "I was once from a village, dear. But... no more village is left."

Orin's stomach dropped. "Fleshers," he muttered, the word tasting bitter on his tongue.

The transformation in Lena was instant. She recoiled, clutching the bundle close. "There, there, my child. Mommy's got you. Mommy has always got you."

Her gaze snapped to his, sharp and furious. "How dare you say such things. Such evil things in front of my beautiful girl!" She paused, her eyes wild, and for a moment, he thought she might attack.

But then, just as suddenly, she began rocking again, humming that same twisted lullaby. "If my husband were still here... well, he's not." Her voice broke, but before he could even process it, she was smiling again. "There, there, don't cry," she whispered to the bundle.

Orin glanced at Maurelle. She looked as bewildered as he felt. The baby... he realized with a sinking feeling that he hadn't heard a single sound from it.

"Can I... can I hold her?" Maurelle asked, her eyes darting nervously to his.

Lena's face lit up. "Of course, dear." She lifted the bundle and handed it over with surprising tenderness.

Orin's heart froze as he saw Maurelle's expression twist in shock.

"Is she not the most beautiful girl you've ever seen?" Lena cooed.

Maurelle didn't respond. She just stared at the bundle, her face pale. Orin took a step forward, his throat tight. "She's... very beautiful," Maurelle whispered, carefully handing the baby back.

"We almost didn't make it out," Lena murmured, her smile almost... proud.

Orin's heart hammered as Lena stood, clutching the swaddled bundle close. She took a step forward, but her foot caught on the hem of her half-pulled-down dress. Everything seemed to slow as she stumbled, the bundle slipping from her arms and falling to the ground.

"No!" Lena screamed, diving after it.

The bundle hit the dirt and unraveled, spilling its contents. Orin felt the wind leave his lungs as he stared at the heap of dirty rags lying at her feet. "My baby!" Lena wailed, frantically gathering the scraps of cloth. "Don't worry, Mommy's here. Mommy will put you all back together."

She knelt there, trembling, her fingers shaking as she tried to reshape the rags into the form of a child. A tear slid down Orin's cheek as he watched her cradle the empty cloth. He knew that pain. He knew that madness. If it hadn't been for Maurelle, he might have ended up the same: lost, shattered, clinging to memories that weren't really there.

"Let me help you," Maurelle whispered, her voice trembling.

She reached out to gently adjust Lena's dress, but the woman's hand shot out, striking her to the ground.

"You little bitch!" Lena shrieked, rising to her feet. "You tried to kill my baby! You're jealous of the love I have!"

"Lena, stop!" Orin shouted, grabbing her shoulders and pulling her back as she aimed a vicious kick at Maurelle's ribs.

"She's mine! My baby!" Lena's voice rose, wild and furious, as Orin forced her down, holding her still. "Mine, mine, mine!"

"Are you okay?" he asked Maurelle, who was clutching her side, gasping for breath.

She didn't answer. Instead, she pushed past him, marching right up to Lena. "You stupid woman! Can't you see you're holding nothing? Your baby's already dead!" The words exploded from her before she could stop herself.

Lena froze, her eyes wide, uncomprehending. She began to rock again, her humming low and broken. Orin shot Maurelle a look, but she was already kneeling beside Lena, pulling her tattered dress back up over her shoulders.

"Your baby is… very beautiful," Maurelle murmured softly.

Lena blinked, a fragile smile flickering across her face. "Yes, dear… It's just her and I now."

Orin slumped back, exhaustion washing over him as he watched Maurelle rub Lena's shoulders gently. There was something both soothing and terrifying in the woman's lullaby. He leaned back against the tree, the warmth of the fire lulling him. Despite every-thing, he felt his eyes growing heavy as that eerie, broken melody filled the air.

"Mommy loves you, yes she loves you. No one else will ever have you. You are mine, yes all mine. And I will love you till the end of time. Sleep well through the night. Don't let those bad dreams bite. Sleep well through the night. I'll be with you till you die..."

And then, mercifully, darkness took him.

Orin woke with a start, blinking in the pale morning light. The fire from the night before was little more than a smudge of blackened ash, and Maurelle was curled up beside it, still asleep. He stood, muscles protesting, and looked around. There was no sign of Lena.

"She left late last night," Maurelle murmured soft-ly, sitting up and rubbing her eyes. She looked tired, but there was a flicker of relief in her gaze.

Orin nodded, feeling a strange mix of emotions. Relief, yes—how could they have cared for her in that state? But sadness, too. Lena was a broken soul, beyond saving. He turned to the lake, the surface like glass, reflecting the morning sun. They'd have to cross it today, and he had a feeling it would drain every bit of energy they had left.

"Let's eat," he said, breaking the silence. "Then we'll head across."

Maurelle nodded and began picking the bones from last night's toads, while Orin gathered the last of the lakedale bulbs. The world around them began to stir as the flowers slowly opened, signaling the start of the day. Lofen flies buzzed softly, and the familiar croaking of the toads joined in like some strange dawn chorus.

That's when he noticed Maurelle go still, her eyes narrowed, focused on something in the distance.

"What's that?" she whispered, pointing toward the edge of the dead forest.

Orin squinted, following her gaze. "Let's find out."

They made their way cautiously through the twisted, lifeless trees. As they drew closer, a chill settled in

Orin's bones. Two figures dangled from the gnarled branches of a sefmore tree—one large, one small. And then the light caught a flash of blue fabric, shimmering faintly in the dappled light.

"Lena... what have you done?" Maurelle breathed, her voice barely a whisper.

Orin's heart sank as they stepped closer. Lena hung limply from a thick vine tied cruelly around her neck. Beside her, the swaddled bundle—the rags she'd cradled so lovingly—swayed softly from another vine. His throat tightened as he took it all in, the sadness and desperation that had driven her to this final act.

They stood in silence, the weight of it pressing down on them. There was nothing left to say. Without a word, they turned and walked back to the fire, leaving Lena swaying gently in the breeze. Orin looked at Maurelle. Guilt flickered in her eyes, and he could see the question forming there, heavy and painful.

"There was nothing you could have done," he said quietly. "She was already lost."

Maurelle tried to smile, but it didn't reach her eyes. Orin knew she felt responsible, somehow. Maybe if they'd stayed with Lena longer, she wouldn't have ended up like that. But deep down, they both knew she had been beyond saving long before they'd met her.

They packed up their camp and made their way to the lake's edge. The water sparkled in the morning light, impossibly clear, stretching out like a shimmering expanse of glass. Maurelle's laugh broke through the stillness.

He kicked off his boots and rolled up his pant legs, wading into the cool water until he found two large lily pads floating near the shore. "Wrap your clothes in this and use a branch to hang on to. It'll keep you from drowning along the way."

They stripped down, bundling their gear carefully in the lily pads. Orin glanced at Maurelle, who was already clutching her stick tightly, her gaze steady.

"You ready?"

She smiled back. "Are you?"

The water was freezing, sapping what little strength Orin had left, but they pushed forward. Their makeshift floats kept them from sinking under the weight of exhaustion. Hours dragged on, each stroke becoming a battle as the sun dipped lower and lower in the sky. Orin glanced back often, watching as Maurelle fell further behind, her movements sluggish.

"Almost there!" he called, knowing it wasn't true.

They were still hours from the opposite shore, and every now and then, a dark shadow flitted beneath him, making his pulse quicken. His mind whispered that it was just a trick of the light. But deep down, he knew better. He paused, waiting for Maurelle to catch up.

"I... I can't..." Her voice was weak, her grip on the branch slipping.

"Just hold on," he urged, pulling her closer. He wrapped his arm around her waist, holding on with everything he had left. "Almost there."

The hours stretched endlessly, the night creeping in. His limbs were numb, his chest burning with every strained breath. But, as the first light of dawn began to pierce the sky, his foot brushed against something solid. He pushed forward, dragging them both up onto the bank, collapsing in a heap. His muscles screamed in agony, trembling uncontrollably as they lay there, gasping.

"We'll rest a few minutes," Orin managed, his voice barely a rasp. Maurelle nodded, and within moments, she was out cold.

More than a few hours passed before Orin woke again, the sun high in the sky. He groaned, every bone in his body aching as he turned to Maurelle and nudged her shoulder gently.

"Time to wake up."

She moaned softly, rolling onto her back. A tired but triumphant smile spread across her face. "I didn't think we were going to make it."

Orin chuckled weakly, the sound rough in his dry throat. "Neither did I."

They dressed slowly, strapping on their weapons and gathering what little food they had left. As they looked out over the dead forest that stretched before them, Orin turned to Maurelle. "Let's keep moving."

The days blurred into one long march, the once towering trees shrinking down to brittle shrubs. The dirt under their feet gave way to jagged rocks, forcing them to scramble over boulders and navigate narrow ledges. Exhaustion settled deep into Orin's bones, but every night, as they huddled together, they talked quietly, sharing stories of the old days.

Orin told Maurelle about Shira and Cal, about Ferkin and the adventures they had as children. She would laugh, but when it came time for her to share, she always remained tight-lipped, offering only small, cryptic glimpses of her past. Even so, Orin began to think of her as a sister—someone he could trust, someone who'd seen the same darkness he had.

The terrain grew steeper, the air thinner, until finally, they crested a massive boulder and looked up at the red stone cliffs towering before them, disappearing into the clouds.

"We're here," Orin breathed, the words a mix of disbelief and relief.

He turned, pulling Maurelle up beside him. They stood there, gazing up at the sheer rock face, knowing it would be their next challenge. But for now, they would rest.

"We'll start the climb tomorrow," Orin said, leaning back against the cliff base.

The stars above glittered like scattered diamonds, brighter than he'd ever seen them. He wondered what the people of Ballator were like, if they would help them fight the fleshers... if they even existed. He glanced at Maurelle, already asleep beside him, her chest rising and falling softly. She'd come so far.

Orin closed his eyes, the weight of exhaustion pulling him down. As he drifted off, he wondered if he'd ever see the forests of Terra again... or if this was as close to home as he'd ever get.

19
Kellop and Flup

Kellop's paws thudded against the brittle ground, each step echoing like the crackle of dead leaves. The forest around him was a graveyard of skeletal trees, their bark peeling away to reveal rot beneath. His ears flattened against his skull, his breath came in ragged gasps, and the air itself felt heavy, suffocating. Something was wrong—something worse than before.

Beside him, Flup darted erratically, his wide eyes darting upward in terror. "Kellop, look!" he choked out, skidding to a halt. "It's bigger... so much bigger! They don't see it! They don't see it!"

Kellop froze, his heart pounding as he followed Flup's gaze. The Eye of Mother loomed above, a massive, swirling orb of crimson and gold, pulsing with a dreadful energy. It had grown, consuming more of the sky, its tendrils of light stretching toward the moon like greedy hands. The sight made his fur bristle.

"It's going to swallow it soon," Kellop whispered, his voice barely audible. "We have to go. Now."

"Where?" Flup's voice cracked. "The forest is dying. Time's broken and they don't see it!"

Kellop's jaw tightened. "We warn Him. He's the only one who can stop this."

The ground beneath them shifted, unstable and wrong. The trees groaned, their branches twisting like claws. The air was thick with the stench of decay, and the stars above flickered in and out, as if unsure of their place. Time itself was unraveling, merging past and present into a chaotic blur.

"I can feel it, Kellop," Flup whimpered. "Everything's shifting. The sun, the moon... it's all mixing together. What if the Eye is doing this? What if it's pulling everything apart?"

Kellop didn't answer. He couldn't. The Eye's weight pressed down on him, its gaze relentless. He grabbed Flup by the scruff and pulled him forward. "We run. We don't stop."

They sprinted through the forest, the trees closing in around them. The ground rippled, cracks splitting the earth as the forest itself seemed to come alive. The Eye's light bathed everything in a sickly red glow, and the shadows stretched and writhed like living things.

"Kellop, we're going in circles!" Flup cried, his voice trembling. "We've been here before!"

Kellop growled, frustration clawing at him. He knew Flup was right. The twisted oak, the patch of dead ferns—they'd passed them twice. Time was folding in on itself, trapping them in a loop.

A deafening crack split the air, and the ground lurched violently. Kellop stumbled, his paws slipping as the earth split open ahead of them. A jagged chasm yawned wide, its depths echoing with a low, guttural rumble.

"Move!" Kellop shouted, dragging Flup away from the fissure. They ran, the forest collapsing behind them, the Eye's light growing brighter, more oppressive.

"It's swallowing everything!" Flup gasped, his voice thin with terror. "What do we do?"

"We warn Him," Kellop snapped, his voice fierce. "That's all we can do."

They burst through the tree line into an open field, the Eye dominating the sky above. In the distance, a figure stood, cloaked in shadow, his gaze fixed on the chaos. Around Him, the ground was littered with the bodies of Dixin fairies, their delicate forms broken and still, their tiny swords clutched in lifeless hands. Their wings, once iridescent, were now dull and cracked, their eyes wide and unseeing. The army of the dead lay scattered like fallen leaves, their final stand etched in the dirt.

Kellop skidded to a stop, his chest heaving. "The Eye... it's consuming everything. Time is unraveling."

The figure turned, his eyes glowing with an other-worldly light. "You've seen it," he said, his voice deep and resonant. "The end begins."

Kellop's heart sank. "Can you stop it?"

The figure looked up at the Eye, his expression one of glee. "I have done what is about to be done. I have given what has yet to be given. I have taken, what has still to be taken." He turned to Kellop and Flup, his face a distorted flash of sickening glee. "My children are already gone and have yet to arrive. The Lands of the future have fallen. All will bow to the Thorned King of Time. The king of this world. The fallen one. I am the casted down."

From within the Eye of Mother, orbs of light emerged. At His will, they descended upon the two Wooden Gobels, who were frozen in place. He lifted His hand towards them, His fingers curling like the claws of a predator. "Now live forever in me, as I live in you."

Kellop and Flup tried to scream, but no sound escaped. Their bodies twisted, their forms warping as time itself seemed to tear them apart. Their fur peeled away, revealing raw flesh that bubbled and split. Their eyes bulged, then melted, their mouths stretching into silent howls. The orbs of light burrowed into them, searing their insides, their very essence unraveling. They were trapped in an endless moment of agony, their minds fracturing as time looped their torment over and over.

The Thorned King watched, His laughter echoing across the desolate field. Around Him, the dead Dixin fairies seemed to stir, their lifeless hands tightening on their swords as if in one final, futile act of defiance. But they were already gone, their light extinguished, their hope crushed.

The Eye of Mother pulsed, its crimson tendrils reaching further, consuming the stars, the moon, the very fabric of existence. The Thorned King spread His arms, His shadow stretching across the land. "All will bow," He whispered, His voice a venomous promise. "All will break."

And as Kellop and Flup's silent screams echoed in the void, the world itself began to unravel, piece by piece, into the maw of the Eye.